TAKEN BY SURPRISE

"Alyssa, do not question my good conscience!" Harris said, turning to her. A stern frown returned to his lips. "There is more at stake."

"More what—" Alyssa began, mystified and frustrated. "Tell me. I'm listening."

"More than I will discuss with you." As he held her gaze, his frown melted away and a half-smile formed on his lips again. "But I must say, if I'm ever in trouble, I hope you will come to my defense."

She suddenly found her chin captured in his right hand, and he stepped closer.

"You are very valiant, sweet Alyssa," he whispered, his lips almost upon hers.

She stood frozen, captured by the unexpected husky sound of his voice and the warm strength of his hand on her chin. The depths of the emotion in his eyes held hers. Then his lips descended to hers, moving over her mouth, firm and questing. . . .

Books by Linda Madl

BAYOU ROSE

A WHISPER OF VIOLETS

THE SCOTSMAN'S LADY

THE SCOTSMAN'S BRIDE

BRIGHTER THAN GOLD

SILK AND SECRETS

Published by Zebra Books

SILK AND SECRETS

Linda Madl

ZEBRA BOOKS

Kensington Publishing Corp.

http://www.kensingtonbooks.com

ZEBRA BOOKS are published by

Kensington Publishing Corp.
850 Third Avenue
New York, NY 10022

All Kensington titles, imprints and distributed lines are available at special quantity discounts for bulk purchases for sales
promotion, premiums, fund-raising, educational or institutional
use.

Special book excerpts or customized printings can also be created to fit specific needs. For details, write or phone the office
of the Kensington Special Sales Manager: Kensington Publishing Corp., 850 Third Avenue, New York, NY 10022. Attn.
Special Sales Department. Phone: 1-800-221-2647.

First Printing: November 2002
10 9 8 7 6 5 4 3 2 1

Printed in the United States of America

To Evan Marshall, my agent

In Appreciation to
Robin Edmunds, Elizabeth Grayson, Mary Kilchenstein,
Margaret Ohmes, and Kayla Westra
for their friendship, help, and support.
And to my husband for his love and patience.

One

"I'm being banished," Alyssa said aloud to the empty carriage. Involuntarily, her hand flew to her lips to stem the unhappy words, but it was too late. The syllables hung in the air, invisible, vibrating—so that she heard every dismal implication. She was alone in a carriage bouncing along a foggy lane in a foreign land—in Cornwall, to be precise. Her family, the Lockharts of Boston, had sent her away to a cold and dreary place.

Slowly she lowered her hand into her lap and waited. Listened. *Banishment.* It sounded just as harsh as it had the first time. So what happened now that she'd admitted the truth to herself? Did giving it a name change anything?

Nothing. She was still on her way to a place she'd never seen, to stay with people she'd never met. Even the tightness in her belly remained as uncomfortable as ever.

If Aunt Esther were here, chattering in her ear, as the dear lady had during the entire two weeks of the Atlantic crossing, Alyssa would probably never have uttered the word. Never admitted to herself that this was a trip into exile because of an unfortunate prank. Never faced reality.

"But you've always known the truth," she told herself. Once she'd spoken aloud, it hardly seemed strange to continue. "Yes, you've always known the truth, but it was so darned hard to face." She lifted her chin in defiance. "No, I will not view this as punishment. I will see it as a pilgrimage to the homeland of my favorite authors."

Her frown softened. Dickens, Austen, the Brontës, and especially Robert Louis Stevenson. She loved Stevenson's adventure novels—pirates and smugglers. He and the others had always made her want to visit England's green shores. The way her life had been going, she wasn't going to enjoy a European wedding trip from Mama and Papa, like Opal and Twyla had. Her sisters and their husbands had toured London on their honeymoons, and then they had gone on to Paris and Rome with a stopover in Munich. And no doubt Mama and Papa would provide an elaborate journey for her brother Winslow.

"No such fine itinerary for me," she muttered aloud again, taking in the shabbiness of the Trevell carriage. The crushed velvet upholstery was well worn and the brass lamp appeared to be out of oil and badly in need of polishing. She was traveling to Cornwall to spend the fall with the Trevells, distant country cousins upon whom Papa had prevailed to take her in. She knew nothing of these people beyond the fact that there'd been a recent death in the family. They couldn't possibly be glad to have a visitor at such a time.

She did know, however, without it being said, that her parents didn't give a fig whether the Trevells were in mourning or ruled a cottage or a manor. They just wanted her out of Boston, out of sight, and out of mind. She was an embarrassment, a scandal, and an unworthy daughter.

"And you have no one to blame but yourself, Miss Alyssa Marie Lockhart." Her frown deepened, and she pulled her Persian lamb jacket closer against the October chill. She was in disgrace, and she knew exactly why. "But I didn't have to let them put me on a steamer to Southampton," she reminded herself. "I could have run away."

Abruptly the carriage lurched to a stop, throwing Alyssa forward. She caught herself on the opposite seat, bumping her knees and knocking her Persian lamb hat askew. As she struggled to right herself, she heard men's voices shouting from the road ahead. Their tone was harsh with anger, but their words were unclear.

What on earth? she wondered as she scrambled onto the seat and straightened her hat. A thrilling thought made her gasp. Highwaymen? Like the legendary Dick Turpin? But he wasn't Cornish—and he'd lived a century ago.

She pressed her cheek against the cold windowpane to see what was happening. A line of workingmen on foot barricaded the narrow lane. No caped highwayman on a gallant steed, only forbidding, hollow-cheeked men in baggy clothes powdered with something white. Flour? Two men carried torches, flaming bright orange against the fog. Others carried long, flat wooden sticks that she recognized as cricket bats. From the fierce set of their mouths and the narrowness of their eyes, she didn't think they were out for a game.

One of the men wore a clerical collar, of all things. He was a tall graceful fellow whose black clothes were dowdy but brushed and comparatively clean. Separating himself from the group, he slowly walked toward the carriage. The reined-in coach horses whickered and fidgeted, their harnesses jingling. When he reached the equipage, he spoke to the Trevells' coachman, a thin, haggard man named Whittle who wore a mourning band on the sleeve of his blue livery. Whittle had met Alyssa at the Launceston train station. He answered from his seat, more anger in his voice than fear. A note of familiarity colored his tone, as if he knew the clergyman.

However, Alyssa couldn't quite understand their exchange. Since her arrival, she'd found that the Queen's English varied a good deal even in its homeland. More than once she'd had difficulty understanding what she was certain must be plain English to a Britannia native.

As she watched, the clergyman turned away from the coachman and shook his head in disbelief. When he caught sight of her with her cheek pressed against the glass, he smiled. Caught rudely staring like a schoolgirl, she pushed away from the window. But that did not prevent the man from striding up to the door and pulling it open. As he climbed into the carriage, it creaked and sagged under his weight.

Shocked by his forwardness, Alyssa hastily scooted across the seat into the far corner. He smelled of stale tobacco smoke and sour beer, like the stable boys at home when they returned from the tavern. She wasn't frightened, exactly. After all, the man appeared to be a churchman. Still, it was all rather strange.

With a grace extraordinary in so tall a man, he settled himself opposite her. For a moment they stared at each other. Alyssa kept her hands clasped in her lap and met his gaze without a blush or a blink. He was a handsome man, in an oily way. He sat back in the seat and made no move to remove his hat as he assessed her.

"Good day, miss," he said at last.

Alyssa nodded in reply. Nothing about him was what she would have expected from a clergyman. His long chin was covered in a dark, well-trimmed beard. Deep lines framed his mouth; and his brown eyes reminded Alyssa of someone, but she couldn't think who it might be at the moment. His white shirt was dingy, though his coat was brushed. His dark hair was pulled back in a long slick queue. What concerned Alyssa most was that despite the smile that spread across his face—more a smirk, actually—there gleamed in his dark eyes the light of a fire burning deep inside. This was no ordinary man. This man thrived on the energy of a mission.

"So Elijah told me true," he said, his smile still in place. "You're not who I thought to find here."

"And who might you be, sir? And those men with you?" Alyssa asked, flustered and annoyed with his bad manners. She'd never been one to stand on formalities, but the least he could do was introduce himself. "And whom did you expect to find in this conveyance, anyway? The Trevell crest is on the door."

"A Yank, are you?" At last he removed his battered, black wool cap to reveal a high forehead. "I am the Reverend Zebulon Whittle." His accent was understandable, yet more like a workingman's than a seminarian's. "Those gentlemen, those miners and their families be my congregation."

"Miners?" Alyssa glanced out the window once more at the white streaks on their clothes. "But the white dust?"

"Clay mines," the Reverend Whittle explained. "They dig out the clay to make the fine china you ladies like to put on your tables. Just as dirty a job as mining coal, only the dirt be white."

"Oh," was all Alyssa could think to say.

"And you're to be the houseguest at Penridge Hall? Miss . . . ?"

"Lockhart," she supplied. "Yes, as a matter of fact, I am. How did you know?"

"Elijah, my brother, told me." He gestured toward the coachman's box above.

She realized that was who the reverend reminded her of— Whittle, the coachman.

The Reverend Whittle leaned back in the seat, his keen scrutiny unrelenting. "Elijah has worked for the Trevells since he was a lad. As a gardener, footman, whatever they require. Loyal to a fault, my brother is. And what would a handsome young woman like yourself be doing traveling to a place like Penridge Hall with no chaperone?"

"I have a chaperone," Alyssa corrected, lest this stranger misunderstand her circumstances. "My Aunt Esther broke her ankle in Southampton. She looked the wrong direction before we started across the street and a hansom cab knocked her a glancing blow. She is unable to travel. So while she is recovering with a friend, I'm going ahead without her. I'm expected at Penridge Hall shortly."

"Oh, have no fear." Reverend Whittle grinned as he flopped his cap back on. "I've no intention of keeping you, but I did think you should be told what you'll find at that fine manor, just on the chance that you don't know."

"Know what?" Alyssa asked, hesitating to engage in gossip, yet curious. "I know about Lord Penridge's death some three months ago, and that his widow and cousin are in mourning. I can only hope my stay will not be a trial for them."

The reverend smiled, the corners of his mouth turning up in what appeared to be genuine amusement—but not the sort a man of the cloth should enjoy. The expression made her tug at her skirts to be certain her ankles were covered. "I'll wager the new lord won't find you a trial, me dear. Oh, no. But do you want to go where murder has been committed?"

"Murder?" she breathed. What nonsense was this? "What murder?"

"Why, of Lord Alistair himself," Reverend Whittle said, lifting a hand with dirty fingernails into the air as if he could hardly believe she didn't know. "My brother is too loyal to utter a word against the Trevells, but I, on the other hand, feel it is my duty to inform you of what a house of transgressions you be walking into. Oh, yes, the new lord got old Doc Lewellyn to declare that his cousin died of natural causes. Couldn't have been too difficult. Old Lewellyn is so blind and deaf he can hardly tell the beat of a heart from the tick of a clock. But, 'twas murder, all right. Those two Trevells have fought over everything all their lives. Ask anyone in the county. Now the young Trevell newly returned from India has himself a title and a manor house. And his cousin Alistair lies amoldering in his grave."

Alyssa didn't know what to think or say. A rumor of murder was news to her.

The reverend leaned forward, his elbows on his knees. He lowered his voice as if to speak in earnest. "Now I ask you, is Penridge Hall a place for a young lady like yourself to be going?"

She took a deep breath and scrutinized the Reverend Whittle closely. She saw no reason to let his gossip unnerve her. People too willing to share rumors were always suspect. "If the doctor saw nothing to report to the police, then what you say sounds more like tittle-tattle than fact to me."

"'Tis more than atittle-tattle, I promise you," the reverend said, sitting back, clearly affronted. "I simply feel, Miss Lockhart, 'tis my Christian duty to warn you. I would have spoken to your chaperone if the lady had been here, but as it be— well, you know the truth of it now. The Trevells be a strange lot. The old lord ran things with an iron hand as did his father before him. Time will tell what we can expect from the new lord. But look well about you, Miss Lockhart. There be a murderer at Penridge Hall, and his title may well be Harris Trevell, the new Lord Penridge."

"I thank you for your concern," Alyssa said, fussing with the fit of her gloves and wishing the strange clergyman out of the carriage.

"'Tis a pretty place, Penridge Hall," he continued as he reached for the door handle. When he climbed out, the carriage bobbed back to its normal balance. He turned to face her. "You'll like the place on first sight. Everyone does. But the Garden of Eden was beautiful, too, Miss Lockhart. The garden was the doom of mankind. Remember that and beware. Beware. Good day to you."

Before she could say more, he closed the door and slapped the side of the carriage, the signal to the coachman. Instantly the vehicle lurched into motion.

Still curious, she slid back across the seat and pressed her face to the window again to see if the miners were still there on the road, but they were gone. Only the Reverend Whittle stood at the roadside. The way ahead was clear except for the fog.

The reverend raised his hand in farewell and soon disappeared into the gray mist behind them as if he'd never existed. The carriage moved on, the horses' steps quick and sure.

She settled back into the seat, relieved he was gone and mystified by his sudden appearance. Just what had all that been about? Murder at Penridge Hall? What nonsense. But she was glad that Aunt Esther had not been along to hear the story. The poor lady would have been shocked into a fainting spell, no doubt. She would have worried herself to a frazzle during their entire stay.

Alyssa turned the clergyman's mysterious hints of foul deeds over in her mind. Murder? This could be the beginning of an adventure. A real exploit. Of course, in time she would learn that it was a silly tale started by a gossipmonger, or a devoted friend of the poor dead lord, or possibly an enemy of the new lord. But who were those miners? And why had they looked so grim? And whom had the Reverend Whittle really expected to find in the carriage?

Another lurch, but this one only jolted Alyssa against the carriage wall. She grabbed the velvet cord handle to steady herself. They had turned at the top of a hill and started downward, into a valley. Woods and fog closed in around them, thicker and darker than ever. Cold apprehension wriggled in her belly.

What did she really know about these Trevells? They were cousins of Aunt Esther's great-great-uncle somebody, an obscure transatlantic relationship that had been respected down through the generations, since some long-ago relative had landed in Boston. Though the relationship had been maintained, it had never been held close. What did Aunt Esther or Papa truly know about them?

Alyssa took a deep breath. She knew there was a Lady Penridge, the widow, and a little girl and the new lord himself, Lord Penridge. Beyond that . . .

Until now she'd assumed they would be like Boston relatives except they would have that wonderful refined English accent and look like people out of a Dickens novel. But what if she were wrong? What lay ahead? A dark place full of shadows and ghosts? A house more a castle than a residence, full of dungeons with torture chambers and secret passages prowled by a murderer?

She pursed her lips. Maybe she should have run away. How

far would her carefully hoarded pocket money have taken her? St. Louis? Kansas City? New Orleans?

"New Orleans," she whispered. Now *that* would have been an adventure. Maybe she could have learned how to use one of those writing machines and gotten a job with it.

Or maybe she could have gone farther west, to Kansas, and become . . . what did they call them? Harvey girls? It was said Mr. Fred Harvey only accepted respectable young ladies to wait tables in his fine train station restaurants and that the girls often found husbands for themselves among the customers. Of course, she could hardly expect to find a man Mama or Papa would consider suitable at a lunch counter in an Atchison Topeka & Santa Fe Railroad station, but then she wasn't having much success in Boston, either.

She shook her head again. The fact was she hadn't had the heart to run away. She'd gotten no farther than mentally composing her runaway note when she'd had the vision of Mama reading it, then wailing over her disappearance.

Papa, grim-faced, stomping around the house and then sending a private investigator after her. The imagined tears, screams, and vapors had been too much. As much as she longed to try her own wings, she could not trouble Mama and Papa so. She could not inflict such pain—in addition to the family embarrassment she'd already wrought.

The horses' pace quickened. They must be nearing Penridge Hall. Full of doubts, yet more curious than ever for the first sight of her destination, Alyssa once again pressed her cheek against the windowpane.

Fog swirled ahead of the horses almost as if it had taken on a life of its own, arching up gracefully then falling away, parting miraculously as they approached a large, two-story gatehouse. The rooms above the arched passage were lit with lanterns, the yellow light casting a welcoming glow into the darkness. She only had a moment to note the crenellations above, topped with obelisks that gave the granite structure a deceptively delicate fairy-tale appearance.

The gateman, a boy really, waved at the coachman and nodded to Alyssa. She responded with a wave. The horses' hooves struck the graveled drive, and the carriage swung around the circular path. The fog seemed to close in around them again. She could barely see the outline of a sizeable mansion ahead. The coach turned again, forcing her to scoot across the seat to the other side to continue searching for a glimpse of the house. She squinted, hoping to catch sight of more detail.

As the carriage neared the door, the last wisps of fog magically fell away. At last she had her first real view of Penridge Hall.

Two

Against the mist stood a simple, gray granite facade with a two-story entrance porch centered toward the drive. From either side of the house's wide façade, long identical wings stretched out, creating a huge U shape. The roofline was decorated with crenellations and obelisks at the corners like the gatehouse. Dozens of chimneys dotted the slate roof. Lacy vines traced up the walls. Masses of green shrubbery nestled close to the foundation. Alyssa was impressed with row upon row of tall windows. From them, too, fell the golden glow of lamplight, brightening the dark afternoon and warmly greeting her.

She sighed with relief and pressed her hand to her pounding heart. The reverend was right; Penridge was impressive. But he was wrong, too. There was nothing sinister here. It was a wonderful place—almost fairy-tale-like. And she wasn't easily impressed. She'd been entertained in the finest homes Society's four hundred had to display—the great Gothic mansions built along the Hudson and the lavish dwellings in the exclusive neighborhoods of New York and Boston. But none of them could compare to this. None had been built three centuries earlier. None appeared to have grown where they stood, from the ground like an element of the landscape. None of them looked as though their mistress was as likely to appear at the door in a full skirt with a whale-boned bodice as she was to step out in a modern trim skirt with a high-necked shirtwaist.

When the carriage pulled to a stop at the entrance porch, Alyssa became aware of dogs barking and a flurry of activity at the porch door. She touched her hat to make certain it was straight. A stray tendril required a hasty tucking into place. She wanted to make a good impression on her English hosts.

Coachman Whittle appeared at the door and opened it for her. "So sorry about the interruption in our journey back there, miss. My brother, he don't mean to give offense, and I hope you don't take none. Since he found religion, he believes he's obligated to save everyone."

"That's all right, Whittle." Alyssa took the hand he offered and climbed down from the carriage. What a relief it was to stand on solid ground after the long bumpy ride across the moors. "Your brother's unorthodox introduction did no harm."

"Bless you, miss, I am grateful for that," he said. "I will have your luggage into the house straightaway. In the meanwhile, Mr. Tavi here will see to you."

Alyssa shook the wrinkles out of her skirts, then looked up expectantly at the man she'd heard come out onto the step. The sight made her blink in astonishment.

He stared back at her calmly, resignedly, as if he were accustomed to being regarded with surprise. He had a clean-shaven, olive complexion, dark liquid-brown eyes, and a sensuously shaped, though expressionless, mouth. Instead of a butler's black tailcoat, he wore a tan, high-necked military tunic with brass buttons. On one of his arms was a black crepe mourning armband like the coachman's. But it was his headgear that captured Alyssa's attention. The white turban made him appear . . . quite tall.

"Good afternoon, Miss Lockhart," he said in a deep, softly accented voice. He placed his fine hands together below his chin, as if about to pray, and bowed ever so slightly. To Alyssa's wonder, his turban, which appeared heavy, remained perfectly in place. "Welcome to Penridge Hall. My name is Tavi. I trust you had an uneventful journey. If you need anything during your stay here, you must not hesitate to call on me."

"Yes, the trip was fine," she murmured distractedly, unable to stop staring. He was hardly the sort of butler she'd expected to find at the Trevell's. So exotic, so mysterious. Mama's friend, Mrs. P. J. Grogan of New York, had a real English butler. Unlike Tavi, the man had been bland and grandly understated.

Tavi stepped aside and gestured for her to precede him into the house. "Her ladyship and his lordship await you inside."

"Thank you, Tavi." She was vaguely disconcerted by her reaction to the butler, but she offered him a smile. What other surprises was she going to find at Penridge Hall? Taking a deep breath, she stepped through the doorway into the narrow entrance porch that quickly gave way to a large front hall. She found herself treading on plush Oriental carpets rather than stone flags.

Pulling off her gloves, she walked into an area more like a receiving room than a hall. In here the draperies were closed against the chill of the fading afternoon, and lamps burned. A bowlful of roses by the window filled the room with a floral scent. Modern tufted chairs and tables stood around the cheery fire burning in an enormous, ancient hearth. Firelight played shadows across the ornate plastered ceiling.

Before the fireplace stood a blond woman wearing black crepe and a widow's black beribboned cap. At her side stood a little girl dressed in a similar fashion. The woman smiled slightly in greeting, held out her hands, and strode gracefully across the room. The dark-haired child did not follow.

"Alyssa—may I call you Alyssa? We are family, are we not?" the lady said, her voice light, yet throaty. She was almost as tall as Alyssa with an elegantly slender figure, a flawless complexion, fine wide-set sapphire blue eyes, and a small but full-lipped mouth. Her fair hair was simply smoothed back in a chignon. Even dressed in black, the whole effect was severe yet beautifully ethereal, almost

Madonna-like. "No need to stand on ceremony, is there? I am Gwendolyn. I do hope your journey has not been too exhausting. And it is such a shame about Aunt Esther. We were so sorry to hear about the frightful accident. I understand it is unfortunately a common thing, what with you Americans accustomed to traffic on the opposite side of the street. I trust she is resting comfortably at her friend's home."

"Yes, please call me Alyssa." She found her hand clutched in Gwendolyn's firm grasp and a light kiss bestowed on her cheek. Though she'd never seen this woman in her life, she returned the greeting, brushing her lips against the perfumed cheek. It was such a relief to be greeted warmly, as if she were family. "The trip was fine. Aunt Esther was very disappointed that she had to remain in Southampton."

"I shall write her immediately of your safe arrival and assure her that we are pleased to have you here." Gwendolyn took Alyssa's arm and walked her toward the fire. Alyssa was aware of Tavi lurking behind them. "Esther must join us as soon as she is able to travel. Oh my, I haven't even allowed you to take off your wraps. Tavi, take Miss Lockhart's jacket. And I have neglected to introduce my daughter. Miss Alyssa Lockhart, this is my daughter, Meggie. Meggie, dear, do come meet your cousin from America."

As Alyssa shrugged out of her coat, tousle-headed Meggie walked to her mother's side. The child looked to be about ten years old and bore some resemblance to her mother. She was also dressed in black, and even wore a black beribboned cap atop her dark curls. With a scowl, she bobbed a perfunctory curtsy.

While Tavi took her coat and reticule, Alyssa offered the child her warmest smile. "How do you do, Meggie."

Meggie's glare never wavered.

Gwendolyn sighed. She turned to Alyssa, an appeal for patience on her beautiful face. "Meggie misses her father terribly."

"Of course she does," Alyssa said, suddenly feeling awkward and out of place. "I'm sure you all do. I'm afraid my visit is ill-timed."

"But Alistair would have been so pleased to have our American cousin visit us," Gwendolyn said, forcing a tight smile. "You mustn't allow the mood of the house to trouble you. Alistair's sudden loss has been painful for us, but time will heal our grief. I have little doubt of it. We must move on. Alistair would have expected no less of us."

"That's very kind of you." Gwendolyn's words of welcome eased the tight awkwardness in Alyssa's chest. She was going to like this woman.

"Did I hear the carriage?" A deep, preemptory voice boomed from the other side of the fireplace.

"Yes, indeed, Harris." Gwendolyn turned. Alyssa followed her hostess's gaze.

"Ah, so I did," the man said, halting in the doorway. He wore a black frock coat and cravat. His gaze, gray and steely, immediately engaged Alyssa's.

Unwillingly, she sucked in a breath, but she could not break away from his gaze. So this was the new lord. He was hardly a Dickens character. Instead of a paunchy, balding, bejowled gentleman like Mr. Fezziwig, Lord Penridge was tall, fit, clean-shaven—and hardly jolly. She wondered, as he assessed her, if she was as unlike his expectations as he was hers.

"So our American cousin has arrived." His voice was caustic, his smile cold. Though Alyssa stood in front of the fire, a chill crept over her. Clasping his hands behind him, he released Alyssa from his gaze only to turn to the lovely Gwendolyn as he strolled casually across the room.

Alyssa forced herself to turn back to the fire. But he was so much more interesting than she'd expected, she couldn't resist the urge to glance in his direction again. She longed to take in more details—the line of his brow, the wealth of dark brown hair, the crisp whiteness of his linen against the tan jaw.

"Indeed, our guest has arrived, Harris," Gwendolyn said as if she found nothing in the least disturbing about the man's sudden presence. "Alyssa is here safely at last."

"Evidently," he said. Once again she could feel him eyeing her over Gwendolyn's head. His keen assessment conveyed the distinct impression that he wasn't pleased she had arrived at all.

She struggled to control her quickened breathing and finally summoned her courage to return his stare once more.

"Harris, you are purposely being boorish," Gwendolyn scolded lightly with a half-smile. "Welcome our guest. Alyssa Lockhart, may I present Harris Trevell, Lord Penridge. Be kind, Harris. The girl has journeyed a great distance."

"Indeed, she has," he said, his gaze unrelenting, challenging. She stared back unabashedly this time. In spite of his cold frown, he was handsome. He was broad-shouldered, narrow-hipped, and long-legged. More simply put, he was a hero out of a storybook—though his dour demeanor disqualified him for the role of Prince Charming. His physical presence made Alyssa feel acutely alive and clumsy all at once.

"Miss Lockhart," he said, offering her a slight bow. No "so jolly good to have you at Penridge" prattle. He clearly was not pleased to have her here, and she was glad he was honest enough to forego the lie. He continued, "May I call you Alyssa since you will be spending some time with us?"

"Yes, of course," she stammered, feeling off balance like a gauche schoolgirl who barely knew how to behave in formal company. "I would prefer that. And I should call you 'my lord'."

Gwendolyn frowned and stared into the fire.

Her question seemed to catch him off guard. He hesitated before he laughed for the first time, a rueful sound. But his white teeth flashed in a face brushed golden from hours in the Indian sun. Flutterings stirred inside Alyssa, light and strange in their newness.

"My lord?" he repeated, irony in his voice. "Does that

sound strange to you? It does to me. I am accustomed to being addressed as 'colonel.' But 'Harris' will suit me fine."

"Ignore the man." Gwendolyn leaned close and looped her arm around Alyssa's. "He is only being difficult. You will find us a very informal household. Let me show you the house, and then you can take some refreshment and rest before supper."

Leaving Harris behind, Gwendolyn bustled Alyssa off toward a door opposite the one through which she had entered. They crossed another carpeted hall, Gwendolyn leading the way. To Alyssa's surprise, there was nothing in the least castle-like about the house. The shabby condition of the carriage in no way reflected the richness of Penridge. The furnishings, for the most part, were the height of Victorian fashion, deep red velvet and dark, soft leather in that charming combination of mismatched reds and greens, textures, and patterns that only the English seemed to be able to assemble as if it all fit together.

They climbed a rich, dark wood stairway and walked down the cavernous hall. Gwendolyn explained that in the late 1860s a fire had gutted the house. The interior had been completely rebuilt since, incorporating modern conveniences for the family including an up-to-date kitchen and water closets.

What a letdown. Not a single shiny suit of knightly armor loitering in a corner. No flashing swords crossed over the hearth. No echoing great hall, with a minstrels' gallery at one end and a dozen lances fanned out against the opposite wall. Nothing inside Penridge Hall was like the old manor house and castle stereoscopic pictures she had studied before the trip.

Alyssa hid her disappointment. Gwendolyn was clearly proud of her home and enthusiastic about its modern luxuries and rich decoration. She pointed out the new furnishings, the fine craftsmanship, and the valuable artwork with great pride. Her pleasure soon vanquished

Alyssa's disenchantment; she, too, found herself pleased with the house. So it wasn't what she expected. That needn't make it any less charming.

She was especially pleased when Gwendolyn showed her into the bedchamber where she would be staying. The light spaciousness of the room made her take an audible gasp.

Gwendolyn smiled. "I am so pleased you like it."

"It's delightful." Alyssa walked into the center of the room to take in all the lovely details. The chamber was decorated in blue-and-white chintz covers, cushions, and draperies. The ceiling, like all the ceilings in the house, was patterned with ornate plaster decoration. A cheery fire burned in the pretty blue-and-white Delft-tiled hearth opposite the poster bed. On the far side of the room was a long windowseat, a gilt dressing table with a bowl of roses stood against one wall, and here, too, the scent of roses filled the air.

"I hope you will be comfortable," Gwendolyn said as Alyssa walked over to peer out the window at the foggy rose garden below. "This chamber has not been used for some time," the widow continued. "Alistair was a private man. He was not inclined to have houseguests. But I saw to it that Jane and Tavi aired and cleaned the chamber thoroughly."

"But it's immaculate." Alyssa moved from the window around her steamer trunk, which had been placed in the middle of the floor, to the fireplace. She extended her hands toward the warmth of the flames. The heat immediately drove away the chill that had settled over her in the receiving room. She was going to enjoy a comfortable exile, indeed, if she didn't have to face his lordship too often.

When she turned to Gwendolyn, she caught a glimpse of Meggie staring at her from behind her mother's skirts. "I know I will be perfectly comfortable here," Alyssa said, acting as if she'd not been dismayed by the child's resentful glare.

"Splendid," Gwendolyn said, pressing her hands together in a gesture of pleasure. "And you are such a lovely, tall creature, Alyssa. I do so look forward to introducing you to Vicar Carbury and his daughters. He has two girls nearly your age. Delightful young ladies. I know you'll enjoy their company. I don't want your stay to be a gloomy one."

"I'm sure I'll be most comfortable and well entertained," Alyssa said, wishing to reassure her hostess.

Gwendolyn smiled that poignant smile again, blue veins barely visible beneath her translucent skin. The shoulder-length ribbons of her black cap trembled. Alyssa feared her arrival was taxing the lady's strength.

A knock at the door distracted Gwendolyn. "Tea, my lady," came a woman's voice from the hallway.

"Come in, Jane," Gwendolyn said. "I hope you do not mind, Alyssa, but I was sure that you would like the opportunity to rest before supper and to freshen up. So I took the liberty of ordering tea served in your room. This is Jane. Since you did not bring your own maid, she will see to things for you."

In the doorway the maid stood nearly hidden behind a huge tray of china and silver. China rattled as she bobbed an awkward curtsy. "Where shall I put it, my lady?"

"Put the tray by the windowseat," Gwendolyn directed. "When you have finished serving tea, unpack Miss Lockhart's things."

Gwendolyn turned back to Alyssa and once more offered her a cheerless smile. "Supper is served at half past seven. Of course, we dress for the evening meal, even though the household is in mourning."

"Of course," Alyssa echoed.

"We shall leave you to rest." Gwendolyn hesitated, then, without warning, she embraced Alyssa. "I am so delighted you have come, my dear. Your youthful spirit will be good for us at Penridge."

"Thank you, Gwendolyn," Alyssa stammered, returning the brief embrace.

With that, Gwendolyn left the room, drifting through the

doorway like a shadow of the woman she must be when she wasn't weighed down by grief. Silently, Meggie followed her mother, her head bowed, her gaze avoiding Alyssa's. But when the child reached the door, she glanced over her shoulder, a haughty, narrow-eyed gaze skewering Alyssa; then she, too, disappeared through the doorway.

Jane heaved a soft sigh as she closed the door behind the pair. She was a woman of motherly figure with wisps of gray hair at her temples, a care-worn but pleasant face, and an uncertain pucker around her mouth. Spying Alyssa's look of bafflement, she said, "Master Alistair's death was a great blow to Lady Penridge. I'm not certain that she and Miss Meggie are as recovered as they thinks they are."

"Of course, their grief must still be a burden, " Alyssa said, thinking of what the reverend had said about the late lord's death being a murder and wondering if Gwendolyn or Meggie had heard that rumor, too. How would it make them feel?

Without further comment, Jane bent over the tea tray to pour. "There are sandwiches here for you, miss, if you be hungry."

Gwendolyn's sudden exit left Alyssa feeling strangely dispossessed—not in the least hungry. His lordship's frown had done nothing to reassure her, either. Although on the surface the Trevells' welcome had been warm, at the moment she felt more alone than she had when she was riding in the carriage across the foggy moor. Maybe her visit—despite her hostess's protests—was a mistake. The timing was so unfortunate. At best, her stay should be a short one, but where else could she go? Aunt Esther's friend, Mrs. Taddington, hardly had room for another guest.

"How do you take your tea, miss? Milk, lemon, or sugar?" Jane asked.

Alyssa turned to the maid and watched the woman pour steaming water over the tea in the silver strainer placed in a dainty porcelain cup. She liked her tea clear with just a touch of sugar, but she knew that was very un-English. "How do you drink your tea, Jane?"

"Me, miss?" The maid straightened. With brows arched in surprise, she regarded Alyssa solemnly. "Why, miss, I like mine with lots of milk and two lumps."

"Well, then, Jane," Alyssa said, determined to make herself at home as she'd been bidden to do—to make this unwanted and ill-timed journey as much of an adventure as she could. "I'll try lots of milk and two lumps also."

Three

Whitened with hot milk and sweetened with lumps of sugar, the tea's steaming warmth soon restored Alyssa's spirits. She and Jane companionably settled into unpacking the steamer trunk. Though Jane went about the business with feigned indifference, from the way she fingered fabrics and eyed lacy details, it was clear the maid was taking stock of Alyssa's wardrobe. She said little at first, clearly too well trained to voice her judgments. However, the lift of her brow as she removed each new garment from the trunk indicated she found the quality more than acceptable.

Alyssa was glad that she'd accepted her mother's advice that it was *de rigueur* to take somber-hued clothing—gray, lavender, white, and black—to wear in the mourning household.

As they worked, Alyssa made small talk. She had so much to learn. At first, Jane confined her remarks to answering questions. Eventually, Alyssa got her to talk about her background. She was from a Cornish family, unmarried, and had spent most of her life in service. She'd been with the Trevells for several years, though she'd trained as a girl and had served most of her life in a Devon establishment.

Through Jane's chatter, Alyssa learned that the most recent houseguest had been Colonel Trevell himself upon his return from India only three months earlier. He had, of course, stayed in his old room, where he still dwelled, even after becoming Lord Penridge.

"He brought that Tavi fellow with him," Jane said, hanging Alyssa's favorite blue dinner gown in the gilt wardrobe in the corner of the room. Disapproval edged her voice. "We were all glad that the colonel returned. But none of us ever thought that foreign batman of his had come to stay for good."

"A batman?" Alyssa repeated, uncertain about the meaning of the term.

"A batman is an officer's orderly," Jane explained. When Alyssa seemed still at a loss, she added, "You know, a gentleman has a valet. An officer has a batman."

"Yes, I see," Alyssa said, enlightened by the comparison.

Jane continued, "So you see why we below stairs asked ourselves, what is a batman doing getting himself up like he is good enough to be a butler? And him a foreigner and all."

Reluctant to hear the maid out about an ambitious fellow servant, Alyssa said, "The unexpected passing of a family member sometimes calls for changes."

A knock on the door prevented her from saying more.

Being closest, Alyssa opened the door. Tavi stood before her, his face solemn and his dark gaze riveting. His presence immediately upon the heels of Jane's negative comments made Alyssa uneasy. "Yes, what is it, Tavi?"

The turbaned butler put his hands together and inclined his head. It was such a submissive gesture, yet it never seemed to diminish the man's dignity. "His lordship wishes to see you in the library before dinner, Miss Lockhart."

Alyssa's heart sank a bit. So his lordship was going to question her about the reason for her visit. She knew it. Why else would he ask to see her alone? Any mention of that fateful night at Blandfield's made Papa's face turn so red she'd never had the courage to ask him how much he'd told the Trevells. She suspected he had not told them much. But a man like the perceptive, all-business Lord Penridge would hardly be fooled by her father's abrupt request to take in his daughter for an extended visit. Penridge would ask questions.

"Then I shall be glad to meet his lordship in the library at half past," Alyssa said, careful to keep any concern from her expression. She could handle this with dignity. She might have made a bad decision once, but she would not act like a penitent for the rest of her life.

"Very well," Tavi said. "I shall inform him so, miss."

She closed the door softly and turned to see Jane watching her.

"Which gown would you like to wear to dinner, miss?"

"Something blue," Alyssa said. Her best color. She always had more confidence when she knew that she looked good. "Definitely something blue."

When Alyssa descended the main stairway, she saw Tavi standing at the foot as if keeping watch for her.

When he saw her, he gave that little bow and said, "Please follow me to the library." He led the way toward a wing of the house that Alyssa had not toured earlier. Night had fallen outside. All of the draperies were drawn, and the house was dark, though lamps burned in every hall they passed through. Thick carpets muffled their footsteps. Lights even burned in a large salon they crossed, but the fireplace was cold. Their shadows gyrated across the walls and paneling—Tavi's large turbaned head, her full evening skirt—creating distorted, tortured shapes.

Finally, Tavi stopped at a door at the end of the salon. With a flourish he placed his large hands on the polished brass doorknobs, pulled opened the double doors, and stood at attention.

"Miss Lockhart to see you, my lord." Then he stepped back and gestured for Alyssa to enter.

She stepped to the doorway without comment and peered into a vast room. It was more like a ballroom than a library. A few bookshelves lined the walls and a grand piano sat in the bay window at the dark end of the long chamber. She could see Lord Penridge awaiting her in front of the farthest fireplace. He was leafing through a book.

"Watch your step, miss," Tavi murmured, touching her arm and indicating the stone banister.

Alyssa saw that she had to descend three stone steps into the "library" where the glow of the two blazing fires in fireplaces on the same wall gleamed on the wood floor. The cold of the stone balustrade chilled her, but she mentally gathered her composure about her, like gathering up her skirts, and went down the steps with her head held high. As she walked across the enormous hall toward her host, her footsteps echoed self-consciously on the polished floor. Penridge closed the tome he was holding and set it on the fireside table.

"Good evening," he said, appearing to smile, but his eyes were so dark she couldn't read their true expression—or even be certain of their color. With a strange flutter in her breast she also noted how Lord Penridge looked just as handsome as he had earlier. She could not resist smoothing the hair at her temples. She should have paid more heed to her coiffure.

"I am pleased to see you are looking restored," his lordship said.

"Yes, I'm feeling quite refreshed, thank you," she said, silently reminding herself to say the right things and not impulsively blurt out what was on her mind, as she was prone to do. "It was a longer trip than I had expected."

"I'm afraid our Cornish roads make for slow going," Lord Penridge sympathized. "And I heard about the interruption of your trip by Reverend Whittle. I apologize for the inconvenience. Ever since Whittle ordained himself a man of God, he oversteps his authority from time to time. I will see that he is spoken to about waylaying innocent travelers."

"His call *en route* was a bit surprising," she admitted. She was not going to say anything about the reverend's claims of murder in the Trevell household. No one else seemed to think the previous lord had been murdered. Why should she bring up what was probably only a cruel rumor? "But I'm none the worse for the surprise."

"Brave girl," Lord Penridge said, his eyes lingering on her before he turned toward the fire. Alyssa was troubled once more by the urge to smooth her hair.

"Rest assured that the days of Cornish smugglers and pirates are long over," he added. "And the good reverend is the closest claim we have to a lawless highwayman around here."

Alyssa's cheeks warmed. Did the man read minds? Nonsense. How could he know that she'd been fantasizing about a handsome highwayman when Reverend Whittle and his men had waylaid the Trevell carriage? She turned toward the fire and prayed that the dimness of the room hid her blush. "I'm sure the roads of Cornwall are quite safe."

He paced around her to the other side of the hearth. "Please, sit." He gestured to one of the cushioned chairs that flanked the fire. When she had lowered herself to the seat, he took an iron poker from the tool rack and knelt on one knee before the flames.

Alyssa watched him, observing that he had not rung for a servant to stoke the fire but had chosen to do it himself. She clasped her hands in her lap apprehensively and waited for the questions to begin. He surely had not asked to see her in a private audience to apologize for the reverend's bad behavior.

"Let me begin by saying that we are pleased to have you here at Penridge," he said, intent on the fire.

"I realize this is a very awkward time," she murmured. That was the appropriate thing to say, wasn't it?

"Nevertheless, we are pleased to be of service to our American kinsmen," he continued. "I regret pressing you for details of something that might be unpleasant. However, it is clear that there is a specific reason for your visit.

Be assured that your father was circumspect. But because I shall be acting as your guardian while you are here, I should like to enquire as to what it is."

Well, there it was, right out in the open. Alyssa shifted uneasily in her chair. It was a relief to have the issue out, yet she hesitated, glancing at his handsome face, lit only by the firelight. She had decided, when she realized that night at Blandfield's what a gaffe she'd made, that she was not going to apologize for it. She might grant that her actions had been ill considered, but she was not going to bow her head in shame. Gracious, her brother Winslow pulled one stunt after another, and Papa merely smiled—with a trace of pride, if she was not mistaken—at his son's high jinks. High jinks. When Winslow did something that embarrassed the family, it was called high jinks—not a scandal.

Alyssa scrutinized her host. He was studying her, waiting for her reply, no hint of impatience on his face, no tension in his movements. She suspected the man was capable of the patience of Job if it gained him what he wanted. How much should she reveal? How much detail need she tell him? He was right; he was her guardian. Papa had made that clear to her before she left.

Yet, old as Penridge was—he had to be at least thirty—confessing to him was hardly going to be like revealing the truth to a kindly, white-haired uncle. She drew a shaky breath and her hands grew cold. The man was tall, vital, and entirely too masculine for a girl to forget that she was—a girl. Gracious, what should she say?

"All I ask is to know the truth," he prompted when she did not respond. "On my word of honor, I shall keep what you say in confidence. We need never speak of it again. But to do my best for you as my ward, I must know the facts."

"Yes, that seems fair," she agreed. There was no reason to delay. The truth was the truth and would not change with time. "You see, it all started when Winslow, my brother . . ."

She cleared her throat. "My brother called me a skinny red-head."

His lordship blinked and then stared at her as if her words were the last thing he'd expected to hear. After a pause, he turned back to the fire and said, "Go on."

"I know it sounds childish." She took another deep breath, surprised to find that the epitaph still had the power to upset her, to anger her. Anger fueled her courage. "He called me a skinny redhead. And he said that none of his friends would dare be seen on the dance floor with a bag of bones like me."

She glanced at his lordship to see how he was taking this revelation. His mouth worked in a strange way and he coughed. He placed the poker on the tool rack and stood up, his action graceful and easy.

"How old is your brother?" he asked.

"He's a year younger than I," she said. "He's eighteen."

"He has much to learn. Sometimes young men say the opposite of what they are truly thinking." His lordship settled into the chair across from her, his face a study of solemnity. She wasn't sure what he meant by that. He turned to her with one raised brow and said, "I gather you had to do something to disprove his assertion."

"Yes, well, it just happened that the school I was attending, Blandfield's, was putting on a Roman mythology program of classic tableaus. You know, scenes from famous myths. It's a theatrical tradition they perform every year. It is quite highly praised."

"A laudable effort, I'm sure," his lordship said without looking up from the fire.

"And all very tasteful," she was quick to add. There was no reason why he should think ill of the school or her teachers. It certainly wasn't their fault that she'd taken it into her head to show up Winslow. "All the girls wear body stockings and are draped in fabrics like Roman ladies or gentlemen. Everything is posed behind a scrim. The gauzy effect makes the tableau quite artistic and dreamlike. It also makes it difficult to see who is playing what part. Or that a girl is playing a man's part. It's all quite anonymous."

"I understand," he said. "Go on."

"At least, I thought being behind the scrim was anonymous," she said, remembering how, when she'd gone out in the theater audience during rehearsal to judge the effect for herself, all she could see was shadows and outlines. "I'd been selected to play Hercules, because of my height. Well, on top of Winslow's taunt, it was just too much."

"Ah, I see." He glanced at her, his gaze speculative this time. For a moment she thought she saw him struggling against a smile before he spoke. "One insult heaped upon another?"

"Exactly," she agreed, surprised at how well his words described her feelings. His understanding was like having a little weight taken off her shoulders. She took a deep breath. "It took some doing, but I managed to trade places with the girl who had the part of Venus rising from the sea."

"Clever." He leaned an elbow on the arm of his chair and rested his chin in his hand so a finger obscured his mouth.

Her courage wavered.

"What happened?" he asked, his gaze resting on her now.

"I miscalculated," Alyssa admitted, uncertain how to tell the next part.

"Miscalculated?" he prompted.

"You see, I never considered that my height and my hair might give me away."

His gaze flickered to the curls she'd piled atop her head, much as she'd worn her hair as Venus. She liked the style because it made her look grown up. "Your hair is a rather distinct rosy copper," he observed.

"Yes, so when I stood up from my shell, rising from the sea . . ." Alyssa paused, careful to keep from sounding as if she were wailing in dismay. "The top of my head showed above the scrim."

He choked off a cough—or was it laughter?

"Need I say more? Unfortunately, Mama and Papa and some of the audience knew exactly who had *not* worn her body stocking."

His lordship's fit of coughing subsided and he was silent for a long moment.

"I only intended to brag of it to Winslow," Alyssa added in a small voice, "not have the whole world know that it was I in her altogether, behind the scrim."

"Indeed," was all he said.

Alyssa risked a glance in Penridge's direction, her heart thrumming faster than normal. How was he taking this? He didn't seem particularly incensed. Papa had roared loud enough to wake the dead. Mama had gabbled, "How could you? How could you?"

But the expression she saw on her host's face surprised her. If she wasn't mistaken, a genuinely amused smile tugged at his lips, an expression that he tried to resist but could not. Not at all the sort of reaction she'd expected from the cold man she'd met upon her arrival.

Finally he asked quietly, "What did your brother say?"

Alyssa was feeling braver now. "Winslow hasn't spoken to me since that night."

"That's poor sportsmanship on his part," his lordship observed. "Your parents?"

"Miss Blandfield suspended me from school immediately. Mother was furious. She had used her influence with friends to get me accepted there. It is very elite—*trés chic*, if you're New York or Boston society. And it was the third school I've been suspended from in two years. I'm afraid I always offend some teacher along the way. And the day after the tableau, my sisters sent telegrams from New York. I don't know how they found out so quickly, but they did. And they were outraged. Papa says I've shamed the family."

"So it was time for you to leave home for a while," Lord Penridge finished for her, meeting her gaze.

"Yes, well, that's it, the whole sordid tale." She tucked her feet beneath her chair, clasped her hands in her lap, and waited for a lecture.

"And while you are here, your parents would not take it amiss if you followed in the path of Miss Jennie Jerome and found a suitable husband," he added. "Some proper royal such as Randolph Churchill."

"Nothing as ambitious as that," she stammered, embarrassed by the quick shift to the subject of marriage. The man certainly understood her parents. They had hinted that she might redeem herself if she found a husband in England. "I'm afraid they think that because no one here knows my story, some gentleman might consider . . ."

"Umm—so I take it there will be no young American bloke turning up on my doorstep in search of you?" He studied her with a sidelong gaze that told her the answer to the question was important though she couldn't imagine why.

"You mean a suitor?" she asked. "Oh, dear me, no. Mama is certain I've ruined my chances forever."

"I daresay the scandal is hardly as dire as that," his lordship said, but his amused smile was gone. This time he settled a curious gaze on her. His dark eyes gleamed softly in the firelight, scrutinizing her as if he were seeing her anew. "However, I do think it wise to keep the story of you being sent down from Blandfield's over a naked tableau to ourselves."

Alyssa drew a deep breath. "That little prank wasn't one of my wisest decisions."

A sudden shadow crossed his face, and he sat back in his chair and turned to the fire once more. "Don't blame yourself overlong, Alyssa. We have all made unfortunate decisions. As much as we may regret our actions later, we soon learn that the world does not come to an end, even if we wish for it. Even pray for it. Life goes on. We deal with our mistakes as best we can."

Alyssa watched him gaze into the fire, bemused. Orange light flickered over his face; his handsome features that had softened somewhat as he'd listened to her story became hard and uncompromising. She knew his thoughts had drifted far beyond her silliness. What regrets filled his thoughts? He'd lived so many more years than she. He'd seen more places, known more people—men and women.

Women. That thought disturbed Alyssa and tantalized her. What other women had he shared a fireside with? Did they have firesides in India? All she could conjure at the moment was a stereoscope picture of the Taj Mahal. Surely there were beautiful women—dark-eyed beauties who knew how to please men, voluptuous creatures, honey-skinned, veils hiding their mouths, bangles flashing at their wrists, bells tinkling on their toes. Sensuous sirens who whispered into his ear, touched his lips, and danced for him until his dour mood was conquered.

A knock on the door echoed through the library. It jolted Alyssa out of her fantasy.

"Enter," Lord Penridge called without taking his gaze from the fire.

Alyssa turned to see Tavi walking across the chamber, his footsteps nearly silent. He stopped on the other side of his lordship's chair.

"What is it, Tavi?"

"My lord, you asked to be informed immediately when the poachers were apprehended."

Penridge looked up at the butler, his expression even harder than it had been a moment before; his voice was deep and harsh. "The game warden caught the culprits?"

"Yes, my lord. What is the phrase? *Red-handed*—I believe. He wanted to know if you wished him to take them to the sheriff."

Penridge stood up, his movement swift and tense with anger.

"Yes, straight to the officials." He spoke with the command of a medieval lord, master of the manor who wielded the power of life and death over his people. The cold imperiousness of it sliced through the silence of the library and sent a shiver through Alyssa. "Be sure the sheriff knows that I shall tolerate no leniency in this matter."

"I understand, my lord," Tavi said, giving a slight bow and already retreating backwards. "I will convey your wishes to the warden."

As the butler left the library, Penridge remained standing in silence with his back to her. Alyssa could not prevent the memory of Reverend Whittle's accusation from creeping into her mind. Lord Penridge was clearly not a man to push. But was he a murderer?

The sound of the dinner gong drifted through the open door.

"Ah, dinner is served." Penridge turned to Alyssa, shadows of anger miraculously absent from his eyes and the line of his mouth. He was her handsome, elegant host once more. "I apologize for that unpleasant interruption. And I want to thank you, Alyssa, for your honesty with me."

"It was only fair for you to know, my lord," she said.

"Harris." He gave her a patient smile and offered her his arm. "Remember, you are to call me Harris. Cousin Harris if you must, but that sounds terribly stuffy."

"Yes, it does . . . Harris." It made her feel enormously grown up to call this man by his Christian name. Still, she hesitated for a fraction of a second before she took the arm he offered. After her confession and his vow to keep her secret, he seemed slightly less remote than he'd been upon her arrival. When she finally laid her hand on his arm, she found it hard and unyielding, yet warm.

"I do hope you will make yourself at home at Penridge Hall," he said as he led them toward the steps. "Make use of the library, and there are books in my study, too. The stable is at your service if you like to ride. I'm positive Elijah can find a suitable mount for you. All I ask is, no Lady Godiva style of riding."

She laughed.

He looked down at her again and gave her a smile—not one of pleasure—but, nonetheless, a smile.

Oddly, his gentle mockery eased her awkwardness. "I love to ride, but I promise to be quite conventional."

"Good." He placed his hand over hers. His fingers were warm and his hand so large that it covered hers completely. He led them up the steps. "Let's see what Chef Hugo has prepared for us this evening, shall we? He's a troll of a man who has only recently taken over the kitchen, but I have it on good authority that he makes a delicious curry—one even Tavi will tolerate—and he devises the most delightfully sinful sweets."

"Sounds wonderful." Alyssa smiled at Harris. Despite everything—mourning household and rumors of murder—she was very glad she'd decided against becoming a runaway.

Four

Dinner that night was an elegantly simple affair in the mahogany-paneled dining room. A tall silver candlestick of many white tapers lit the three place settings at the head of the long table.

Gwendolyn greeted Alyssa and Harris when they entered. She was heartbreakingly lovely in a fashionable black dinner gown appointed with an exquisite diamond, pearl, and jet necklace and earrings suitable for a widow. To Alyssa's relief she explained that Meggie was taking her supper in the nursery.

Attentively, Harris seated Gwendolyn while Tavi seated her—as was only proper, Alyssa told herself. Then Tavi seated Harris —it was still difficult for her to think of him as simply Harris. From the head of the table Harris guided the conversation toward her voyage. He asked innocuous questions about the weather, shipboard activities, Aunt Esther, and the presence of other notable passengers that she was glad to answer. She relaxed.

As he had promised, he said nothing of her confession. The three of them passed the meal discussing the trials and delights of travel, with Gwendolyn doing a good deal of the talking. Alyssa smiled politely and offered her opinion when it seemed appropriate, and gave a mental sigh of relief. Harris's understanding was going to make her stay so much more comfortable than she'd thought it might be.

She cast him a grateful smile. As if he understood completely, he smiled back, a small, you-are-welcome expression. They shared her secret—he would not tell. Like a special camaraderie—it made her feel positively giddy. She savored the feeling and tried to hold up her end of the conversation without betraying her emotions.

Tavi served, moving silently and efficiently around the table, hardly noticed as he took away empty plates and served fresh ones. No other servant entered the dining room; none was needed. The meal consisted of oxtail soup, lamb with mint jelly, roasted potatoes, and peas. A confection called trifle was served for the sweet. All was very satisfying. Each dish was tasty and well prepared, not at all what Mama had given Alyssa to expect of English fare. She assumed that Chef Hugo could be thanked for that. Soon after the sweet plates were removed, they retired for the evening with the excuse that Alyssa was tired from her travels.

It wasn't until she was preparing for bed with Jane's help that Alyssa even gave the menu a second thought.

"And what was served in the dining room tonight, miss?" Jane asked as she helped Alyssa unhook the buttons down the back of her dress. "Chef Hugo don't allow any of us into his kitchen anymore. We could smell such good things. We don't even have a kitchen maid except for the scullery girl who helps wash up. He seems to have frightened her to secrecy."

What an odd question, Alyssa thought, as she described the menu. "Why is Chef Hugo so fussy about who's in his kitchen?"

"Why, because of the master's death, to be sure." Jane hung the blue bodice in the dressing room wardrobe.

"But he died of natural causes, didn't he?" Alyssa asked, thinking back to what the Reverend Whittle had told her. Perhaps Jane had heard the rumor, too.

"And food poisoning is natural enough, I suppose," Jane said, reaching for the skirt as Alyssa stepped out of it.

"Food poisoning?" she repeated, her hand unconsciously going to her stomach. Was that a grumble she felt?

"A strange case it was and an awful way to go." Jane shook her head. "Painful. The poor man suffered on for several days."

"Did anyone else fall ill?" Alyssa asked.

"No, not another soul." Jane opened a dresser drawer. "Which nightgown would you like tonight, miss?"

"Whatever is on top," Alyssa said, too curious to care about what she would wear to bed. No wonder rumors of murder were flying, she thought. "Isn't that odd? I mean, for no one else to take sick from food poisoning?"

"There be those who think it was," Jane said, with a shake of her head. "And there were those who took offense and left. The last cook had been here for thirty years. I can tell you she didn't take kindly to being told bad food had come out of her kitchen. Peter, the butler, left, and Robert, the footman, and Meggie's governess. Offended they was, too. I was surprised Elijah Whittle didn't go. Be that as it may, that's why Penridge Hall is understaffed. Master Harris was fortunate to be able to prevail upon an old army acquaintance to send his cook. But Chef Hugo, being a Frenchman, didn't set well with some below stairs."

"I suppose not," Alyssa agreed, still considering the revelation. Food poisoning? No one at the dining room table had eaten as though they feared anything. In fact, she remembered clearly that Harris had seemed to have a healthy appetite. Only Gwendolyn toyed with her meal. But then, she had eaten the trifle with some enthusiasm.

Alyssa stepped out of her petticoats and realized that Jane was staring at her.

"'Tis nothing to concern yourself about, miss," Jane said. "We've all been eating the food from the kitchen for years, before the master's death and since. Not a one of us has fallen ill."

"Of course," she stammered, rubbing the sudden chill from

her bare shoulders. "It's just the shock of it. I'd thought the old lord had died of a heart seizure or apoplexy. Something sudden, but . . . I'd never considered . . ."

"Poisoning," Jane finished, clutching a folded nightgown against her bosom and motioning for Alyssa to turn around so she could unhook her stays. "Us neither. But that was the way it was. And those who wouldn't accept the fact are gone. Replaced. Master Harris saw to that. And there's nothing to fear now."

Alyssa glanced over her shoulder. Jane regarded her with an open, honest gaze—almost a challenging expression. The maid obviously wasn't afraid, and it seemed she didn't want the houseguest to entertain doubts, either.

"I'm sure you're right," Alyssa said, wanting to believe Jane. Free of her stays, she began to strip off her camisole. Yet, the truth was she hadn't thought to be afraid until Jane had told her not to be.

"Now," the older woman held out the gown, the neck open for Alyssa. "I think you should wear this one. 'Tis heavier than the others, and the nights do get cool here. Probably cooler than you expect."

"Good advice." Alyssa ducked into the garment and pulled it down over her body, grateful for the warmth.

"I'll bank the fire," Jane said, turning toward the hearth. "When the winter cold sets in, I'll warm your bed with a pan. You'll be comfortable here, Miss Alyssa. We'll take good care of you. You'll see."

After Jane was gone, Alyssa lay awake in the dark, speculating about all that she'd seen and learned—hungry miners, rumors of murder, a resentful child, food poisoning, a mysterious butler, a handsome host gallantly willing to keep her secret. Where would it all lead?

She didn't know, but the memory of the private smile Harris offered her at the dinner table lingered fresh in her mind. The clarity of the intimate expression on his lips stirred warmth in her so strong that fears of poisoning dried up and shrank away. Alyssa fell into an exhausted, dreamless sleep.

"I regret that we can do little entertaining while you are here," Gwendolyn was saying as Alyssa watched the afternoon sunlight turn the tea she was pouring into liquid amber.

They sat at a table that had been set up on the gravel garden path. Tavi, silent as ever, had appeared with the tea tray and sandwiches. The fog of the day before was gone. The sky above was blue, the October sunshine was warm, and the breeze was just strong enough to stir the white linen tablecloth. Bees hummed drowsily over fragrant, late-blooming roses, and autumn leaves rustled in the trees.

Ordinarily, Alyssa loved the afternoon ceremony of steaming tea and sweet cakes, translucent china cups, lacy napkins, and light, meaningless chitchat. But her visit had come at such an awkward time that today, her first full day at Penridge, it seemed more important to concentrate on her hostess than to indulge herself in the pleasure of the ritual.

"But, of course, I understand completely," she hastened to say with her hands folded politely in her lap. She offered a small smile to Meggie, who sat on a stool at her mother's feet. The child stared back, a furrow between her dark brows, her resentful frown unwavering. "Please know that I don't wish to impose in any way," Alyssa added, deciding to ignore the child's bad humor. She didn't even want to think how she'd feel if she had just lost her father.

"Ladies."

She glanced up as Harris appeared at the garden doorway, dressed in riding breeches, shiny black boots, and a well-cut gray coat. The breeze ruffled his dark hair.

The sight of him made her heart give a little leap. She frowned at her reaction. It really wasn't proper for her to be having these feelings about her host. Nevertheless, she was glad to see him.

She had spent the morning exploring the library where she and Harris had met the night before. With sunlight streaming through the high windows, the place hardly bore any resemblance to the sinister cavern that it had seemed then. The shelves offered a good collection of reference books, biographies, histories, natural sciences, and even some novels. She chose one of the latter to take to her room to enjoy later. She'd even sat down at the piano and played a tune for her own amusement. There was no one about to listen, which was just as well. She was an indifferent musician at best. Still, she liked to play and the music soothed her mood.

In the grand salon through which Tavi had led her the night before, she lingered to study the portrait of Alistair Trevell, the thirteenth Lord of Penridge, Harris's cousin. The deceased. The portrait was draped with crepe, the sign of a household in the deepest mourning.

She tilted her head to better study the man whose likeness was rendered in oils, noting a family resemblance. Alistair was older and heavier than Harris. However, he had the same strong chin and broad, intelligent brow, gray eyes, and dark brown hair. Yet there was something about Alistair's mouth that distinguished the two men, a petulance, a sour twist of the lips. It was enough to make Alyssa suspect that the late Lord Penridge might have been more than just cool and aloof like Harris. He might have been an unpleasant man with a quick temper at times.

What had Reverend Whittle said about the two of them fighting? Sure, cousins brought up together, like siblings, tangled now and then. She and Winslow fought, but that hardly meant they were ready to murder each other. What had come to pass between the two men that would lead people to think that one would murder the other? Greed for a title? If she were asked which of these men looked like the sort who would murder for a title, she would have to say the late lord, not Harris.

At midday, Harris put in no appearance, to her disappointment. He was out seeing to business affairs at the mine, Gwendolyn had explained as they lunched in the breakfast room, a meal of bread, cold meats, cheeses, and fruits. Gwendolyn and Meggie had been occupied with lessons all morning, and some of the work spilled over into the lunch conversation.

Meggie was such a pretty child, Alyssa thought sadly. She had her mother's round blue eyes and her father's dark hair, and a complexion that should have been rosy-cheeked. But her black mourning gown and cap made her appear wan and pasty. If only the girl would smile and laugh so she looked like a child instead of a wary old woman gazing out of a little girl's body.

"I'd be glad to help with your lessons." Perhaps schoolwork would be a way to overcome Meggie's hostility, Alyssa thought. "My brother and I used to make games and songs out of learning our geography lessons."

Meggie glowered like a small thunderstorm sitting at the luncheon table.

"How nice for you and your brother," Gwendolyn said. Then she graciously gave a list of excuses as to why Alyssa's help was unnecessary.

In the afternoon Alyssa had explored the garden, which was a lovely place full of meticulously trimmed evergreens and intricately designed flowerbeds amid graveled paths. She found a comfortable bench and spent some time reading. But by teatime, faced once again with the gloomy Gwendolyn and the resentful Meggie, Alyssa was beginning to feel a bit unwelcome.

When Harris appeared at the garden door, it was nearly like being rescued by a hero out of a novel.

"What's this I hear about imposing?" he asked from the doorway.

"There you are, Harris," Gwendolyn said, a smile lighting her face. She set her teacup down and began pouring another cup for him. "I am so glad you are able to join us as you promised. I was just explaining to Alyssa that our entertaining here at Penridge is restricted by our mourning."

"Indeed." He sat down between Alyssa and Meggie. He touched the girl's shoulder and asked her how her lessons had gone. Meggie shrank from him and muttered an unintelligible response. A perplexed expression crossed Harris's face, but he turned and smiled politely at Alyssa. "I believe I heard something about imposing?"

"I was just saying that I didn't want to impose," she repeated.

"If that's true, then why are you here?" Meggie demanded, speaking directly to Alyssa.

The abruptness of the question left her momentarily speechless.

"Miss Lockhart has come to visit her British kinsmen," Harris replied instantly, accepting the teacup from Gwendolyn without looking in the child's direction. "There's nothing amiss about that, Meggie. It has been three months since your father's passing. While a ball with dancing might be inappropriate at Penridge, inviting friends and relatives for a visit is perfectly acceptable now."

Meggie's frown deepened.

With a forced smile, Gwendolyn turned to Alyssa. "Yes, I was about to say the same. And though I'm unable to accept invitations, you would be welcome in the homes of our acquaintances."

"Indeed," Harris said. "We must invite the Littlefields for tea."

"The Littlefields?" Gwendolyn almost spilled her tea. Her smile vanished and she glanced cautiously at Alyssa. "Of course, they are our neighbors. I suppose, Harris, that you want Alyssa to meet Byron?"

"Byron?" Harris echoed as though the idea was the last thought on his mind—and it lacked appeal. He set his teacup down without drinking from it.

"Yes." Gwendolyn's smile returned but it was not quite as

enthusiastic as before. "Alyssa needs to meet young people her own age. There's Byron. And the vicar's daughters, Edith and Lucy. You remember, Alyssa? They are the delightful girls whom I mentioned last night."

"Yes, the vicar's daughters are charming young ladies." Harris turned to Meggie. "You like Edith and Lucy, don't you, Meggie?"

Abruptly, the silent child leaped to her feet. Her glass of lemonade shattered on the gravel path. The movement was so quick that Alyssa was unsure whether the spill was by accident or design.

"No, I don't like them," Meggie railed. Tears streamed down her cheeks, and her face was livid with anger. "They are silly and empty-headed. They giggle and giggle over a sheep-faced look cast their way by any young man. Even on the day of Papa's funeral. I think you're horrible, all of you. Planning parties and Papa only just laid to rest. How can you?"

"Meggie—" Harris began, reaching for the child's shoulder. His voice was filled with consternation and patience.

But Meggie shrugged away, escaping his hand and facing him with a glare. Her fists were clenched at her sides. Then she turned her scowl on her mother and Alyssa. "I hate you all," she hissed, but her eyes rested on Alyssa. "Most especially you for coming now."

Alyssa stifled a gasp, shocked at the child's outburst. But before she could say anything, Meggie dashed into the house.

"I am so sorry for this, Alyssa," Gwendolyn said, as she rose from her place. "No, don't trouble yourself, Harris. I'll see to her. Please finish your tea."

Alyssa turned to Harris. "Perhaps it would be best to delay any teas or dinners on my behalf. After all, you know the truth—I'm not here to be feted."

"No, do not blame yourself for Meggie's behavior." Harris placed a comforting hand on the back of her chair. The gesture touched her, like being taken into his confidence. But she could not dismiss the turmoil she was causing him and his family. "Meggie is taking the death of her father very hard," he said.

"It is to be expected," she said, trying to think of a way to spare her host any more awkwardness.

"She and my cousin were close," Harris went on. "Perhaps even closer than she is to her mother. And Gwendolyn tells me Meggie has always been a sober child, given to dramatic scenes."

"Nevertheless," Alyssa said, growing unhappier by the minute with the upset she was causing. "I don't want to offend Meggie's sense of proper mourning for her father."

"Nor do I." His face dark and troubled, he released the back of her chair without looking at her. "Nor do I intend to encourage hysterics. Gwendolyn and I are in agreement on this. Meggie's grieving has turned morbid. Her taking exception to your visit is purely arbitrary."

She thought Meggie's behavior expressed anger, not grief.

"It has been three months since Alistair's death." He took up his teacup again, a strength and finality in the gesture. "The obligations of deepest mourning have been met. A simple tea with neighbors, providing Gwendolyn feels up to it, shows no disrespect to Alistair's memory. We will invite the Littlefields, Sir Ralph and Lady Cynthia, to tea at the end of the week. You will enjoy meeting them. They are our nearest neighbors and very nice people."

"I'm sure they are," Alyssa echoed, gazing down at the shattered lemonade glass that Tavi had begun to clean up. She wondered what form Meggie's grief would take at the Littlefields' tea party.

She saw no more of Meggie that day. When she asked about the child at dinner, Gwendolyn assured her that Meggie had calmed and was resting comfortably. Alyssa was glad of that.

But her relationship with Meggie did not improve. At

lunchtime the next day Meggie only mumbled a greeting when Alyssa had seated herself at the table.

"I'd like to write to Mama and Aunt Esther," she said over a light lunch of vegetables and roast chicken served by Tavi. "Where might I find stationery and ink?"

"Of course you should write your mother," Gwendolyn said, dabbing a napkin to her lips. Mother and daughter had once again brought schoolwork to the table, leaving Alyssa to feel a bit like an outsider. But after Meggie's outburst at tea and Harris's revelation about the child's temperament, she was beginning to understand Gwendolyn's need to distract the child with lessons.

"You'll find pen and ink in the morning room," Gwendolyn said. "Tavi will show you where the room is. Use my writing desk. Use whatever you like. Elijah takes the post into the village daily. Actually, you can ride into the village with him if you like. Or order the carriage, for that matter," she said in a rush of eagerness to offer her guest amusement. "And the Littlefields have accepted our invitation to tea. They will be here tomorrow."

"Thank you, Gwendolyn." Alyssa happened to glance across at Meggie, who was studying her with narrowed eyes. "I'm looking forward to meeting your neighbors."

"Are you going to write your mama about how boring it is here?" Meggie asked, in a light mocking voice and with a smirk. "If you do, maybe she will let you come home."

"Margaret Trevell!" Gwendolyn frowned at her daughter in horror. "How ungracious."

"On the contrary." Alyssa waved the rudeness aside, even as the rebel in her soul stirred. Meggie could not know how impossible it was for her to return home right now. Nor was she going to allow an angry, grieving child to get the better of her. She met Meggie's gaze across the table. "I wish to write my mother and Aunt Esther about how lovely Penridge Hall is, and how much I'm going to enjoy a long stay here."

Meggie's smirk vanished.

"Excellent," Gwendolyn agreed, casting Alyssa a look of understanding. "You see, Meggie, Alyssa likes Penridge. As a mother, I know her mama will be delighted to receive a long, chatty letter."

Meggie's fork clattered to her plate. She glared at Alyssa, who ignored her as the conversation with Gwendolyn turned to the fineness of the day. A moment later, Meggie shoved back her chair and excused herself, claiming to have a stomachache.

"I'll be right up, dear," Gwendolyn called after the girl hurrying from the room. "This is so unlike her. She was never a demanding child. She was always happy before Alistair's death. She adored her father and he her. I don't know what to do but keep her occupied with lessons. She has always loved her schoolwork."

"I understand completely," Alyssa said.

"We will both heal in time," Gwendolyn said with a somber smile. "Please excuse me. I'd best go see if she needs some remedy."

Alyssa lingered at the table, enjoying the view of the garden that the tall, mullioned breakfast room window afforded. The afternoon shadows were already growing long from the angle of the autumn sun. Yellow leaves swirled through the air on the breeze. She knew the garden air would be fresh and cool. Maybe she would ride with Elijah to the village, just to get out.

It was a moment before she realized that she was not alone. In the corner by the door, Tavi waited, motionless, silent. He was waiting for her to leave so he could clear the table.

Feeling awkward, she rose. "I'm sorry. I don't mean to keep you from your duties."

"It is quite all right, miss," he said, with no smile, no frown, only that polite nod of his head. "Take your time."

"No, I'm finished," she said, folding her napkin and placing it on the table. "Thank you."

"The morning room is straight down the hallway," Tavi directed. "Third door on your right. Would you like me to show you the way?"

"No, I can find it." She walked out of the room, forcing herself not to rush. She'd dealt with servants all her life, but the Lockhart staff had been like family. People she'd grown up with and were more like relatives, who hurried you along when you needed prompting or indulged you when indulging was called for. She did not feel quite so comfortable with the staff of Penridge Hall. She wasn't certain that she would ever feel comfortable with Tavi with his white turban and quiet, mysterious ways.

Third door on the right. She stopped, peering inside through the partially opened door to see a pleasant room in yellow and lace with windows facing west. She could see a black enameled, mother-of-pearl inlaid writing desk at the window. The scent of dried rose petals wafted through the open doorway. Unmistakably a lady's domain. A large potted palm sat next to the desk. Red tapestry cushioned chairs with white antimacassars and a mahogany tea table were arranged near the cold hearth.

"What a pleasant room," she murmured to herself. She was already anticipating settling herself in the desk chair and composing letters to Aunt Esther and her mother. Aunt Esther would especially love reading about Penridge Hall.

Gently she pushed the door open. She'd taken one step into the room when a small but heavy object struck her head. The blow took her by surprise. She reached up to fend it off, but she was too late. It struck her shoulder. Then liquid splashed as the object tumbled to the floor. Thin liquid splattered her hair, her face, and the front of her gown.

She waved her hands and uttered a helpless cry of surprise. Touching her face, her fingers came away dripping black. She gasped. Ink. She felt a rivulet of it run down her neck. Black blotches soaked the bodice and skirt of her new lavender gown—the one that was already becoming her favorite.

"Hah!" Meggie jumped out from behind the palm, the

black crepe of her mourning gown rustling with her hasty movement. She laughed a harsh, humorless cackle and pointed at Alyssa. "I got you! I got you! How do you like Penridge now?"

The child's face was hard and cold—like a little apprenticed witch.

Having a brother, Alyssa had dealt with more than one prank. Unfazed as she was, the sight of Meggie's contorted face gave her pause. Her blood ran cold.

"Meggie?" Gwendolyn came charging down the hallway. "What is this? Meggie? Alyssa? Are you in the writing room?"

Speechless, and holding her ink-covered hands out to avoid touching anything, Alyssa turned to face Gwendolyn.

"What—" Gwendolyn halted at the sight.

"Just a prank," Alyssa managed to say at the moment. She didn't know whether to be offended, angry, or pitying of the poor bereaved child.

"Prank?" Gwendolyn looked blank as she stared at Alyssa in disbelief.

"When I opened the door—" Alyssa began to explain.

"I put the ink bottle on the top so when Miss Lockhart opened it, the bottle fell on her." Meggie had stopped laughing. She clapped her hands and grinned, clearly pleased with herself.

"Why would you do that?" Gwendolyn brushed past Alyssa into the room and rang for a servant. "Miss Lockhart is our guest. Alyssa, I am so sorry. I'll have Jane help you immediately. Meggie, where did you learn such things?"

Gwendolyn had turned to Meggie. The mild scolding did nothing to dampen Meggie's defiant glare at Alyssa.

The wave of shock had disappeared. Fuming, Alyssa glared in return.

The message passed between them, Meggie and her. This was to be more than just a prank. This was war. There would be more tricks. Skirmishes and ambushes designed to dismay, demean, and discourage. Alyssa understood. She and Winslow had battled almost as viciously at times. She recognized anger, frustration, and demands for attention—better than Meggie could imagine. She felt petty and childish, but she held Meggie's gaze so the child knew she understood the challenge, and she was not afraid.

Jane scurried into the room. The sight of an ink-stained Alyssa brought her to a gasping halt. "Oh, miss, ink in your hair and on your lovely lavender gown, too. Let's see what we can do. We might be able to get it out with lemon juice. Come along."

Alyssa resisted Jane's prompting long enough to be sure that Meggie was still watching her. She wanted the child to hear her message. "Yes, Jane, let's see if we can do something about the ink. And after I've bathed, then I'll write my letter in my room. I'm eager to tell my mother and Aunt Esther about my long stay at Penridge, just as I planned."

"I'll send pen and ink up to your room," Gwendolyn offered.

"Thank you," Alyssa said, glad of Gwendolyn's support.

Before she followed Jane out of the room, Alyssa caught Meggie's gaze once more and had the satisfaction of seeing the girl's eyes widen in comprehension and annoyance. Her prank had failed.

Five

Harris did not take the news of the prank well at dinner that night, which Alyssa had learned was always an adult affair. Frowning as Gwendolyn told him about the ink bottle, he turned to Alyssa.

"Were you able to remove the stains?" he asked, studying her face and hair. This was not the sort of attention she wanted from him.

"Yes, from me, but I'm afraid the gown is another story," she said as Tavi served the beef and Yorkshire pudding. "However, I really don't think we should make too much of it. It was just a practical joke."

"But this is not acceptable behavior toward a guest," he said, with indignation. "Meggie is old enough to understand that."

"Please, don't discipline her on my account," Alyssa said, understanding how any harsh punishment would be just another mark against her in Meggie's mind. Though she did not fear the child, she saw no reason to make matters worse.

"You are her mother." Harris glanced at Gwendolyn. "What do you think?"

"I scolded her, Harris, and made her give up her tea. What more can we do?"

"Very well," he said, taking up his knife and fork. "But if there is any more trouble, we may have to consider another course. Perhaps send her away to school."

"Not yet," Gwendolyn pleaded, clearly troubled by the possibility. "She'll come around, Harris. You'll see."

"I think she needs her family now," Alyssa said before she realized she had no real right to express an opinion.

But no one contradicted her. And so it was left.

The next morning after breakfast, she finished writing the letters she had intended to write, making no mention of the Reverend Whittle stopping her on the road, or of an ink bottle atop a door, or of a report of food poisoning. Mama and Papa would hardly think those things reasons for her to return home, and her ailing aunt did not need to know about things that would worry her.

Alyssa confined the letters to describing the house and the gardens and expressing her anticipation of meeting the neighbors and the vicar.

She lunched alone. Gwendolyn sent word that she and Meggie would have a tray sent up to the schoolroom. A wise move, she thought, considering how things were going. Harris was off at the mine as usual. She knew, though, that everyone would be at home to receive their guests for tea at four o'clock.

After lunch she walked to the stables, peering into the stalls to inspect the horses. After all, Harris had told her she had the use of them if she liked. At home she had her own little mare and rode most every day. She missed Cookie and the company of the horses, stable dogs, cats, and good-humored grooms.

Elijah and a lone stable boy, Johnnie, were surprised to find her wandering alone and unannounced in the stables. Still, they were delighted to show her around and tell her the names of each animal, even the coach horses. She loved the smell of hay and horses and the smoothness of well-groomed horseflesh under her hand. Before long she was feeling quite at home in a way she had not felt in the house.

"His lordship's mount, Pendragon, a fine black steed, is out now, of course," Elijah said as they passed two empty stalls.

"Master Alistair's horse was sold last month upon Lady Penridge's request."

At the stall of an elegant bay gelding, he said, "Here is Pilgrim, Lady Penridge's horse. She doesn't ride as much as she did once. And here is Mistress Margaret's pony, Piskie. A good little mount. Then we have a couple of mares. You might like to try Knacker or Smuggler. Knacker tends to chew her bit. Noisy but dependable."

"She looks very nice," Alyssa said, rubbing the muzzle the chestnut mare presented to her. She moved on to the next stall where a dapple-gray mare with black points gazed at her. "What is Smuggler like?"

"Smuggler's a bit spirited, miss," Elijah said, with warning in his voice.

"I'm used to a little spirit." she smiled at the gray mare that studied her with a glint of mischief in its dark eyes. "I'd love to ride her."

"Are you sure, miss?" Elijah cast a skeptical glance at her.

"She reminds me of my Cookie at home," she said, conscious of her first attack of homesickness.

Elijah nodded, seeming satisfied. "I'll have her ready for you in the morning."

The prospect of a morning ride put a bounce in her step as she walked back to the house to dress for tea. By the time the guests arrived, Alyssa was beginning to feel a bit more at home.

"I expect you are finding our little island of England quite different from your home in America," Byron Littlefield said as he stirred his tea, his pinkie finger raised in the air. He was a pleasant enough young man, tallish, and he cut a fine figure, dressed in the height of fashion. But the modishness of his waistcoat did not make up for a premature receding hairline of fair curls, the watery paleness of his blue eyes, his long nose and pointed chin, or his overconfident grin, which he cast at Alyssa over a plate of watercress sandwiches.

She smiled bravely in return. No doubt Harris and Gwendolyn thought they were doing her a favor, but the prospect of being paired with Byron for the remainder of her stay in Cornwall was dismaying, to say the least.

They were sitting around the tea table set up in the garden, this time in the shade of a giant oak on a carpet of grass. It was another glorious fall day awash in golden sunlight, filled with the scent of late-blooming flowers and enlivened by the flitting of the last of the season's butterflies. The perfect setting for tea. So much more suitable under the circumstances, Gwendolyn confided to her before the Littlefields arrived, than having a formal tea in the salon where they normally entertained.

"Yes, Miss Lockhart, do tell us how you find Cornwall different from your home," Lady Cynthia chimed in. She was a few years older than Gwendolyn, with dark hair tucked under a simple lace cap, a sallow complexion, and dark eyes that followed every move Gwendolyn made like a wary puppy.

"I hardly know where to start," Alyssa said, mentally debating about how honest to be. Mama had brought her up to understand that her obligation to be an amiable guest was as essential as her hosts' obligation to be hospitable. She wanted Harris, who was standing behind Gwendolyn across the table from her, to be pleased to have her in the company of his neighbors.

"For one thing, everything here is so very much greener than at home. The roads are narrower. The air is a bit damper. But the trains are quite comfortable. The roses and rhododendrons are absolutely sumptuous."

A smile of pride lit Sir Ralph's round face. "We have first-rate trains. To be sure. You like it here, then?"

"Everyone has been most kind," she said, unable to resist a glance in Meggie's direction. The child was seated between her and Gwendolyn. Meggie met her gaze, sniffed impertinently, and reached for a strawberry tart. This was their first confrontation since the ink bottle incident. Obviously, Meggie felt no remorse.

"It is a pleasure to entertain Alyssa," Gwendolyn said, her voice soft and lifeless. "We are doing our best to move on after Alistair's death."

Lady Cynthia's polite smile vanished. "Yes, it must be difficult for you, Lady Penridge. After all that you had to go through with the staff and all . . ." Her words trailed off.

"Gwendolyn is bearing up admirably." Harris, holding his teacup, placed his free hand briefly on his cousin-in-law's shoulder.

A wan smile of appreciation crossed Gwendolyn's beautiful face. She turned her head slightly toward him and touched his hand lightly in response.

The casual but intimate gesture sparked an unexpected flash of envy in Alyssa. She sipped her tea to cover the emotion. The envy bred a flicker of guilt. Harris had every right to comfort his cousin's widow. But, oh, how she would like him to praise her so—to touch her hand, to smile at her like that.

Byron sipped his tea, his gaze darting around the circle of them at the table. She prayed her jealousy did not show. And she wondered if he felt the same tension in the group that she sensed from the moment of the Littlefields' arrival. Surely the awkwardness was just that of the first gathering after a painful loss. Whatever it was, there seemed too many awkward silences.

"Go on, Miss Lockhart," Byron urged, setting down his cup. "What else have you discovered that has intrigued you during your visit?"

"One of the things I'm enjoying most is the house," Alyssa said, vaguely aware of Tavi moving around the table, offering a platter of sandwiches, biscuits, tarts, and scones to each guest. She also noted that once accepted, the food remained untouched on the guests' plates. "Penridge Hall is all tradition on the outside and modern innovation on the inside. Gaslights and all," she added.

"Alistair's doing," Sir Ralph said in a soft but accusatory tone.

"Well, of course, after the fire he modernized the house," Lady Cynthia said defensively. "Why renovate the house to its old-fashioned state?"

"And a fine job he and Gwendolyn did of it, too," Harris said.

Another long, awkward pause stretched over the table.

Alyssa sensed that they were talking around some issue that they all knew about but no one dared mention. Something sensitive or embarrassing.

"Have you heard about the wedding, Miss Lockhart?" Byron asked brightly.

"No," she said, relieved that he was changing the subject. "What wedding?"

Meggie silently gestured her desire for more tea.

"I quite forgot about Lucy's wedding," Gwendolyn said, reaching for the teapot.

Her usual graciousness oddly absent, she began to refill Meggie's teacup without offering the other guests more.

When her mother had finished pouring the tea and milk, the child busied herself with the sugar and lemon.

"Lucy Carbury, the vicar's daughter, is getting married in a few weeks," Gwendolyn explained. "There will be a lovely celebration in the assembly room in Launceston. Mrs. Carbury and the girls have been planning the event for weeks now. I cannot go, but, of course, you must, Alyssa. Everyone in the district will be there. There will be music and dancing."

"It sounds very festive," Alyssa said, vaguely aware of Meggie fiddling with her black pinafore and squirming in her chair.

"Then we shall see to it that you go," Harris said, studying her over Gwendolyn's head. The severity of his expression did not make her think that he was particularly pleased with the idea.

"Indeed, it will be festive," Byron said, smiling more broadly at her now. "You must promise to save a dance for me, Miss Lockhart."

Abruptly, Meggie stood, rattling the china on the table. "May I be excused, please?"

Gwendolyn looked quite startled. "But I thought you liked—Chef Hugo made the strawberry tarts just for you."

"I had one." Meggie shrugged in a manner that said she felt she had fulfilled her obligation. "May I go now? I have schoolwork I wish to finish."

"Let her go, Gwendolyn," Harris murmured.

"Of course you may go, dear." Gwendolyn tugged on the hem of the rumpled pinafore. "Say your good-byes to Sir Ralph and Lady Cynthia and Mr. Littlefield."

"Good-bye." Meggie offered the guests a tight smile and a quick curtsy.

"That's my girl," Gwendolyn said. "I will be up soon to see what progress you have made."

Meggie dashed into the house.

"My, how she has grown." Lady Cynthia engaged Gwendolyn in conversation about Meggie and then the garden.

Sir Ralph asked Harris about a problem with poachers, which seemed to interest Byron.

When Alyssa picked up her teacup and took a sip from it, she knew immediately why Meggie had been so eager to leave. She nearly gagged on the foul-tasting liquid. Instantly she brought her napkin to her mouth to stifle the involuntary reaction. She didn't want to repulse anyone, nor did she want to embarrass her host in front of his guests.

Her tea was full of salt. Salt smuggled in pinafore pockets, no doubt. Another of Meggie's pranks.

She held the napkin to her mouth a moment longer and prayed that no one at the table had noticed, but the observant Tavi was instantly hovering at her side.

"Is there anything wrong, miss?" the butler asked in a low voice. She thought she actually detected concern in his tone. "Are you all right?"

Alyssa cleared her throat. "My tea is cold. Please bring me another cup."

Tavi stared into the teacup, then into her face, scrutinizing her as though he thought she might be fibbing—or something worse.

"Do you feel all right, miss?" He peered into her eyes and searched her face for something dire—like poisoning symptoms?

Alyssa stared back. What was she supposed to do? Grab her throat and turn blue? Or perhaps she should slide out of her chair onto the grass and begin to foam at the mouth.

When she merely blinked at him expectantly and held out her teacup, making it clear she was giving no more explanation, he answered, "I'll bring you another cup immediately."

She folded her hands in her lap and waited. No reason to give Meggie the satisfaction of making a scene. Winslow had taught her that lesson. Having hysterics over a prank only made the culprit victorious.

Neither Harris nor Gwendolyn seemed to have noticed that anything was amiss.

As the others talked, Alyssa glanced upward at Penridge Hall. Was Meggie watching from above, waiting to see how she reacted to her teacup full of salt? Very likely. Was that a small figure in black at the stairway-landing window that overlooked the garden? Tall palms sat in each corner of the landing. Because of the fronds, Alyssa couldn't be certain if someone was there, spying. In any case, she purposely turned to Lady Cynthia, smiled, and leaned forward, pretending to listen with great interest to the conversation about roses.

From the corner of her eye she saw a vague movement at the landing window. Then it was gone.

* * *

That evening, Alyssa sat at the dressing table, preparing for dinner and wondering what to do about Meggie. How was she ever going to make the child see that she was not the enemy?

Jane bustled into the room and began to see to Alyssa's dinner gown and shoes.

"And did you meet Mr. Byron, Sir Ralph's nephew?" the maid asked as she brushed the hem of the gray dress they'd agreed upon. "What did you think of him, miss? A handsome lad, is he not?"

"He seems very nice," Alyssa said, pursing her lips at herself in the mirror. Now the servants were matchmaking.

"Yes, he is a right nice young gentleman," Jane said. "He's looking for a wife. So they'll be trying to pair you two off. The Littlefields, that is. Did I tell you that my sister is in service at the Littlefields'?"

"No, you didn't," Alyssa said.

"So, we share stories sometimes." Jane brushed diligently at the dress sleeves. "Not often, mind you, but you know, sometimes on our days off, sister and I talk and things come up about family."

"I suppose it's unavoidable," Alyssa said, attempting to follow where Jane was leading.

"Sister says that Sir Ralph hardly lets Lady Cynthia out of his sight these days," Jane said. "The poor lady is a bundle of nerves with him always looking over her shoulder."

"I thought she was uncomfortable."

"Elijah said the Littlefields didn't stay long today," Jane continued as she worked.

"They were here over an hour." Alyssa picked up the hairbrush and began to brush her hair. "Is that not proper enough for a tea?"

"Yes, proper enough." Jane examined the neckline of the dress. "It's just that this was their first visit since that fateful night. You know, the night that Master Alistair took sick with food poisoning. They were here, at the table. I was curious as to how they'd react when they returned."

"Now that you mention it, they didn't eat much," Alyssa said, remembering how the strawberry tart Meggie had eaten and the scone she herself had taken were among the few items consumed.

"Oh, Chef Hugo will take exception to that," Jane said, as if the thought pleased her. "There weren't any harsh words between Sir Ralph and Master Harris then?"

"No, none that I heard," Alyssa said, turning to look at the maid. But there had been that awkwardness that she couldn't quite put her finger on. "Why do you ask?"

"There are bad feelings between the Trevells and the Littlefields," Jane said. "At least, there were between Sir Ralph and Master Alistair."

The news surprised Alyssa. "But Gwendolyn and Harris talked about the Littlefields as if they were old friends."

"Well, the vicar and Master Harris was trying to make that so," Jane said, picking up the shoes to examine them. "That was part of the reason for the dinner that night. With the help of Vicar Carbury, Master Harris wanted to mend fences with the Littlefields. Master Alistair was not too keen on the idea, but he seemed to go along with it."

Puzzled, Alyssa turned back to the dressing table mirror. "What was the reason for the bad feelings?"

Jane sat the shoes down and stepped back to examine the dress at a distance. Then she turned to Alyssa. "I don't want to be one to tell tales, but being a guest at Penridge Hall, you probably should know—and I doubt her ladyship or his lordship will tell you under the circumstances. But everyone in Cornwall knows the story."

"What story?" Alyssa asked, knowing she shouldn't be encouraging the maid to repeat tales, but . . . well, how else was she to learn things around here?

Jane crossed the room to the dressing table, where she put down the clothes brush and took the hairbrush from Alyssa. "About five years ago, before the fire here at Penridge Hall,

Master Alistair told Sir Ralph that he wanted to buy some land from him to build a seaside cottage for Lady Penridge."

Alyssa sat quietly, listening as Jane began to brush her hair.

"So Sir Ralph sold him the land," Jane continued, her thoughtful brushing becoming more vigorous as she told the story. "But instead of building a cottage on the land, Master Alistair built a clay mine, Wheal Isabel. Named it after his mother. He brought in the most efficient steam engines and pumps. Sir Ralph took exception. He accused Master Alistair of purchasing the land under false pretenses and of failing to show him the neighborly courtesy of offering him a part in the business scheme."

"I see," Alyssa said. "So then, I assume the Littlefields have not been guests at Penridge Hall on a regular basis since that time."

"That's so, except for the night that Master Alistair took ill," Jane said. "That's why all of us below stairs were surprised that Master Harris invited them to be the first callers at Penridge since Master Alistair's death."

"Yes, it is interesting," Alyssa said, understanding better the reason for Gwendolyn's uncharacteristic lack of hospitality and Lady Cynthia's wariness. "Perhaps Master Harris wants to continue to pursue the course of peace that he'd embarked on earlier."

"Perhaps," Jane said. "It's true that Master Harris is not like the man who left Penridge for India ten years ago."

"How so?" Alyssa asked, trying to imagine Harris any different from how he seemed now.

"He's older, of course." Jane stopped brushing, the brush poised in the air. She stared off into space, obviously searching for her response. "Not so angry. He was an angry young man when he left here for India. But not so now. He's quieter. Not that scared or hurt kind of quiet. It's the kind of quiet that says he knows things. You know what I mean, miss? Like he has learned more than the rest of us. He's been places like

India, and he's seen things and learned things the likes of which we can't imagine. Strange things."

"What was he like before?" Alyssa asked, not sure she understood what Jane was trying to say. "What happened to his parents? How did he come to live at Penridge?"

"His parents was burned up in a fire in their London town house," Jane said. "Master Harris was but a boy of five, I believe. His nanny saved him from the flames. But his parents didn't escape. Weren't no other family to take him in. So the poor little tyke came here to live with his aunt and uncle. That was Seymour and Isabel Trevell, Master Alistair's parents. Lord Seymour dismissed the nanny straightaway and brought Master Alistair and Master Harris up together."

"So young to lose his family," Alyssa said, saddened and more curious than ever about Harris. "What was he like as a boy?"

"As a boy he always had a smile on his face, except when he and Master Alistair had a fight," Jane said as she resumed brushing Alyssa's hair. "Confident, he was. He always had a greeting for all of us. He was an easy one to serve, miss. Not that he isn't now, but there's something cool about him that wasn't there before. He's not sunny and open like the old days. Of course, he was but a boy of ten years when I first come to Penridge, but I thought he'd grow up to be the same kind of man. Smiling and easy to talk to. That's been a disappointment, that he didn't grow into the man he promised to be. I suppose travel to a foreign place makes changes. Don't get me wrong. He is still a good lord to serve, miss. I have no complaints. "

Alyssa studied Jane's reflection in the mirror. The woman was telling the truth as she saw it. Harris was not the boy she'd known. But then how many people grew up to be the person they promised to be? Was that good or bad?

Take her, for example. She kept hoping that growing up would make her a better person. How long was it going to be before she outgrew being the brash, heedless girl she was?

Jane ceased her brushing. "Now, how would you like to do your hair for dinner tonight, miss? In the curls on top, your favorite? Or something different?"

She studied herself in the mirror once more.

There in the glass was the same girl she'd known all her life, the tomboy: straight hair a little too coppery, a brow too broad, big eyes too wide-set, a jaw too square, a mouth too wide and full. She was everything unfashionable.

"Something different," she said. "Please, Jane. Something feminine. Something that makes me look grown up and mysterious. Something that makes me pretty."

"What nonsense is this, miss?" Jane said with a chuckle. "You are pretty. Not fashion-plate pretty, granted. But them big eyes and this thick, silky hair—it's the kind of pretty the men never forget. I'm sure Mr. Littlefield didn't overlook your good looks. How about something simple and elegant for tonight? Let's smooth it back this time. Something to wear to dinner and maybe to the wedding so as to catch Mr. Byron's eye."

"Yes," was all Alyssa said, staring at her girlish face and lanky hair reflected in the mirror. But it wasn't Byron's eye she wanted to catch.

Six

"That way leads up to the moor, miss," said Johnnie, the stable boy, when Alyssa reined in Smuggler to study the fork in the bridle path.

It was a clear morning. They'd begun riding along an avenue of beeches in Penridge Hall park. The long lane of trees led down into a stand of woods where a stream ran, bubbling along clear and cool over the rocks and boulders. It had rained during the night and autumn leaves had fallen so that a carpet of gold covered the forest floor. Fairy-tale-like woods, she thought, misty green, gold and mossy.

After all, this was Cornwall: the legendary home of King Arthur, Merlin, and King Mark. A place where a witch or a wizard might pop out from behind a knurled tree to demand, Who goes there? Or maybe a knight in shining armor on a white steed would appear, Lancelot or Tristan, in search of a damsel to rescue.

The scenery was lovely; however, the fork in the path, and the accompanying rumble she could hear from just beyond the woods, were the most interesting things they'd yet encountered.

"It leads to the moor and where else?" she asked, listening to the regular chug of large machinery in the distance.

"To the moor and on to the mine, the Wheal Isabel," Johnnie said, his long, youthful face sober and earnest. He couldn't be more than a day over fifteen, and he seemed a bit intimidated by her. She found that amusing. Why would anyone be afraid of her?

Elijah had refused to allow her to ride alone, which she was accustomed to doing at home. He'd sent Johnnie along to act as groom. She was more than a competent horsewoman. She could outride Winslow and his friends any day. She liked quiet time in the open air with a good horse, like Smuggler, under her.

If she were alone she would have rearranged her riding habit, thrown her leg over Smuggler's side, and ridden astride, which was more comfortable and better for the horse. A solitary ride: no words, just the wind in your hair and silent communication with the animal—that was invigorating. Satisfying. It was primal and real. You could smell the scent of the horse and taste freedom.

She glanced at Johnnie. Still, she decided, Elijah was probably right to send her off with an escort until she knew her way along the paths and had demonstrated her abilities. And Johnnie was a good guide, informative but not intrusive.

"What is the noise?" she asked.

"That's the steam engine you hear rumbling, miss," Johnnie said. "The mine is not a pretty place. And the miners are rough men. I don't think his lordship would want you to go there."

"Really? He didn't mention it." Few things had more appeal than the forbidden. She continued to gaze up the path. Harris was there somewhere at the mine, where he went every morning just like a workingman. She'd thought English lords were men of leisure. At least that's what Mama had told her. "Let's go have a look, shall we? I've never seen a mine." She urged Smuggler up the rocky path.

Johnnie followed, as she knew he would. The poor boy had no choice.

At the edge of the woods the ground gave way to rolling, treeless hills covered knee-deep in yellow gorse—the moor. The well-used rocky path stretched ahead of them, cresting the hill and disappearing in the direction of the noise and the tall stone smokestack belching dark smoke into the clear sky. White powder covered the mine building roofs and the mounds of earth around them.

So this was the clay mine, the Wheal Isabel that had caused such hard feelings between the Littlefields and the Trevells, if Jane's story was to be believed. And why shouldn't she believe it?

The scent of the sea reached her on the breeze, though no surf was in sight. She could not hear any breakers over the din of the steam engine. She knew the coast must lie just beyond the moors to the north, nearly in view of the mine.

She rode on, leading the way. Johnnie jogged along behind on the raw-boned bay saddle horse. Alyssa wondered where the wagon road to the mine was. There had to be one: a road that allowed equipment to be brought in and the clay to be taken out. The path she and Johnnie rode was probably Harris's private way to Wheal Isabel.

Closer to the mine, at the foot of the hill, the path connected with the wagon road she'd been looking for. As she and Johnnie turned onto the road, she heard the sound of voices and many feet moving. Looking toward the cottage rooftops opposite the mine, she saw a crowd of men marching around the bend nearly at a run. White powder covered their shoulders and their caps, much like the men she remembered with Reverend Whittle when he stopped her coach on the road to Penridge. They were shouting as they marched, their words unintelligible, the tone angry. Before she could think what to do the crowd swarmed about them.

Smuggler began to prance. Alyssa fought for control of the mare. Angry faces glared up at her, eyes bright with hostility. Heated voices were raised loud enough that she could hear their shouts over the steam engine noise, but in the excitement she still could not make out what they were saying. One thing was clear, though: rage hung over the mob like an invisible storm cloud.

"Go back up the path, miss," Johnnie shouted, riding up beside her to shield her from the onslaught of the mob.

Alyssa couldn't imagine why she should fear these men. She'd done them no harm. But the fury on their dark faces convinced her. If she fell off Smuggler into the swarm, she'd be in danger. With trembling hands she struggled to bring Smuggler around toward the path again, but the men blocked her way, shouldering against the mare until the animal was almost too frantic for her to control.

"Make way," came the sound of a familiar voice. "Step aside, I say."

Relief flooded through her. Alyssa glanced around to see Harris on horseback fighting his way through the mob toward her. He wore no hat and was in his shirtsleeves and waistcoat as though he'd hurried out of the office to his horse.

At first his demand, shouted over the voices and the engine rumble, went unheeded. The men shoved against Pendragon, too.

"Out of the way," he ordered again without raising a hand to a single man as he expertly reined his big, black hunter through the throng. His lips were thin with determination. He sat tall and erect in the saddle, his sun-darkened complexion in contrast to his white shirt. Even without coat and hat he looked more like Colonel Trevell, military man, than Lord Penridge. "Do not waylay the lady."

When he reached her side, he frowned at her. "What are you doing here?"

Faced with his displeasure, her relief vanished. "I just was out for a ride—"

"Later." He grasped the bridle of her mount and turned back to the mob. "Disperse. Be on your way."

"Not until you hear us out, Lord Penridge," someone called.

The multitude moved, swirled, and flowed around them like a swarm of angry beetles. Alyssa, Harris, and Johnnie could not pass unless they made way.

"What is it then?" Harris asked, though Alyssa felt certain that he already knew what the men wanted.

"Food," a mob member shouted. "Our families are starving."

"That's right, they want food," the Reverend Zebulon Whittle cried, suddenly appearing out of the sea of unfamiliar faces. They parted for him. He swaggered forward to stand at Pendragon's head. "The pilchard run is late this year. And there's precious little grain to be had in these parts. What there is costs a man his first-born child. What are you going to do about it, Penridge? These men have slaved their hearts out for you and your cousin. They have brought you a fortune. What will you do in return?"

"You have even taken the poachers from us," a voice called from the back of the mob. "Had them thrown in Launceston gaol, you did."

"Yes, and I can tell you why," Harris replied. "Poachers steal from Penridge and from you, taking game where they have no right and selling it to you at unfair prices. If game is what you want, talk to my game warden. He can grant a few licenses."

"There ain't enough birds for all of us," another voice called.

"It has been a bad year for the farmers and for the fishermen," Harris said, speaking to all of the men. "The result is that prices are high for everyone. Who is without food? Show me your hands."

An ugly grumble resounded through the crowd. Hands went up all around them. Her fear forgotten, Alyssa stared in dismay at the lean faces of the miners milling around them. Now that they had quieted she could see their gauntness, the hollowness around their eyes, and the loose hang of clothes on thin bodies. Most of them, she was sure, had wives and children at home who must be hungry, too.

Hastily, she dug into the pocket of her riding habit for the treat she'd taken from the sideboard for Smuggler.

"I have an apple," she piped and held it up for all to see.

The mob fell silent. Not a man made a sound as they stared at the fruit in her hand. In the silence she realized what a silly thing she'd done. One apple would hardly feed the lot of them. But it was what she had to give. She leaned down from Smuggler and shoved it at the miner nearest her. "Take it home, please, sir. For your wife and children."

The miner's eyes grew round with surprise. With respect he touched his clay-dusted cap and accepted the apple. "Yes, miss, I will."

"A generous offer, Miss Lockhart." Reverend Whittle smirked at her. Alyssa blushed at her foolishness.

Harris touched her hand, a comforting gesture. "And what do you have to offer these men, Reverend?"

"The courage to face you and ask for what they deserve," Whittle said, a victorious grin revealing a mouthful of yellow teeth. "What say you, Penridge? Your men work hungry. Their families starve. And you lecture them about high prices. The lady offers only an apple. What do you offer?"

Harris's face grew hard and his eyes narrowed. He did not like Whittle, no doubt about it. "Do not cast me the villain in this drama, Whittle. And do not take me for my cousin. No one has ever starved who gave me a decent day's labor. I will have grain shipped in and priced fairly for you. Grain for Wheal Isabel workers and their families. Does that suit you?"

The miners' mutterings took on a slightly more positive tone.

Reverend Whittle studied Harris. "It is a beginning, Penridge. For now it'll do."

"Then be on your way home or to your shift," Harris said to the miners. He still held Smuggler's bridle.

In twos and threes the men began to melt away from the mob. Mutterings continued, but most of the men seemed satisfied with the promise of grain.

"If the grain doesn't arrive soon," Whittle said, his grin

gone, replaced with a fiery challenge in his eyes, "you can be sure you will hear from me."

Alyssa stared at the clergyman who was pointing at Harris. And she'd thought the man just a nosey cleric the day he'd waylaid her coach. Here he was threatening Harris.

"I never doubted that." Harris's voice was even but his mouth twisted with distaste.

Whittle turned away and began to talk with some of the miners who still crowded around him. Deep in conversation, the group strode down the road toward the village.

"Now, what on earth were you doing out here?" Harris demanded, finally releasing the bridle and turning his full attention on her.

"We were just riding," Alyssa said. Then, remembering Johnnie, she added, "Johnnie didn't want me to come this way, but I wanted to explore."

Harris glowered at her as if there were a thousand things he wanted to say, but she guessed that he chose not to say them within earshot of the groom.

"Go to the office and get my hat and coat," he ordered the lad without taking his gaze from her face. "Then catch up with us. I shall see Miss Lockhart home."

With a nod of obedience and obvious relief, Johnnie wheeled the rawboned mare around and cantered toward the mine.

"This way." Harris gestured toward the rocky path she and Johnnie had come down.

"You don't think there will be more trouble, do you?" she asked, silently debating whether he was still concerned for her safety or angry with her.

"Not really," Harris said over his shoulder as he rode ahead of her toward the cover of the woods. "Most of the miners are good men. Honest as the day is long and hard-working, too, when they feel they are being treated fairly. But sometimes circumstances make it difficult for the best of men to stand by their principles."

"Influences like Reverend Whittle?" she ventured.

Harris glanced at her, then rode on without saying any more. When they reached the trees, he halted both horses and turned to face her.

"You will not ride in the direction of Wheal Isabel in the future," he said. "Ride the bridle paths. Ride to the village, if you like. I'll not lock my guests up like prisoners because the miners are unhappy. That would be an insult to you and the miners. But sometimes feelings run high. I will insist that you stay away from the immediate neighborhood of the mine and the miners' cottages. Is that clear?"

Alyssa gave an emphatic nod. The mob had frightened her, and she knew the fear was plain on her face.

"You're pale." he leaned closer, scrutinizing her. "Are you sure you're all right?"

"Yes." She took a deep breath and wished she'd thought to pinken her cheeks with a touch of rouge before she'd left the house. "Truly, it was all such a surprise. I'm fine now. I'll do as you ask in the future."

"Good." Harris looked away and sighed. "This is an old problem, this one with the miners, their wages and food. Alistair was constantly beleaguered with it. Life in Cornwall has never been easy—for miners or farmers or fishermen. I never envied my cousin for having to deal with it. There was a time when I thought I'd gotten the better end of the deal—not being the Penridge heir."

He gave a rueful shrug of his shoulders. "Now the problems that were Alistair's are mine to sort out, anyway."

Hardly the words of a murderer, Alyssa thought, a sweet ribbon of relief uncoiling inside her. Funny how she longed to disprove the rumor of murder that Reverend Whittle had so eagerly told her on her first day in Cornwall. Murder? One cousin against the other, the reverend had implied with a sly smile. Nonsense. The man she'd just heard speak regretted his cousin's death and had no desire to take on his responsibilities.

They turned as the sound of hoofbeats reached them. At the top of the path, Johnnie appeared. He slowed his horse and guided it down toward Alyssa and Harris.

"Here you are, my lord," he said, handing over Harris's coat and hat.

Harris donned his hat and shrugged into his gray coat. "If you're feeling up to it, let me show you some of the other bridle paths that you might find more pleasant," he said, leading Alyssa down the fork in the path she'd rejected earlier. Johnnie followed them. With the angry faces of the miners still lingering in the back of her mind, she gladly allowed Harris to lead the way.

Taking on the role of host, Harris turned the conversation to mundane things about the countryside's trees and ferns. Obviously he wanted to put the violent scene with the miners behind them.

And she thought it was forgotten until, at a bend in the path, he halted and faced her.

"That was a generous offer with the apple," he said. A small smile lighted his face.

The blood rushed to her cheeks as she recalled the foolishness of holding up one apple before a mob of hungry men. "I didn't realize—I just meant to help, though I know it was inadequate."

"No, I didn't mean that." A light shadow of regret crossed Harris's face. "I mean to say, your gesture was a genuine, heartfelt one. I believe the miners appreciated it. You charmed them, my dear."

It was a compliment, paternally given. She didn't know what to say.

As he studied her, a slow smile came to his lips again. "Don't underestimate the power of a generous gesture, Alyssa."

With that, he reined Pendragon on down the path, resuming his narrative about the flora and fauna.

Vaguely pleased with the unexpected praise, she resumed her part as guest, asking questions when appropriate.

Harris's voice was deep and pleasant to her ear, and the information he recounted was of interest. Riding along the stream, with gold-and-orange oaks and hawthorns arching overhead and obscuring the sky, she had no idea whether they were riding north, south, east, or west. The fact seemed of little importance. The air was heavy with the scent of leaf mold. Clear water sang over the rocks. Harris talked of foxes and badgers, nightjars and merlins, hedgehogs and otters. His company was enough for her now. She hoped this interlude would last for a long time.

All too soon, the trees parted and they were riding across a meadow toward an elegant, half-timbered Tudor cottage with a sagging slate roof and a pair of stone chimneys. The small fenced garden was wild with flowers of all kinds; some she recognized—clover, daisies, and cornflowers—and others she didn't. The air smelled of clover. Bees and butterflies danced over the plants, basking in the sunshine. It was a vision right out of a storybook.

She glanced apprehensively at Harris's back. Though she didn't recognize the place, she suspected with regret that it heralded the end of their ride.

His conversation about how many old Cornish hedgerows were actually the remains of ancient wildwoods left as boundary markers stopped in mid-sentence. He was staring at the wagon, stacked with furniture, sitting at the garden gate. Rope in hand, Elijah Whittle stood on the top of the load, bent over a small, dark wooden table.

"Whittle? What are you doing?"

Elijah halted and glanced around to see Harris and Alyssa at the edge of the woods.

"My lord." The coachman struggled to straighten, bracing

his hand against his back. "I'm taking this furniture up to Penridge Hall."

Harris frowned and urged Pendragon toward the wagon. "Lady Penridge's orders, I assume?"

"Yes, my lord," Elijah said, clearly uneasy and confused by Harris's sharp questions. "She is inside choosing what she wants."

Harris said nothing more as he rode up to the garden gate. The frown on his face told Alyssa something was wrong.

"Where are we?" she asked as he dismounted.

Johnnie jumped down to take Pendragon's reins.

"This is the Woodside Cottage," Harris said, studying the structure with some critical thought that made his frown deepen. "This will be Gwendolyn's residence one day."

Of course, the dower house. A charming place. Before Alyssa could dismount, Harris had opened the garden gate and was striding up the path toward the door. She seemed to be forgotten. If this was to be her home, why should Gwendolyn's presence at the dower house trouble him?

She scrambled off Smuggler without waiting for Johnnie's help. Curious to see the cottage—and since Harris had not forbidden her to do so—she hurried up the path after him.

He'd already disappeared from the entry when she got there. Beyond the small hallway she found herself standing in a large keeping room with a massive stone fireplace and low, axe-hewn ceiling beams. The outline of a large carpet remained on the polished wooden floor.

She stepped farther into the room, sniffing the air. It was stale and stuffy; the house needed a good airing. Yet, even on the cool day with a cold hearth, light flooded in through the mullioned windows, making the unused space light and pleasant. What a shame that such a place stood empty and without a family to fill it with laughter and warmth.

She could hear the movements of servants on the floor above. Probably Jane and Lady Penridge's maid, Blanche.

From the adjacent room she could hear the murmur of Harris and Gwendolyn's low querulous voices.

Slowly, quietly so her boots didn't make noise on the bare floor, Alyssa walked toward the next room. She intended to make her presence known, but saw no reason not to eavesdrop as she went.

"It is only a few things," Gwendolyn said. "I especially wanted that wonderful old embroidery frame."

"I thought we had settled this," Harris said. He added something more, but his voice was so low that Alyssa could not make out the words. She thought she heard him say "proper."

Then Gwendolyn said, "You know I hate this place, and I know you do not like the idea of us living out here alone with things being as they are . . ." Gwendolyn's voice softened and Alyssa could hear no more. Hesitantly, she took a step toward the doorway.

"I understand, Gwendolyn, but—" he began, his words fading into a murmur.

"But it is not going to be easy," Gwendolyn replied, regret in her tone. "Meggie is taking things so hard. And now we have a houseguest who must be chaperoned . . ."

It was time to make herself known. Alyssa reached the doorway.

"Hello," she greeted, peering into a modest dining room with more mullioned windows and a brass chandelier hanging from the ceiling center.

Gwendolyn and Harris turned toward her with a start.

Gwendolyn's hand rested on Harris's arm in a beseeching, almost possessive manner.

"Alyssa." The widow's eyes widened in surprise. This morning she was dressed in a simple black gabardine gown without jewelry. Her fair hair was drawn back into a coil at her nape. Even in the shadows of the room, it gleamed from beneath her widow's cap. She had managed as always to make plain mourning look soft and exquisite.

Recovering from her surprise, she offered Alyssa a small smile, but she did not remove her hand from Harris's arm. The familiarity of the contact brought home to Alyssa with a pang the depth of Gwendolyn's relationship with Harris. He and she shared more than the grief of losing a loved one. They were linked in ways, Alyssa realized, that she would never know about or understand. They shared a history, years of memories. Harris might have spent time in India, but still there had been family gatherings. Had Harris taken part in Alistair and Gwendolyn's wedding? Had he been at Meggie's christening? Summer holidays by the sea and winter nights by the fire?

They shared layers and folds of emotions that she had no knowledge of or right to delve into.

"Harris did not tell me you were here, Alyssa," the widow said, offering a restrained smile of welcome.

"Alyssa and I met unexpectedly on the moors during her morning ride," Harris said, as if their encounter had been of little consequence. He glanced at her briefly before returning his gaze to Gwendolyn.

"This is a lovely cottage," Alyssa said to fill the silence.

"Yes, isn't Woodside quaint?" Gwendolyn said. "I have always liked this cottage and its furnishings."

The statement made Alyssa glance at Harris. Hadn't she just heard the widow claim otherwise? He did not react.

"That is why I decided to find a place for some of the pieces at Penridge Hall," Gwendolyn continued. "Alistair never wanted me to remove anything from the cottage even though no one lived here, but Harris is more understanding."

She smiled at Harris, but he said nothing.

"Would you like me to show you the rest of the cottage?" Gwendolyn offered, removing her hand from his arm at last.

"Alyssa has had a difficult morning." Harris seemed suddenly restless. He caught her eye.

Despite her curiosity about the cottage, she took the cue. She'd already annoyed her host once this morning by riding where she was unwanted. She wasn't going to linger here, where she was also useless. "Perhaps another time, thank you, Gwendolyn."

"As you like." The lady inclined her head politely.

"I will see you off to Penridge, Alyssa," Harris said without moving.

"Yes, of course." She offered her hostess an awkward farewell smile and backed out of the dining room.

"Do what you like, Gwendolyn," she overheard Harris say as she crossed the keeping room toward the entry hall. "You know how I feel about it."

Then Alyssa quickened her steps, hurrying out of the cottage, conscious of the hollow echo of her riding boots on the flagstone walk.

Outside, Johnnie helped her onto Smuggler. Elijah was still tying the furniture to the wagon.

Harris reappeared, his frown deeper than ever. He clapped his hat onto his head with finality as he strode through the gate. He swung up on Pendragon easily and cantered off toward Penridge Hall in silence.

Alyssa followed, mystified.

This time Harris made no effort to be a congenial host. They rode the rest of the way home at a canter without exchanging a word.

It was a good thing, too, because when they rode up to Penridge Hall, Tavi was awaiting them at the top of the front steps with a stranger at his side.

Seven

"There you are, Penridge." The fellow standing next to Tavi hailed Harris in a hearty voice, but Alyssa felt his gaze rake over her, taking in more than the cut of her riding habit. She shifted uncomfortably in the saddle under his scrutiny.

"Dundry," was all Harris said in greeting as he drew Pendragon up and dismounted.

Dundry was a man of medium height, with ruddy coloring. He wore the quality suit of an affluent tradesman and the laughing smile of a man who took few things seriously.

"Captain Dundry has just arrived from Bristol, sir," Tavi announced unnecessarily. He took Pendragon's reins as if he were accustomed to such duties.

Johnnie's little brother was leading away the visitor's plain chestnut as Johnnie jumped down to catch Smuggler's bridle.

"So I see, Tavi." Harris seized Alyssa by the waist and swung her down from Smuggler's back. His hold on her was firm but gentle, yet the grimness on his face never wavered. "Show him into my study."

"Not before you introduce me to the lovely lady, I hope," Dundry said, smiling appreciatively at her. The blatant interest was enough to make Alyssa blush.

Harris hesitated out of annoyance, Alyssa sensed.

"Miss Alyssa Lockhart, may I introduce Captain Cecil Dundry, Her Majesty's Army retired," Harris recited, clearly put off by the captain's behavior. "Miss Lockhart is our houseguest."

"Ah, so you are the little American," Dundry said, as if the knowledge filled some gap for him.

"How do you do, Captain?" Alyssa noted Harris gave no explanation as to who Captain Dundry was. She offered her hand politely. "And what brings you to Penridge Hall, sir?"

"I'm an old friend of the colonel's, Miss Lockhart." The man shook her hand enthusiastically with a crushing grip. "And I'm doing very well, thank you. Even better now, in fact."

Harris frowned. "Wait for me in the study, Dundry," he repeated in a low, harsh voice. "In the future, use that entrance to the house."

"Right, old chap, in the study," Dundry said with a good-natured smile and the touch of his hand to his bowler's brim. "So nice to have met you, Miss Lockhart. I hope to see you again soon."

"That would be nice," Alyssa replied politely, with a questioning glance in Harris's direction. He offered her no helpful information.

As soon as Dundry was in the house, Harris turned to her.

"Don't concern yourself with him." Gone was the relaxed warmth of the host with whom she'd ridden along the stream a short while ago. Gone was the man who'd smiled at her impulsiveness. Gone was the man who regretted his cousin's death. It was as if returning to the house changed him.

Her own mood darkened with disappointment and confusion.

"And remember what I told you about riding, too," he warned with a frosty frown, once again the cold host who'd greeted her the night of her arrival at Penridge. "Do not ride in the direction of Wheal Isabel again. Johnnie, you heard that, too?"

"Yes, your lordship," Johnnie said with an overeager nod.

"Good," said Harris, holding Alyssa's gaze for a moment longer. His eyes had grown dark and stormy, but she could not discern the cause.

Turning away, he said, "Good day to you."

He strode into the house with the arrogant, purposeful stride of the lord of the manor.

Later that afternoon, from the library window, Alyssa saw Captain Dundry ride away. Whatever his reason for calling at Penridge, he was not to be a houseguest.

Dinner that night was subdued. Harris made brief mention of the miners' unrest as a caution to Gwendolyn. She listened courteously, then spent the rest of the time at the table chatting about the pieces of furniture she'd brought to the hall. She was quite excited about the new acquisitions. She remained preoccupied with arranging the pieces into the next day.

Alyssa amused herself with horseback riding in the morning within sight of the house. Later she played the piano in the library and sang to herself. Once she thought she glimpsed Meggie watching her from the door at the end of the long room. But when she stopped playing and called to the child, no one answered.

The following morning brought new excitement. It began when Alyssa sat up in bed.

People were stirring in the house. She'd heard them—Jane and Gwendolyn's maid treading lightly and briskly up and down the hallway with tea trays and the like. Tavi, too. She knew that Harris was always up and out early to see to estate and mine business.

She planned to ride out and explore the bridle paths Harris had shown her. She reached for her wrapper lying across the foot of the bed. A hank of hair fell into her face, but she ignored it. Snagging the garment, she stretched and yawned, shoving her arm into the sleeve. With little more on her mind than heading for the water closet, she blindly poked her toe into her slipper.

Sharp pain lanced through her searching toe.

"Ooow!" she yelped. Hurt and shocked to full awareness, she drew back her foot and scrambled backward onto the bed.

"Here? What's this?" Jane burst into the room without knocking. "Are you all right, miss?"

"I don't know." Alyssa cradled her big toe and leaned over to examine it. The skin was red with irritation, but she saw no blood. Then she peered over the edge of the bed at her blue, satin-lined leather slippers. "Something bit my toe."

"Bit your toe?" Jane ventured into the room and with hands on knees bent over the slippers, too. "What—why, there's something in there! I can see it."

Curiosity replaced Alyssa's pain and surprise. "Let's see." She hopped off the bed and reached for the slipper.

"Oooh, be careful, miss." Jane cried, shrinking away toward the doorway.

"It can't be more than a mouse or a frog." Alyssa gave the slipper a slight shove with her toe. That should dislodge any frog. Frogs had been Winslow's favorite prank animal. Nothing happened. She crept closer and peered into the slipper more closely this time.

"There is something in there, with quills." She picked up the slipper this time and shook it more emphatically. Out the prickly object came, hitting the carpet with a bounce and rolling across the floor toward Jane. Screaming, the maid fled into the hall.

Alyssa wasn't certain what it was, but she could see that it was an animal of some kind. Not a mouse—no fur. Certainly not a frog—no smooth skin, no warts. This thing had prickly bristles. It remained on the carpet, huddled in a small, spiny ball.

From somewhere, even over Jane's screeching, Alyssa heard a high-pitched giggle. She knew exactly who was at the bottom of this. Irritated, she straightened. Pranks with animals always made her angry on the creature's behalf. It was one thing to bedevil a person for whatever reasons. It was quite another to make a poor creature suffer, too. Meggie was not going to get away with this prank.

Alyssa rounded toward the door, ready to hold the wicked little girl accountable this time. She launched herself straight into a solid white shirtfront.

Large hands grasped her shoulders and brought her up short.

"What the devil is going on in here?" Harris demanded, looking down into her face. His grip on her was almost painful. "What is it, Alyssa? There's enough caterwauling in this end of the house to send Lucifer hightailing into the next shire."

"Uh, I was just . . ." Looking up at him in his shirtsleeves, with flecks of shaving soap still on his jaw, left Alyssa quite speechless. The scent of his soap sent a thrill spiraling through her middle.

"Something bit Miss Lockhart, your lordship," Jane wailed from the hallway. She wrung her hands. "Something big like a rat. I saw it. It was coming for me, it was."

"There are no rats in this house, Jane." Tried patience edged Harris's voice. Abruptly, he released Alyssa. "At least, there had better not be."

Alyssa shoved the hank of hair out of her face and attempted to find her tongue. "It's not a rat. Whatever it is, it's over there." She pointed to the ball of quills on the carpet.

Harris looked, but it took a moment for him to locate what she was pointing at.

"This little thing?" he asked, walking toward the motionless ball in front of the hearth. He knelt down on one knee, cupped his large hands around it, and lifted the ball for her to see. "This is nothing more than a fuzz-peg," he said, looking up at her and Jane with derision in his eyes. "A hedgehog."

Alyssa stepped closer. "Hedgehog? I've never seen a hedgehog before." But on closer examination she could still see nothing beyond the spines. "Do hedgehogs frequently make nocturnal rounds of the guest chambers at Penridge?"

"You have got me there." Harris frowned as he, too, scrutinized the creature. "Jane, fetch Miss Meggie. We shall see what she knows about this."

Jane left to do as she was told.

"How do we make it uncurl?" Momentarily forgetting her disheveled state, Alyssa nudged the creature gently with her finger.

"When it feels safe, it will uncurl," Harris said, studying the prickly animal in his hand. "Which probably will not happen this morning. Hedgehogs are gentle creatures, for the most part."

"So it's afraid?" she asked. "It won't shoot its quills like a porcupine?"

"No, nothing like that, but it will bite if surprised or angered," he said, "and the bite can fester into a dangerous wound. Judging from its size, I'd guess this is a young one, born this spring."

"You sound like an expert." Alyssa smiled at him, touched by his interest in the creature. She was talking to Harris the man, not his high-and-mighty lordship. She resisted the urge to wipe shaving soap from his jaw with the corner of her wrapper.

"Not really," he said, a nostalgic smile forming on his lips. "But when Alistair and I were boys we had an old gardener who had great respect for hedgehogs. Fuzz-pegs, he called them. He encouraged a colony to make their home in a wild corner of the garden. They eat the slugs and snails, he said. Every wise gardener wants a fuzz-peg, or so he claimed. He wouldn't tolerate any mistreatment of them. Well, good morning, Meggie."

"Good morning, Cousin Harris," Meggie said, dropping a quick curtsy toward Harris and casting an uncertain glance in Alyssa's direction. She was already dressed for the day in her black pinafore with her dark curls tidily pulled back by her cap. She clasped her hands behind her, angelic-like. "What do you have there, Cousin Harris?"

"Actually, I was going to ask you what it is," Harris said, holding the ball out to her. "And what is it doing in here?"

"A hedgehog?" Meggie said, her face serious and her eyes wide. "I have no idea how a hedgehog would get into Miss Lockhart's slipper."

"It was in her slipper, was it?" Harris eyed Meggie in a manner that warned against lies. "Do not dissemble with me, Miss Meggie. What do you know about it?"

"Why would I know anything?" Meggie said, her young face taking on a chilling expression of brazen defiance.

"How did you know it was in Miss Lockhart's slipper?" Harris asked. "I recall a certain recent prank with an ink bottle."

"Yes, there was the ink bottle . . ." Alyssa said, catching Meggie's eye to remind the child that they both knew that there'd been more than just the ink bottle. There'd been the salt in her tea.

Meggie pressed her lips together in annoyance, but said no more.

Rapid footsteps could be heard from the hall.

"What is it?" Gwendolyn said, sweeping breathlessly into the room. "I was dressing. What happened?"

"It seems we have a hedgehog in the house." Harris offered the creature to Gwendolyn. In Alyssa's slipper, to be exact."

At the sight of the spiny ball, Gwendolyn gasped and retreated hastily. "But how—"

"That's what I'm trying to ascertain," he said, turning to Meggie again.

"You think Meggie—" Gwendolyn frowned uncertainly and moved to her daughter's side. "I hardly think it's fair to jump to the conclusion that my daughter is responsible for this."

"You have another explanation for a wild creature being in Alyssa's chamber?" Harris asked.

"Perhaps one of the servants . . ." Gwendolyn said.

They all turned to look at a bewildered Jane, who was cowering in the hallway.

"I do not think so," Harris said.

"Then, I—no, I don't know," Gwendolyn said, clearly reconsidering her earlier words. "What do you have to say about it, Meggie?"

Defiance flashed in Meggie's eyes again, and she puckered her lips in irritation.

But there was more than just defiance in Meggie's eyes. Defensiveness lurked there as well. Defensiveness filled with pain and uncertainty, with fear and loss. With loneliness and bewilderment. Her heart touched, Alyssa's anger wilted. How could she hold a grudge against such a woeful miscreant?

Still, there was a lesson to be learned for the prankster.

"Well, however the poor creature got in here, we must do something for it." Alyssa took the ball gently into her own hands and held it up to Meggie's view. "Look how frightened it is. Wrapping itself up like that to keep safe from strange voices and smells. Did you say it is a youngster, Harris? It probably wonders where its parents are. Wouldn't it be frightening to find yourself alone in a strange place?"

Meggie stared at the ball in Alyssa's hands. Her head bobbed up, and when she looked at Alyssa, her defiance wavered. A shadow of regret darkened her eyes.

"Indeed," Harris agreed, meeting Alyssa's gaze.

She knew from the narrowing of his eyes that they were thinking the same thing.

Still on his knees, he took the creature from Alyssa and continued to speak. "Without his mama or papa or any brothers or sisters, he is quite unprotected. We cannot turn him out alone, can we? The foxes or the dogs might get him."

Meggie shook her head, her gaze fixed on the creature in Harris's hands.

"Besides being alone and afraid the poor thing must be hungry," Alyssa added, building as much sympathy as she could. "I wonder how long it's been since the little fellow has eaten. We owe him a meal. Don't you think so, Meggie? And a home."

This time when Meggie looked up at her, the child's eyes were filled with regret. Her lips trembled. She nodded rapidly.

"Home?" Gwendolyn repeated, looking from Alyssa to Harris as though they'd lost their minds. "What sort of a home?"

"Jane?" Harris called.

The maid crept back into the room. "Yes, sir?"

"I believe we have an old bird cage in the attic," he said. "The big one that Aunt Isabel kept her grumpy old parrot in."

"Yes, sir, I know the one you mean," Jane said. "I'll fetch it, straightaway."

"And a flowerpot and some straw," Harris said, looking at Meggie. "You can get those things from Elijah."

"Me?" Meggie said, pointing a finger at herself.

"Someone has to take care of this poor creature," Harris said. "I can hardly ask a houseguest to do it, and you do know where things are."

"And since you are the youngest in the household," Alyssa agreed, "you should have an idea about how a young, lost fuzz-peg must feel. As soon as I'm dressed, I'll go with you to find Elijah."

Alyssa held the creature out to Meggie. "Well, take him. I must dress."

"Harris, do you honestly think—?" Gwendolyn began.

"It's all right, Gwendolyn. Take him, Meggie."

With a wary look of astonishment, the child obediently held out her hands. Once the animal was in her possession, her expression changed to wonder.

"His spines don't hurt that much." Surprise filled her voice and a smile came to her lips. Obviously she had handled the creature with gloves when she'd planted it in Alyssa's slipper.

"No, they don't hurt much." Alyssa stuck out her big toe to demonstrate her point. "See, no blood."

It wasn't until Harris rose from where he'd been kneeling that Alyssa realized she'd practically shoved her naked toe in his face. Her cheeks heated with the embarrassment of it. A little too brightly, she asked, "What else do we need to know about our new guest at Penridge, Harris?"

Fortunately, he didn't seem to notice her discomfiture. "As I recall," he said, "they like toys."

"Toys?" Meggie repeated, holding the hedgehog closer to study it. "Yes, I see the marking. Look. It has a white stripe down its side here. What kind of toys, Cousin Harris?"

"They all have different markings if you look at them closely enough," Harris said, a faraway look in his eyes as he recalled past days. "I remember your father and I finding a spool in their nests. And buttons. Yes, they like small round things."

"I have some odd buttons," Meggie murmured, her head bent over the animal. When she looked up at Harris, the tension had left her face. Her mouth was still sober, but her eyes were bright with excitement and wary pleasure.

"Mama? Go find my buttons for—" Meggie began.

"First things first, Meggie," Gwendolyn said, placing her hands on her daughter's shoulders and bending over to speak into her ear. "First, you'll have your breakfast. Then we'll see about the buttons. And he will need a name," she added, joining in the conspiracy.

Alyssa almost heaved an audible sigh of relief. She'd begun to fear that the woman didn't understand that she and Harris were trying to coax Meggie out of her troublemaking and into another interest.

"A name?" Meggie looked anxiously at Alyssa. "What do you think we should name him, Miss Lockhart?"

"I don't know," she said. "I'll leave the name to you. But I believe something very English would be appropriate. Something very Cornish."

"King Arthur," Meggie piped without hesitation.

Alyssa smiled. Such a pompous name for such an unassuming creature.

Meggie glanced around at the adults gathered in the room, searching for approval. "We'll call him King Arthur."

"King Arthur it is," Harris said with a wry twist of his mouth. He met Alyssa's gaze, and she was certain he thought the name as extravagant as she did. But no one would make a critical remark about it for Meggie's sake. "Now, I am pleased to have a king under my roof, as well as an American heiress."

"We are a distinguished household, indeed," Gwendolyn added agreeably. She turned her daughter toward the door. "Bring the king downstairs, dearest. We'll find a basket for him until Jane searches out the cage and you've finished your breakfast."

"By then I'll be ready to see what Elijah can do for us," Alyssa called after them.

"Yes, I'd like that," Meggie said over her shoulder as she and Gwendolyn left the room.

"Brilliant," Harris said when Gwendolyn and Meggie were out of hearing. "She hasn't looked that interested in anything since before her father died. A pet may be just what she needed. Even a prickly hedgehog. I told you to trust your impulses."

"So you did," Alyssa said, pleased with her own inspiration, pleased with hearing praise from Harris once more. "Let's hope the king can distract her for a while."

"Indeed."

Before Alyssa realized what he was doing, Harris took both her hands in his and held them. The warm physical link made her heart beat faster. She sucked in a quick little breath as he squeezed her hands gently and leaned forward to kiss her—on the lips.

A light, quick brush of a kiss, too sweet to be brotherly. Yet, too brief to be anything more. Too quick to even get a taste of him. Her face heated with a blush. She was certain he could feel the heat when he touched her cheek with his thumb.

"Thank you, Alyssa, for Meggie's sake," he said, gazing into her eyes with a soft smile.

There she stood in her nightgown with her wrapper barely pulled around her and her hair in wild disarray. She must look awful. But even as she thought that, her body warmed, her breasts suddenly seeming heavy and her nipples sensitive to the woven texture of her nightgown. She longed for him to touch her again.

Suddenly he stepped back from her and frowned. Had he read her mind?

"And I know Alistair would thank you, too," he added, abruptly releasing her hands almost as if he'd forgotten he was still holding them. Then he turned and left her bedchamber.

She stood in the middle of the floor, basking in the warmth of Lord Penridge's approval. Her hands still held the heat of his grasp. She touched her lips where she could still feel the whisper of the kiss he'd given her. Then she clasped her hands together and held them to her heart. Merciful heavens. He'd kissed her. On her face a smile of secret pleasure stretched from ear to ear.

Eight

Alyssa and Meggie fell into a partnership necessary to care for King Arthur. Jane and Gwendolyn seemed glad to be rid of the responsibility of the strange little creature and the angry child.

So it was Alyssa and Meggie who put King Arthur in the big birdcage salvaged from the attic. It was they who went out to the stable to get from Elijah the clay pot and the straw for King Arthur's bed. Alyssa borrowed an empty spool from Jane's sewing basket. Meggie retrieved her favorite buttons from her toy box so King Arthur would have amusement.

Elijah also told them that fuzz-pegs liked bread and milk. From Chef Hugo they pirated the necessary food in a saucer. But still to Meggie's disappointment, King Arthur remained curled up in his protective ball.

"He cannot stay like that forever, can he?" She sat on the edge of her breakfast room chair. It was late afternoon, almost teatime. The cage had been set up on a low table next to a small palm tree in the window. She sighed. "It's just too much for him, isn't it? Will he die of the loneliness, do you think?"

Alyssa knew that it was possible for a creature to die from loneliness. People did. Gracious, she understood the pain of losing your family—or almost losing it through her own foolishness—but she wasn't going to give in to the pain. Nor would she allow Meggie to do so.

"Let's go study hedgehogs in the library," Alyssa suggested, reaching for Meggie's hand. "I saw some books there that might help us learn how to make him feel at home."

Meggie hesitated, her hands remaining in her lap. She studied Alyssa's hand as if it were something foreign and forbidden. Alyssa pressed her lips together and waited for Meggie to decide. This was the final test.

"We can't help him if we don't know anything about him," Alyssa said. Silently, Meggie nodded, then with a cautious twist of her lips, she took Alyssa's hand. Alyssa smiled at the child reassuringly, and off they went to the library, where they pulled books off the shelves, sat down at the library table, and began their search.

"This book says they are born in litters of two or three urchins," Meggie read aloud, her head bent over the dry narrative of a huge natural science volume. "The mother is called a sow and the father a boar. They don't have any hair or spines when they are born."

"Interesting," Alyssa said, musing over another tome. "It says here that their natural enemies are foxes and some dogs, like your Cousin Harris said. But hedgehogs can kill snakes."

"So they are brave," Meggie said, apparently enlightened and impressed. "I know King Arthur is brave."

"Without a doubt," Alyssa agreed, trying to keep her smile of satisfaction to herself. "It says here that they hibernate."

"Hibernate?" Meggie looked at Alyssa.

"Sleep through the winter," she explained.

"Like fish sleeping at the bottom of the lake when it freezes over?" Meggie asked.

"Yes, like that," Alyssa said. "That's a very good explanation."

"So is King Arthur going to hibernate here with us?" Meggie asked with a frown. "That won't be much fun."

"We've got to get him to eat first," Alyssa said. "There will be plenty of time to decide what to do with him when winter comes."

Meggie agreed. Except for their hour in the library doing

research, she was never far from the cage that first day though the creature remained in his protective ball.

It wasn't until that evening as Alyssa was dressing for dinner that King Arthur deigned to show his face. She heard Meggie's whoop of delight echo up the stairs and into her room, and she knew exactly what all the noise was about. With a laugh, she jumped up from the dressing table where she'd been sitting as Jane fixed her hair and ran down the stairs.

She found Meggie kneeling next to the cage in the breakfast room. The child was already in her nightgown and wrapper.

"He's eating," Meggie whispered as if afraid of frightening the creature that fortunately seemed unaffected by her earlier shout. In the cage, King Arthur was slurping at the milk and bread. Meggie's eyes were bright with excitement and her face lit with the natural glow of childish pleasure as she watched. "See, he's eating. Look."

"It's a good sign," Alyssa said, relieved to see that the creature wasn't going to starve itself to death.

"He has a handsome face, don't you think?" Meggie observed. "Furry. A pointed black snout and shiny black eyes just like the illustration. The white stripe on his side makes him quite distinguished, don't you think? And look at his little round ears."

"Furry legs, too," Alyssa said. "Five toes. Look, his back legs are longer than his front legs like the book described. That's why he moves so wobbly."

"Yes, I see," Meggie said, pressing her face against the wire cage and smiling at the creature's strange gait.

As they watched, the hedgehog fed on the milk and soggy bread with a little pink tongue. His slurping and smacking filled the breakfast room with as much noise as a sty full of famished pigs.

"He's not exactly a quiet fellow, is he?" Alyssa observed.

Meggie giggled.

Alyssa smiled. Interestingly, a confession had become unimportant compared to the fact that Meggie seemed to have forgotten her hostile feelings. Still the question remained and Alyssa had to ask, "I wonder how he got into the house."

"Johnnie and his brother found him in the straw behind the stable," Meggie said without looking at Alyssa. "I traded some tea cakes for him. Maybe if they'd left him alone, King Arthur's parents would have found him."

"I'm sure they are looking for him," Alyssa said, though she had no idea what kind of parents hedgehogs were. None of the books had been clear on that point.

"Looks as if he's finished," Meggie said.

King Arthur wobbled away from the saucer, sniffing at the flowerpot and straw. With only a slight hesitation, he snuffled his way into the clay container. He nosed the straw and then began to circle.

"The book said he has a very acute sense of smell," Alyssa said. "But what is he doing?"

The creature circled again and again with its nose to the straw like a dog. Then it lay down among the toys that Meggie had put in the cage for it.

"He's going to bed," Meggie said, a soft smile of satisfaction on her lips.

"Another good sign," Alyssa agreed. "You've done it, Meggie. You've made him feel safe enough to uncurl, eat, and go to sleep."

Meggie looked up at her, glowing with a heart-wrenching smile. With a start, Alyssa wondered if Harris and Gwendolyn truly understood how much poor Meggie missed her father, how huge the loss was for the child.

"Whatever happens, King Arthur will have us," the little girl said with an emphatic nod. "Even if his parents never come back for him. We'll be here for him, won't we?"

"Yes, we'll be here," Alyssa said, understanding at last. No wonder Meggie had fought against her stay. With her father gone, a houseguest stole away the attentions of the only people Meggie felt she could rely on. And now a hedgehog was more than just a distraction for her; oddly, the funny little lost beast was filling the dead man's place.

In the days that followed, Alyssa arranged a routine for King Arthur: feeding several times a day and seeing to it that his cage was set out in the garden daily. While the hedgehog became accustomed to Meggie and Alyssa's presence, he continued to be shy of others. At the faintest hint of a stranger approaching, even Jane or Gwendolyn, he would roll up into a ball. So once Meggie had finished her morning lessons, Alyssa and she occupied themselves with King Arthur's needs.

Meggie discovered he also liked fish, especially salmon, and ham, too. Eagerly she offered him each tidbit and watched him eat with pleasure. His antics with the spool made her laugh. As the animal became at home with them, Meggie began to act more like a normal child. Her sour face faded. She smiled more often. The shadows of anger disappeared from her eyes. Sometimes she even joined Alyssa at the piano when she heard music in the library.

By Sunday sullen clouds had replaced the sunny autumn weather. Gray and heavy, the mist nestled down over the countryside like a hen settling over her brood, leaving the moors hidden and the woods misty, protected from the outside world.

Jane advised warm clothes and a heavy cloak for church. Alyssa heeded the advice, choosing her clothes carefully because she wanted to make a good appearance. Once again as Penridge Hall's houseguest, an American, she would be scrutinized by the neighbors.

But the carriage had barely gotten under way before she was glad that she'd taken Jane's advice and chosen her best and warmest clothes. Despite the four passengers seated companionably in the carriage, the ride was a cold one.

"Mr. Byron Littlefield should be attending services this morning," Gwendolyn murmured as she arranged her black skirts on the seat with Meggie at her side. Her black bonnet framed her face attractively. Today, she wore no veil, an indication she was out of deepest mourning.

"I suppose so," Harris said, gazing out the window at the bleak moors. He and Alyssa were seated with their backs toward the driver's box, facing Gwendolyn and Meggie. The faint spicy scent of his shaving soap reached Alyssa. She could hardly believe her good fortune in being seated next to him though he took little notice of her.

"I mention Byron for Alyssa's benefit," Gwendolyn said, smiling indulgently at Harris. She leaned toward Alyssa to speak in confidence. "Harris just does not understand how a young woman must anticipate these meetings with a young gentleman in order to make the most of them."

Alyssa nodded politely. Seeing Byron Littlefield again held no special interest to her. Still, it was helpful to know that he would probably be at the church. She would be obliged to speak to him.

Encouraged, Gwendolyn continued. "And the Carbury girls will be there also—Lucy, the bride-to-be, and her sister Edith. Mrs. Carbury and her daughters never miss the vicar's sermons. You'll enjoy meeting them."

"I'm sure I will," Alyssa agreed politely once again.

Across from her, Meggie frowned and pulled a face she made certain only Alyssa saw. Meggie had little fondness for the Carbury girls. Alyssa almost laughed aloud, amused by Meggie's reaction to the mention of the vicar's daughters and pleased with the new sense of intimacy that had developed between them.

"I shall ask them to Sunday dinner," Gwendolyn said with a self-satisfied smile.

"The Carburys?" Meggie nearly choked in her surprise and displeasure.

"Yes, the Carburys," Gwendolyn said, glancing sternly at her daughter. "You know that we frequently invited them to Sunday dinner before your father . . . the vicar amused your father."

"Invite the Littlefields as well," Harris said without turning from the carriage window.

"The Littlefields?" Gwendolyn sounded as thrilled about inviting her neighbors as Meggie sounded about inviting the vicar's daughters.

"Yes, the Littlefields," Harris said, clearly perplexed and offended about the cool reception to his suggestion. "Why not? It's perfectly appropriate to entertain neighbors, we agreed. Chef Hugo always prepares enough for guests on Sunday."

"The food is no constraint," Gwendolyn conceded.

"Is there another problem?" Harris asked, studying his kinswoman.

Alyssa bit the inside of her cheek, reminding herself to be invisible during a family disagreement.

"No, of course not," Gwendolyn said, suddenly concerned about the creases in her skirt. "But they were just at Penridge for tea."

"And why not to Sunday dinner as well?" Harris asked. "It will be nice to have a gathering at the dining room table again after these long, dark months."

"Yes, indeed," Gwendolyn said without enthusiasm. "That would be nice."

Alyssa glanced at Harris, wondering if he realized that he might be pressing the widow to cast aside the protection of her mourning too soon. But he returned to viewing the moors outside.

When she followed his gaze, she saw the roof of a square, stone chapel just beyond the crest of a hill. The cross atop its steeple was barely visible through the fog. Along the chapel lane strode groups of men and women obviously dressed in their modest Sunday best. They walked with their heads bowed—in reverence? Or out of weariness? Or as protection against the chill Cornish mist?

"I don't remember seeing that chapel on the way to Penridge," Alyssa said with a glance at Harris. "It was so foggy that afternoon."

"The miners prefer their own church these days." Gwendolyn's tone was sharp with disapproval.

"Is this Reverend Whittle's chapel?" Alyssa asked, realizing the reverend must have been on the road the day she arrived because he'd been meeting with his men at the chapel. But he'd been expecting someone. Someone other than her.

"Yes, it is now, but it wasn't his in the beginning," Harris said, still watching the people thoughtfully. "It was a Wesleyan chapel when built. The congregation and its leadership have changed several times over the decades. For the most part, the little house of worship has served the miners well."

"But Whittle?" Gwendolyn said, disbelief in her voice and a frown of distaste on her lips.

"The Reverend Whittle is something of an unknown," Harris admitted in a surprisingly neutral tone for a man who had just faced-off with the odd reverend only a few days earlier. "Does he protest and demand for the miners' benefit or for his own ambition? There is no doubt he loves the power of his position. Just what is his motivation? Time will reveal the truth."

The carriage slowed to pass another group of worshipers walking along the road toward the chapel. They were singing a hymn, their voices out of tune but at full, fervent volume. When they glanced up at the passing carriage, their faces were somber as they sang. These were workingmen, mothers with babies in arms, children with the sweet youthfulness already worn from their faces by labor. But they sang, their spirits untouched, and their voices raised in melody.

Alyssa was reminded of the angry men she'd encountered at the entrance to Wheal Isabel the day of her first horseback ride. Were any of them among these worshipers? Bitter, aggrieved men who wanted better things for themselves and their families. But today, on Sunday, with their washed faces, hair brushed, go-to-meeting clothes pressed, and a hymn on their lips, they appeared quite sober and peaceful. Hardly a fearsome mob.

"As a local clergyman, perhaps we should invite Reverend Whittle to Sunday dinner," Harris said, still watching the people.

"Harris, don't you dare," Gwendolyn said with a gasp. "When I think of the tribulations that man brought on Alistair . . . I only accepted his assistance in calling on the miners for Alistair's sake. I do not consider him fit social company."

"I but jest, Gwendolyn." Harris turned away from the carriage window, his brows raised, his mouth twisted ruefully. "Calm yourself."

"That is hardly a suitable jest." Gwendolyn snapped. Her pretty face had gone pale and her generous mouth thinned. "I know Alistair had his faults, but he did not deserve to have to deal with an uncouth upstart like Zebulon Whittle."

"It's all right, Gwendolyn." Harris patted her knee briefly in a pacifying gesture. "I'm sorry I made thoughtless mention of the reverend."

Gwendolyn sat back, her spine pressed against the seat, her hands clutched in her lap, her lips trembling as if she might weep. She avoided the gaze of everyone in the carriage.

Concerned for Meggie, Alyssa glanced at the girl to see how she was taking her mother's emotional display. Eyes wide and mouth pinched, the child studied her mother's face.

"Cousin Harris did not mean it, Mama," Meggie cried. In alarm and desperation, she clutched at her mother's skirt with one free hand. In the other she clutched a hand-picked bouquet of late-blooming forget-me-nots.

"I'm sorry, I didn't meant to upset you, Gwendolyn," Harris said in a gentle voice. "Do you wish to go home? We don't have to stay for services if you don't wish it."

Meggie stared at Harris. "But I brought flowers for Papa's grave."

"No, I am all right." Gwendolyn sniffed and blinked the

tears away. "It's just at times, I quite forget what has happened. I think Alistair might suddenly appear and take my arm and lead me into the dining room or to the garden. Sometimes, I hate everyone who made his life difficult."

"I know." Harris leaned forward and reached for Gwendolyn's hand this time. Bowing her head, she gave it to him. "I can hardly believe he's gone myself," he sympathized.

The carriage turned into the churchyard. Beyond the window, Alyssa could see square gravestones and tall, haloed Celtic crosses that lined the way. The bells began to toll, a low ringing. She was surprised to smell the scent of the sea on the air.

"You are right, of course, Harris," Gwendolyn said, raising her head and struggling to put on a public face. "It is time for us to make our appearances at church and invite people to Penridge for Sunday dinner, as has always been the Trevell tradition of hospitality."

"There's the brave Gwendolyn I know," Harris said, patting her hand and offering her a small smile.

Alyssa glimpsed the faintest quivering of Meggie's lower lip. How could they forget the child? "And Meggie is a brave girl, too," she announced in her annoyance. "She has flowers for her father's grave."

With a start, as if they just remembered that the two were sitting there, Gwendolyn and Harris turned toward Alyssa and Meggie.

"Of course Meggie is brave," Harris said after a beat. Releasing Gwendolyn's hands, he leaned across Alyssa to take the little girl's hands.

"You are being very courageous, Meggie," he said. "I know it's been hard for you and your mother to lose your father. But things will get better. You'll see. We each must do our part, day by day, to help. Do you understand?"

Alyssa's heart warmed to see him include Meggie in his praise.

Meggie nodded, her gaze locked on Harris.

"Good, then we put on our brave faces and go into Lanissey Church," Harris continued, "to hear the good Vicar Carbury and greet our friends and neighbors and pay our respects to your father."

Alyssa wondered if he saw the child's desperate need to believe in him.

Nine

Nine

The ancient gray stone structure, Lanissey Church, with its Gothic windows and square belltower, sat on the banks of the Fowey River, stalwart and enduring against the onslaught of time and the elements. Gravestones cluttered the churchyard. Bare trees lined the far riverbank. The river flowed calmly toward the sea. Alyssa alighted from the carriage thinking what a stoic setting it was, cheerless yet soothing in its eternalness.

When everyone had disembarked, she followed them inside. The Trevells' footsteps echoed on the flagstones as Gwendolyn led Harris, Meggie, and Alyssa into their pew. Across the aisle, Sir Ralph, Lady Cynthia, and Byron already filled the Littlefield pew. Nods of greeting were exchanged.

Byron Littlefield pointedly continued to smile at Alyssa until she smiled in return.

Alyssa had hoped for some warmth inside the church, but the sanctuary was so cold, their breath puffed into little clouds in the frosty air.

In a pew at the side, Alyssa saw a small woman in a gray gown and bonnet. Beside her sat two young women. The girls smiled at her briefly, then turned their attention to their hymnals while casting covert glances in the Littlefields' direction.

"Mrs. Carbury and Lucy in blue and Edith in plum," Meggie whispered into Alyssa's ear.

As the organ music began, Alyssa drew her cloak around her. Cold as the church was, the sound qualities of the sanctuary were excellent. She twisted around to find the source of the music. At the back of the church, in the small balcony above the vestibule, a boy pumped away at the small pipe organ bellows. A thin man sat at the keyboard, wringing music out of the organ that soared throughout the sanctuary. Pipes reverberated and hummed, sending gooseflesh up her arms. Chords trembled in the air. And so the long service began.

Just as Gwendolyn had said, the vicar's wife and daughters paid rapt attention to their patriarch's words. Regardless of the service's length, Alyssa took pleasure in the music—the hymn-singing and the offertory solo, played well on a modest instrument. Still, by the end of the service she was quite chilled and eager to be on her way home to a warm fire and hot meal. Yet there remained the obligatory greeting of acquaintances in the churchyard and the visit to Alistair's grave.

As the organ music reached its soaring conclusion then faded, the parishioners filed out of the church. The day had grown even colder, and more fog had crept in, shrouding the river. Little but the churchyard, its gravestones, and lich-gate remained visible.

"Vicar Carbury, it is my pleasure to introduce our American houseguest." Harris drew Alyssa to his side. "Miss Alyssa Lockhart has come to visit us for a time."

"A pleasure to have you with us, Miss Lockhart," the vicar said, shaking her hand with a cool, loose grip. His smile was broad, however. He was in every way exactly what she had expected of an English vicar: esthetically thin, pale, with bright, intelligent eyes and a small mouth. "Lady Penridge has invited us to dine with you at Penridge Hall today. We are very pleased to accept your invitation. You must meet my wife and daughters."

He summoned the ladies Meggie had pointed out earlier. Alyssa found herself inundated by Lucy, Edith, and Mrs. Carbury.

The girls were delighted to meet her, chatting enthusiastically, asking about how her Atlantic crossing had been and commenting that her clothes were of the latest style and fabric. They might be the vicar's daughters, but clearly they were very much of the material world. In fact, Alyssa thought they were delightful girls with their pale hazel eyes, brown hair, and fine enough complexions to be called pretty. Moreover, they were full of energy and curiosity. She liked them for their good spirits and lively interest, though the latter bordered on gossipiness.

She noticed as she talked with them that Harris, Gwendolyn, and Meggie had moved away from the parishioners and were walking among the gravestones. They were headed toward a foggy corner, toward Alistair's grave, no doubt.

She wondered if she should be there for Meggie's sake. "Excuse me, please, I wish to join the Trevells," she said, edging away from the Carburys.

"We shall see you at dinner," Mrs. Carbury said with a wave.

"Yes." Alyssa turned to catch up with Meggie.

Byron Littlefield stepped into her path. "Miss Lockhart, I knew we'd meet again soon."

"Yes, good to see you again, Mr. Littlefield," Alyssa said, looking beyond him to see Harris, Gwendolyn, and Meggie stop at a grave marked by a new headstone and barren earth. The fog swirled in from the river, nearly obscuring them from her sight.

"And how is your visit going?" he asked, little concerned about her apparent interest in something else.

"Very nicely, thank you," she said, trying to slip around him without appearing to make an obvious escape attempt.

"What do you do to amuse yourself?" he asked, following her and chuckling as if she couldn't possibly have the imagination to manage without his help.

"We're making a pet of a hedgehog," she said, at a loss to think of any other recent occurrence to mention. She was really intent on watching Meggie.

"A hedgehog?" Byron exclaimed with a snort. "My goodness, you *are* desperate."

"The creature is really quite interesting." She didn't much care what he thought. All she could think of was the tension and misery that filled the carriage just before they arrived at the church. She prayed that a visit to her father's grave would be good for Meggie.

As Alyssa watched, the child brushed autumn leaves off the top of the headstone and then bent down to place the forget-me-not posy on her father's grave. Gwendolyn said something to her. Harris offered Meggie his hand, pulling her away from the grave. Then Gwendolyn stepped closer to Harris. He put his arm around her, drawing her closer yet, encouraging her to put her head on his shoulder. She was weeping into a black lace handkerchief. Meggie pressed close to her mother's skirt, hiding her face.

The sight of the dismal trio—grieving for a cousin, a husband, and a father taken from them too soon—almost brought Alyssa to tears.

"Their husband and father is sorely missed," she said with a soft sigh.

Byron was watching the Trevells now, too. He cleared his throat noisily. "I do not like to speak ill of the dead, but nobody liked him, you know. Alistair Trevell was a tyrant. Ruled the Wheal Isabel and Penridge Hall like a despot. He thought nothing of insulting his wife, his kinsman, or his neighbor. The whole county knew what a boor he was. There are even those who think he deserved to be murdered. That is, if he was."

"You are right. There's no point in speaking ill of the dead," she said, offended even as she recalled that Jane had told her about the bad feelings between the Littlefields and the Trevells. And here it was again—the word *murder.* A chill crept into Alyssa's bones. "Who would have murdered Alistair Trevell? And why?"

"Believe me, I take no pleasure in telling you the truth,

Miss Lockhart." Byron pulled a long face and his regret almost sounded sincere. "Any number of people might have decided they'd had enough of the man. A vengeful servant. A disgruntled miner." He paused before adding, "An ambitious kinsman."

Her heart rebelled against any hint of Harris being the villain. She studied Byron Littlefield. How much did he know about his uncle's complaints against the Trevells? How much would his uncle's charge of unfair business dealings trouble him?

"Perhaps a resentful neighbor?" she wondered aloud.

Byron appeared unsurprised. "Undoubtedly some would say so," he continued pleasantly enough, hooking his thumbs into his waistcoat pockets. "I thought you should know for your own welfare. The Trevells have always been ones to think too well of themselves. His late lordship was no saint, as I'm sure the Trevells would like you to believe."

Alyssa watched Gwendolyn lean against Harris's shoulder. Envy twisted uncomfortably in her belly. At the same instant, another question gathered form and drifted to the surface. Had Gwendolyn heard the rumors of murder? Was she aware of the whispers that Harris had killed his cousin to inherit the title? Surely not. How could she stand there with her cheek against the fabric of his coat, smelling the scent of his shaving soap, and suspect that Harris had murdered her husband? How could she entertain such an idea and accept his touch or take comfort from his words?

Harris momentarily pressed his cheek against the top of Gwendolyn's bonnet, a gesture so tender it made Alyssa's throat ache with unshed tears. How could such a man be a murderer? She struggled against her concern for Meggie and her uncertainty that Harris might not be her storybook hero after all.

Abruptly she turned away. "I don't believe any of it," she said aloud, hoping the words would banish her unpleasant musings.

"It's all right, you know," Byron said, his voice low and comforting, his lips close to her ear.

"What?" she asked guiltily, startled to find that he was still at her side. She turned to him, mystified. "What's all right?"

"Nobody thinks any the less of you because you are a Trevell houseguest," Byron said with a tolerant smile.

"I'm not concerned about what people think of me," she said, exasperated with him and herself. "I realize that you believe you're doing me a favor by telling me these things, but the Trevells are my hosts *and* my distant relations. I would appreciate it if you would keep your speculations to yourself."

"Of course," Byron said without contrition, but as if he'd expected no less from her. "I understand your position. I will not speak of it again. I look forward to seeing you at dinner later."

"Ummm," she said, turning again to see Gwendolyn take Meggie's hand and begin to walk toward the carriage awaiting them in the church lane.

Harris lingered beside the grave, his top hat in his hand, his gaze on his cousin's gravestone. What was he thinking? Was he missing his cousin? Did he resent Alistair's death for saddling him with responsibilities he claimed he had never wanted? Or was he pleased to be left alone to comfort Alistair's beautiful widow and child?

Alyssa saw no grief or sadness on Harris's face when he turned away from the grave. What she saw was the stony face of a cold and wrathful man.

One glance down the table—alive with the gleaming silver, sparkling, gold-flecked Murano crystal, and green-and-white Wedgwood china—made it easy for Alyssa to understand why the Carburys and the Littlefields so readily accepted Gwendolyn's invitation to dine. Nothing about the Sunday feast revealed that the house was in mourning. Or that Gwendolyn had been up inspecting the table setting before breakfast.

The menu included saddle of lamb, aspic of salmon, a cheese soufflé, sauces and creams, pickles and cheeses, breads and jams, wine and sherry. The room was redolent with the smells of good food.

Harris sat at the head of the table with Lady Cynthia at his right. Gwendolyn sat at the foot of the table with Sir Ralph on her right. Lucy, Edith, Mrs. Carbury, and the vicar were arranged in between. Meggie, who was allowed to join the adults on Sunday, sat on the same side with Byron and Alyssa, who were seated next to each other. Alyssa forced a smile and silently cursed Gwendolyn for her misguided matchmaking.

Now that Byron had hinted at murder and revealed that Alistair Trevell had enemies, she'd rather have been seated near Lady Cynthia or Sir Ralph. Though in truth, Byron had told her no more than Reverend Whittle had—a mere rumor, really—but hearing the information from an additional source gave it credence that had to be dispelled. In their company she would have a better chance to learn more about what had happened between the Trevells and the Littlefields.

Despite the gloom outside and the bad feelings between the families at the table, the conversation flowed easily from the weather to Lucy's coming nuptials and on to the county fair. The discussion flowed with enough good humor to relax everyone.

Harris and Gwendolyn played their parts as host and hostess with aplomb. Meggie grinned and observed her table manners with great care. She was clearly pleased to be part of the adult party. Harris smiled frequently, praising the vicar's sermon and complimenting Mrs. Carbury on her lovely daughters. Gwendolyn flattered Sir Ralph on the cut of his new waistcoat and encouraged Byron to partake of another serving of the lamb. If anyone at the table feared poisoning, they certainly were not eating like it today. The dishes were served and cleared away by Tavi and Elijah, who'd exchanged his coachman's coat for a footman's livery. Every plate she saw leave the table was nearly clean.

During the meal, Alyssa observed that Lucy was happy and content with her match and thrilled with her wedding plans. But Edith clearly had a crush on Byron Littlefield. It was impossible to tell if he had noticed or not. For Alyssa's part, he bestowed entirely too much attention on her.

"I understand you enjoy riding," he ventured, cutting into his second portion of lamb.

"Yes, I ride now and again," she replied, avoiding the mention that she rode nearly every morning.

"Then we must ride together some day," Byron offered, raking a pleased glance over her.

"How nice that you ride," Edith said from across the table, obviously eager to engage Byron in conversation. "I've never had the courage to climb atop a horse. They are such large animals. And tall. But I do enjoy a drive on nice days."

"Perhaps Mr. Littlefield will take you out for a drive," Alyssa volunteered.

Byron choked and frowned at her. "Perhaps we could all go," he suggested.

Surprised by his diplomatic response, Alyssa glanced at Byron and considered revising her opinion of him slightly.

"If it was not so late in the autumn, we could all go out for a drive and a picnic," Lucy suggested.

"Yes, picnics are nice," Edith said, suppressing a nervous giggle and a hopeful glance in Byron's direction. "Do you like picnics, Mr. Littlefield?"

"Well enough," he said around another bite of lamb, and then devoted himself to his food.

"Yes, picnics are nice," Alyssa agreed, smiling and deciding to release him from the obligation. "But, alas, the season seems over for now."

"Would you like to meet King Arthur, Mr. Littlefield?" Meggie asked in a small but proud voice.

"King Arthur?" Byron echoed in surprise. He cast a questioning glance at Alyssa.

"The hedgehog," she reminded him.

"Yes, your entertainment," he said with a laugh.

"He's an entertaining little fellow when he isn't curled up in a ball," Alyssa said.

"How original," Lucy and Edith chimed together. They launched a barrage of questions about Meggie's hedgehog. The girl responded with pleasure.

Alyssa looked around the table, pleased with the apparent success of the dinner. The Vicar and Mrs. Carbury doted on their daughters' every word. At the far end of the table, Lady Cynthia spoke to Harris with a selfconscious duck of her head. But once the lady glanced up as she was talking, catching Alyssa's eye. She glimpsed uneasy interest in Lady Cynthia's gaze. At the other end of the table, Sir Ralph seemed quite fascinated by Gwendolyn, but he frequently glanced toward his wife and Harris.

When Tavi brought the cigar box to Harris, Gwendolyn took her cue to rise and excuse the ladies to take tea in the salon. Thankful for winning her freedom from Byron, Alyssa got up from her chair.

"We must have a look at King Arthur," Lucy suggested.

Edith agreed. "Please introduce us to your spiny friend, Meggie."

Meggie, who'd disliked the vicar's daughters until now, beamed with gratification at the suggestion.

"Let's do," Alyssa said, taking Meggie's hand and leading the way into the breakfast room. "We'll join you in the salon soon, Cousin Gwendolyn."

King Arthur responded to visitors in his usual way. He curled up into a ball. But Lucy and Edith were not put off by his shyness. It was Edith who picked him up and rubbed his back in a circular movement until he uncurled for them. They treated him to a slice of apple. They studied him in the cage, plying Meggie with questions about the spool and the buttons, about the flowerpot and the straw. They were amused to learn the creature favored salmon.

"Only the best for our Cornish hedgehogs," Lucy joked.

"And he prefers white bread to brown," Meggie added with authority. The smile that spread across her face betrayed her pleasure in the company of the vicar's daughters.

By the time they entered the salon, giggling and laughing over the absurdities of a hedgehog's preferences, Tavi had served tea. Lady Cynthia was sitting on one side of the room, a teacup in her hand and an uncertain expression on her face.

Gwendolyn sat on the other side of the salon, a strained smile on her face and a teacup also in her hand. "We were just discussing the best London shops to order covers and fabrics from," she said a bit too brightly. Apparently leaving the men in the dining room had not improved Lady Cynthia's case of nerves.

"The shops in Launceston and even Plymouth have so little to offer," Mrs. Carbury agreed dutifully. She'd taken herself to a chair by the fire, which needed stoking. There was a decided chill in the air.

"Here, let me pour for you young ladies," Gwendolyn offered, moving to the tea table and taking up her duties as hostess. She poured for Lucy, Edith, Alyssa, and Meggie. The girls continued their conversation on a sofa near the window, chatting nearly like old friends.

"Alyssa, we are dying to know," Lucy began, glancing conspiratorially at her sister, who sat on the other side of her, "you said you have two sisters."

"Yes, both are married and proud mothers," she said, wondering what it was that the girls were "dying" to know.

"We were wondering if they have hair like yours," Edith finished with an embarrassed laugh.

Alyssa chuckled softly as an annoying blush stained her cheeks. She wished her hair would not win her so much attention. "Truthfully, I'm the first redhead in the family since my grandmother. My sisters are quite conventional blond beauties."

"Do not be sorry for it," Lucy said, frowning slightly as if she feared she'd given offense.

"For all they say about red hair being out of fashion," Edith said, "have you noticed how the men can never resist it?"

"No, I haven't noticed," Alyssa said. Her red hair was an attribute she would have done without.

Oddly, Lady Cynthia flicked a glance in her direction. "Might I have more tea?" she asked, holding her cup out toward Gwendolyn.

"Certainly." Gwendolyn rose from her chair and started toward Lady Cynthia.

At the same instant, the lady rose from her chair. The cup she was holding rattled on its saucer.

The abrupt movement startled Gwendolyn, who held the teapot. Steaming tea splashed from the flowered Wedgwood spout and cascaded down Lady Cynthia's skirt. The lady screeched and spun away.

"Oh my, I'm so sorry." Gwendolyn stepped back, dismay on her face.

Lucy had the presence of mind to grab a napkin and give it to Gwendolyn, and Edith took the teapot. Alyssa rescued the teacup from Lady Cynthia's hand and seized a napkin for her skirt.

"It's all my fault, really," Lady Cynthia cried in distress and raised her hands helplessly into the air. Then she clutched Alyssa's arm as if she feared Alyssa were going to escape. "Oh, oh, what—"

"Don't fret, Lady Cynthia." Alyssa squeezed the lady's hands reassuringly, but she wondered why the woman seemed so intent on catching her attention. "I'm sure we can sponge the stain out with some cool water if we get right to it. This way to the butler's pantry. It's all right, Tavi. I'll take care of Lady Cynthia."

Alyssa ushered the lady from the room.

"That was so clumsy of me," Lady Cynthia babbled, but her voice lacked conviction.

"Just an accident," Alyssa said, though she didn't believe it. The lady had created the calamity, no doubt about it. "Let's see how bad this is."

As soon as the door to the butler's pantry was closed behind them, Alyssa dampened a cloth and began to sponge Lady Cynthia's skirt. The woman brushed her hands away. "Don't worry about the stain. This gown is no great loss. I just didn't know how else to get a moment alone with you."

"But, why . . . " Alyssa stared at the woman in bewilderment.

"I've seen how you look at Harris," Lady Cynthia said, her eyes brimming with tears. Her grip on Alyssa's arm was strong, her fingers cold, and her voice full of urgency. "You are so young. Be careful. Do not tread where you have no right. I learned that lesson the hard way. It was a terrible mistake. How I have suffered. Do not believe everything the Trevells tell you."

"What would they lie about?" Alyssa asked, surprised and embarrassed. Was she so obvious in her admiration for Harris? Had other people seen how she felt about him? Or was this poor woman mad?

"You do not understand," Lady Cynthia said, seizing Alyssa's arms and searching her face. "Alistair, Harris, and Gwendolyn had a long and unpleasant history."

"I wouldn't know about that," Alyssa said, pulling away.

"And you do not want to know,'" Lady Cynthia concluded, her anxiety now almost palatable. "Believe me. The Trevells use people to their own purposes. No one escapes. Turn your attention to Byron, my dear, even if you do not care for him much. He is a bit of a braggart, but he will not hurt you, however boring he may be."

The door swung open and Gwendolyn stood there. "Are you having much success, my dear? That was so appalling of me to spill the tea all over your gown. Pray do not tell me this is a new gown, Lady Cynthia. I shall feel most dreadful if you do."

Immediately, Lady Cynthia released Alyssa and put several steps between them. "It's quite last season's fashion, Lady Penridge. You mustn't trouble yourself over it."

"I am so relieved," Gwendolyn said, clasping her hands together and smiling sweetly.

Alyssa could do little more than gape at the women as they examined Lady Cynthia's skirt and determined that the stain had faded considerably with her sponging. Lady Cynthia tossed aside the towel and strolled through the door, her arm linked through Gwendolyn's, chattering about what a fine cook Chef Hugo was.

Still bewildered, Alyssa followed them out of the butler's pantry. Lady Cynthia seemed to have discovered her confidence. But what on earth had the woman been trying to tell her? What warning was Lady Cynthia trying to give?

What was clear and troubled her most was that Lady Cynthia had noted her feelings for Harris. So she was wearing her feelings on her sleeve. Mama had scolded her about that more than once. She had never learned to mask her emotions, a definite disadvantage in Society where nuances counted for everything.

Harris was all wrong for her; she knew that. He was an older man, one to be admired, certainly, but not to be sought. But if she were seeking him, what other woman would she be trying to displace? Gwendolyn? Or was there someone else? Lady Cynthia herself, perhaps?

Alyssa shook her head. Hardly. No, the lady was nice, but she lacked the style and sophistication she imagined Harris would find attractive.

Still, Harris and a woman other than herself . . . The unpleasant possibility washed over her like ice water after a hot bath.

Ten

The thought pursued her into the night and the next morning. After breakfast, as she gazed out the library window at the opposite wing of the house, she unhappily continued to wonder what Lady Cynthia had meant about treading where she had no right. What *could* she have meant except that she had, well, had an affair with a man other than her husband? Was that man Harris? Did her husband know?

What *did* the ever-present, keen-eyed Sir Ralph know? Sir Ralph who the neighbor Alistair Trevell, Lord Penridge, had deceived.

Alistair Trevell, master of a lucrative estate that his cousin Harris had inherited but said he didn't want. Alistair Trevell, husband of the beautiful Gwendolyn, whom, it appeared, his cousin Harris also may have inherited—and, perhaps, *did* want.

Shivering despite the warmth of the fire, Alyssa reluctantly confronted the questions she'd been avoiding: could the rumors possibly be true? Could Alistair have been murdered? And could it be—yes, she had to face it—could it be that Harris had murdered his cousin Alistair in order to gain his title and his estate *and* his wife?

Even if it were true, how would she ever know? Would there be evidence of such a thing? And where would it be? In Harris's bedchamber? Or his study?

Her curiosity about Harris's study had been piqued several days earlier when Jane mentioned, as she'd rattled on about her household chores, that only Tavi was allowed to clean the master's study. How strange, Alyssa had thought at the time. Now she wondered if there was a more sinister reason for keeping all but his trusted servant out.

The study was the place where Harris went to tend to estate business: a room in the same wing as the kitchen, but farther down the hall near the back stairway to the servants' quarters. The wing that she could see from the library window had its own entrance from the far side of the drive. Occasionally, when she was in the library, she would see horsemen arrive or the gamekeeper's small trap come through the fairy gate and drive up to that door. It was the entrance that Harris had instructed Captain Dundry to use.

Her father had had such a room in their home, a place where business acquaintances came and went, where deals were struck and cigars were smoked. Though she, Winslow, and her sisters seldom entered their father's sanctum, the place was not forbidden to them. It was just a room that smelled of stale smoke and, in rainy weather, of wet wool and damp leather. It held little of interest. What did they care for a globe, maps, and receipts? Papa's business diary, a humidor, a couple of hunting trophies—a buck and a badger—and a couple of fat leather chairs? Little that told them anything they didn't already know about the man who used it—their papa.

But would Harris's study tell her more? The day she looked out upon was gray and gloomy, like her speculations. What secrets did his study hold? Was any of it her business?

Most certainly not. However, she would not—could not—convince herself that she should leave well enough alone. After the events of Sunday, she had to know more.

She'd seen Harris ride away earlier, on his way to the mine, she supposed. Gwendolyn and Meggie were occupied with lessons upstairs in the schoolroom. Jane was busy with her daily chores, as would be Tavi, she calculated.

Uncertainly, she chewed on her lip as she gazed out the

window at the other wing of Penridge Hall. Its mystery
drew her. Being a snoop was not an admirable thing. On
the other hand, now seemed as good a time as any to investigate.

Before she could talk herself out of the idea, Alyssa
turned from the window and started off. Through the grand
salon, down the hallway, past the magnificent staircase and
the comfortable wood-paneled receiving room, a glimpse
of the dining room. At the hallway to the kitchen she paused,
listening to the clatter of dishes and the voices of Chef
Hugo and the scullery maid.

She saw not a soul as she went, giving her courage. She
forged on past the yellow lady's morning room and on toward Harris's.

At the short flight of stairs that separated the wing from
the main house, she hesitated again, still chewing on her
lip. She listened for a sound that might indicate anyone was
close by. Silence.

She stepped down the stairs and went into the first large
room she found.

It was the billiards room, spacious, dark, and unoccu-
pied at the moment. The curtains were partially drawn. The
billiards table squatted in the center of the room. Leather
chairs lined the walls. A card table and chairs sat in front
of the cold fireplace. The faint scent of cigar smoke clung
to the air. A glass trophy box containing a sizeable red fox
hung over the mantelpiece. The hearth looked as though it
had been unused for some time; its blacking appeared fresh
and thorough. The lamp globes gleamed from disuse. It appeared Harris was an infrequent billiards player.

She turned and saw for the first time the closed door
across the hallway. Harris's study? Her reluctance gone,
laid low by her curiosity, she walked out of the billiards
room and straight to the door.

Cautiously, she put her hand on the knob and turned it.
It was unlocked. She opened the door and stood on the

threshold. The sight nearly choked her. She stifled the sound.

The room was a clutter of objects—trinkets and treasures, shiny and rich—disarrayed on the cabinets, bookshelves, the table and floor. Brass urns. Ebony statues. Silver trays. Rolled rugs. Baskets and beads. Lamps and books.

She stepped farther into the room, staring in open-mouthed wonder. A huge tiger pelt was draped over the length of the sofa. Yards of fine folded fabric were stacked on the sofa's arms. The silver and gold threads glittered, even in the dim light of the study. This was like stumbling upon the treasure cave of Ali Baba and his forty thieves. Gold, silk, and gems.

Was this booty from Harris's stay in India?

Awed, she continued to scan the room until her gaze fell on a brass-trimmed, mahogany box on the hearthside table. Next to it was lying a white jade dagger, its hilt decorated with gold. She picked up the dagger to admire the delicate craftsmanship and the translucence of the jade. The blade was sharp. Overall, the dagger was exquisite, but she had no idea whether it was truly useful or ceremonial art. Carefully she laid it down on the table.

The wooden box on the table was about the size of a generous picnic basket. It had a hinged top and many drawers down its front, the type of box she'd seen missionaries carry on expeditions to store an assortment of things such as specimens. It was so close at hand, she naturally opened it first. Half expecting to find more jewels, she peered into the top compartment. Instead of precious stones, she found herself gazing at a variety of glass-stoppered bottles, corked vials, and tiny envelopes of powder.

She picked up one of the bottles to read the label QUININE FOR MALARIA. She put it back and picked up another. LAUDANUM FOR PAIN. The label of the vial she selected next was indecipherable. Then there was "Aromatic spirits of Ammonia" or smelling salts, she concluded. "Oil of cloves for toothache." Another jar, unlabeled, was full of a white powder she did not recognize. Another jar was labeled "arsenic." Poison—but it was used for other things, too, she thought, malaria among them.

Hastily she dropped the jar back into the box and decided to look in the drawers. There she found absorbent cotton, sticking plaster, muslin bandages, thread and needles. Another drawer offered paregoric for loose bowels and a bottle of syrup of ipecac to induce vomiting. The last drawer she pulled open was full of instruments that she surmised were for surgery. Scissor-like tools, scalpels, pliers of several sizes.

With a shudder, she refrained from touching them. The sight made her think of the dentist. She'd not suffered at the hands of one yet and did not care to entertain the thought.

"Who—Miss Lockhart?" Tavi's voice boomed from behind her, louder than she'd ever heard him speak.

Alyssa jumped. Drat it. Embarrassment tugged at her as she turned, but she took a deep breath and decided to brazen it out.

"May I help you find something?" he demanded in a tone that was anything but helpful, perhaps even sarcastic. He strode into the room, glaring at her. He offered no bow and his usual humble demeanor was gone. "No one is permitted in here but his lordship and myself."

"I didn't realize," she said, simulating dismay. "He told me I might borrow a book. And when I walked in, well, there are so many wonderful things . . . "

"This box should be locked," Tavi said, his eyes narrowed. Hastily he crossed to her side, studying the wooden box as if he expected to find something amiss. Satisfied that nothing was gone, he snapped the lid closed. "Where is the lock?"

She shook her head. "It was unlocked when I found it."

"It's his lordship's medicine chest." Distress furrowed his brow. "It should be locked at all times."

"Perhaps his lordship forgot to lock it," she said.

The turbaned butler continued to search the tabletop and the floor for the lock.

The gleam of brass on the carpet caught Alyssa's eye. "Is this it?'" She bent to pick up the small brass padlock.

"Yes," he said, eyeing her as if he thought she'd brought it out of her cuff. He snatched the lock from her hand and latched it on the box. "May I show you to the morning room?" he offered, his frown still in place.

"No, thank you," Alyssa said, disappointed. Frantically she searched for a delaying tactic. She'd only begun to investigate Harris's study. "I'll find my way as soon as I select a book. His lordship said I might borrow a book."

Tavi appeared uncertain. "I'll wait."

Alyssa stifled her exasperation and smiled. "I won't take long."

Crossing to the bookshelves, she began to read the titles, which were all related to estate management. Hardly her cup of tea. She could feel Tavi's gaze on her back, scrutinizing her, making her feel awkward and disliking her for possibly putting him in a difficult position with his master.

She drew her fingers across the spines, but nothing among the books looked remotely like the sort of thing that would interest her. She wasn't learning anything about Harris from this visit, either. She might as well be on her way. Then she saw a long, thin spine that looked like it might be a nice book of illustrated poetry.

"Here we are," she said aloud and smiling cheerfully. "This looks interesting. Thank you, Tavi." With the book tucked under her arm, she swept out of the study, up the few stairs, and on to her room.

She closed the door and leaned against it, taking a deep breath. That was an adventure. One not especially instructive, and it had earned her an enemy. Yes, definitely, she was not Tavi's favorite in the household.

However, her adventure wasn't a colossal failure, either. Perhaps she hadn't had the time to search Harris's study, but she had borrowed a book. That meant she had an excuse to return.

What had she learned? The book still tucked under her arm, she crossed to the windowseat overlooking the rose garden and sank down onto the cushion. If Harris had a woman in his life, there was no outward evidence of her on his desk or the mantelpiece. But had she, indeed, found evidence of murder?

Well, not evidence, but perhaps cause for suspicion.

The medicine box had been a most intriguing find. Full of medications, necessary gear, curious substances. No doubt it had been an important part of Harris's equipage in India. Soldiers had to be prepared for injury or illness.

Still, she didn't like what niggled at the back of her mind. Many of those substances were poisonous. Who knew what sort of exotic potions—drugs or powders—one might find in a mysterious place like the Asian subcontinent? Perhaps there was even a poison that appeared to affect its victim like food poisoning. What an unwelcome thought. She leaned her forehead against the window. Her heart beat slower, heavier.

"Alyssa? Alyssa?" Meggie's voice came from the stairway down the hall. "Lessons are done. It's time to feed King Arthur."

Despite her dark thoughts, the eagerness in Meggie's voice brought a smile to Alyssa's lips. The nigglings whispered that she really didn't know anything for certain. There were more important things to tend to, like a little girl who was finding herself again after a great loss.

"I'm coming," she called to Meggie. Rising from the windowseat, she tossed the book and her doubts aside. "Let's feed King Arthur his lunch."

* * *

The unsuccessful expedition into Harris's study curbed her curiosity for a day or so. She directed her energies toward Meggie and King Arthur. The change in the little girl since they'd adopted the hedgehog was amazing. She smiled more often and her cheeks took on color, making her resemble the other apple-cheeked children Alyssa had seen in Southampton.

The hostility that she had felt at first every time the child looked at her had vanished. Now Meggie sought her out, not just to take care of King Arthur but also to share a walk in the garden or a story from a book. They discovered that they both liked stories, the more exotic the better. They even went riding, Meggie on Piskie and Alyssa on Smuggler. Though they never rode out of the sight of the hall, Meggie seemed to enjoy herself immensely.

Grief and anger no longer shadowed Meggie's eyes. The change almost made Alyssa lighthearted. Little was said, but she wasn't the only one who felt the difference. On fair days when lessons were done, Gwendolyn, with a sweet smile so much prettier than her strained expression, quietly turned to tending her garden. Jane went about her chores, humming with obvious relief. She had no more messy pranks to clear up after. Harris smiled when he greeted his niece, sometimes ruffling her hair.

It was just such a moment when Harris displayed his affection for Meggie and the child gazed up at him in response that Alyssa glimpsed the worship in the girl's eyes. With a pang of sympathy, she realized Meggie adored her uncle. So the child was another female enthralled by his spell. She was glad for Meggie's sake that he made no more mention of sending her away to school.

The days that followed were pleasant, almost halcyon. For long hours, Alyssa gave no thought to the rumors of poison or murder or Lady Cynthia's strange behavior. Byron Littlefield called once to pay his respects during an afternoon horseback ride. Alyssa declined his invitation to join him. He took no offense. With a confident smile, he offered to call another time.

The next day a letter arrived from Aunt Esther. Her leg was mending nicely, she wrote, and her friend's daughter and three children had arrived for an extended stay while her son-in-law was away on a business trip. The household was bulging at the seams—children on cots and servants doubled up in the attic.

Alyssa was especially thankful that peace had been achieved with Meggie. There certainly would be no room for her at the home of her aunt's friend if her welcome wore thin at Penridge Hall.

That evening after dinner, she answered her aunt's letter, assuring her that all was well, that her company was missed at the hall, and that she, herself, was making new friends. She did not write about Byron Littlefield. The *last thing* she needed was for Aunt Esther to write home speculating about potential suitors. She also never mentioned her and Harris's confrontation with Reverend Whittle and the miners. Why worry Aunt Esther about their local troubles? Instead she wrote of King Arthur, of Lucy and Edith and the wedding, and of Gwendolyn's lovely rose garden that still offered a few late blooms.

By the time she signed and sealed the missive, she was yawning and quite ready to go to bed. Jane bustled in to stoke the fire for the night. She had turned down the bed earlier, when she'd helped Alyssa undress.

"It's going to be a cold one tonight," the older woman said, busying herself with the coalscuttle. As if to mark her words, a gust of wind rattled the windowpanes.

Alyssa gathered her wrapper closer and rose from the writing desk. She hardly had time during the day for letter writing now. Meggie needed her. Keeping up with the little girl wore her out sometimes.

"Yes, I can feel the chill already creeping across the floor," she said, anticipating the warmth of the downy counterpane as she scurried across the cold floor. How quickly the damp penetrated the carpet, stealing up into the soles of her slippers.

Hurriedly she plopped onto the edge of the bed, kicked off her slippers, shrugged out of her wrapper, and thrust her feet under the thick covers.

The pain was sharp—immediate—stinging.

She yowled. It lanced up through her toes and the tender pads of her feet.

Jane started. "Miss—what?"

Trying to free herself from the pain, Alyssa gasped and kicked at the source. Drawing her feet away from it, she yanked aside the counterpane to discover what was attacking her.

Nettles covered the sheets. Dozens of spiny little green burs—barbed, needle sharp. She swung her legs over the edge of the bed, but she dared not step on the floor. The nettles clung to her toes and feet, and stepping on them would drive the barbs deeper into her flesh. She whimpered with pain and frustration.

"No, let me get them," Jane rushed to the bedside and knelt down to help. But the nettles were too sharp for her to remove with her bare hands.

"Don't hurt yourself, Jane."

"I won't, miss." Ever resourceful, the maid grabbed a corner of her apron and began to pluck at the spiny things. The nettles clung to the white cotton. She worked quickly as Alyssa clutched the bed linens against the pain and tried not to wriggle her feet. But she couldn't keep from sucking in a noisy breath of discomfort.

"My heavens," Jane exclaimed. "I'm getting them as fast as I can. I never saw the like. Nettles. Nettles everywhere."

"What is it?"

Alyssa and Jane glanced up to see Tavi standing in the

doorway. His face was dark with concern. Neither of them had heard him knock or open the door.

"Miss Meggie is up to no good again," Jane burst out before Alyssa could say anything. "She put nettles into Miss Lockhart's bed."

"Meggie?" Everything inside Alyssa protested. "No, no, not Meggie. She's over that."

"Well, who else then?" Jane's lips thinned, and her eyes narrowed as she picked at the nettles. "Must have come in and done it after I turned your bed down but before you come upstairs to write your letter."

"Ow!" Alyssa winced as Jane pulled a bur from inside the arch of her foot.

"I'm sorry, miss," Jane said, hesitating for the first time. "There's just a few more here."

Alyssa bit her lip to keep from yelping again. She watched Jane tug gingerly at the burs.

More commotion at the door nagged her. When she looked up again, a scowling Harris stood there instead of Tavi.

"What is this?" he demanded, both hands on the doorframe and a frown on his face. His cravat was gone and he was in his shirtsleeves as if he, too, had been undressing for bed. "Tavi told me there is some trouble."

"Nettles in my bed," Alyssa said, trying to make light of it. But it was impossible to smile with needle-like pain shooting through your feet.

"Are you all right?" he asked, striding into the room in a flash, his gaze riveted on her toes. He stopped at her bedside, peering over Jane's shoulder.

"No actual damage," she said, embarrassed that her bare feet were the object of his perusal again. It really wasn't proper. "Ow!"

"I'm so sorry, miss," Jane repeated, still at her task, her apron full of the burs.

Suddenly, Harris was on his knees beside Jane, reaching

for Alyssa's foot, wrapping long, steely fingers around her anklebone.

"Bring a lamp over here, Jane," he ordered as he examined her foot more closely, careful not to disturb the burs.

The heat of his touch surged up Alyssa's calf and into her body. Melting warmth pooled in her belly. That odd feeling returned and flowed into her breasts again, the fullness, the sensitivity. Gazing down at his head bowed over her legs and the sensation of his hands on her bare skin brought heat flooding into her cheeks, but no one seemed to notice. This truly was improper. She attempted to pull her ankle from his grasp.

"I'm not going to hurt you," he said, his gaze still on her foot, his grasp unyielding. Her pain was overwhelmed by other sensations. With the feel of his hand on her leg, Alyssa thought she was going to swoon of embarrassment—or pleasure. "Who did this?" he demanded.

"Looks like more of Miss Meggie's pranks to me, Master Harris," Jane began again as she held the lamp for Harris so he could see better.

To Alyssa's shock, Harris began plucking the nettles from her feet, his touch light and quick.

"I know them nettles weren't there when I turned the bed," Jane added.

"No, I don't think it was Meggie—ow!" Alyssa winced again.

"I'm sorry," Harris said, glancing up into her face, a furrow between his brows. "That was a particularly nasty one."

"I know it can't be helped," she muttered between clenched teeth.

"It might be best if you did not look while I'm doing this." He bent over her foot again, his hold on her still firm as he continued to work.

"All right," Alyssa said gazing up at Jane, who was holding the lamp.

"A good soaking will take away the pain," he said. She

could feel his fingers working swiftly. "I have some salts that will help in my medicine stores."

"That's right," Jane agreed. "A good soaking will do the trick. Take any soreness right out."

"There, that's it, the last one," he said, looking up into her face. "Better now?"

She sighed. "Yes, much."

When she smiled, he looked truly relieved. His thumb stroked the arch of her foot ever so gently. She relaxed, willing to allow him to do that for as long as he liked.

"You are certain you are all right?" he asked, glancing down to see that he was stroking her foot. He frowned. To Alyssa's disappointment, he released her immediately.

"Yes, I'm fine," she said, tucking her feet back under her nightgown and trying to ignore the blush that stained her cheeks once more. "It was just uncomfortable, not really life-threatening."

"I will send Tavi up with the salts." Harris rose, still frowning. "Then I'll have a word with Gwendolyn about Meggie."

"It couldn't have been Meggie," Alyssa protested. "She is in bed and has been for some time, hasn't she? Where would she get such things? Surely Elijah permits no nettles in the garden."

"Then who else?" he asked, looking at Alyssa as if she should know better.

"I don't know," she said, annoyed that she was unable to offer a better theory, something that would protect Meggie. "But she's been so good since we made a pet of King Arthur. I just can't believe . . ." She let her words trail off as she saw the stony look come over his face. "What are you going to do?"

"I will discuss it with her mother first," he said as he turned away. When he reached the door, he turned back toward them. "Make Miss Lockhart comfortable, Jane. I do not know what is going on here, but I will not have this kind of nonsense at Penridge Hall."

He disappeared down the hallway toward Gwendolyn's room.

Eleven

Alyssa didn't sleep much that night. It was another two hours before her bed linen was changed and the pain sufficiently soaked from her feet so she could comfortably crawl under the covers. But lack of sleep didn't keep her from being up in the morning in time to talk to Harris again. Whatever happened, she did not want to be the reason that Meggie was punished—especially when she didn't think that Meggie was the culprit.

Who else would do such a thing? And why? Those questions churned through her head both awake and in her dreams as she slept. By dawn no answer presented itself. She awoke knowing that whatever she did, she had to convince Harris that the villain wasn't his niece.

She dressed hurriedly, without waiting for Jane's help, hoping to catch him alone at breakfast. She thought she was early enough, but when she reached the breakfast room, she found Harris, Gwendolyn, and Meggie already seated at the table. All three heads turned toward her as she stood in the doorway.

Gwendolyn looked tired, her hair uncharacteristically untidy and her face pale. Harris was dressed for business, freshly shaved, combed, brushed, darkly grim. But it was Meggie's face that troubled Alyssa most. Meggie glared at her, her mouth set in a belligerent pout and her chin thrust forward in defiance. Tears streaked her cheeks. Disappointed that she was too late to speak to Harris alone, she went to her place and stood behind her chair.

"Good morning, Alyssa," Harris said, gazing at her with concern. "How are your feet this morning?"

Alyssa blushed as the image of his strong, warm fingers stroking the arch of her foot flashed through her mind. "Much better, thank you. The salts you sent up helped a great deal."

"Alyssa, I'm so sorry," Gwendolyn began, her hands in her lap, appeal on her face. "I just can't expl—"

"May I join the discussion?" Alyssa asked, glancing at Meggie again. She did not want to hear Gwendolyn blame the child, too.

"By all means, join us, but there is nothing to discuss," Harris said, reaching for his teacup without looking at any of them. "Meggie is leaving for school in three days. I've dispatched a telegram this morning requesting admittance to an excellent school in Exeter. I'm certain they will be willing to take her."

Alyssa turned to Meggie. "Is that what you want?"

"No," Meggie cried, pounding her little fists in her lap. "I didn't do it."

"I believe our cousin Harris is making the best decision," Gwendolyn said. "I completely approve. We cannot go on like this."

"But, Meggie didn't put the nettles in my bed," Alyssa said, speaking first to Gwendolyn and then to Harris. "She says she didn't, and I believe her."

"I believe there was another incident you didn't tell us about," Harris said. "Tavi mentioned something about salt in your tea?"

"Why didn't you tell us about that?" Gwendolyn asked.

"Because I thought it would only serve to aggravate matters," Alyssa confessed, silently reproaching Tavi. "And it happened while the Littlefields were here. I didn't want to make a scene. What does that have to do with this?"

"Then you weren't protecting Meggie?" Harris asked.

"No, I was not protecting her," Alyssa said, annoyed at

finding herself in doubt. "Nor am I protecting her now. If I thought she'd done this, I would say so."

Meggie's face contorted into a thundercloud of outrage and despair. "But I did not do it," she wailed. "I didn't. I do not want to go to some school in Exeter."

"The arrangements are made," Harris said, quite dispassionate toward his niece's pleas.

Had the man no heart? Alyssa wondered.

"No more tears," he continued, rising from his chair and laying his napkin down on the table. Breakfast was over. "You will make new friends and learn new manners."

"I don't want to make new friends," Meggie sobbed.

"That is enough." Gwendolyn cast a severe frown at her daughter. "Of course you will make new friends."

"The subject is no longer open for discussion." Harris strode from the room.

"Meggie, I'm so sorry," Alyssa began, and then she decided she would not leave it at that. She had not tried her best. Determination brewing, out the door she went, skirt in hand to keep it from tripping her. She hurried after Harris, who was headed to the stables.

She whisked by Johnnie and Elijah and found Harris in Pendragon's stall, cinching up the girth one more notch.

"I think you are being very unfair," she declared to his back without preamble—and before her courage deserted her. She wasn't being impulsive. Meggie's future was important.

He slowly pulled the stirrup leather into place then faced her. "And just how is that?" he asked coolly, resting one arm on the saddle. "The child's grief appears to be the source of her misdeeds. I cannot allow her to upset the lives of everyone else at Penridge Hall."

"I understand that and I would not argue against school if I thought it would help," she said. "But it is because of her grief that you must let her stay. Don't you see how important you and Penridge are to her? This is her home. You and

Gwendolyn are her family. She's lost her father, and now you are taking her from her mother, too. Have you no pity?"

"Sweet Alyssa, do I seem so insensitive to you?" he asked, studying her, his expression shifting from harsh authority to cool exasperation. "Do I seem pitiless?"

"I believe you are too severe," she said, deciding she had his full attention now, and she would make use of it. "Meggie does not need a soldier's discipline. She needs the compassion a child deserves."

"I assure you that I am not without sympathy for her," he said, turning back to the saddle. "I lost my parents when I was young."

"Then you know how she feels," she said, recalling the story Jane had told her of Harris losing his parents at age five. "So why must you send her to school when you know yourself how terrible it is to be sent off into the unknown?"

He turned to her, his frown less stern, his gaze keen, searching. "Is that how you felt about coming here? That you were being sent off into the unknown."

The question surprised her. She had not been thinking of herself at all.

"No, it's not the same thing," she stammered, though she knew with a pang in her heart that he was right. She'd felt a sense of loss when her parents sent her away. And she'd been frightened, though she'd never let them see it. "I'm not a little girl," she said, squaring her shoulders to mask her reaction now.

"I'm glad," he said, and seemed genuinely so, his frown altering almost into a smile. Then he returned to adjusting the saddle. He spoke over his shoulder as he worked. "It's true I know something of how Meggie feels. It is a painful time. Confusing. Bewildering. She feels abandoned, though she knows better. She's adrift. She may even feel as if the loss was her fault somehow, even though she knows that was impossible."

Alyssa listened, wondering how much of what he was

telling her was what he knew about Meggie's feelings and how much was his own boyhood experience.

"She is suffering. The problem is," he continued, "she seems to want to make the people around her suffer, too."

"Don't you see she will get over that?" Alyssa said, holding her hands out in appeal. "Her behavior with King Arthur is proof that she can. She has been better behaved this last two weeks. You've seen it. Give her more time. Think of this prank with the nettles as a relapse if you must. But how can you in good conscience send her away?"

"Alyssa, do not question my good conscience!" he said, turning to her. A stern frown returned to his lips. "There is more at stake."

"More what—" she began, mystified and frustrated. "Tell me. I'm listening."

"More than I will discuss with you." As he held her gaze, his frown melted away and a half smile formed on his lips again. "But I must say, if I'm ever in trouble, I hope you will come to my defense."

She suddenly found her chin captured in his right hand, and he stepped closer.

"You are very valiant, sweet Alyssa," he whispered, his lips almost upon hers.

She stood frozen, captured by the unexpected husky sound of his voice and the warm strength of his hand on her chin. The depths of the emotion in his eyes held hers. Then his lips descended to hers, moving over her mouth, firm and questing.

She hesitated at first, her eyes wide open and her hands fluttering at her sides. How was she to respond? This was a man's kiss. The feel and scent of a man so near, so intimate was more than her mind could make sense of. The delicious, rough texture of his wool coat sleeve scratched against her throat, and his leather and spice scent filled her head.

She surrendered, involuntarily, no longer caring about

how she should do it. Grasping the lapels of his coat, she
tilted her head back and attempted to give in return, to taste
him, to know more of the feel of his lips, the heat of his
mouth.

He took her offering. For a moment she thought she felt
his tongue teasing her lower lip. A low groan escaped her.
Her insides turned into liquid heat, and she tingled all over.
Seeking more, she leaned into him. She didn't care if she
ever took another breath again. She just wanted this thing
with his mouth and her mouth to go on and on and on.

Abruptly his hands caught her hands on his lapels, and
he held her away from him. He took a deep, wary breath.

"I should not—" He stopped.

"Should not what?" she asked, suddenly cold. "What?"

"I am your guardian, just as I am Meggie's," he said,
thrusting her farther from him and firmly putting a full step
between them. His painful grip on her hands and the lock
of hair that had fallen across his brow was proof that the
kiss had affected him as much as it had her.

"It is my place to protect you, not to take advantage." He
released her hands and went to Pendragon's bridle.

"But you kissed me before," she said, touching her lips,
which still tingled with his warmth. "The day we found
King Arthur."

"That was different," he said without turning toward her.

"How so?" she asked, unwilling to let him dismiss it.

"It was a gesture of gratitude," he said, making some ad-
justment to the bridle. "Let's keep that kiss and this one to
ourselves, shall we?"

"And what was this?" she asked, her insides still unset-
tled.

"A lapse." He took up Pendragon's reins and led the stallion out of the box, past her. "Trust me, I would not send
Meggie away if I did not believe it vital to her welfare. I
am sorry if you find that pitiless."

"Then you could order me to go away just as easily," she said, unable to keep the accusatory tone from her voice.

"As you said yourself, your situation is entirely different." He led the stallion out into the stable yard. "But if I thought it necessary, yes, I would send you away."

She followed, unhappy with his tone. Obviously, he'd given sending her away some thought.

Elijah and Johnnie were busy cleaning stalls at the far end of the stable. Alyssa glanced in their direction, but they were intent on their chores. They couldn't have seen Harris kiss her. Nor would anyone at the house. Nevertheless, she brushed her hand across her lips again, certain that the world would know she'd just been thoroughly kissed.

In the stable yard, Harris halted and prepared to mount the black.

She could think of no more arguments to pose for Meggie's sake.

He stopped before he put his foot in the stirrup and turned toward her again.

"I know it's not easy for you and Meggie to part now that you have become close over King Arthur," he said.

"But I honestly think she is innocent," Alyssa pleaded.

"I know you do, and I admire your loyalty." Harris swung up on Pendragon and regarded her indulgently. "Please don't make it difficult for Meggie to leave by continuing to protest."

"I didn't think about that," she said, ashamed of herself for not considering Meggie. "Naturally, I don't want to make anything worse for her."

"Good," he said. "Then I can count on you to help her pack and come to terms with going away to school."

Apprehensively, she gazed up at him, astride the great black horse, and she nodded. "Of course."

He smiled, apparently pleased with her agreement. "It may have been wrong of me," he said softly. She knew he was referring to their kiss. "But I am *not* sorry," he added.

Then he wheeled Pendragon around and spurred the stallion off in the direction of Wheal Isabel.

Bewildered, confused, and unhappy, Alyssa wrapped her arms around herself and walked back toward the house. So much for convincing Harris of Meggie's innocence and saving her from being sent away. She had succeeded at nothing.

Nothing but receiving her first real kiss.

She halted and tentatively licked her lips. The taste of him was still there, salty and spicy. She sucked in a deep breath to prevent her belly from quivering and threatening to melt again. The kiss had not been what a romance novel would deem a searing one, but there had been more in it than any guardian should bestow on his ward. Much more. He'd been right about that.

But had he kissed her because he found her desirable, because she was a kinswoman he was fond of, or because it was a way to stop the argument and get his way?

Guiltily, she glanced at the house. No one at the windows. No one could have seen her anyway, she was certain. But there was still the nagging guilt that she and Harris had done something forbidden. Had he really meant to call it wrong? Whatever it might be termed, she didn't think the kiss was something to tell anyone about, just as he said.

She resumed her walk toward the house, thinking to return unnoticed. Jane would be going about her usual morning chores. Gwendolyn and Meggie would be commencing to pack. She should see if she could help and be of some comfort to Meggie, as she'd promised Harris.

When she reached the garden door, though, she found Tavi holding it open for her.

She stared at him, wondering why he couldn't be dusting the study instead of at the door to note her return. "Thank you, Tavi."

"Miss Lockhart." His expression was as bland as ever as she stepped through the doorway.

"Where are Lady Penridge and Miss Meggie?" she asked, certain that he knew she'd been in the stable with Harris and that he didn't approve.

"In Miss Meggie's room," Tavi replied, closing the door. "I fetched the trunk from the attic for them, and Jane is preparing it for packing."

"Thank you," Alyssa said, moving toward the stairs. "I'll go up then and see what I can do."

"Yes, miss." He bowed, his hands humbly pressed together. But she was beginning to think there was nothing humble about Tavi, the butler. No, indeed. He saw far too much and knew too much to remain indifferent to the actions and affairs of the residents of Penridge.

The next two days were a blur of activity, of laundry and pressing, mending and folding, sorting and airing all the things that were to go to Exeter with Meggie. The school had sent an affirmative telegram in reply to Harris's request and attached a list of clothing, linens, and personal items required for Meggie's stay.

Neither Gwendolyn nor Alyssa spoke of the prank or Meggie's reluctance to go to school. To lift the child's spirits they went about the packing with a smile and as much excitement as they could muster. Even Jane contrived to make a happy event of the chore.

There was no time to talk to Harris again, and there was no need, Alyssa decided. She'd made a promise to him to help Meggie, and she would keep it.

Besides that, what was there to say to him after the kiss? He'd pronounced it a mistake. Not one he was sorry for— though perhaps he was just trying to make her feel better. However, he'd been clear; he wanted to forget it, to act as if it had never happened. She could act that way, but she'd never forget. *He'd kissed her*, for heaven's sake. She'd been kissed in a way she'd never been kissed before, and she knew with all her blossoming womanly instincts that he'd kissed her with passion. She'd remember that kiss to her dying day.

But what did you say to a man after a kiss like that?

She could, however, do her best for Meggie. They met in the breakfast room, feeding King Arthur and talking over Alyssa's future care of the hedgehog. They even took one last, short horseback ride. Though they never talked of school or Meggie's leaving, planning the sequence of King Arthur's day and saying farewell to Piskie seemed to mollify Meggie's unhappiness and allay her fears.

When the morning of departure arrived, everything was ready for Meggie's trip, and the child seemed resigned to going off to school.

"I hope there will be no tears," Harris said, lingering over the breakfast table after Gwendolyn had taken Meggie upstairs to put on her cloak and pack the last of her things. Instead of riding off to the mine early, he'd remained at Penridge to see Meggie off.

"I admit tears would make parting difficult." Alyssa silently prayed, too, that there would no weeping. She didn't think she could remain dry-eyed if Meggie cried.

"I thank you for helping with Meggie," he said, toying with a spoon on the table. "Your patience and cheer over the last couple of days have not gone unnoticed."

"It's the least I could do," she said.

From the hallway, they heard the child's quick steps on the wooden floor. She appeared in the breakfast room doorway. Her purple morning bonnet was tied jauntily under her chin, and her cloak was wrapped around her.

"Here I am," she announced with a brave smile. "I'm ready to go. Mama is having Tavi bring down the last trunk. But I want to talk to Alyssa. May I, Cousin Harris? I must ask her to do something for me."

Harris gave them a tolerant smile. "Of course, ladies.

While you make your final decisions about King Arthur, I shall go out and see that Elijah and the carriage is prepared for your journey."

As soon as Harris was gone, Alyssa asked, "What is it?"

Meggie's smile faded. She walked around the table to sit on the edge of the chair next to Alyssa's.

"There is one more thing," she said, her lips beginning to tremble. She looked up at Alyssa, her big, solemn, round eyes growing watery with unshed tears. "Will you do one thing for me?"

Alyssa braced herself against the tightening of her own throat. "I will do whatever it takes to make you smile."

"Will you find out who murdered my papa?"

Alyssa sucked in a shocked breath. She had wondered if Gwendolyn had heard the rumor, but she'd never thought about Meggie. That someone would breathe such a thing to a little girl was unthinkable. "Where did you hear that?"

"Johnnie from the stable told me," she said, her lips beginning to tremble in earnest this time. "He said . . . Oh, Alyssa, it is so terrible."

Great tears began to trickle down her cheeks.

Alyssa groaned, struggling to keep her composure. "What, sweetheart? What did he tell you?"

"He said that everyone knows the truth," Meggie sobbed out, her soulful eyes big and round as saucers. "He said that everyone knows that Cousin Harris murdered Papa." Then she wailed, clutching at Alyssa for comfort.

"Oh, sweetheart." Alyssa's heart ached as she gathered the child close. She pressed Meggie's head to her bosom. Frail shoulders shook with pain and sorrow. She absorbed as much of the child's sobs and hurt as she could, hoping to give comfort. She would have wept, too, if she hadn't been so angry.

"Tell me it's not true," Meggie begged.

"Of course it's not true," she said, not caring that she didn't know whether it was or wasn't. No child should have to live with the cruel doubt that another beloved family member had murdered her papa. "Have you asked your mama about this?"

Meggie stopped her sobbing long enough to give Alyssa a beseeching look. "I don't want Mama to hear the rumor. She would not be able to bear it. Promise me you will not tell her."

Alyssa heaved a weary sigh. What a web.

"Promise me," Meggie insisted. "Mama must never know."

"I promise," she said, dozens of things running through her mind—how to console Meggie and to rebuke one heedless stable boy. She pulled her handkerchief from her sleeve and began to dry Meggie's eyes. "I promise I won't tell your mama, and I promise that your cousin did not murder your papa. You must not trouble yourself over a silly rumor. You must go to school and make your place there. You will do well, I'm sure of it. You'll make new friends and go to new plays and eat Devonshire cream and berries. You'll be quite the worldly lady by the time you come home for Christmas holiday."

"I'm so glad it's not true." Meggie dried her eyes as instructed and nodded. "I love Cousin Harris, you know. I could not bear it if he was Papa's murderer."

"Well, he is *not*." Alyssa knew as she spoke the words that, she *must* learn the truth. It would never be good enough to tell Meggie he was innocent only to make the child feel better. She had to know the truth for herself—and for Meggie. "Better now?"

"Yes," Meggie said, a smile of relief on her face. "Do you really think they will serve Devonshire cream and berries at school?"

"On special occasions, at least," Alyssa said, praying the school would not let her and Meggie down.

"Will you be here when I return for Christmas?" the child asked, wiping away her last tear. Hope shone in her eyes.

"I hope I will be," she said. Heaven knew she had nowhere else to go or nowhere else she'd rather be. "I will read Mr. Dickens' ghost story to you if I am."

"Yes, I'd like that." Meggie gave a rapid nod of her head. "The one with Tiny Tim."

"Of course, the very story that is my Christmas favorite," Alyssa agreed and they laughed softly.

The sound of Harris's boots preceded his approach. They fell silent, waiting. When he appeared in the doorway and saw them together, watching him, a tentative smile came to his face. "I heard laughing. No tears?" he asked.

They smiled at the same time and shook their heads. Secretly, Alyssa tucked her handkerchief into Meggie's hidden cloak pocket.

"Then Elijah is ready whenever you are," he said.

Meggie grinned, slid off the chair, and ran toward him, her hand outstretched for his. "And so am I ready, too, Cousin Harris. I know everything is going to be all right. Alyssa told me so."

"Excellent." Harris's smile of gratitude as he took Meggie's hand warmed Alyssa's heart. Then he turned away to walk the child toward the waiting carriage.

Twelve

After the departure of one small girl, Penridge Hall seemed oddly empty, Alyssa thought, as she carried King Arthur's food from the kitchen to the breakfast room. Chef Hugo still glowered over the fact that a hedgehog was being fed from his larder, but he did not say so to her. As possessive as he was of his supplies, he'd apparently decided a hedgehog did not seriously threaten his reputation.

She sat the food in the cage and watched King Arthur sniff it and then sniff at her, his little black nose twitching in the air, catching her scent and seeking another's. His beady eyes squinted at her skeptically as though he didn't feel she was adequate to the task of feeding him. Obviously, he'd become accustomed to having a larger audience.

"I miss her already, too," Alyssa said to the pet.

Perhaps part of the reason the house seemed so empty was because Gwendolyn's maid, Blanche, had accompanied Meggie to Exeter. The young woman had relatives in the city and was delighted to be assigned the task of seeing Meggie to the school. But the absence of the maid wasn't enough to explain the emptiness. It was Meggie's energy—positive or negative—that filled so much of the house. Now it was gone.

King Arthur finally sniffed around his cage to his food dish and began to slurp at the milk and bread. She would remember to sneak some salmon from the table for him next time it was served.

Relieved to see the animal eating, she sat back in her chair.

As long as the hedgehog didn't starve himself for want of Meggie's company, the only worry she had was how to find a murderer, if there was one to find. She would have the truth for Meggie's sake. Although she was uncertain of how to go about discovering the facts, she had an idea about where to begin to ask questions.

She found Jane in Meggie's room. The little girl's chamber was strewn with discarded garments and keepsakes that Meggie had gone through in a rush, choosing what to pack. Gwendolyn was in the room, too, standing in the middle of the floor looking miserable and overwhelmed.

"I am afraid it is one of my beastly headaches," Gwendolyn moaned, lifting the back of her hand to her forehead in an elegant gesture.

"I can finish here, my lady," Jane said, picking up a petticoat from the floor.

"Go lie down, Gwendolyn," Alyssa urged, stepping into the room. "I can help Jane finish."

"I miss her already, you know," Gwendolyn said. "But I suppose Harris is right. School is the place for her now."

"She even seemed to be looking forward to it when she left." Alyssa hoped to make Gwendolyn feel better.

"Yes, she did seem happy to go in the end, and I'm glad of it," Gwendolyn said. "I believe I will lie down. Call me for tea, won't you, Jane?"

"Yes, my lady." Jane stood back from the doorway to allow Gwendolyn to leave. "Can I bring you anything, my lady?"

"No, I will be all right if I lie down," Gwendolyn said, looking back at Alyssa. "Until tea."

"Of course," she said.

Once Gwendolyn was gone, she and Jane resumed sorting through the dolls, books, and games. It wasn't long before the right opening to begin her questions came.

"I never thought I would say it, but the house echoes without that child here," Jane said as she put items into the appropriate boxes and drawers.

"You admit it then?" Alyssa asked with a smile as she slid a handful of books onto a bookshelf. "You miss Meggie already."

"Yes, well, when she was not up to her pranks, she was not such a bad sort," Jane admitted. "But school will be good for her."

"Perhaps," Alyssa said. "You've been at Penridge Hall for a long time, haven't you, Jane? Didn't you say so the first night I was here?"

"Yes, miss, I've been here nigh onto nineteen years," Jane said with a sharp nod. "I've been here near as long as you are old. Why do you ask?"

"I was just wondering," Alyssa said. "You told me Master Harris lost his parents years ago. What was he like when he came here?"

"He didn't do things like pranks," Jane said. "No, not him. And see how he has turned out?"

Another woman in the household under Lord Penridge's spell, Alyssa thought wryly. "Tell me, what was it like for him then?"

"Well, I suppose it was hard, losing his parents in the fire like he did and then his nanny, too." Jane paused to gaze into the near distance as she recalled the memories. "Master Harris and Master Alistair were both only children with a year difference in their ages, five and six. That was before my time, mind you. By the time I came to Penridge Hall, he and Master Alistair were ten and eleven, and a pair they were, too."

"How was that?" Alyssa asked.

"Well, they was always at each other," Jane said with a shake of her head. "Of course, you expect that of boys. One always trying to best the other. It's in their male nature, ain't it? But this was different. It weren't always good-natured, boys-will-be-boys kind of thing. They was always out to defeat each other."

"Was there some reason for the competition?" Alyssa forgot that she was supposed to be folding a towel and settled on the edge of Meggie's narrow bed.

"Sure, there was," Jane said. "I didn't see it at first, then one day the old man, the old Lord Penridge, Alistair's father—he berated Master Alistair when he did not whup Master Harris as quick as he thought he should. Told him if the boy wanted to be a son of his, he'd have to be a better fighter than that. He expected his son and heir to be a winner."

"He sounds like a real taskmaster," Alyssa said.

"That wasn't the end of it." Jane became agitated as the memories freshened. "The old lord would say like things to Master Harris. No matter what those boys did, the old lord expected better of them. He purposeful set the boys at each other. Boxing, wrestling, horse racing, cricket. Even shooting—who could bag the most birds in the least time. There wasn't nothing that the old lord didn't turn into a contest to prove who was most worthy of the name Trevell."

"That doesn't sound like a very happy home," Alyssa said, thinking of the pressure that would put on a boy who already felt he'd been abandoned.

"It wasn't, I can tell you," Jane said, her eyes bright with indignation. "It wasn't. The old lord was impossible to please in the house, too. And after he died, quiet-like in his bed, God rest his soul, we all thought things would get better."

"And did they?"

"At first, yes." Jane picked up a stray stocking and went to the clothes press with it. "Master Alistair had married Miss Gwendolyn. She being so beautiful and all. A fine lady of the manor. But little by little, Master Alistair became as much of an old tyrant as his father. He didn't have two boys, one of them an heir, to pit at each other's throats, so he put his efforts into the clay mine business. Like they say, the apple don't fall far from the tree."

"And Master Harris, what did he do?" Alyssa asked.

"Why, he must have had his fill of it all." Jane waved her

hand in the air. "He had bought his army commission before the old man died. A captain he was already before Master Alistair and Miss Gwendolyn were wed. Shortly after the wedding he went off to India."

"So he saw Alistair and Gwendolyn married before he left?" Alyssa asked.

Jane said nothing, just pressed her lips together and turned away to close the clothes press. "He was Master Alistair's groomsman, he was."

Alyssa studied the maid's back. "Something else happened? You've told me this much, Jane. Why not finish the story?"

Jane frowned over her shoulder, as if she did not like the tale nor the telling of it. "Well, there are those who make a great deal of it, but I think it was all the old lord's doing. Constantly comparing them two boys against each other. Betrayal was just destined to be."

"Betrayal!" Alyssa sat forward in anticipation. "Jane? What betrayal?"

Jane turned and glanced toward the door where Gwendolyn had exited. "No one has spoke of it since it happened so long ago. The whole affair of Miss Gwendolyn Blakethorn. As boys they fought over who rode the fastest horse and who cheated on the cricket pitch. By the time they were young men, nineteen and twenty, the stakes were higher."

"Higher? How?"

"Women."

"Gwendolyn?" Alyssa asked with a gasp, understanding beginning to dawn. "Miss Gwendolyn Blakethorn and her family came to Penridge Hall as Master Harris's guests," Jane said, studying Alyssa to see if she needed to explain more. She did not. "She and he, they'd met while Master Harris was at Sandhurst. When they arrived here, with her mama and papa all proper-like, you could see in their eyes they had a real fondness for each other."

"Master Alistair decided to win her?" A chill slipped down

Alyssa's spine. Was this the history that Lady Cynthia had spoken of?

"Indeed, that seemed to be what happened." Jane resumed her picking up. "She was lovely—still is, of course. Her father was a banker. Wealthy. Well-connected, but not Society."

"So Harris courted Gwendolyn. He introduced her to Alistair, who won her away," Alyssa said.

Jane cast her a sidelong glance, and then whispered, "I heard it was more seduction than winning."

"You mean Alistair seduced Gwendolyn away from Harris?" Alyssa said, speaking louder than necessary in her surprise.

"That was the betrayal," Jane said with an emphatic nod.

"But you said that Harris was Alistair's groomsman at the wedding. There must not have been hard feelings. Not serious ones, anyway."

Jane shrugged. "Hard to say. Master Harris made a brief but polite toast at the wedding breakfast and left for India almost immediately."

"But he had an army commission." Alyssa said. What had Harris been feeling when his cousin married the woman he'd brought home to meet the family? Had he been jealous? Bitterly so? Or had they, Gwendolyn and he, found their love was not as great as that of Gwendolyn and Alistair's? "Wasn't he expected to leave?"

"He'd never spoken of going to India," Jane said. "He were a captain in a mounted guard. There'd been talk of a position with an embassy guard on the continent. Maybe Gibraltar. Nothing so far away as India."

"I see," Alyssa said. And years later, Harris, the rejected suitor, returned. And then Alistair died under suspicious circumstances, leaving Harris heir to a title and widowing a beautiful woman whom Harris had once courted. No wonder the gossips had been having a field day.

"And what do they say below stairs?" she asked. "Who else would have benefited from Master Alistair's death? You said yourself that he wasn't well liked. That he became as much of a tyrant as his father. You told me about the bad feelings with the Littlefields."

"Well, I guess there is some sense in that." Jane hesitated in her work long enough to consider the thought. "And they were here the night of the dinner when Master Alistair first took sick. Even Mr. Byron was here, sitting across from the vicar's daughters."

"So it is possible that one of the Littlefields poisoned Master Alistair?" Alyssa said, secretly relieved to discover someone else had good reason to commit the murder. "If he really was poisoned, that is."

"More than Master Harris had a reason to think on poisoning Master Alistair." Jane straightened and reared back to explain. "Sir Ralph or his nephew Byron. Sir Ralph refused to go to church on Sunday for a while, until the vicar convinced him he should, even if Master Alistair was sitting in the pew across from him. And we was all surprised Sir Ralph didn't go to court over the land and the clay mine. But even if he took up the notion to do murder, why did he wait until Master Harris returned from India to do it? Sir Ralph could have done away with Master Alistair long before that."

"Maybe Harris's return gave him the cover he'd been looking for," Alyssa speculated. "Someone else to cast suspicion on."

Jane shook her head and stopped putting a pinafore on a hanger. She turned to Alyssa as if to take pity on her. "It's worse than that, Miss Lockhart. Sir Ralph doesn't have to make Master Harris look bad."

"What are you saying, Jane?" Alyssa asked.

"Do you truly want to know what happened that night? You might not like the tale."

"Yes, by all means," Alyssa touched the older woman's arm and gestured for Jane to sit down in a fireside chair. "Tell me everything."

Jane drew a long, weary breath and began. "It was a strange night. Spring. Began with a full moon, but soon the clouds come in, running fast across the sky bringing in the mist and then the fog. By the time dinner was over, it was nigh impossible to see from the house to the gatehouse. So the Littlefields took their leave a bit early. Peter Pendeen was the butler then. He saw them off. Master Alistair was just beginning to feel ill."

"Had the evening gone well?" Alyssa wanted to see it all, feel it all. "What was the mood?"

"It had gone all right, I guess," Jane said, closing her eyes briefly as she called up memories. "Elijah helped Peter serve. Robert the footman were away that night. His mother was deathly ill. Master Alistair wouldn't have foreigners or women serve at formal dining. So Tavi didn't serve and he was right offended, too. Didn't say nothing, but I could tell. That was the way of it. Tavi and I helped in the pantry out of sight but where we could hear most everything. They wasn't real jolly at the table, but all seemed to be well enough. Edith and Lucy had a lot to say, as always, and the vicar filled in the conversation when it got too quiet."

"Then what happened?" Alyssa asked, feeling the mystery begin to unfold.

"Master Alistair said he was dizzy when the brandy and cigars were served and then took sick during the night," Jane recalled. "A stomachache—severe-like—then some vomiting. He moaned something dreadful. Peter called Elijah, and Elijah sent Johnnie for Dr. Lewellyn. It was dawn by the time the old doctor arrived."

"How was Alistair by then?" she asked.

"Actually, he was better by daylight," Jane said. "The doctor said it was food poisoning and gave him some remedy. Told him to stay in bed and eat bland things until his stomach settled."

"This must have upset Gwendolyn," Alyssa said.

"Yes, she was in a state," Jane said. "She went into the

kitchen and took Mrs. Brodie to task herself. But, you know, when she was with him, she was calm and patient. Never let him see how upset she was. She was at his bedside the whole time, fetching and carrying for him. Wasn't nothing she wouldn't do for him. I stayed with Meggie, read to her and took her for walks. Lady Penridge didn't want the child to be troubled by her father's pain. I heard about what was happening in the sickroom from the other servants and Peter. He kept us all informed."

"And Harris?"

"Master Harris was nearby most of the time," Jane said. "Except when he went to the mine to see to Master Alistair's duties."

"And Tavi, where was he during all this?" Alyssa asked.

"He was always lurking around, whether we liked it or not," Jane said with annoyance. "Peter didn't like the man. Didn't approve of having a foreign servant in the house. Never allowed him to serve in the dining room. Tavi was considered Master Harris's personal man."

"Did Alistair follow the doctor's orders?" Alyssa asked.

"Yes, did just as the doctor said, but it didn't help." Jane gave an unhappy shake of her head. "He had another spell of pain and vomiting that night. By the second morning, he was weaker than ever. Lady Penridge wanted to send for the doctor again, but Master Alistair wouldn't have it. He called old Dr. Lewellyn a fool. That upset Lady Penridge. She said they should send for another doctor, then. But he wouldn't have that neither."

"Why not?"

"He said it was too late."

"Go on," Alyssa urged.

"That night it stormed something awful." Jane stared at the cold fire grate, her sight was on the past. "Like the wrath of God, the lightning was in the sky with the wind and blowing rain hard enough to sting the skin like bees. I don't know if the Almighty was particularly fond of Master Alistair, but I

swear he didn't seem to take to what was happening at Penridge Hall that night."

"Alistair was worse?"

"He'd been in pain all day," Jane said. "We'd been frantic
to find something that would set on his stomach. Something
he could hold down and gain strength from. But nothing
seemed to help."

"The mood in the house must have been pretty dismal?"
Alyssa said.

"It was." Jane clasped her hands in her lap and hunched her
shoulders. "Lady Penridge was about at her wits' end, but she
never let Master Alistair see it until finally she had to get
some rest, late that night. He was still restless and moaning.
Master Harris told Lady Penridge to go rest and that he would
sit with Master Alistair. Least, that's what Peter told us later.

"Lady Penridge had gone to her room. Master Harris was
with his lordship. Peter was bringing a tray up from the
kitchen, and he heard it. He was standing outside the door."

"Heard what?" Alyssa asked.

"He heard Master Alistair call Master Harris a murderer,"
Jane said, gazing straight into Alyssa's eyes. "Murderer. He
addressed his cousin with that word."

For a moment Alyssa couldn't breathe. Couldn't speak.
"Surely, Peter misunderstood the conversation."

"*Murderer* is a plain, clear word, miss."

"Did anyone ask his lordship about the scene?" she asked,
hoping for some clarification that would hint at innocence.

"Wot? Ask the man if he murdered his cousin?" Jane stared
at Alyssa as if she thought her temporarily mad. "How proper
is that? I mean wot would you say? 'Excuse me, your lordship, but did you poison your cousin like the butler says?' I
should think not! That'd be 'most the same as accusing him
of the deed, wouldn't it, now? Don't none of us below stairs
believe that. I'm just telling you the tale Peter told us that
night in the kitchen. He left the next day as soon as Master
Harris told us that Master Alistair had died in the wee hours

of the morning. Cook had already packed up and left the day Dr. Lewellyn raised the idea of bad shellfish."

"And now do you believe Peter or the doctor?" asked Alyssa.

"I'm not certain." Jane examined her work-worn hands. "I saw that shellfish earlier in the day, laying out in the cool room on the marble, and it all looked clean and fresh to me. Nevertheless, I can tell you this, miss, I don't believe anyone in this house is in danger unless they make too much of the tales told."

She heard the warning in Jane's words, but she had more questions. "Does Lady Penridge know any of this? I mean, did she hear Peter's story?"

"I doubt it, miss," Jane said. "Peter knew not to spread tales to his betters. And her constitution wouldn't hardly bear it. She were up day and night nursing her husband until the end. She were exhausted and now, well, wot's done is done. Wot would be the use of telling her any of it? Some reap wot they sow. I'm inclined to think that's wot happened to Master Alistair. The late lord's harvest was a bitter one. Wouldn't be here if I didn't believe that. Now I have to get on with my work. And I'd be obliged if you didn't mention to anyone that I told you all of this. Master Harris was firm that he didn't want us dwelling on the events of that night."

"No, of course, I won't say anything," Alyssa agreed, her insides fluttering with dismay and denial.

"Don't get me wrong, miss," Jane said. "I like Master Harris well enough. Nobody official brought charges of murder, so who am I—or who is Peter Pendeen—to say different? Service in this house has been a bit easier with the late lord gone, may he rest in peace. I don't have no quarrel with the new Lord Penridge."

"Thank you for telling me what you know." Alyssa remained in her chair as Jane got up and went on with the dusting and sweeping.

Her own legs were too weak at the moment to hold her up.

Rumors were one thing, but Pendeen was an eyewitness, in a way. Maybe Jane didn't care if murder had been committed. Gwendolyn had no idea of the truth and accepted it all at face value. What else would a wife, a new widow in uncertain health, do?

But Alyssa couldn't accept that. Not for Meggie's sake. Not for Harris's sake—for she still wasn't ready to believe that a man she had come to like as much as she did Harris could have committed murder. To believe it would be to lose all confidence in her own judgment.

Did Harris know what Peter Pendeen claimed to have heard? Pendeen was no longer part of the household—out of fear for his own safety or because of the shame of serving bad food? Just what *did* Harris know? It seemed only fair to ask.

But Jane had a point: such a question had to be put delicately.

Thirteen

"I thought I'd join you for a ride this morning," Alyssa said when Harris walked into the breakfast room the morning after her intriguing talk with Jane. During the night she had decided that there was no point in delaying the miserable task. She would ask Harris for the truth in a private setting. A morning ride seemed like the perfect time and place. She had been waiting for him at the breakfast table for nearly a half hour, dressed in her riding habit, with her unruly hair tucked firmly beneath her hat. She looked her best, she hoped.

He halted and raised his brows. "You did, did you?"

"You don't mind?" she asked, feeling a bit daunted. His reception was cooler than she'd wished for. He'd never offered to ride with her, but she'd hoped that if she presented herself, he would agree to join her. "I haven't had a serious ride for some time," she added.

"We can ride as far as the stream," he said, as if he were obligated to do so. He walked to the sideboard to serve himself. Tavi appeared from the kitchen with fresh tea. "Have Elijah saddle Smuggler for Miss Lockhart," Harris ordered.

Pleased, she smiled to herself and wiped her hands on her napkin with relish. She'd feared that he might be avoiding her after their kiss. What was the proper word to express her pleasure?

"Capital!" she said.

Harris paused in serving himself that strange fish the

British liked for breakfast and turned toward her. "What was that?"

"I said, capital," she repeated with a grin.

He chuckled; warm and deep, hardly the sort of sound a murderer would make, she thought. "I see we will have you fluent in the native language in no time," he said.

She smiled at him, and he smiled in return.

"And, may I ask, where did you hear that particular exclamation?" he asked.

"Byron Littlefield," she replied.

His smile faded. "Ah, Littlefield. Tavi told me he called the other day and asked you to go riding with him—but that you refused."

Alyssa shrugged. "Meggie and I were busy with King Arthur." She glanced at Harris, wondering if Tavi had told him about her visit to his study, too.

He merely nodded, making no further comment. Yet she had the distinct impression that he was pleased about her refusal of Byron's invitation.

"I'm learning to like the native food, as well," she said, nibbling on her toast. "I've developed a passion for lemon curd."

"Then by all means satiate your appetite," he said, his smile returning. "Tavi, more lemon curd for Miss Lockhart."

The remainder of their breakfast conversation was light and of little consequence. Upon finishing, they headed directly to the stable, where the horses awaited them. The morning was clear and cool, perfect for a ride.

"Have you heard anything from Meggie?" Alyssa asked as they set the horses at a brisk walk through the fairy gate and down the avenue of beeches. To her disappointment, he instructed Johnnie to ride with them as groom. The boy followed at a respectful distance.

"The school telegraphed yesterday that she had arrived and that all was well," Harris said. "Gwendolyn's maid should be returning tomorrow."

"Well, that sounds good," she said, truly relieved to hear the news, but at a loss as to how to continue her enquiry.

He made no reply.

They rode farther in silence. Asking him forthrightly about the murder had seemed so sensible earlier, but now, she didn't know where to begin.

She cleared her throat.

"Was there something you wanted to ask me?" He glanced in her direction. He'd slowed the pace so they were riding side by side.

"Yes, well, actually there is," she said. He was giving her an opening, but still, it was awkward.

"Then, out with it." He cast her a smile of wry amusement.

Alyssa steeled herself. "I was wondering if you are aware of the rumors circulating about you and your cousin's death?"

Harris's smile disappeared, and he turned away to watch the bridle path winding into the wood ahead of them.

"You wound me, Alyssa," he said at last. Was that truly the hint of a frown she saw? She urged Smuggler onward so she could see him better, but he did not look at her and she could not be certain.

"I thought you were going to ask me about our kiss in the stable," he continued.

Immediate embarrassment warmed her cheeks. Their kiss had never been far from her mind. In fact, there were moments when she thought she could taste him still, feel the throbbing of her body from his touch. "You said it was best forgotten," she stammered.

He glanced at her—*unhappy* was the only word she could think of to describe his expression. It surprised her.

"So I did," he said without looking at her again. She sensed that he did not intend to give her the opportunity to read anything more from his face. Shadows cast by the winter-bare woods overtook them, and the path narrowed. He took the lead, speaking over his shoulder. "It is best forgotten. Shall we simply say that your valiant fight on Meggie's behalf moved me?"

His approval made her heart flutter; but she did not like the way he had so easily changed the subject. She persisted. "And the rumors?"

"Yes, the rumors," he echoed with a note of irritation in his voice. "This is not something that you should be troubling yourself about. However, to answer your question, I know there is vague talk that Alistair was murdered—poisoned, to be precise. Is that what you mean? Naturally, as the Penridge heir I have motive," he said dismissively. "It's the kind of rumor that some petty gossip starts whenever a lord dies before his time and a kinsman inherits."

So he knew something of what was being said about him. That was a relief. "Yes, well, there is more than just suspicion to the rumor," she said.

"What more do you speak of?" he asked, his voice light but edgy now.

"There is a story that Alistair actually accused you of being his murderer on his deathbed."

With deliberation, Harris halted his horse and looked over his shoulder at her. "Yes, and . . . ?"

"Supposedly he pointed his finger at you," she continued, drawing Smuggler up beside him. "And he called you *murderer*. Of course, I don't believe it . . ." Further denial died on her lips.

He stared at her, his expression inscrutable—at first. Then she realized she had surprised him. He glanced away briefly. When he turned back to her, he seemed recovered.

"I certainly *hope* you don't believe it," he said, his voice still light as if he wanted to laugh but couldn't quite manage it. "Because if I were the murderer, you have just made a terrible mistake."

"What do you mean?" she asked.

"If I were the murderer," he said, leaning close, his eyes narrowed and an unpleasant smile on his face, "I'd be concerned about how much you know. I'd be concerned about what questions you'd been asking and of whom. Suppose I did murder my cousin? How wise would it be to speak to me of the deed, to tell me all the things you've heard? Wouldn't you be afraid? You should be."

"Of course, you're *not* a murderer," she said, with more outward confidence than she was beginning feel in the face of his anger—or was he baiting her? "Or I wouldn't have spoken of it to you. I was afraid that you didn't know what people are saying. I thought it was the only honest thing to do. To tell you what is being whispered behind your back and to ask for the truth."

He studied her for a long moment. "Who in particular is saying what?" he asked, finally urging Pendragon onward.

She followed, wondering if he should know that even Meggie had heard the rumor.

Then, unexpectedly, he halted Pendragon and peered over his shoulder at her. "Has Gwendolyn heard this rumor?" he asked, urgency in his voice.

"I don't know." Disappointment twisted in her heart. Gwendolyn was the first one he thought of. Not Meggie. Nor her. He was worried about Gwendolyn's regard for him. "If Gwendolyn has heard anything, she hasn't spoken of it to me. But who is spreading the rumor is not the point, Harris."

"Not so," he said softly, riding ahead again. "A murderer might spread a rumor to deflect attention from himself."

This was a new thought. Of course, the real murderer would want to misdirect people. If he—or she—said Harris was the murderer, people would believe the obvious of an ambitious kinsman. "But your old butler? He wouldn't have—"

"Pendeen?!" Harris halted the black again and turned on her with a ferocity that made her tug hard on Smuggler's reins. "Peter Pendeen is spreading this tale?" he demanded. "The old eavesdropper. Alistair always complained about Pendeen listening in and telling all to anyone, especially below stairs. That is one of the reasons I was relieved when

he gave notice after Alistair's death. And what did he have to say?"

Alyssa swallowed with difficulty, feeling like the talebearer now. "Ah, well . . ."

"Out with it," Harris said.

"Jane said that the night that Alistair died, Peter Pendeen came downstairs and said that when Gwendolyn had left Alistair's room to rest, you stayed behind. He overheard Alistair accuse you of being his murderer. He said that Alistair actually pointed at you."

After a moment's silence, he looked back at her, one eyebrow raised in query. "What if I told you that all he said was true?"

"If you are trying to frighten me," she said, annoyed with his baiting, "I will warn you it is not easy to do. My brother has spent his entire life attempting the same thing."

"Then let me say this another way, Alyssa," he said, raising his chin, his eyes narrowing, his gaze glittering with bitterness. "If I am the murderer, would I tell you the truth?"

"I may be impulsive, but if I believed you guilty, I would never have asked you what happened," she said, surprised and touched by the bitterness in his voice. But it did not frighten her. Who had wounded him so that he was so quick to distrust her? "Tell me what happened that night."

He studied her a moment longer. If he had something more to taunt her with, he apparently thought better of it. "Alistair told me he believed that he had been poisoned," he began. "The man was in terrible pain and had been for several days. I'm not certain how lucid he was. I had wondered about the possibility of poisoning, but couldn't bring myself to think murder possible at Penridge. Nothing was missing from my medicine chest. I had been concerned enough to check its contents when Alistair fell ill. I argued with Alistair about his claim."

He gave her a sideways glance. "I do not know what Jane told you about my cousin and me, but many of our exchanges were heated. In that last conversation, things were no different. Ultimately he pointed his finger at me and said, 'Murderer. Murderer.' He said it twice, just like that. Then he choked and had to wait a minute before he could speak again. When he did, he said, 'Find him. I'm counting on you, Harris. Find my murderer.'"

"And Pendeen was already on his way to the kitchen before your cousin finished what he was saying," Alyssa concluded softly.

"Precisely," he said.

"Isn't there a test or something to rule out poison?" she asked. At home she read the newspapers when Papa neglected to remove them from the breakfast table. Front-page murder cases were her favorite stories. She'd learned a great many things a young woman of good breeding had no business knowing, one of them being that poison could be detected in a dead body, even a long-buried one. "You could prove the rumor wrong."

"I tried to suggest to Gwendolyn that there might be questions about Alistair's death without going into detail," he said with a shake of his head. "She was in such a state. She wouldn't hear of doing any tests. When I talked with Doctor Lewellyn, the coroner, he said Alistair was probably delusional because of the pain and the laudanum prescribed for him. In the grief of the moment, I had little concern about anyone accusing me of murder. Then Sir Ralph, magistrate, ruled Alistair's death to be of natural causes. So no test was done."

"Sir Ralph is magistrate?" She couldn't help repeating the information, it was so unexpected.

"Yes, he is," Harris said. "So you see, the circumstances of Alistair's death have not been officially questioned by anyone."

"Except Alistair himself and the local gossips," she said, urging Smuggler to follow as Harris began riding again. How convenient if Sir Ralph himself had murdered Alistair. "Are you going to leave it at that? Don't you want justice? Don't you want the murderer to answer for his crime? Don't you want to grant your cousin his deathbed request?"

"That depends on the cost," he said, only slightly ahead of her now. "At this late date, there is only one way to be certain whether Alistair was murdered or not."

Having a fair idea of what that involved, she grimaced.

Harris rode on. "You know what suffering Gwendolyn and Meggie have been through. I am not about to upset them by allowing Alistair's body to be exhumed for reexamination."

"I see, yes, of course," she murmured, gazing at his broad back with admiration, ready to exonerate him and to replace him on his story-book hero pedestal.

"I'm glad you understand," he said. "But, do I want to know the truth? Do I want justice? Yes, I do. Even when the truth is learned and justice served, it will change nothing. Gwendolyn will still be without her husband and Meggie without a father."

"Yes, I see." But your name would be cleared, she wanted to argue, though his mind seemed made up.

They'd reached the end of the woodland trail. Up the hill the trees parted and the land opened onto the moor that surrounded the clay mine.

He turned to her as she rode up to his side. Smiling, he leaned toward her and reached out, touching her chin with his thumb in a gesture of affection not unlike one he might bestow on Meggie. Her heart fluttered nonetheless.

"So, my sweet Alyssa, don't trouble yourself over me and my good name," he said with a rueful smile, as if he'd read her mind again. "I can live with the suspicions. Finish your ride and go home to read in the library or borrow another book from my study, if you like. Yes, Tavi told me. But please cooperate with him in the future. You put him in quite a dither. Go now. Johnnie, see Miss Lockhart home—ride by way of the millstream and the waterfall. You haven't seen our waterfall, have you? Good day."

He spurred Pendragon away, leaving Alyssa with the sinking understanding that he did know what was being said about him—and that being unjustly accused of murder was a sacrifice he was willing to make for Gwendolyn and Meggie.

The millstream and the waterfall were lovely, moss-covered and sparkling with mist. She would have preferred to see them in Harris's company; however, the side trip gave her the opportunity to take Johnnie to task for telling Meggie the rumor that her cousin had murdered her father. Johnnie hung his head in remorse.

The rest of the way back to Penridge she had time to consider what Harris had told her. His sacrifice for a grieving widow enriched Alyssa's admiration of him. On the other hand, it disappointed her. As much as she liked and admired Gwendolyn, as much as she understood that her jealous feelings stemmed from her crush on Harris—a *tendre* as some called it— she did not like to think that he was willing to give up his reputation for his old sweetheart. It seemed foolish. How could she explain the feelings to herself? If he would sacrifice his good name, what else would he sacrifice for Gwendolyn? Then there was Meggie to think of, too.

She returned to Penridge Hall, where she passed the remainder of the morning playing the piano. That afternoon, after attending to King Arthur, she made up her mind to find out as much from Gwendolyn about Alistair's death as she could without upsetting her. Gwendolyn might even want to talk about it, Alyssa reasoned, if the subject was brought up gently.

But when she went to the receiving room, the warm, wood-paneled chamber off the entry hall where tea was served now that it was too cold to sit in the garden, she found Gwendolyn with guests. One of them was the last person on earth she expected to find at Penridge Hall—the Reverend Whittle.

The sight of him, especially after the way Gwendolyn had spoken of him, was such a shock that Alyssa started as she stood in the doorway. The reverend and the other guest, a man she did not recognize, rose when they saw her.

Gwendolyn smiled as if nothing were amiss. "There you are, dear. We have guests for tea today. I believe you met the Reverend Whittle—at least he has indicated so. And this is Dr. Lewellyn."

Whittle smiled that sly smile of his and gave her a nod of acknowledgement. "Miss Lockhart, how nice to see you again."

"Reverend." Alyssa returned his greeting coolly. She was not particularly pleased to see him. The man, handsome in his devilish way, made her skin crawl. He certainly had some gall to sit down at Penridge's tea table after the nasty confrontation he'd created at the mine only a week earlier.

"Dr. Lewellyn is a long-time family friend," Gwendolyn said, gesturing to the small, unfamiliar guest.

"How do you do, Dr. Lewellyn," Alyssa said, offering a polite smile to the elderly gentleman dressed in shabby gray elegance. He had a balding head and blue eyes grown cloudy with age. She ignored Whittle and moved to sit next to the doctor.

Meeting the doctor was almost enough good fortune to make up for the displeasure of finding Whittle present. She had come down to tea hoping to encourage Gwendolyn to talk about that night or at least what she knew about the rumors. And here was the very doctor who had been called to Alistair's bedside.

"Miss Lockhart, my pleasure," the doctor said with a kindly smile. "I've heard so much about you from everyone. And now, at last, we meet."

"Everyone?" It was disconcerting to think of herself as the topic of strangers' conversation. She cast a questioning glance in Gwendolyn's direction.

"I think the doctor is referring to the Carbury girls," Gwendolyn said. "Ah, here is Tavi. Sit down, gentlemen. Let's have our tea."

As Tavi set down the tray, the men resumed their seats.

The doctor began with the usual questions about her visit. Had she seen this or that? Had she met so-and-so? What did she think of a particular site? She enjoyed answering him. While he appeared rather aged, his wit was quick enough and his interest in people sincere. He appeared hardly the doddering old fool that Whittle had portrayed him to be.

The reverend watched Gwendolyn as Alyssa talked, a supercilious smile on his face. It was clear to her that he was pleased indeed to be sitting at tea with Lady Penridge. Somehow she didn't think Harris would be so pleased if he knew.

At the first appropriate opportunity, after the polite questions had been answered and Gwendolyn had served them, Alyssa asked, "What brings you to Penridge Hall, Reverend?"

"Like you, Miss Lockhart," the reverend began, "Lady Penridge and I are concerned for the miners' welfare. These are difficult times with the price of food so high."

"So you have said," Alyssa said, silently wondering if she looked as baffled as she felt. Gwendolyn had spoken disparagingly of Whittle in the carriage on the way to church. If that was how she felt, how could she tolerate him at her tea table? How could she work with him, even in charitable works, when she disliked him so? Alyssa glanced from the serene widow to the smug reverend. She could only assume that Gwendolyn, despite her personal feelings, was behaving as the good lady of the manor.

"The late Lord Penridge and I were very concerned about the children's welfare." Gwendolyn bowed her head over her teacup. "Dr. Lewellyn and Reverend Whittle have been my loyal supporters in my endeavors here at Penridge and at Wheal Isabel to aid the suffering. They have carried on without me these last three months during my mourning."

"It is the least we could do for you under the circumstances," the reverend said, leaning toward Gwendolyn. His gaze almost literally caressed the lady, tender and rapacious all at once. Alyssa struggled against the vision of a blond Red Ridinghood in black at the mercy of a big, bad wolf in a cleric's collar, the beast's tongue lolling out in anticipation.

Clearly, the reverend found Gwendolyn attractive. She merely offered the reverend her innocent widow's smile as she set down her cup to pour tea.

"And I have been extending credit for my services and offering some *pro bono*," the doctor said, selecting a scone from the tea tray. "Sick babies need care. The children must eat. My payment can wait."

"That is very good of you, Doctor," Gwendolyn said.

"The last shipment of grain was not near enough to feed the number of hungry families there are." Reverend Whittle stirred his tea ever so politely, yet he hadn't mastered Byron's skill of the pinkie in the air. Where had a former wrestler learned such manners? "The next shipment promised by his lordship has yet to arrive," he added.

"Does Lord Penridge know the shipment is late?" Gwendolyn asked.

"Yes, my lady, he does," the reverend said. "He said it should arrive any day now."

"Then I'm sure it will be here soon." Gwendolyn nodded.

"Your new chef is excellent." The doctor washed down his scone with tea. "Excellent. No more problems?"

"None," Gwendolyn said, turning toward him.

Alyssa looked from the doctor to the widow, assuming they referred to the chef because of the food poisoning.

"I understand Mrs. Brodie is cooking for a solicitor's family in Penzance," the doctor said, eyeing a sandwich on the tray. "Bit of a comedown for her."

"I have no hard feelings there, and I wish the family and Mrs. Brodie well." Gwendolyn turned to the reverend and added, "Whatever is left from our tea, I will have Chef Hugo pack up for you to take to the sick."

"Bless you for your generosity, Lady Penridge." Reverend

Whittle's smile literally glowed—hardly the formidable countenance he had shown to Harris. "When you feel your grieving permits, you will once again be welcome to join me in my calls to the sick."

Gwendolyn nodded gravely. "Perhaps, in time. In time."

"Of course, dear lady, I do not mean to obligate you until you're feeling up to it," Whittle said, offering Gwendolyn an artificial smile of sympathy.

"Perhaps I could help," Alyssa said, once again remembering the gaunt, grim faces of the miners and their women on the road to the church. "I mean, if something needs to be done, I'd be glad to lend a hand."

The three turned to her as if she'd uttered a heresy.

Reverend Whittle opened his mouth to respond, but Gwendolyn spoke first.

"That is helpful of you, dear, but it is the lady of the manor's responsibility to visit the sick, offering food, medicine, and inspiration where she can. It is I they look to."

"I only thought . . ." Alyssa's voice trailed off, leaving her feeling as foolish as she had when she'd offered her meager apple to the mob of miners.

"I know you meant to be of assistance," the reverend said, grinning at her. "But you understand so little."

Alyssa frowned at him.

The doctor rose from his chair. "I really must be on my way. A few more calls to make before the day is done."

"Let me see you to the door," Alyssa offered, jumping up partly to escape Whittle and partly in hopes of speaking privately with the doctor.

"How kind of you, Miss Lockhart," the doctor said, offering his arm. She took it, and they strolled toward the entry hall.

"I understand you've been of great service to the family before and after the death of the late lord," she began, "So unfortunate, the food poisoning."

"We don't like to talk about it," the doctor said, pursing his lips. "If you are troubled, think no more of it. The new chef seems quite reliable, though who would have thought Mrs. Brodie would let something like that happen? I would have laid odds on the certainty of her kitchen. Always one of the best, Mrs. Brodie was, to my mind, until this thing happened."

"And only one person fell ill?" she probed, hoping she didn't appear to be too obvious. "One would think with food poisoning that more than one person would become ill."

"It's because of the individual servings," the doctor explained. "That particular shellfish was tainted. Whelk was a favorite of Alistair's. Mrs. Brodie knew that. The shellfish served to the other guests was fresh enough. The late lord admitted his portion tasted off, but because there were guests at the table, he did not want to openly complain to Cook."

"I see," she said, thinking how a host keeps appearances up in front of guests at all costs. Her papa and mama did the same. All smiles at the dinner table, but later, Cook would know if something didn't suit.

"At a dinner like that, an intentional poisoning would pose the same problem, you see," the doctor continued. "Yes, I've heard the rumors, too. How would only Alistair's food be poisoned, unless it was by one of the servants? I think that's highly unlikely. Alistair's symptoms didn't fit strychnine. Its effects are immediate, creating rigidity in the body and convulsions that would be an obvious indication of poison, and digitalis is much the same. Arsenic is more difficult to recognize."

"And what were Master Alistair's symptoms?" Alyssa asked.

"He was feeling unwell when the Littlefields left," Dr. Lewellyn said. "Dizzy, he told me. Food poisoning can strike that fast. Sometimes it takes up to two days. Then vomiting, loose bowels, fever, chills, and general weakness—eventually delusions. *All* symptoms of food poisoning. So you see, my dear, it had to be bad shellfish. Seldom fatal, but in this case, it was."

"Who was serving that night besides Peter Pendeen? Do you know? Did Tavi serve?"

"No, not Tavi. I believe Gwendolyn said Elijah served that night," the doctor said. "Peter Pendeen and Elijah are both old and trusted servants of the Trevells. Nothing suspicious there. No reason to suspect Mrs. Brodie, either, other than for bad luck and a bit of carelessness. But she did take the news hard. I don't think she'll speak to me again. But so be it."

"No, I suppose not," she said, thinking how she would feel if someone told her a dish she had prepared caused a death. Guilty, frustrated, angry—and, perhaps, all too willing to spread a rumor about poisoning.

"Put your mind at ease, Miss Lockhart," the doctor said, reassuringly patting her hand. "Eat hearty. You are safe enough at Penridge."

Alyssa thought she probably was, but one tyrannical lord had thought so, too. And look where he was now.

Fourteen

Alyssa's cheeks burned with embarrassment, and her body grew warm and restless as she gazed at the book she'd borrowed from Harris's study. It lay open on her lap. She was sitting on the windowseat in her chamber studying the illustration with care. A man and a woman were sitting with their legs apart, and appraising each other's privates, which were drawn in great detail—the shading of hair, the deep color of the woman's secret places, the enlarged condition of the man's member. The woman was holding something long and round in her hand, something sausage-like.

She frowned. What on earth were they doing, and what was that thing the woman held? Why would she want something to eat at a moment like that? It must be for something else . . . Abruptly she slammed the book shut. Her hands trembling, she threw open the window and allowed the cool air to take the heat out of her face.

Had she known that the subject of the book was the myriad ways of men and women coupling, she never would have taken it from the shelf. Well, maybe she would. But she'd wished she'd been better prepared for the revelations she'd found between its covers. It wasn't just the nudity—she'd seen nude drawings before—it was . . . the detail. And the actions. She'd never seen anything like it, though she'd heard such books existed.

Hesitantly she cracked the book again, peering at the random illustration from the corner of her eye, as if a sideways glance would make it less shocking. But the picture was just as startling, and she noticed details this time that she had not seen before. The woman, nude and open and smiling. The man equally bare, his male endowment much larger than she would have expected. He was also smiling.

The book fell open wider. She studied the picture closer. There was languid intent on both of the faces. Was that passion? The woman appeared to be pleased with what was happening, and the man appeared to be devoted to his actions with the woman. Did her sisters do this with their husbands? she wondered. Did Mama do this with Papa? *Surely* not.

She bent over the illustration. If this book showed the truth, then all she'd learned, mostly through innuendo and euphemism, was a lie. Women enjoyed what men did to them. And if this book was to be believed, women did personal things to men that they likewise enjoyed. What would it be like to be seen and touched like that by a man? She shivered, but not from the cool breeze. What would it be like to have Harris touch her that way? And how would it be to touch him?

Whispering, ghostly sensations flowed over her, teasing and tickling her skin. She closed her eyes against the feelings, only to see, in her mind's eye, the man and woman from the book come to life—except that their faces were now hers and Harris's. A hollow lightness filled her, bringing a long, low sigh.

She closed the book with a snap, with finality this time. She shouldn't be having these thoughts or seeing these images. Time to return the tome to Harris's study—before tea, she decided. Before he returned from the mine and realized what she'd borrowed. Before she gave way to more impossible fantasies. Her face grew warm again—this time at the thought of *him* paging through the illustrations. Without further hesitation, she went to the study.

The door was locked. No surprise. So she went into the billiard room and rang for Tavi. The butler soon appeared.

"I'd like to return a book," she said, holding the volume close to her skirt so he could not read the title. She prayed that he did not notice her blush, either.

"Very good." He opened the door for her and stepped into the room, looking around as if to satisfy himself that all was as it should be. He turned to her. "Will you be long, Miss Lockhart?"

"I'd like to choose another book," she said, walking past him, the book still pressed against her skirt. The scent of spices engulfed her as she stepped into the dim room. Somehow it was already a familiar scent. She liked it. "I will be a few minutes."

"As you wish." He lit the desk lamp for her. "I shall return shortly."

He bowed his way out of the room, leaving the door slightly ajar. The air was heavy with perfume and spices.

Satisfied he was gone, she skirted around the table in front of the fireplace, slipped behind Harris's desk, and went straight to the bookshelf where she'd found the naughty book. Finding the empty slot, she replaced the book and sighed with relief. Silly though it was, she wasn't ready for the knowledge it had to impart. She was old enough, but she sensed it wasn't yet time.

Relieved to have that done, she turned to look at Harris's desk. On it lay papers, arranged in neat stacks, none appearing, at first glance, to be particularly personal. No photographs. Only official documents, letters about the mine, receipts, and bills of lading. Nothing from Captain Dundry, whoever he was. The telegram from Meggie's school was the nearest thing to a personal document on the desk.

Disappointed, she turned to the other things in the room, the crates, baskets, and trunks. The medicine chest on the table was locked, the shiny brass padlock fastened in its proper place. She drew a finger down the graceful, shiny brass urn on the table next to the chest. An ivory carving of a horse caught her eye. She walked around the table to examine it more closely. From one thing to the next, she browsed until the tiger skin drew her to the sofa with the colorful stack of gleaming gold-and-silver silk on its arm.

She stroked the tiger fur from a big fellow, thrilled with its silkiness and the fierce boldness of the contrasting yellow-orange and black stripes. Then the silk caught her eye—sheer blue silk woven with gold thread, the likes of which she'd never seen. A soft gasp escaped her. No Boston dressmaker, no New York designer had ever shown her and her mother anything like this.

Greedily she picked up the fabric and unfolded the length, taking pleasure in the soft smoothness of it in her hands, cool and shimmering. Like water washing over the skin but leaving light and color instead of wetness. Irresistible. Addictive. She sank down on the sofa and touched the fabric to her cheek, closed her eyes, and abandoned her senses to it.

"I see you've found the silk," Harris's voice sliced into her reverie.

She froze, the silk still pressed against her cheek. If he had to walk in on her, why couldn't it have been when she was reading something intellectual or philosophical so she could appear wise and learned? But, no, here she was, digging through his imported goods like a gauche girl. Turning slowly, she looked over her shoulder to see him standing in the doorway. He'd obviously left his hat and riding crop with Tavi, but he was otherwise dressed as if he'd just returned from the mine.

"Yes, the silk is alluring," she said, letting it drop into her lap. Would honesty extricate her from this awkward moment? "And the tiger skin impressed me, too. I just came to return the book I borrowed. I hope you don't mind."

"Not at all," he said, leaving the door open and moving to his desk, where he laid down the post he was carrying. "I brought the silk from India because it would tempt ladies like you."

"It does that," she said, admiring the fabric in her hand once more. "And the tiger skin? Did you shoot him yourself?"

"Yes, I did," Harris said. "A man-eater—killed six villagers in as many months. It had to be taken down."

"Man-eater!" Alyssa gasped, jumping to her feet to stare down at the skin. "But weren't you frightened? I mean, he is huge."

He chuckled. "Alyssa, you are supposed to admire my courage, not question it."

"Of course I admire your courage," she stammered. "I was just wondering how it felt to hunt an animal that I've read will stalk its stalker."

"Indeed, a tiger is dangerous, big and intelligent, and I do not mind admitting that to hunt and be hunted gives one pause," he said, returning to the post. "The creature had to be shot, so I did it. What else catches your eye? Everything you see here I intend to use in starting an import business. It is helpful to know what strikes a fashionable lady's eye."

"The silk is wonderful," she said, holding it up again. "How do the Indian ladies wear this? I mean, do they wrap it about themselves like one sees in the pictures?"

When she looked at him again, he was watching her closely.

"Yes, they wear it in a traditional style called a *sari*," he said.

"That's the term I've heard." Taking the silk by a corner, she held a length of it up before her. "It is just wrapped around them? No seams? No tapes or buttons?"

"Actually there are several ways it can be draped," he said, dropping the envelope he'd been holding and moving toward her. "In one part of India it is traditionally worn in a pantaloon fashion."

"Truly!" she said, surprised to think that an ancient culture had discovered what western women were just finding for themselves.

"But I imagine you have seen pictures of the classic style

draped over the shoulder. I will show you." He came to a stop in front of her. "The *sari* is a beautiful costume, graceful and feminine, cool and colorful. Six yards of fabric, anything from the sheerest cotton to gold-embroidered silk like this, unstitched, yet perfect for every woman's figure."

He reached around her, encircling her and taking the fabric from her, his fingers brushing against hers. His warmth burned into her. Startled, she tried to step aside, but bumped into him.

"No, don't run," he said, a soft chuckle in his voice. "Just turn around. I'll show you how it's done."

Obediently, she turned her back to him. What on earth was he doing?

She stood very still lest they make contact again. He lifted the fabric, its gossamer weight floating on the air, settling gracefully down across the front of her.

"The ladies wear a basic undergarment," he said, bringing the silk up to her waist and speaking over her shoulder, his lips dangerously close to her ear. "A fitted bodice and a long petticoat. Nothing so confining as stays. We shall pretend that your gown serves as such. They begin by pleating the fabric across the front like so. Seven deep pleats. This fullness gives them the freedom to move."

"I see," she said, breathless from his nearness. She could feel his hands on her waist, burning through the thick fabric of her stays as he fashioned the pleats. She dared not move lest she find her derriere pressed against his lap. Despite the layers of cloth between them, the spark of his touch made her feel as if she might as well be naked in his arms.

She expelled a shaky breath.

"Are you all right?" he asked, resting a hand on her shoulder.

"Yes," she managed to say.

"I'll allow you to tuck this into your skirt," he said as his hands slipped away from her. She stood clasping the silk against her, suddenly feeling abandoned. Then, understanding his instructions, she lifted the part of her bodice that overlapped her skirt and tucked the silk into the waistband.

"Turn," he instructed, holding up the length of fabric so that it wrapped around her as she turned. He smiled at her. Forgetting her self-consciousness, she did as he ordered. Turning, the silk wound around her, soft and whispering, clinging and lustrous.

"You have chosen well." He was behind her again, draping the silk over her shoulder, his mouth so close this time that his breath stirred a tendril of hair.

"Can you see yourself reflected in the brass urn?" he asked, bending closer. "See how the blue silk becomes you? See how beautiful you are?"

Reflected in the urn she saw a young, red-haired woman with a decidedly feminine figure, wrapped in deep blue and gold. The vision was exotic and, yes, beautiful. Behind her stood a tall, handsome man, his gaze intent on her. She knew he wanted her. For the first time in her life she understood what it meant to feel like a woman, a desirable woman.

She realized his breathing had quickened just as hers had.

A hand on her waist, he pulled her closer, tightening the fabric across her breasts. She leaned against him, aware of his strength and size. Aware once more of a sensitivity and fullness in her breasts that only he seemed to inspire.

Suddenly he uttered a harsh, frustrated sound and his hands gripped her arms. The next instant his lips descended on her neck. His mouth was warm, firm, and hungry. Her knees went weak, but she managed to stay standing. The onslaught of sensations was so strong it overwhelmed all else. She closed her eyes, savoring the heat of his mouth moving up her neck to her earlobe. Every part of her tingled with life, yet she was too weak to move, to resist, to respond. All she could do was pray that his mouth would find hers again. And she would let him taste all of her that he wanted. She turned her head slightly when he reached her ear. He kissed it, his lips tugging gently on the shell. She whimpered. Another shiver passed over her.

"Sweet Alyssa," he murmured. "You tempt me so."

A knock sounded at the open door, cold, harsh, sharp.

Harris released her. The sanctuary of his arms gone, she swayed a moment before she regained her balance.

"Enter," he called, turning away abruptly. With his head bowed, he moved to stand behind his desk, facing the door as if nothing had happened.

Tavi entered.

Drat. She struggled with the fabric.

"My lord." The butler bowed, hands together, his gaze darting from her to Harris, obviously seeking to learn what had been going on. "Lady Penridge says that tea is served in the grand salon," he said.

"Yes, that's why I returned early from the mine," Harris said, shuffling through the post once again. "I promised we'd have tea together. Tell her ladyship that Miss Lockhart and I will be right there."

"Yes, my lord." Tavi cast her a curious look, clearly taking in the blue silk draped around her, and then he left the room, leaving the door still open.

Alone with Harris once more, she pulled the fabric from over her shoulder. Then, with trembling hands, she sank down on the sofa and attempted to pull the pleats from her skirt.

"I apologize for being so bold," Harris said without looking at her.

"There's nothing to apologize for," she said, pulling the last of the pleats free. "I asked about the *sari.*"

"In the future, please borrow your books from the library and not off my bookshelves," he said, without looking at her.

"Of course," she said, pushing the fabric from her and rising from the sofa, though she was still dizzy. "You have been most generous to me, and I wouldn't dream of repaying that generosity by compromising you."

His head came up with a start. "Alyssa, my compromise is

not the problem. I think we have established that my reputation is taking a bit of a drubbing already. However, I will not have your good name sullied while you are here. I know that Tavi can be trusted to keep what he sees to himself. Unfortunately, I cannot be as certain of the rest of the household. You are my ward, and there are certain lines we should not cross."

"Not even if there is something *more* between us?" she asked, the desire she'd seen in his reflection—the desire she'd felt coursing through her body still fresh in her mind.

He gazed straight into her eyes, stern and forbidding. "There is nothing *more* between us, Alyssa. Do you understand me?"

"I understand," she said, though she didn't. Surely he knew his own mind. Yet, how could he look at her like that, kiss her, hold her, and then deny it all? Had she misjudged his expression, his touch, and the whisper of his passion in her ear?

Still trembling, she stepped hesitantly toward the door. "I—what you have here is so beautiful. I wish you good fortune with the import business. It's bound to be a success. Who could resist such beautiful things?"

He eyed her. "Indeed, who could resist?"

Tavi was waiting for her when she reached the hallway. He closed the study door behind her, his gaze never leaving her face. It was clear he knew that she was not welcome in the study again.

Shaken, Alyssa retreated to her chamber.

She pleaded a headache to excuse herself from tea. Never had she done such a thing before. She'd always thought little of people who used their health as a reason for refusing an invitation they did not want to accept, but she could think of no other explanation for missing tea. Claiming to have a previous engagement would hardly be believable. She knew no one beyond the Trevells. After the liberties she'd allowed Harris, she simply could not bring herself to face either him or her hostess.

By dinner she had regained enough of her composure to make an appearance, but she had no appetite. She could not meet Harris's gaze directly nor Gwendolyn's. Deception was not her strong suit. She felt so awkward in Harris's presence that she was certain that Gwendolyn would notice. But the widow seemed to find little amiss except Alyssa's uncharacteristic silence. When she remarked on it, Alyssa claimed to be missing Meggie.

Harris cast her a small, sympathetic smile. "We all miss Meggie," he agreed.

"Yes, we do," Gwendolyn agreed, accepting Alyssa's explanation without question. "But I believe school is good for her. I had a letter from her today. She is already making new friends."

Alyssa had said it not just as a cover for her awkwardness, but because it was true. Meggie had been her distraction, her company, once they'd become friends over King Arthur. Now there was only her and Gwendolyn, who seemed occupied with her roses, her needlework, and her mourning. She was very particular that her gowns, caps, and jewelry be proper. And there were many household duties. The housekeeper had also been one of the servants to leave over the late lord's death; since then the lady of the house had more to see to than normal.

Alyssa counted on King Arthur to help her fill her days. That and letter writing to Aunt Esther about life at Penridge and to Meggie about how the hedgehog was faring.

But the next morning when Alyssa entered the breakfast room to feed King Arthur and to have her own breakfast, she found the cage door standing open and the cage empty.

"Oh, no." Frantically, she glanced around the room. Where could he be? She lifted the tablecloth and scurried around the entire table, then peered under the sideboard and around the potted palms. Nothing. Panic rising—what would she tell Meggie?—she summoned Tavi.

He appeared in the kitchen doorway looking as displeased to see her as she was to see him.

"Tavi, was the cage door open when you came into the breakfast room this morning?" she asked.

"No, miss," he said, a harsh gleam in his eye. She was more conscious than ever that he disliked her. "But it was open when Lady Penridge returned with it."

"Lady Penridge?" she gasped.

"Yes, miss," Tavi said. "This morning she took the cage from the breakfast room."

"But I always see that King Arthur gets his fresh air," she said, confused. Was Gwendolyn taking over the care of the hedgehog?

"Yes, I know, miss," Tavi replied. "I don't think it was fresh air that Lady Penridge was concerned about. She went off in the direction of the pond behind the stable. I believe she freed the creature, miss. When she returned, she told me to clean the cage and see that it is returned to the attic. I regret that I was delayed performing that task."

"No!" She didn't like the sound of that at all. She'd spent enough time around the stables at home to know about the fate of unwanted animals. Surely there was some mistake. "King Arthur is Meggie's pet. I promised to take care of him until she returns for the Christmas holiday. Lady Penridge knows that."

Tavi stepped back, clasping his hands behind him and saying no more.

"Where is she? Where is Lady Penridge?" she demanded. "There has been some misunderstanding, and I must talk to her."

"I believe she is in the garden with Elijah," Tavi said, apparently unconcerned about her doubts.

The day was gray and windy, but she didn't take the time to find a wrap. She went out the garden door and was caught immediately in a cold gust. The chill brought momentary tears to her eyes. She wrapped her arms around herself as she forged on, around the corner and straight to the rose garden.

No one was there. The last of the roses had faded with the onset of November. Only a few brave leaves clung to the rose canes. She hurried on through the garden, up the hill to the square stone structure that served as the garden shed. Another gust of wind caught at her skirts. Her fingers stiff with cold, she grabbed the latch of the shed door, pulled it open, and slipped inside.

Enough light fell through the small window for her to see the large room lined with rakes, clippers, shovels, trellis, pots, and buckets. At the far end of the potting bench stood Elijah Whittle and Gwendolyn. Open-mouthed, they stared at her.

"Alyssa, dear, where is your cloak?" Gwendolyn asked.

"I wore none," she said. "I must speak with you."

"Yes, what is it? Elijah won't mind," Gwendolyn said. "We were just taking stock of our gardening supplies for the roses. I fear with the confusion of the late lord's death, ordering supplies for the rose garden was neglected. Now, what is it, dear? "

"Did you release King Arthur?" Alyssa asked, too upset to think of caution before the servants. "Is it true?"

Gwendolyn heaved a weary sigh, as if she'd been much put upon. "Yes, I did, Alyssa. I'm afraid I've never been fond of house pets. The poor creature was entirely too much fuss and bother and completely out of place in the breakfast room."

"We could have found another place for him," Alyssa said.

"Don't you see, dear?" Gwendolyn said. "The thing is such a nuisance. It is a wild creature that should be fending for itself in the out-of-doors."

"But he's so young, he hardly knows how to feed himself,

and we promised to care for him until Meggie comes home," Alyssa said, already wondering how she was going to break the news to the child in a letter. "She will be so disappointed."

"It is good of you to take your promise to Meggie so seriously," Gwendolyn said. "But don't be concerned. Two months from now when she returns, she will have forgotten about the poor silly beast, I assure you. It has served its purpose to distract her from her grief. He's quite at home outside, isn't he, Elijah?"

"Quite, my lady," Elijah said, nodding in agreement. "He will find himself a place to hibernate now that he is out in the cold. Then he will be back next spring. Miss Meggie can visit him in the garden. He's a welcomed guest here."

"I'm sure that knowledge will be a comfort to Meggie," Alyssa said, fighting to keep sarcasm out of her voice and wondering how likely it was that the poor creature would survive that long.

Clearly satisfied with the solution to what she saw as a problem, Gwendolyn returned to studying the catalog she held. "Elijah and I were just considering adding some new roses to the rose garden," she said. "It's such a pleasure to plan a garden when the weather has turned bleak, don't you think? Have you any favorites, Alyssa?"

"I am afraid I don't know much about roses," she said, unable to escape from the sorrow she knew Meggie would feel when she learned her pet was gone. Gwendolyn's reasoning that King Arthur was a wild creature might be true, but she clearly had no idea how disappointed her daughter would be to return from school and find no pet waiting for her. It was on the tip of her tongue to ask Gwendolyn whether she had discussed the hedgehog's fate with Harris, but on second thought she decided not to. She was too likely to give away her feelings about him, and then Gwendolyn would know, and he'd asked her to keep their relationship on a ward-and-guardian level. She'd probably already said more than she had a right to.

Someone pounded on the shed door. "Lady Penridge." It was Jane calling from outside.

"Enter," Gwendolyn called.

Jane burst into the shed on a gust of wind, a plain black cloak swirling around her. "My lady, Tavi sent me to tell you that Reverend Whittle is here and he wants to see you. He will speak only to you, he said."

"He must have some mission of charity in mind," Gwendolyn said with a sigh. "Have him wait in the receiving room. I shall be right there."

Gwendolyn laid the catalog down on the potting bench. "We can finish this business about the rose supplies later. Now, Jane, let's go see why the Reverend Whittle is calling."

As soon as the shed door had closed behind them, Alyssa turned to Elijah.

"Do you have a trap?" she asked. "Perhaps with food in it we could lure King Arthur back."

"Now that you mention it, I might have something down below here," he said, bending down to look through the clutter beneath the potting bench.

Alyssa waited while he sorted through the things. As she listened to his mumblings and rummaging, her gaze fell on the catalog. She went to the bench and reached for it, leafing through idly. What sort of roses did Gwendolyn wish for during the cold days? It was an attractive publication, the promise of colorful, delicate blossoms indeed a mood lightener considering the dreariness of the day. She put the catalog down on the bench. And sitting next to it, her gaze fell upon a glass jar. The label, written in faded ink, read ARSENIC.

"Elijah?"

"Yes, miss," he said, straightening to look at her.

"What do you use arsenic for in the garden?" she asked.

His gaze went to the jar. "We mostly use it for rats when the cats don't do their job in the stable. I keep it in here because this shed is usually locked."

"That's wise," she said, eyeing the poison. So there was another source of poison at Penridge besides Harris's medicine chest. "And you have the key?"

"No, miss, not me." he said. "Tavi has the keys. Either I or Lady Penridge request it when necessary. If you please, miss, I don't have a trap that wouldn't hurt the little fellow. But I can tell you that fuzz-peg will probably turn up in the spring, ready to do his job with the slugs and snails."

"I'm sure you're right," she said, turning to leave. Her mind was buzzing with speculation and irritation with herself. Why had she concluded there would be only one source of poison? "Thank you, Elijah. I'll leave you to your work."

She escaped to her room, where she sat down at her writing desk, not to write to Meggie of King Arthur's return to the wild. There would be time for that later. But, while the facts were clear in her mind, she began a list of who had a motive to kill Meggie's father *and* had access to poison.

Fifteen

Much as she disliked the idea, Harris had to be at the top of the list of possible murderers. There was no avoiding it. The rumor named him specifically. She wrote out his name on the blank paper, then stared at it as she distractedly chewed on the end of her pen. He had the obvious motive. She turned in her chair to gaze out the window as she mentally sorted through what little she knew to be fact.

First, whether Harris's explanation of his cousin's finger-pointing was true or not, the servants believed a murder had been committed, and the victim himself believed he'd been poisoned. Though it was impossible to see a solid connection, Harris's return from India seemed to have stirred up whatever led to his cousin's demise.

Second, Harris had the obvious motive: inheritance of the Penridge barony—and the possibility of regaining his sweetheart. That thought made Alyssa's heart sink. But she could not allow her personal feelings to color her investigation. Her goal to learn the truth must be foremost. Still, that didn't mean she couldn't pray that the facts would exonerate Harris.

What else? He had access to several poisons in his medicine chest. Who knew what he'd learned about potions and poisons in a dark, exotic place like India?

But her trip to the garden shed had proved that he was not alone in having that access. Resolute, she began to contemplate more possibilities.

What about Gwendolyn? She penned "Lady Penridge" on

the paper. The spouse was often a suspect—she knew that from her newspaper reading—but why would Gwendolyn murder her husband and the father of her daughter? Alistair had been the source of her social position, privilege, and wealth. But to be fair, if Harris were on the list, Gwendolyn should be there, too.

Alyssa wrote on. What about Sir Ralph, whose motive was vengeance over unfair business dealings. The glare he aimed at Harris during Sunday dinner as his lordship talked to Lady Cynthia had been positively murderous. No doubt he, too, had a garden shed stocked with arsenic. As magistrate, Sir Ralph was in the perfect position to protect himself—or someone else. Which brought her to the next suspect: Byron Littlefield.

She scribbled Byron's name on her list. As Sir Ralph's heir, he might share his uncle's bad feelings. After all, it was his inheritance that was diminished by Alistair's defrauding of Sir Ralph. Was that motive enough to make Byron commit murder? She tapped the pen against her nose. Somehow she could not envision Byron being passionate enough to kill anyone over anything, unless someone had insulted his latest choice in waistcoats.

With a shake of her head, she chided herself for her mean-spirited judgment.

Other suspects? What about Reverend Whittle?

She jotted down the clergyman's name. Would he commit murder on behalf of his miners, out of resentment, or in a move to gain power? Or perhaps out of some misguided zealotry? He clearly disliked the Trevells and considered Alistair his foe, and Harris, too. But how would he poison a lord? He had not been at the dinner table the foggy night Alistair fell ill. His only connection with the household was his brother Elijah.

Alyssa sucked in a breath of surprise. She hadn't thought of that before. Elijah had access to the garden shed and served at the table as footman. Was he more in sympathy with his brother's cause than he appeared to be?

Then there was Tavi. The man was a mystery. Besides the fact that Tavi and the late lord did not like each other, Jane had mentioned that Tavi had a wife and child in India whom he wanted to bring to England. Was Alistair somehow an impediment to that goal? What if Tavi wanted a better position in the household. Would he commit murder to gain the title for his own master, thus elevating himself? If so, Harris might know nothing of it.

The thought brought a low moan of dismay and enlightenment from her.

With a flourish she wrote the butler's name below Reverend Whittle's on the list. She studied the name closer, watching the black ink dry. She'd not thought of that layer of motivation before. How devious was the butler? What did he know of drugs and poisons? Like Harris, he had access to the medicine chest.

Her gaze skimmed back up the list. Who else? Vicar Carbury and his family had been there, too. She shook her head. No, the vicar had no motive.

Another question: where did Lady Cynthia and her confusing warning fit into all of this? What did it have to do with Alistair's death? Had the lady attempted to mend the fence between Alistair and Sir Ralph and earned the anger of one or both men? Possibly, but Alyssa felt strongly that Lady Cynthia's cryptic words had been in reference to a romantic relationship. Had she attempted to flirt with Harris and been rejected? Perhaps. Had she flirted with Reverend Whittle? He was an attractive man and certainly wouldn't be above a flirtation. He'd made that plain the first day Alyssa had met him.

"Oh, my." This new light on events made her sit back in her chair and reassess it all. Maybe there was a reason for Sir Ralph's sharp-eyed gaze on his wife at Sunday dinner. Were there other clues that she had missed? She must review other moments and comments that might be meaningful.

Tired of staring at the paper with Harris's name glaring at her from the top, she laid down her pen and rose from the desk. She strolled across the room and stretched out on the bed, careful not to get her shoe soles on the counterpane. Here she could think with fewer distractions. She stared up at the lacy patterns of the canopy above.

There were two questions to answer. *Who* and *how?*

If neither the butler, Pendeen, who'd served the meal, nor the cook, Mrs. Brodie, who'd prepared the food, had motive to murder their lord and master, then how had it been done? If one of Alistair's dinner guests had poisoned him, how had the poison been administered at the dinner?

She closed her eyes, envisioning the dinner table that night. The guests would probably have been seated much as they had been at the Sunday dinner she herself had attended. Sir Ralph on Gwendolyn's right and Lady Cynthia on Alistair's right. Where would Harris have sat? Near the head of the table with Lady Cynthia and Alistair or at the foot with Gwendolyn and Sir Ralph?

Suddenly, Alyssa was seated at the table next to Harris. Crowded around were all the guests, even the Vicar and Mrs. Carbury. Lucy and Edith giggled at her from the other side of the table. Each of them turned at least once to glare at Alistair at the head, the Alistair she'd seen in the portrait, the man with the petulant lips. Sir Ralph, Byron, Lady Cynthia, even Tavi was there.

Then they all receded into the shadows, and it seemed only she and Harris shared the candlelight. He ignored his cousin. His gaze was meant only for her. The intensity of it sent a pang of desire through her. He was dressed in formal attire. At her side he was large, handsome, elegant, and all male— so masculine, it sent a thrill through her.

The smile on his face as he regarded her was full of tenderness, that precious glimpse of desire she'd seen in his reflection in the brass urn. She didn't care in the least who had murdered Alistair.

He offered her a glass of dark red wine. "Drink, my sweet," he coaxed, putting the glass to her lips. She drank.

At the head of the table, barely visible in the shadows, Alistair began to choke. Harris's gaze held hers over the rim of the goblet. Alistair grabbed his throat, and his face began to turn purple. Harris continued to ignore him. There was nothing to do but drink, to please Harris, to taste what he had to offer.

"That's it," he whispered as she swallowed sip after sip. "Drink. Drink."

The dying Alistair, the guests, and the table vanished. She drank until they were lying together, floating on blue-and-gold silk. Her limbs were numb. Harris had drugged her, but she didn't care. He loomed over her, gazing into her face, her eyes, searching for some confession that she was unable to give because she didn't know what he wanted her to admit.

Her skin was bare, and so was his, but she was not ashamed or embarrassed. This was a dream, and she didn't have to make sense of where their clothes were or be afraid he would not find her desirable. She smiled at him and touched his face.

In a low, beguiling voice he whispered praise. She was beautiful, he said. She believed him. The belief made the air heady and sweet. The light shimmered. His skin burned on her skin. His lips sipped tantalizingly at her mouth. Her body warmed beneath his caressing hands, his cunning fingers. The power and heat of him was strong and seductive. She gave herself up to all the sensations he cajoled from her, the sweet melting of her being, the honeyed ache to know his touch, to allow him to fill her.

She was helpless, and he knew it. She sighed. Was that such a bad thing?

A crash brought her up and out of her doze.

"Miss!" Jane scurried into the room without waiting to be

invited and wrung her hands. "Something has happened. Something awful. Elijah just brought word. There's a riot over the grain shipment, and the miners, they have Lady Penridge. Holding her prisoner, they are."

"Prisoner!" Alyssa sat up, her brain foggy, still filled with seduction and desire. She grappled with Jane's message. "Miners? Lady Penridge? Where is . . . wait! Does Lord Penridge know this?"

"He does," the maid said. "He and Tavi are in his lordship's study laying their plans and unlocking the gun closet. He said to tell you to stay in the house until he gets back."

"What happened?" she asked, standing to face the maid and praying that the intimate caresses she'd been dreaming about weren't evident on her face.

"Her ladyship left with Reverend Whittle to parcel out the grain at the little chapel on the moors, and Elijah went with her," Jane said. "You were here in the garden shed when I come to her with that message."

"Yes, I remember," Alyssa said, her groggy mind beginning to make sense of things. "Surely the reverend's congregation wouldn't turn violent," she said, even while remembering how close to violence they had been that day she and Harris had confronted the hungry miners near Wheal Isabel.

"I don't know about that, miss." Jane shook her head. "But it's a fine thanks to his lordship for trying to help them. Attacking the poor, widowed Lady Penridge."

"I must talk to Harris," Alyssa said, more to herself than Jane. As an army officer Harris surely knew what he was about and needed no advice from her. "Maybe there is something I can do to help."

"Yes, miss," Jane said, following her out of the room.

Alyssa wasted no time in finding him in the study. The door stood open as she rounded the corner. She could see him, Tavi, and Elijah Whittle loading shotguns and laying them across the desk. She studied his face, the remnants of her dream still with her. How handsome he was, even wearing his harsh soldier's mask. How she wished to be something special to him, rather than just his ward.

She marched into the study. "Jane told me the news. Surely you don't think they'd harm her?"

"I don't know," he said, looking up from a box of shells. His eyes were cold and narrow, and there was a growl in his voice. "I never thought they'd do a thing like this—detain a Trevell and make demands like some outlaw rabble."

"What exactly are they asking for?" she asked.

"They want to talk to me," he said. "Apparently the grain shipment was unsatisfactory. They refuse to release Gwendolyn until I make an appearance. How *dare* they!? This is Whittle's doing. Forgive me, Elijah."

"Nothing to forgive, my lord," the coachman said with resignation. "He's my brother, and I know as well as any what he's capable of. He's stirred the miners up to a frenzy, he has. Making things harder for everyone. Some of them have weapons, Miss Lockhart. Her ladyship is right frightened, she is."

"But he's not capable of hurting Gwendolyn," Alyssa said. "I'm almost certain of it."

"And why do you say that?" Harris stopped loading his pistol and looked at her.

She hesitated. Did he not know? Had he never seen the gleam in the clergyman's eyes when he spoke to Lady Penridge? "Reverend Whittle was here for tea two days ago. He was concerned then about the grain shipment. But I could tell then that he likes her—too well to hurt her. He is just trying to alarm you."

"Perhaps, that and demonstrate his power over the miners," he said, gazing down at the shells.

"If they have weapons," said Tavi, who no longer seemed like a dutiful servant, but a soldier, preparing himself and his lord for battle, "it is best to be armed when you face them." He held out another pistol for Harris to take.

Gunmetal gleamed in the light of the lamp that had been

lit against the gray afternoon shadows. The sight of it chilled Alyssa, but not because she was frightened of firearms. She'd done her share of skeet shooting—a fashionable pastime on a country estate. Actually, she could outshoot her brother Winslow. She could handle guns without fear. But she also understood the violence the weapons could do and that thought sent cold dread into her bones.

"Quite so, Tavi," Harris said, accepting a pistol. "See to Pendragon, Elijah, and a horse for Tavi. Saddle Lady Penridge's horse as well. She will be returning with us."

"Yes, my lord." The coachman started toward the door.

"Tack up Smuggler, too, Elijah," she called. "I'm going along."

The three men froze, each staring at her.

"Alyssa, you will stay here," Harris said, his tone firm. He expected no argument.

"Perhaps if a woman is with you there will be less chance of trouble breaking out," she said.

"If you are with me, there is a chance of you being hurt," he said, his frown deepening. "I don't need to be explaining to your father how you came to be injured in a miners' riot."

"But what if Gwendolyn is hurt?" she persisted, surprised at how easily the logic came to her lips.

"I will see them all hung," he said with cool decisiveness. He flicked open the pistol and eyed the shells in the full cylinder.

"Think of Gwendolyn." She just knew that she had to go with him. "What if, God forbid, some unthinkable thing has happened? Shouldn't another woman be there?"

He studied her for a long moment, clearly unhappy to be contemplating what she suggested. But he understood exactly what she meant. Tavi and Whittle watched in silence, each tense. She knew they didn't want her to go along. She had to strengthen her case with Harris.

"Are there other women there, Elijah?" she asked.

"Yes, miss, a few," he said reluctantly. "But not gentle-women. They be miners' wives."

"Then leave the guns here and take me along as assurance to the miners of your peaceful intentions," she pleaded.

Harris studied, but she could only guess what he was thinking, what factors he was weighing. Would her presence be a weakness or strength in the minds of the reverend and the miners?

"If anything happens, I can outride men on foot," she added, putting forth her final and strongest argument. "I am not being brash or thrill-seeking. I am not being impulsive, my lord. This is important. Gwendolyn might need me."

Finally, Harris flipped the pistol closed. "Saddle Smuggler, Elijah," he said, shaking his head as if he feared he would re-gret his decision. "I don't have time to argue with you."

"The grain was to be delivered to Wheal Isabel where my manager or myself could oversee the distribution of it," Har-ris said as they neared the miner's chapel. Alyssa rode at his side. She'd managed to get him to tell her what had happened. Darkness was gathering on the moor, and Johnnie rode ahead of them, carrying a lantern to light the way. Armed with a shotgun, Tavi rode with the stable boy. Harris carried only a pistol, under his coat and out of sight.

Elijah Whittle had been left behind with instructions to in-form the sheriff and the magistrate, Sir Ralph, of what was happening.

"I wanted distribution of the food to be fair," Harris con-tinued. "Apparently the reverend waylaid the shipment—rather forcibly, I suspect. He took it to the chapel and somehow lured Gwendolyn there to make it look as if the business had my approval. I've had no opportunity to see the condition of the grain or the amount of it."

"What does he hope to accomplish by doing this?" she asked. They turned the horses off the moor road onto the chapel lane. They were close enough now that she could see the crowd of miners and a few women milling around the front of the squat gray chapel. Torches lit the churchyard. "He stands to earn your ill will," she added.

"He cares not," Harris said. "I believe all of this trouble-making is his attempt to make the Trevells look bad. The miners may have had their complaints about Alistair, but they were loyal to him in their way. He opened a mine and offered jobs when all the other mines were closing. Nevertheless, the reverend doesn't have to work very hard to make Alistair look bad. My cousin was frugal in his business affairs and not always a very compassionate man. He made enemies with our neighbors as well as the miners. I've made some concessions, like shortening the shifts and making repairs on their cottages. Gwendolyn has helped with the personal touch by calling on the sick. Still, there is much fence-mending to do. But it cannot be done overnight—not without hurting the mine, which in the long run won't do the miners any good at all. Change takes time and the reverend, crafty man that he is, has succeeded in turning the situation to his advantage."

"But is he truly working for the benefit of the miners?" Alyssa asked.

"He is creating his own world of privilege and influence," Harris said. "It's the worst kind of greed. If there are degrees of greed. When greed's source is vanity and the desire for power, it benefits few. The miners have enormous respect for their church leaders. They look to them for guidance and re-assurance and protection. The reverend gains their confidence by telling them what they want to hear—by blaming the obvious villain for their woes. I want you to be prepared for him to say some outrageous things. Lies, most of it. But unfortunately, not all."

"I understand."

"I hope you will," Harris said, eyeing her with a doubtful glance, the sort that said he believed her too young to truly comprehend. "I will order him to release Gwendolyn as quickly as possible. When he does, I want you to ride with her back to Penridge Hall without delay. Johnnie will go with you. Tavi and I will work out whatever needs to be settled here. Do you understand? I'm counting on you to do as I say. No arguments. I do not want you and Gwendolyn here if things turn ugly."

"I will do as you say," Alyssa said, praying she had the courage to do as she promised when the time came. "I'll get Gwendolyn back to the house as soon as possible."

"Good," he said. "One last thing—do not allow the reverend to draw you into the conversation. This is between him and me."

She nodded.

As they rode up to the chapel, the crowd gathered around two large wagons turned toward them, then quieted. She searched the crowd, looking for the familiar faces she'd seen on the road to church on Sunday. But today she saw only lean, sour faces. The coldness in their eyes sent a shiver through her.

These had to be the same folks she'd seen on the road to the chapel on Sunday, but their mood was ugly. They were angry, resentful, dissatisfied, and ready to argue and demand. Many carried cricket bats or tools that might be used as weapons. She could see a man standing on the lead wagon, lean and wolfish, wearing a shabby black suit, his shoulders righteously squared—the reverend himself.

"Greetings, your lordship," he called, mockery in his voice, a snide smile on his lips, his dark eyes lit with devilment. He stood on the wagon, hatless, his hair tied back in its slick queue, his presence commanding the attention of all in the churchyard. He was taking great pleasure in the turmoil he'd wrought. She knew in that moment, however impossible it was, that she wanted Zebulon Whittle to be Alistair's murderer.

"So good of you to come and see how miserable your promise of food is." He sneered at Harris. "And I see you

brought the generous Miss Lockhart to witness your embarrassment."

Harris halted his horse.

She drew Smuggler up next to him.

"What is this all about, Whittle?" Harris asked, ignoring
the reverend's taunt. "And where is Lady Penridge? If she has
come to harm, make no mistake, you will find yourself cooling your heels for a long while in Launceston gaol."

"Lady Penridge is safe inside." The reverend gestured toward the chapel. "The wagoners are there, too. The good lady
came here with me of her own free will to help with the dispensing of the food."

A murmur of approval ran through the mob.

"And is she here still of her own free will?" Harris rested
his gloved hands nonchalantly on the pommel of his saddle.
Alyssa marveled that he could remain so calm and collected
in the face of such hostility and scorn. She held her head up
to show she was unafraid, too. But inside she was ready to retreat.

"Neither of us could anticipate the change in the mood of
these good people when they discovered the grain is wet and
moldy," the reverend said in mock innocence. "A fine lot of
bread this rotten stuff will make them. Do you always deal
with such disreputable merchants or only when you're purchasing goods for charity?"

The crowd mumbled their agreement again, full of disapproval this time.

"I regret that the grain is unusable, if that is so," Harris
said, obviously refusing to be baited by the reverend. Alyssa
was proud of him for it.

"It is so," an angry woman in the rabble shouted back.
"Hardly fit grain to feed a beast, let alone to mill into flour to
feed to my man and my children."

"Then make use of it and feed your beasts," Harris said,
speaking to the woman.

"But we need food *now,*" another voice called from the other side of the crowd.

Turning to speak in the direction of the new voice, Harris promised, "I will see that you have food soon." Then he turned toward the reverend and added, "However, I want Lady Penridge released, now."

"Promises, promises," the reverend taunted.

"That's right," a miner covered in clay dust shouted, his mouth a garish pink contrast to his white face. "You Trevells have always been good with promises. When will you make good on them? Will it be another fortnight before we see grain wagons again?"

"I'll ride out to Launceston tonight to purchase the food myself," Harris said. "I'll guarantee it is good and return with the wagons at the earliest possible hour. *After* you release Lady Penridge."

"Let's keep the lady here until he returns," another voice called. "That'll guarantee his speedy return."

A low, ugly murmur of agreement ran through the mob.

Uneasy, Alyssa glanced in Harris's direction. Instead of quieting the crowd, his promises had agitated them. Nevertheless, he remained resolute.

"I am concerned for your children, too," Harris said, speaking loud enough for everyone to hear him, but never appearing angry, never shouting. "I will deal harshly with the merchant who has sent us the unacceptable commodity. But I am not going anywhere until Lady Penridge is released."

The rabble began to surge again, miners turning to miners to grumble, to protest, their anger feeding on itself. With her nervousness growing, she glanced again at Harris, but he seemed unaffected by the shifting mood.

"How do we know you'll keep your promise?" the reverend said, shrugging as if he had no control over the crowd. "The late lord, God rest his soul, was known to forget his promises once the crisis was over. But if Lady Penridge would be so good as to remain with us until you return, we'd know that all will end well."

"Out of the question," Harris said, directing his remarks to the reverend. "I understand your disappointment in the Trevells. But the lords of Penridge have never submitted to extortion, nor will they begin to do so now."

The crowd shouted its displeasure and rushed forward.

Spooked, Smuggler's head came up and the mare danced in place, pulling against Alyssa's grip on the reins. She struggled for control, fought not to let the tension in the air panic her, too.

Tavi brought his shotgun up, the barrel pointed to the sky, orange torchlight glinting off the gunmetal.

All faces turned toward the weapon.

Alyssa cringed, waiting to hear the shotgun blast split the air.

But Tavi did not fire.

The mob's grumbling quieted, dampened by the sight of the firearm. It was only a temporary lull in the tension. Something had to be done to break the deadlock, to soothe the mood. Or a gun blast would be required.

Alyssa managed to quiet Smuggler. As she brought the mare around again, a face in the crowd caught her eye, the haggard face of a mother she'd seen that Sunday, carrying her child to the chapel, singing as they walked down the lonely moor road.

In the momentary quiet, Alyssa knew what to do. With as much volume as she could muster, she began to sing. "Jerusalem" was the first thing that came to her mind, the hymn that she'd heard them singing that morning, their voices carrying on the cold, foggy air, sweet and true. The same hymn she'd sung in church at home more times than she could remember. A hymn she'd sung with the Trevells at Lanissey Church.

In the torchlight, the mob glared at her. But the churning ceased. She continued to sing, painfully aware of her voice, small and alone, before an angry crowd—aware of her heart beating frantically in her chest, almost louder than her voice. The woman she was watching did not join her.

At her side, Harris remained motionless, his gaze on the reverend. The miners before her eyed each other awkwardly. To her other side and behind her, she was aware of Tavi, unmoving on his horse, the shotgun in his hand.

She continued to sing, peering into face after face. *Sing with me. Sing with me,* she willed. If only they would let the hymn steal the ugliness from the moment. The mob's silence grew enormous, but she sang on, praying silently now. *Sing with me.* She was beginning to feel foolish, almost as silly as when she'd pulled the apple from her pocket and offered it as a solution to their problems. But still she sang.

Suddenly a small voice rang out over the mob, joining hers, that of a child, perhaps. She couldn't be certain. High and a bit off-key, but the words were clear and the voice sweetly steady. Then another, a weaker woman's voice, was raised, its owner attempting to join them. The added voices inspired Alyssa; she sang on, thankful to a music master who had required his choir to memorize all the verses.

As she sang, more voices joined in. The miners directly in front of Smuggler began to sing, grudgingly at first, then with more spirit. The woman Alyssa had seen first was singing now.

Alyssa glanced at the reverend, who still stood on top of the wagonload of bagged grain. He was frowning as he glanced around the mob, searching for faces that might still be with him. Apparently he found few. And he knew better than to scold his congregation for singing a hymn. At last he saw her watching him, and his frown altered into a rueful smile.

He'd lost control, and he knew it. She'd won. Her heart beat quickly but with more confidence now. As if ceding victory to her, the reverend touched his brow in salute. Then he turned to wave to a man at the church door. The man disappeared inside.

Taking another breath, Alyssa began a new verse, aware of the malice seeping away from the crowd, crawling into the darkness, into the fog. When the church door opened again, the man was leading Gwendolyn from the chapel.

Alyssa nearly wept with relief, but her voice never wavered.

Sixteen

Harris was off Pendragon in a flash. Alyssa watched the singing mob part for him, some stepping back almost respectfully. Fearlessly, he made his way to Gwendolyn's side. She was pale, her step uncertain. Her bonnet sat off center and dust streaked her black skirts, yet she seemed calm. He slipped an arm around her, and Gwendolyn looked at him and nodded as if to say she was unharmed. Still she clung to him as he led her to her horse and helped her mount.

"Go, now," he said, loud enough for her, Gwendolyn, Tavi, and Johnnie to hear over the singing. "Return to Penridge. Summon Dr. Lewellyn. I'll come back as soon as I can."

The timing couldn't have been better. Alyssa held the last note of "amen" as long as she dared.

Johnnie was already leading the way down the lane toward the main road, Gwendolyn behind him. Tavi and the gun did not move. Alyssa lingered, waiting to see what Harris said.

He swung up on Pendragon and turned to the miners and the reverend. "I'm off to Launceston to bring more grain. For those of you who have immediate needs for children, someone who is ill, or a breeding wife, come to Penridge. Tavi will dispense food from our personal stores."

A low murmur of approval moved through the crowd.

Alyssa turned Smuggler toward the lane, following Johnnie, Gwendolyn, and Tavi. Harris was behind her. Her throat was sore and her mouth parched, but she rode with a light heart. They'd rescued Gwendolyn.

When they reached the main road, she drew her horse to a halt and turned to him.

"It seems I must thank you," he said, drawing Pendragon up beside her.

"It was a small thing," she managed to say.

"No, it wasn't," he said, gazing into her eyes. His silent gratitude warmed her heart and made her belly flutter. "It was courageous and compassionate, Alyssa, and I owe you thanks. So do the miners, for saving us all from something that could have been very ugly indeed. I'll be back as soon as I can. Tavi, you heard what I said about the stores. Don't let Chef Hugo hold back anything."

"Yes, sir."

"Go safely," she said, wanting to say more, unhappy with the thought of him riding across the dark moor on a cold night, wanting to touch him and thank him for his courage. But she knew there was nothing more she could say that was appropriate.

"I shall," he said, turning Pendragon's head north, toward the road to Launceston. "Take care of Gwendolyn."

He was gone, galloping into the fog and darkness.

"No, do not send for Dr. Lewellyn," Gwendolyn said with surprising strength and determination. She'd just dismounted Pilgrim at the front door of Penridge Hall. Tavi was giving orders for Johnnie to summon the doctor to Penridge. She'd interrupted him abruptly. "I'm a bit shaken, but I do not need a doctor. Do not trouble poor Lewellyn on a night like this."

"There's no need for you to be brave, Gwendolyn." Alyssa dismounted and hurried across the gravel to take the lady's arm. Gwendolyn's composure was impressive, though the strain did show in her pallor and the trembling of her hand.

"All I need is some tea and some rest," she said, accepting Alyssa's support and turning toward the house.

"I'll see to it immediately, my lady," Tavi said, his humble bow incongruous with the gun slung over his shoulder.

"Have Blanche bring a tray to her room," Alyssa said, leading Gwendolyn into the house.

"I'm really all right," Gwendolyn said, accepting her assistance. "Truly I am . . . but you will stay with me, won't you, Alyssa? For a bit? Have tea with me?"

"Of course I'll stay with you as long as you like." Alyssa squeezed the lady's hand. Even through Gwendolyn's gloves she could feel cold fingers. "I could use a bracing cup of tea myself," she added.

"Thank you." Gwendolyn smiled gratefully and patted her hand.

Elijah Whittle and Blanche met them as they entered. A great fuss was made, with the servants scurrying to provide every comfort. Gwendolyn behaved as the gracious lady of the house despite her harrowing experience.

She was soon made comfortable in her chambers. The draperies were drawn against the cold darkness, a fire roared in the hearth, and a tray of steaming tea, soup, sandwiches, biscuits, and fruit was laid out on the tea table.

Having taken a chill, Gwendolyn was made comfortable in her favorite chair with a shawl over her shoulders and an afghan over her legs. Blanche hovered over the tea table, arranging everything just so.

"That will be all, Blanche," Gwendolyn said. "Miss Lockhart will pour for me, will you not, dear?"

"Yes, I'll be glad to," Alyssa said, noting the maid's doubtful gaze at her mistress. "We'll call if we need anything more, Blanche."

The maid bobbed a curtsy and was gone.

"Are you hungry?" Alyssa poured, taking great pleasure

in the steamy warmth wafting up from the spout and the reassuring amber clarity of the liquid as it swirled through the strainer. Life might have its ups and downs, but you could always count on a good cup of tea for comfort. "Chef Hugo has prepared sandwiches and soup. Or perhaps you'd like biscuits with your tea?"

"Biscuits," Gwendolyn said, glancing at the tray with apparent disinterest. "I really could not abide anything more." She sighed heavily as she gazed into the fire. "Was he not wonderful? Your singing was inspired, Alyssa, but he was absolutely heroic."

Alyssa glanced at her. She did not need to hear Harris's name to know who Gwendolyn meant. "He was wonderful," she agreed, passing the teacup.

The lady accepted the tea and held her gaze. "He didn't hesitate a minute, did he? When word came that Reverend Whittle was refusing to release me, he came immediately. I was so frightened. But I had every confidence in Harris."

"He was very concerned," Alyssa agreed, pouring her own tea. She had every confidence in Harris, too, but at the moment she was troubled by the thought of him riding across the moor, alone. There were dangers out there—outlaws, washed-out roads, the cold, the remoteness. He risked much for Gwendolyn and the miners' sake.

"Tell me about it, if you like," she urged, puzzled about how Gwendolyn had fallen into the reverend's hands in the first place. "What did the reverend do? What did he say when he called this morning?"

"He was very persuasive," Gwendolyn began, setting down her tea and considering the question. "He'd mentioned the shipment yesterday when he was here for tea. You remember?"

Alyssa nodded.

"When he arrived today, he told me that the grain was here," Gwendolyn said. "He said he thought this would be a good time for me to come out of mourning enough to be present as the food was given out. I think you'll agree, the reverend can be quite charismatic when he wants to be. Of course, Harris had told me it would arrive any day when I asked him about it. He had been most upset about that appalling confrontation at the Wheal Isabel when you first arrived. He was eager to satisfy the miners. We had not discussed the doling out of the grain, but I thought, under the circumstances, the bad feelings and all, that it would be a consoling gesture if I were present as the reverend suggested. After all, we were enough out of mourning to receive guests. Surely I could do this for the needy."

"I think that was very good of you," Alyssa said. "And Reverend Whittle obviously took advantage of your generosity."

"Indeed," Gwendolyn said with an indignant shake of her head; then tears brimmed in her eyes. She picked up her teacup and sipped from it. "Who would think a man of the cloth would do such a thing? I simply could not imagine how a good deed could turn into such an unpleasant affair."

Alyssa squeezed Gwendolyn's free hand sympathetically, knowing she would have been just as gullible. "The moment Harris received word of your predicament, he called Tavi into consult and sent Elijah to the magistrate. There was no detail about the situation that he overlooked or neglected. He would never let harm come to you."

"I knew it. I knew he would know what to do. No doubt we will hear from Sir Ralph soon," Gwendolyn said, her smile returning. She sipped from her teacup and stared into the fire. "How can anyone believe that dreadful rumor about Harris?"

Then, as if she'd said words she regretted, she glanced at Alyssa. "I can only assume you've heard the gossip. Blanche tells me the servants mutter about it often enough. I assume Jane has said something about Harris having something to do with Alistair's death."

Alyssa hesitated before replying. She recalled Harris saying he'd broached the subject about questions regarding Alistair's death with Gwendolyn. But what else had Gwendolyn heard? Under the circumstances, Alyssa could not anticipate what the lady wanted to hear or should hear.

"As a matter of fact, yes, I had heard some notion of the sort." Casually, she picked up a biscuit and nibbled on it, but it was only tasteless crumbs in her dry mouth. "I did not take it seriously enough to mention it to anyone. I wondered if you'd heard."

Surprise crossed Gwendolyn's face. She regarded Alyssa with great concern. "My dear, you protected me? How sweet of you. But don't believe any of the tales. I do not. Not a word. Heaven knows, Alistair and Harris had their differences. They were like brothers—competitive, always out to get the best of each other. All the good and bad that comes with that. But when the press came, they stood together. Harris would not poison his cousin. Never. Do you think I would be living under this roof if I thought Harris had murdered Alistair? Do you think I would allow my daughter to live here if I believed that? Certainly not."

"No, I'm sure you wouldn't," Alyssa echoed, wondering what more Gwendolyn knew. "Then, if it wasn't murder, what happened?"

"A bad whelk," Gwendolyn said with a wave of her hand to dismiss the gossip. "There was no murder. There is no reason to dispute Dr. Lewellyn's diagnosis. I was with Alistair from the beginning until the last. His symptoms were just like that of food poisoning. How this rumor of murder came to life, I shall never know. I suppose it was because he and Harris were so competitive. People actually believed there was bad blood between them, but that was not so."

Alyssa studied the widow. Gwendolyn appeared to be telling the truth, as she saw it, anyway. Who would want to live under the same roof with a murderer, or someone you thought might be a murderer? What mother would risk her child's safety in that fashion? None. At least, not knowingly.

Alyssa admitted to herself that if she'd not heard about the claims of Peter Pendeen, she'd almost be willing to believe, like Gwendolyn, that there had been no murder—just a painful, unfortunate death.

"It's all so sad." Alyssa shook her head. "For you and for Meggie. And now this turmoil with the miners and Reverend Whittle."

"I'm so glad Meggie is not here to witness any of this," Gwendolyn said.

Shouting from the direction of the kitchen side of the house reached them. Alyssa went to the window to see what was happening. Torches bobbed against the darkness as a small group of miners and some women strode up the drive from the fairy gate. "Reverend Whittle and his rabble are here!" she said, glancing back at Gwendolyn.

The color that had begun to seep into Gwendolyn's face drained away. Her eyes grew round and haunted. "I would not have gone with him today if I'd thought he was capable of such villainy. When he saw the moldy grain, he turned into a monster. Ranting. The miners and their women hung on his every rebellious word. Now they've come to claim what they think is theirs. They'll leave us all helpless and starving."

"Do not trouble yourself over this." Alyssa rang the bell for Blanche. "I'll see to it. Tavi is very efficient and stalwart. I'm sure he will manage, but I'll see how it is going. Blanche, there you are. See to her ladyship while I see to our visitors."

"Alyssa, do be careful," Gwendolyn pleaded. "The reverend is so unpredictable."

"Indeed," Alyssa agreed.

The good reverend was not with the small group of miners who arrived at Penridge Hall. Only a noisy, respectful few, eager for food, had the courage to come to the house and make their way around to the back.

Tavi frowned at her when Alyssa appeared in the larder, but he went on dispensing the grain, smoked hams, bacon, dried fish, potatoes, beans, and other stores. Chef Hugo was sulking in his room as his precious stores were given away, Jane told her. But the scullery maid and Jane were doing their best to help Tavi. Alyssa stood by the door, reminding the recipients, who looked too greedy, that the food was for their sick, the children, and the women with child. More supplies were coming soon. Many stopped to curtsy or touch their caps, offering thanks as if they knew her as a member of the family and liked her.

The food went farther than she expected it to. Tavi's careful work, she suspected. She sent the scullery maid and Jane off to bed when they'd finished tidying the empty larder. She lingered as Tavi locked the outside door, the jingle of his keys echoing in the empty storeroom.

"Do you think there will be more trouble?" she asked.

He turned to her. "It is not likely. The sheriff has been notified and is on alert. But I will keep watch tonight. Elijah will watch from the gatehouse. How is Lady Penridge?"

"She is bearing up well," she said. "How long before his lordship returns?"

"That depends on how fast he works," Tavi said. "But the colonel knows what he's about. I expect him the day after tomorrow."

Alyssa nodded. She knew no matter how fast Harris worked, it was going to be the longest two days of her life.

If Penridge Hall seemed empty without Meggie, it seemed positively desolate without Harris. Alyssa could not concentrate enough to read. Music and singing passed some of the time, but her throat was still raw and she'd lost the heart to sing—at least until Harris had returned. She spent more hours than she should pacing from one window to the next in the hope of glimpsing him riding through the fairy gate.

Gwendolyn spent the morning of the first day recovering from the shock of her unpleasant experience. She'd languished in bed until the midmorning. Then she took a long, soaking bath with Blanche waiting on her. By teatime the sheriff had called to inquire about her welfare and to ask if she wished to press charges. She graciously declined, citing the hardship of the miners as an excuse for their uncharacteristic behavior. Dr. Lewellyn also called to inquire about her health and to say that he'd seen the provisions from Penridge Hall's stores put to good use among those in the miners' cottages who needed it most.

By evening of the second day, Alyssa was at her wits' end, but Gwendolyn found constructive uses for the time.

"His lordship will want a bath," she began after she'd settled herself in the family withdrawing room with her needlework in her lap. She summoned Alyssa and rang for Tavi. "See that everything is ready for him in the bath."

"Yes, your ladyship," Tavi said with an inclination of his head. "It is in readiness."

"Lay a big fire in his chamber," Gwendolyn instructed. "Have we any more apple tree wood to put on his fire?"

"I'll see to it, my lady," Tavi said.

Alyssa listened in silence, envious of Gwendolyn's knowledge of what to do. Despite all that had happened, the lady had managed to keep her wits about her. She had not lost sight of what needed to be done in the household, whether it be cosseting the chef or seeing to the needs of the lord of the house.

"How is our supply of his favorite brandy?" she asked.

"Adequate," Tavi said. "I've set out a bottle."

"The newspaper?" Alyssa said. "He will want his newspapers and the post."

"Yes, of course, good Alyssa." Gwendolyn tapped a finger thoughtfully to her chin. "Dinner? He has been such a hero, I do so want everything to be right for his return. What shall we have for dinner?"

"The larder is still somewhat bare," Alyssa reminded her.

"Chef Hugo is very sensitive on this point," Tavi reminded them.

"I am sure he is," Gwendolyn said with some sympathy.

"I took the liberty of sending Johnnie out to shoot some fowl for the table," Tavi said.

"Excellent, Tavi." Gwendolyn rewarded the butler with a smile of approval. "Harris fancies fowl. What else do we still have?"

"Shh," Alyssa said, sitting up to listen more closely. Part of her had been alert all day for any sound that heralded Harris's return. She was certain she'd heard something on the gravel outside. "What is that sound?"

They all listened intently. A low rumble reached them. The sound of heavily loaded wagons and the jingling of harnesses. Then the barking of the stable dogs began.

"He's back!" she cried.

She was out of the withdrawing room at a less-than-decorous sprint, down the hallway, and out the door in time to see the line of wagons come through the fairy gate. At the head of the line rode Harris on Pendragon.

Exhausted, the black carried his head low. But Harris sat upright, proud, disciplined, and hatless, with dust on his coat and the shadow of two days' growth of beard on his face. But he was all right; she sighed with relief.

The sun had just sunk behind the trees, casting the house in shadows. Lantern held high, Elijah came out of the gatehouse to greet them. Lumbering up the drive behind Harris were six large wagons piled high with bags of grain or stacked with barrels of other commodities.

She was about to strike out across the lawn to greet him when she realized that would be a mistake. She was but a guest, a Trevell ward. She had no right to throw her arms around the lord of Penridge. With effort she remained on the front steps, her hands clasped before her.

"There he is," Gwendolyn cried, coming out onto the front step beside Alyssa. By then he'd spotted them. Gwendolyn smiled and waved, a ladylike raising of her hand.

He lifted his hand in a return greeting.

"Doesn't he look fine?" Gwendolyn said, her gaze still on Harris, a smile of pride on her lips. "A bit exhausted, perhaps, but he is safe."

"Yes," Alyssa sighed once more. As they watched, Harris gave Elijah instructions on where the wagons were to be taken and the horses stabled. Then he turned Pendragon toward the house. When he reached the front step, he swung down, bounded up the steps, and swept Gwendolyn up in his arms.

Alyssa stepped aside, feeling left out and self-conscious.

"Gwendolyn, are you all right?" He thrust her away at arm's length for an appraising look. "I'm so sorry I couldn't stay with you. This trip couldn't be delayed. But you look well—as lovely as ever."

"Harris, it was so terrible," Gwendolyn said, stepping into the circle of his arms and resting her head on his shoulder.

Was she going to burst into tears *now* for his benefit? Alyssa watched the scene with a touch of annoyance.

Then Gwendolyn lifted her head. "I've never been so frightened in all my life. But then you were there, like a brave knight to my rescue. How could I not be well? I shall forever be indebted to you."

Harris gazed into Gwendolyn's eyes. "I will always be here when you need me. I told you that when Alistair died."

Embarrassed to be witnessing such a personal moment, Alyssa clasped her hands behind her and turned to watch the wagons. She should excuse herself, but she didn't know how.

She fidgeted, and suddenly Harris's gaze was on her. "And you, Alyssa, my Joan of Arc. There was no more trouble after your hymn singing? That was a stroke of genius."

His praise made her smile and ache with pride.

"No more trouble," Tavi answered before she could respond. "The music took the fire out of them."

"And they took the stores from our larders," Gwendolyn said, slipping an arm around Harris's and leading him into the house. "But the sheriff was here today to say he has his eye on Reverend Whittle and the miners."

"Good," Harris said. "I'm glad to know he is aware of the situation. And I suppose Chef Hugo is in despair."

"Naturally, he was weeping and babbling in French, but I suspect he can rise to the occasion," Gwendolyn said, gazing at Harris worshipfully. "Have you an appetite after your ride? Tavi has your bath ready. Did you learn any news in Launceston?"

"Only that grain is scarce everywhere," he said. "However, I managed to stock some supplies for Penridge Hall."

They disappeared into the house, linked arm in arm, their heads inclined toward each other, their words intended only for the other.

Alyssa trailed after them, feeling like the fifth wheel on a wagon, feeling lost and strangely frustrated.

Sir Ralph called the next day. Alyssa saw the magistrate ride up and enter the door that led to Harris's study. The two men confined themselves for two hours, Jane told her later. The maid had served them tea but overheard nothing. And there was no opportunity for Alyssa to speak with Sir Ralph. She could only assume they had discussed the incident with Reverend Whittle. Later she saw Captain Dundry call. His stay wasn't long. Whatever was discussed and decided that day in Harris's study, nothing was said of it to the ladies at the dinner table.

As adventurous as the events had proved to be, none had provided Alyssa with useful information to note on her list of murder suspects. Her time was spent being a congenial companion to Gwendolyn. That required little of her. And, for want of anything better, she was forced to sit down at her writing desk and compose a letter to Meggie about the fate of King Arthur. She took her time over the missive, endeavoring to make it sound as if the little creature was off on a grand adventure much like Meggie's own. By the third draft, she decided she was beginning to develop a good story and get the tone right.

Gwendolyn's rapid recovery slowed the day Harris returned. She spent most of the next week languishing on the chaise in her room, sharing tea with Alyssa and idling over her needlework. During the rambling conversations, Alyssa learned that the widow had two sisters, just as she had.

"I am the oldest, and I married very well," Gwendolyn said, smiling at memories she did not explain. Alyssa could imagine how the sisters felt; at least she knew how she felt, constantly having her sisters' success set before her.

"My sisters were so envious when Alistair and I wed," Gwendolyn continued with a nostalgic smile, "that they would not speak to me for days. But then they wanted to be in the wedding, so the silence did not last long. Since, they have done well for themselves, too. One married a banker like Papa, and the other married a London solicitor. But neither achieved my success."

Several times Harris appeared for tea, making time in a busy schedule to sit with them and talk of inconsequential things. Gwendolyn seemed to take strength from his visits. Alyssa warmed at the sight of him. Yet, she was so afraid that her feelings for him were obvious that she felt awkward and tongue-tied, even when he made every effort to include her in the conversation.

"There's much talk about the wedding these days," he began on his third appearance for tea that week. "I saw the vicar this morning, and he apologized for Mrs. Carbury and the girls not calling. They have been much occupied with the wedding arrangements."

"But, of course, it is set for this Saturday, is it not?" Gwendolyn said. Her color was glowing. She looked quite fit, though she was dressed in a black tea gown and was reclining on her chaise. "The Trevells must be represented," she added with a determined glance in Harris's direction. "You have accepted for us, have you not, Harris? I'm in mourning, but that should not keep you from attending."

"Yes, I accepted for the family," he said, stirring his tea thoughtfully.

"And, Alyssa, it is time for you to enjoy something amusing," Gwendolyn said. "Heavens, poor child, we've had nothing but mourning, pranks, and food riots since you have arrived. You must go to the wedding. Byron Littlefield will be there, will he not?" She directed the question to Harris.

The thought of meeting Byron again did not excite Alyssa much, but the opportunity to speak with his uncle, Sir Ralph, interested her. And the Carbury girls were delightful. Like Gwendolyn, she found herself looking to Harris for a response.

"I imagine Littlefield will be there," he said with a nod. There'd been a touch of a smile on his lips until Gwendolyn had mentioned Byron.

"Then, by all means, you must go, Alyssa," Gwendolyn urged with an indulgent smile and an airy wave of her hand. "Harris will take you. I am not up to the gaiety of a wedding yet. But you go. Dance. Be merry."

"Too true," Harris said, looking at her at last. The exhaustion of the all-night ride to and from Launceston was gone from his face. Today, even after a long morning of work, he was clean-shaven and energetic. His cravat was tied immaculately. His coat was pressed and his boots gleamed. The sight of him smiling at her made Alyssa's knees tremble, and the prospect of having him as an escort made her almost breathless.

"Alyssa deserves to get out and enjoy some festivities," he

said with a bemused smile. "I shall be delighted to be your escort to Lucy Carbury's wedding."

"Thank you, my lord." She smiled in return as casually as she could manage. He was to be her escort. She would have him to herself, alone, without Meggie or Gwendolyn. The prospect was more than she'd ever dreamed of. "It will be a pleasure and an honor to attend the wedding on your arm."

As she gazed into his countenance, she prayed her face did not betray the depth of her feelings for him, did not betray what she knew to be true. Even if he was too old for her, even if she would never be more to him than his ward, even if it was possible that he was a murderer, dear Lord, she loved him.

Seventeen

Lucy Carbury made a lovely bride. In a gown of white lawn with tiers of white lace at her shoulders and edging her skirt, she looked virtuous and vulnerable. As she stood beside her groom at the Lanissey Church altar, her dark hair lay glossy beneath a sheer white veil fastened in place with orange blossoms. What a lovely couple she and her groom made.

Alyssa smiled at the couple, happy for them. She was proud of herself for not weeping during the ceremony as she usually did. Weddings always made her cry, even her own sisters' ceremonies. She couldn't say why, exactly. This wedding was more touching than many she'd attended because the vicar, Lucy's father, presided over the ceremony. Otherwise, it was much like the ceremonies she'd attended at home in Boston or New York. A similar litany and vows, blessing, and bestowing of rings. Even during the organ music she remained dry-eyed. Even through the kiss at the back of the sanctuary she shed not a tear. Maybe it was those inquiring looks from Byron Littlefield across the aisle that helped her keep her emotions under control.

With the ceremony over, she and Harris were swept along with the small crowd that pressed into the little parish vestry. Overhead, the church bells tolled the happy occasion. On the table lay the parish record, open and ready to be signed.

Slowly and smug, the groom took the pen from the parish clerk, dipped it into the ink bottle, and set his signature in the book first, signing with a great flourish. He grinned and swaggered.

The crowd chuckled indulgently at his bravado.

"Here, hold this for me." Lucy shoved her bouquet into Alyssa's hands.

Young and delicate, Lucy solemnly took the pen from the clerk and leaned over the book. The sunlight poured through the window, engulfing her in a halo of bridal white. Her lips trembling and solemn, Lucy signed her maiden name beside her groom's with a steady, sure hand. Tears sprang into Alyssa's eyes without warning. In ink, Lucy promised herself to him for eternity. She entrusted him with all her future, with her world and her being. With her body and, in a fashion, even with her soul.

The pure courage of that, the faith in another, the trust in love, struck at Alyssa's heart. She stared at the signature in black ink written in the ledger. Somehow it seemed more binding than the words uttered at an altar. Words vanished into thin air, but this record, kept open to all to examine, was permanent. Writ for all time for any to witness.

That's when the tears she thought she'd escaped rolled down her cheeks. Women did it every day—gave their lives to the men they loved. She was very happy for Lucy. Her groom seemed a handsome and good-natured young man. And heaven knew Alyssa expected to make the same promise to a man one day. But the immensity, the audacity, of such a pledge touched and terrified her.

When Lucy had finished signing, she straightened and gave her groom a sweet, beatific smile. He kissed her soundly. The crowd in the little office applauded.

Lucy retrieved her bouquet, and her groom swept her out of the room.

"It's a happy occasion." Harris pressed a handkerchief in Alyssa's hand and murmured into her ear. "I will never understand why women cry at weddings."

"It's just so . . . so . . . " she stammered, stifling a sob and attempting to dry her eyes.

"I know," he said, putting a hand on the small of her back to guide her out of the office and toward the carriage. "Two lives being made one. It's so beautifully frightening."

She took a deep, steadying breath, surprised yet pleased that he understood. "Exactly."

He smiled at her as if there was more he would say, but the time was not right. "Let's go to the dance, shall we?"

In the carriage he would not be drawn into conversation beyond the most mundane comments about the event. The wedding celebration was held in the assembly rooms over the shops of the nearby village, across the market square from the vicarage. When they arrived, the street was already crowded with carriages and the rooms above were full and stuffy with revelers. The musicians were tuning up in one room, and the hired servants were setting out the supper in another.

The noise and the crowd didn't keep Byron from nearly accosting Alyssa when she reached the top of the stairs.

"Miss Lockhart, you will save a dance for me, will you not?" he asked before he saw Harris slightly behind her on the stairs. Uncertainty flashed across his face. "With his lordship's permission, of course."

"Littlefield." Harris offered a cool greeting as he took Alyssa's hand and placed it on his arm. She stared at his hand covering hers in surprise.

"My lord," Byron bowed. "It was a lovely wedding, was it not?"

"Indeed," Harris replied.

"A beautiful bride and a handsome groom," Alyssa said. "I would be pleased to dance with you, Mr. Littlefield, if his lordship agrees."

Harris inclined his head gravely. "But of course you may dance with Mr. Littlefield if you like."

Confused, Alyssa studied Harris for a moment. He seemed to be giving permission, while his possessive grasp on her arm appeared to deny it. "I'll agree to a dance with you on one condition, Byron."

Byron's face brightened as if he'd discovered the secret of pleasing her. "Anything, Miss Lockhart."

She leaned toward him without releasing Harris and spoke softly. "Dance with the bride's sister first."

"Edith?"

"Please, Mr. Littlefield," she said, glancing in Edith's direction.

Lucy's sister was standing on the edge of a crowd gathered around the bride and groom, a distant smile on her face, a posy clutched in her hand. Despite the noise and the gaiety, she looked quite lost.

"The maid of honor is very happy for her sister, I'm sure," Alyssa murmured to Byron. "But I suspect she's feeling a little eclipsed at the moment. A dance with a handsome man such as yourself would do a world of good for her spirits. Would you do that for me?"

"When you put it like that." Byron grinned with the pleasure of being flattered. "I'd be pleased to dance with the lady. She does look rather fetching today."

"Indeed, I thought so, too," Alyssa said. "Be sure to tell her so."

When Byron was gone, Harris, who'd witnessed the exchange, stepped to her side and smiled at her conspiratorially. "Very nice, Miss Lockhart. Your resourcefulness continues to impress me. I, too, shall dance with the maid of honor in due time."

"My lord," Alyssa smiled her acknowledgment. "That would be kind of you. And you might rescue me from Byron when the time comes," she added. After all, a girl could hope, she thought. "But first, shall we wish the bride and groom our best?"

Lucy and her groom accepted their wishes with smiles and thanks. In the crush of well-wishers, Alyssa and Harris were separated. Mrs. Carbury took up the duty of introducing

Alyssa to other Trevell neighbors and fellow congregation members in attendance.

Alyssa answered the usual questions about her visit with ease now, smiling and working her way through the crowd. The wedding entertainment seemed to be much the same as that at any ball. Eventually she managed to find her way from the dance floor into the card room, where she found Sir Ralph and Lady Cynthia.

Harris was already at another table. He was playing with businessmen and fellow former army officers, she judged from their conversation as she passed. She overheard some talk about the unrest with the miners, but no one seemed inclined to discuss the topic. She didn't linger to hear more

The Littlefields, her quarry though they did not know it, were at a table of gentry, ladies and gentlemen. She greeted Sir Ralph and Lady Cynthia and insinuated herself at their table. The play, a game of Casino, was rather dispirited. She would have found it boring if she were not intent on observing the Littlefields. Sir Ralph played indifferently, to pass the time rather than to win the game. Lady Cynthia had more skill, but she seemed distracted and bored.

Alyssa continued to play as the others left, one by one, to join the dancing or to find refreshment. Finally her patience was rewarded, and she was alone with Sir Ralph and Lady Cynthia. He seemed to have little interest in dancing and devoted his attention to having the waiter fill his cup regularly. Lady Cynthia seemed to be reluctant to leave him.

"Shall we play a game of Loo?" Alyssa asked, shuffling the cards. She had suggested the easy card game so she could concentrate on her goal without seeming obvious. She'd hoped to talk with Sir Ralph without Lady Cynthia present—he was one suspect on her list whom she'd had little conversation with—but perhaps this was best. Introducing the topic of the fateful night at Penridge Hall would seem less obvious with Lady Cynthia there.

"If the game suits you, Miss Lockhart," Sir Ralph said with

a shrug of indifference. "As you might guess, I'm not much of a man for the dance floor."

"Yes, let's do play Loo," Lady Cynthia said, as if embarrassed by her husband's comment.

"It has been a lovely wedding," Alyssa began as she dealt the cards. "I regret that Lady Penridge can't be here to enjoy it—and Master Alistair, too."

Lady Cynthia hesitated as she sorted through her cards. She glanced uneasily at her husband. "Yes, a shame. The late lord's death was such a shock. Now poor Gwendolyn is left alone with a child to raise."

"Yes, unfortunate for Lady Penridge," Sir Ralph said, playing a weak card. He was sinking rapidly into his cups. His speech was slurred, and his card skills were gone. "But Alistair Trevell, the devil take him, had little interest in weddings and such. He'd have made an appearance, then left Gwendolyn to represent him. Go off to count his money or whatever other diversion he'd found for himself."

"Did Master Alistair have some other pastimes?" she asked innocently, taking her turn to play a card.

"He fancied bird-watching," Lady Cynthia offered, glancing uneasily at her husband again. Alyssa sensed the lady would have changed the subject if she could.

Bird-watching sounded so unlike the reputedly tyrannical Alistair Trevell that Alyssa had heard about, she almost laughed. "Bird-watching?"

"A sly one, Alistair Trevell," Sir Ralph said, giving up another trick. He turned to his wife. "Think that's what he told Lady Penridge? That he was out bird-watching?"

Lady Cynthia sat stiff and silent.

"That must have been a terrible night for all of you," Alyssa persisted when the lady said nothing. "The night when Master Alistair fell ill, I mean."

"A dark night, indeed," Sir Ralph said with an ironic laugh. "Lady Cynthia and I went home and waited to see which one of us took sick next. I thought I was a goner, but nary a twinge in the belly. I would gladly reward the little whelk that brought Trevell to his demise if the little bugger was around to accept it."

Lady Cynthia paled. She glanced at Alyssa and then across the room toward Harris's table, fearful that her husband had been overheard.

Abruptly rising, she said, "Excuse me, I really must freshen up. Would you care to do the same, Miss Lockhart? I can show you the way to the ladies' room."

"Yes, I would like that." Alyssa took the hint and followed the lady. She wasn't certain what Lady Cynthia was up to this time, but Sir Ralph was too drunk for her to rely on anything he said. "Thank you for the game, Sir Ralph."

She allowed Lady Cynthia to lead the way. Once they were alone in the room set aside for the ladies to put their cloaks and repair their toilet, she touched Alyssa's hand.

"Do forgive him," Lady Cynthia said. "This past year has been a difficult one for him."

"It's a wedding celebration," Alyssa said, purposely misunderstanding the lady's meaning. "Everyone is entitled to enjoy himself or herself."

"I mean what he said about the late Lord Penridge," Lady Cynthia said.

To Alyssa's surprise, tears gathered in the lady's eyes.

"You see, the past year has been such an ordeal." Lady Cynthia sobbed. "Alistair's death and all the suspicion. The rumors of murder. You've heard them no doubt. It's been so difficult to live with."

"Yes, I'm sure it has been," Alyssa said, wondering what it was that Lady Cynthia truly had to tell her. "But the grief fades. Things will get better."

"No, they are worse than ever," Lady Cynthia said, more tears threatening. "My husband will hardly allow me out of his sight. You think I *like* to sit in the card room and play cards while there is dancing and laughter in the next room? This is the price a woman pays when she betrays her husband."

"Betrays . . ."

"I was a fool," Lady Cynthia hissed. "I loved him, at least I thought I did. I believed he loved me. But he used me."

"Who?" Alyssa asked, even as the answer was dawning. But she had to hear the name from Lady Cynthia to be certain there was no mistake.

"Alistair, of course," Lady Cynthia said, nearly sobbing out his name. "No one knows. Not even Byron. Do not speak of it to anyone. But I must tell someone, another woman. I am so ashamed of what this has done to Lady Penridge. Of course, Alistair and I never saw each other alone again after Ralph discovered us. I knew we dared not. I had never seen Ralph so furious. I thought he might throttle Alistair there in the bedchamber."

Alyssa handed the lady a hand towel while her imagination conjured up a lewd scene between the cuckold husband and the adulterous couple. A darkened room, a tangle of bed sheets, and nakedness. Men glaring at each other, murder in their eyes, their faces twisted in fury. Loathing heavy in the air, especially after the bad business deal.

"You and Alistair were . . . lovers?" Alyssa managed to say aloud. "When did your husband discover this?"

"Only a week before Harris returned," Lady Cynthia continued, gazing off distractedly at nothing. "In that moment of discovery, his anger was so great he might have done murder. But since then, he has cooled. It is I who have suffered. I have not been free since that day. Perhaps I do not deserve to be. Now he goes everywhere I go. Or I must go everywhere he goes."

"And you are certain no one knows?" Alyssa asked.

Lady Cynthia nodded, took a gulp of air, and blew her nose into the hand towel. "He hates me now. If anyone were to die at my husband's hand, it would be me."

Beyond the ladies' room door the musicians began a lively country dance. Voices rose in laughter, and feet shuffled on the dance floor.

Alyssa stared at the lady whose shoulders shook as she wept into the hand towel. Poor thing—she was remorseful and despairing, trapped in a hateful marriage while in the next room a new marriage was being celebrated.

Compassionately, Alyssa stroked the lady's arm. So Sir Ralph had more than one reason to hate the late Alistair, Lord Penridge. More than one reason to commit murder. And the timing made more sense. If Sir Ralph were going to have murdered over disputed property, he would have done it long ago.

Dabbing away her tears, Lady Cynthia seemed to have a second thought. Her tears vanished, and she seized Alyssa's hand. "I should not have burdened you with this secret, but I don't want you to become too involved with the Trevells. They do only what serves their purposes. Alistair married Gwendolyn for her money, you know. He did not truly care for me, either. And once caught, he was a coward," Lady Cynthia said, speaking too rapidly to be convincing now. "Sir Ralph would have called his lordship out, as he said. It is still done these days, you know, dueling, though it is against the law. Alistair probably would have never appeared on the field. Sir Ralph's remedy has been to keep me under his thumb. He is not violent. He is not cruel. He is not a murderer. If anyone says so, they are wrong. You believe me, do you not?"

Alyssa nodded slowly, sadly. It was perfectly clear that Lady Cynthia *wanted* Sir Ralph to be innocent, but did the lady truly *believe* her husband was guiltless?

"I've come to claim my dance," Byron said, bowing to Alyssa.

She'd just stepped out of the ladies' room with Lady Cynthia, who had dried her eyes and was joining her husband in the card room. Alyssa's head was buzzing with what she'd learned. But here was Byron, requesting the dance she'd promised—just when she wanted desperately to sit and think.

"I danced with Edith, as you asked," he said. "Several times, in fact. Lord Penridge danced with her once, too. Now, you and I must dance."

Alyssa glanced around the room looking for Harris, glad to know that he'd danced with Edith, but she did not see him among the onlookers.

"I'm afraid I don't—" she began, glancing at the line of couples that was forming on the floor. She'd never been a success at a dance. Her hair was too red and her height too great for young men to press her for a turn on the floor. She loved music, but she knew few steps beyond the polka and the waltz. She hadn't even learned the wild steps to the new ragtime music that some of the girls at Blandfield School were so excited about.

"You know this dance," Byron said, grabbing her hands and pulling her toward the dancers. "I believe you colonists call it the Carolina reel, or some such?"

"Virginia reel," Alyssa corrected with a laugh as the music began. "Yes, I know it."

"Then this is my dance." Byron drew her out onto the dance floor to join the others. She looked around, hoping that Harris was near. Now was the time for him to rescue her, but he was nowhere in sight. He was probably still in the card room.

She turned to Byron. There was nothing to do but dance. As the steps came back to her, she moved about the floor with less conscious effort. Conversation was impossible during the lively dance, but that could not keep her thoughts from turning back to what Lady Cynthia had told her.

She'd said that no one but Sir Ralph knew of the affair. But what if that weren't true? What if Byron knew? Or the Reverend Whittle? The bride and groom skipping down the center of the dancing couples interrupted her speculation. When it was their turn, she and Byron followed. As she parted from Byron at the end of the row, she swung around to see Harris watching her, a cool, polite mask on his face.

What if Harris knew of the affair?

That's when she noticed that Lady Cynthia was hanging on his arm, smiling, apparently pleased to be watching her and Byron. Behind them, Sir Ralph swayed unsteadily, his color high and his eyes bloodshot from drink. The sight of the Littlefields and Harris together almost made Alyssa trip over her own feet. One of the gentlemen in the line reached out to steady her.

She thanked him and moved on with the music. Harris never came to her rescue.

Eighteen

Nor did he rescue her when a waltz began and Byron whisked her away in his arms again. In fact, to her disappointment, she and Harris never danced.

"It was very nice of you to dance with Edith," she ventured later that evening as they rode home in the dark carriage. Elijah had not lit the inside lamp and Harris seemed to find no reason to do so. The darkness gave her courage.

"She is a charming girl." He sat across from her with his back toward the driver's box and his face shadowed so Alyssa was unable to read his expression. "You were right. She was feeling quite happy for her sister, but neglected," he added.

"I had hoped that you and I might take a turn around the floor," Alyssa ventured, nearly blushing at her forwardness, though she couldn't imagine why. She'd already asked this man if he was a murderer. Why shouldn't she ask him about a dance?

"I know you did," he said, his tone quiet and even. "But this was the opportunity for you to meet new young men, not waste a dance with your guardian."

"I see, yes, of course," she said, feeling let down and strangely annoyed. "Was I successful?"

"Yes, indeed, you were," he said with no variation in his tone. "Quite."

So the next day, Sunday, after church, when Byron sidled up to her and asked if she cared to go horseback riding on Monday, she accepted—right in front of Harris. Why shouldn't she ride with Byron? Harris only rode with her when she trapped him at the breakfast table. She was not going to spend her stay at Penridge riding with Johnnie following in her wake.

Later, at Sunday dinner, Gwendolyn insisted on hearing the details of the ceremony and the wedding celebration. Alyssa did her best to recount it all, except for Lady Cynthia's confession. Harris listened, having little to add. As she told Gwendolyn about who danced with whom, she couldn't help but wonder how much Harris knew about Lady Cynthia and Alistair's affair.

Monday proved a busy morning with a call from Mr. Nigel Hawthorne, the gentleman who'd saved her from tripping during the reel. He asked if she'd go for a drive with him one day. She agreed, surprised and pleased to find that after one appearance at a wedding dance, she'd become such a center of attention.

As soon as Mr. Hawthorne left, she retired to the library to study her list of murder suspects. Eager to note Sir Ralph's additional motive for wanting Alistair dead, she wrote it out and sat back, hoping some new revelation would jump out at her. None came but the obvious. Sir Ralph had two solid reasons to commit murder—fraud and infidelity.

"Did you do it, Sir Ralph?" she murmured aloud. "And if so, how?"

Alyssa stared out the library window, trying to imagine the scene that night around the dining room table. Sir Ralph would have been seated near Gwendolyn, his hostess. He could hardly have jumped up, run to Alistair's end of the table, and sprinkled poison on his host's food.

As she was staring out the window, she saw Captain Dundry ride through the fairy gate at a businesslike pace and enter the entrance leading to Harris's study. Curious. What was he doing back at Penridge?

"Who are you, really, Captain Dundry?" she whispered to herself, peering closer at him. He certainly didn't dress like gentry. If he was Harris's friend, he was apparently not the sort one invited to luncheon or tea. She'd seen him call one other time since their first meeting, but he'd never joined them later in the receiving room or the dining room.

She wondered what Gwendolyn knew about the man.

"I must remember to ask," she muttered. "Discreetly, of course."

She returned to her list. Annoying thoughts of Harris continued to plague her as she worked. Why hadn't he danced with her? She reminded herself that he was her guardian; she was his ward. Like her parents, his goal was to see her properly chaperoned until she was eventually wed.

She must have been mad to think there was any more than that to their relationship—to think she'd seen relief in his face the first time she'd refused Byron's invitation to go horseback riding and thought that . . . well, that he might be jealous. She must have lost her senses ever to have thought their kiss had meant anything. Or to have thought that there was anything significant in his escorting her to the wedding beyond a polite host offering his guest the opportunity to meet potential suitors.

Harris was no doubt in agreement with Gwendolyn about pairing her off with Byron. The whole situation made her want to scream, which would serve no purpose. Screeching herself hoarse would not win Harris nor help her find the truth about Alistair's death. So she would ride the current for now, she decided, a tactic she'd found useful at home. Sometimes creating a storm gained one less advantage than biding one's time.

"Gadzooks, but you look fine, Miss Lockhart," Byron blurted when she greeted him in the receiving room later that afternoon. She was dressed in her best dark blue riding habit and had requested that Smuggler be saddled. Byron did not keep her waiting. He rode up to Penridge exactly on time.

The sincere pleasure on his face when he laid eyes on her lent veracity to his words. He wasn't just flattering her. He was genuinely pleased that she had accepted his invitation to go riding.

She smiled at the enthusiasm of his compliment. She'd taken special pains to look her best, and it was nice to be appreciated. "Thank you, Mr. Littlefield. It's very good of you to say so."

"I say, could we get on to Christian names?" he said, offering his arm to escort her out to the horses. "Please call me Byron. My mother named me after the poet himself, Lord Byron."

"Of course, one of my favorites," she said, continuing to smile at him. What was the point of keeping the poor boy at arm's length? He was nice enough. It wasn't his fault that he would never be the man she wanted to spend her life with. "My mother named me Alyssa. It's a lofty form of Alice, I think."

"I thought it was for the flower," he said, looking puzzled. "Alyssum.'"

"I hadn't thought of that, but I'm sure you're right," she said, flattered again and annoyed with herself for being so dour. "I'd much rather be named for a flower."

They laughed over their inane conversation. She was going to enjoy herself today, she decided. Johnnie was waiting for them with Smuggler and his rawboned old mount. Byron had also brought along a groom.

When she saw Johnnie's horse and he came forward to give her a leg up onto Smuggler, Alyssa protested that they did not need his help.

He shrugged. "His lordship's orders, Miss Lockhart," was all the boy would say.

"Well enough," Byron said cheerfully. "The boy can keep my groom company."

She fumed in silence. She could not say why, but Harris's interference annoyed her.

So they set out on a pleasantly clear November afternoon, with a light, cool breeze blowing at their backs and two grooms following them.

They rode slowly, talking all the time about the wedding and the newlyweds' plans to honeymoon in Brighton. Then they moved on to other topics such as the lack of a quality tailor in the village and the novelty of Byron's uncle's plans to install a telephone at the manor house.

Alyssa did not recognize the paths they took, but it wasn't long before she could hear the rhythmic swell of the ocean and smell the salt air. Then they rode over the crest of a hill and there it was, the sea, dark blue and glittering in the late afternoon sunlight. Gulls soared overhead, their cries just audible over the wind. The rugged coast stretched below them, then away toward the east and the west, dotted with tiny, rocky islands and reefs. It was easy to see why the Cornish coast was so treacherous to shipping

"Do you like it?" Byron asked. She could feel his gaze on her.

"It's beautiful," she said, trying to take it all in, to soak up the beauty of it and save it to savor another time.

"I find it a rather desolate part of the world," Byron said, obviously mystified by her interest. "And to think this is where I find my inheritance."

"But the desolation is the beauty of the place," she said, studying the coastline. "It builds such character in its people: independent, hardy, stoic, and oddly spiritual."

"Spiritual?" Byron repeated in disbelief. "Those Cornish miners? They are ignorant, stubborn, recalcitrant, and sullen."

"You'll find a chapel around every corner, by a spring or built on an outcrop, named for one Celtic saint after another," she said, amazed that he had not noticed. "Indeed, spiritual. I find it rather awe-inspiring."

"That is true about the saints," Byron had to agree, but otherwise he remained clearly mystified by her observation.

She took the opportunity to ask some oblique questions

about Sir Ralph and Lady Cynthia. Byron seemed to like his aunt and uncle well enough. They had no children. He would inherit their fortune and estate. It was Cornwall he was not fond of. He seemed intent on avoiding the topic of the late Lord Penridge's premature death. Out of concern for her feelings, she supposed. She'd been rather stern with him about the topic that day in the churchyard when he'd been intent on slandering Alistair's name. Today he was at first reluctant to talk about that fateful evening, but eventually she was able to draw him into the discussion.

"Of course, I knew Uncle Ralph's feelings over the land and the clay mine business," Byron said as they rode along the cliff-top bridle path. "He'd ranted on about it to me many times, though most of his dealings had transpired five years ago. Reminded me constantly how important it was to my future inheritance."

"And Lady Cynthia," she asked. "Did he talk of it in front of her?"

Byron looked surprised. "A bit. But my uncle is a gentleman. He doesn't talk business in the presence of ladies."

"Of course," she said. "What was it like, that night around the dinner table when Lord Penridge took sick?"

"Dashed uncomfortable, it was," Byron said, looking off into the distance as he recalled the memory. "Lord Penridge said little. Poor Aunt Cynthia sat next to him, hardly knowing what to say. The dinner was the vicar's idea, you know, his and Colonel Trevell's. She was near tears by the end of the evening."

That observation hardly surprised Alyssa. "And your uncle?"

"Uncle Ralph had the easier role, seated beside Lady Penridge," Byron said. "Such a gracious lady. One can hardly blame her for what her husband did. Vicar Carbury and the colonel did most of the talking, them and Miss Lucy and Miss Edith. No business was discussed at the table out of respect to the ladies."

"Did any of the guests at the table get up and move around?" she asked.

"No, Pendeen and that Whittle fellow, the reverend's brother, did the serving," Byron said.

"When the ladies withdrew," she prompted, "and the men began to talk business."

"Oh, no. Things never went that far," Byron said. "Lord Penridge, the late one, stood up and said he was feeling unwell. Uncle wasn't excited about the business anyway. We left immediately. I say, you're not going to bother your pretty head over this, are you? It's all said and done."

Alyssa agreed and turned the discussion back to the scenery. But she had a better picture in her mind now about what had happened on that night almost four months ago.

By the time they returned to Penridge, it was a bit later than they'd intended. They'd become comfortable in each other's company. The afternoon shadows had grown long and the air was cooling. The dark winter night was about to settle in. But the afternoon had been so agreeable, Alyssa couldn't resist lingering on the front step after Byron had helped her dismount.

"May I call again?" Byron asked, his usual overconfidence suddenly subdued. He was standing on the step below her, their faces on the same level. Johnnie had led Smuggler away, and Byron had sent the Littlefield groom home ahead of him. They were quite alone.

"Yes," Alyssa said, suddenly grateful for his friendship and ashamed of herself for avoiding him. He really wasn't bad company. "I'd like that."

"Capital!" He grinned, his gaze still intent on her face, his hat tucked under his arm. He hesitated, making no move to leave. Waiting . . . for what? Was there some British custom in bidding farewell to a caller that she did not know?

Astonished, she realized he was hoping for a kiss. She didn't know how she knew because it had not happened to her before. No young gentleman had ever offered the least indication that he wanted a kiss from her.

She was so flattered that she leaned forward and placed a friendly kiss on his lips.

Byron sucked in a breath of surprise. "Sweet, but too brief," he complained with a bashful smile that astonished her after all his blustering confidence.

She laughed and backed away. "Good day, Byron. Thank you for a most enjoyable afternoon."

He grinned good-naturedly. "I'll be prepared next time."

Tavi opened the door. Alyssa offered Byron a wave and went inside.

She nearly skipped through the house to the stairway and had just reached the landing when she heard Tavi calling to her.

"Miss Lockhart?" The butler stood at the foot of the stairs, gazing up at her.

She halted, her hat in her hand. "What is it?"

"His lordship wishes to see you in his study," Tavi said.

"Now?" she asked. She was eager to change out of her dusty, horsy-smelling clothes.

"He would like to speak to you at your earliest convenience," Tavi said.

"I'll be there as soon as I've changed." She continued upstairs, wondering what Harris could possibly want to talk to her about. She changed quickly, tidied her hair, and returned downstairs.

The study door was standing open when she arrived. A lamp glowed on the desk and a fire burned on the hearth, as if Harris had just stepped out for a moment. She thought about ringing for Tavi, but decided against it. Why trouble the butler when Harris must be nearby and would return any time?

Walking into the room, she was once again intrigued by the chaos of riches stacked everywhere and pleasantly lulled by the scent of spices. The mahogany medicine chest that had set on the tea table was gone, but the brass urn was still there. Guiltily, she glanced at the bookshelf behind Harris desk. The lewd book she'd borrowed was in its place. She was glad of that. She hoped Harris had never realized she'd borrowed it.

Rolled, fringed carpets stood in the corner. The ebony and ivory carvings sat on the mantel. At the side of the fireplace she noted for the first time a cricket bat.

The sight gave her an unexpected vision of Harris. A young man on the cricket field or pitch or whatever they called it. Her knowledge of the game was lacking. But she'd always envisioned him in a military uniform, sober, stiff, commanding, not as a boy intent on swinging a bat or throwing a ball.

On the sofa still lay the tiger skin and the blue-and-gold silk Harris had draped around her as a *sari* only two weeks ago. In truth, she didn't think it had been moved since she had unwrapped herself from it with Tavi glaring at her. Just thinking of that moment brought back the magic silkiness of the fabric against her skin, the warmth of Harris's breath against her ear, the burning as his hand spread across her belly as he worked the silk into pleats.

Suddenly she yearned to touch the silk again. She started toward the sofa. Stroke it was all she wanted to do, savor the smoothness and admire the rich color again.

She picked up the silk. It unfurled almost like a living thing, billowing and surging lightly against the air. Fascinated with the play of the color and the glitter of the gold, she held it up to her cheek again and turned toward the polished brass urn to catch her reflection. It was so beautiful. How was it Harris had made it cling to her? It began with pleats across the front. How many? Seven?

She pleated the fabric until it looked like she remembered it in Harris's large, capable hands; then she tucked it into the waist of her skirt. Next she wrapped it around her hips again and up over her shoulder—so graceful and simple. She admired herself in the urn. Since her last wearing of the silk, she'd stopped dressing her hair in fussy curls on the top of her head. Instead she'd begun to draw it back into a simple bun at her nape. The style suited her, classic and elegant. The simplicity of her red tresses smoothed back did more to make her look mature than all those curls had. The style suited the *sari*, too. All she needed were pearls to dangle from her earlobes and she would indeed be a seductive, exotic beauty.

Behind her someone cleared his throat.

She froze.

"His lordship is on his way," Tavi said.

She turned slowly. The hint of a frown marred the butler's usually bland face. She felt like a little girl caught trying on her mother's clothes without permission. "I'll wait for him," she said, trying to act as if nothing was amiss, which meant she had to resist the urge to shed the silk as fast as she could. "The study door was standing open, and I saw the beautiful fabric."

"And dressed yourself in the native costume of India?" Tavi asked. He never raised a brow, but he might as well have. She could hear the mockery in his voice.

"Yes, well, I was just passing the time while I waited." She rearranged the fabric on her shoulder. She felt like a fool but she would not give him the satisfaction of knowing that. "Will his lordship be much longer?"

"Not much longer at all," Harris said, striding into the room. He stopped just inside the door and appraised her from head to toe. She faced him, hoping he wouldn't mind that she'd decided to try the silk again. His expression was harsh. "I was just looking at one of the carriage horses with Elijah," he said, walking around her, his gaze glued to her. "It seems to have pulled a tendon. Nothing serious. You may go, Tavi. And leave the door open."

The butler put his hands together and bowed out of the room.

"So, the blue-and-gold silk is your favorite," Harris said, stepping back a pace.

"I'm sorry," Alyssa said, eager to explain herself. "I was trying to remember how you, well—"

"Nothing to apologize for." Harris stopped in front of her, his gaze still locked on the blue silk clinging to her gown. "It suits you well."

She blushed and reached for the fabric on her shoulder.

"No, don't," he said, catching her hand before she could pull it away.

His hand was cold from being out-of-doors, but the strength and urgency in his touch was undeniable. She released the silk and found herself staring up into his face.

"Wear it, if you like," he said, his eyes dark and intent. Abruptly, he turned away, went to the door, and closed it.

A closed door was a bad sign. She took a deep, shaky breath, trying to forget the force of his touch, the heat that it had sent through her that had nothing to do with temperature. Taking a deep breath to steady herself, she said, "Tavi said you wanted to speak to me."

Harris took up his usual position behind his desk and said in a voice so low it almost sounded like a growl, "Yes, I have a question for you."

She was in trouble, no doubt about it. She knew all the signs, though she didn't have a clue what this was about. Straightening her back and lifting her chin, she asked, "Yes, my lord, what do you want to know?"

"What in heaven's name did you think you were doing out there on the front step with Byron Littlefield?" he demanded.

Nineteen

"Thanking him for the horseback ride," she said, surprised by the question. It had never occurred to her that someone might be watching her kiss Byron on the front step. Still, they had nothing to hide. "You were there at Sunday church when he invited me. It was a very pleasant ride."

"And for that you kissed him?" he demanded, glowering at her. "A 'thank-you' is sufficient, or do you kiss every gentleman you go riding with?"

"Certainly not," she said, astonished by his reaction to so innocent an act—and affronted by his implication. "Merely a friendly kiss. Almost sisterly. He proved a congenial companion. It was hardly like the one you and I—"

"Do not speak of that," Harris snapped, holding a hand up to silence her. "It has been brought to my attention that Mr. Byron Littlefield is a wastrel, a gambler, and a ne'er-do-well. He is hardly worthy of you, and you would do well to make note of it."

"But I thought you wanted me to see him," she said, irritated, confused, and hurt by his disapproval. "You and Gwendolyn. Matchmaking. Wasn't that the purpose of the tea in the garden and the Sunday dinner and my attendance at the wedding? You said as much in the carriage."

"Seeing him is one thing," Harris said, the anger in his voice receding a bit. "Kissing him is quite another. That should be plain enough."

She stared at him. It wasn't plain at all. One moment he

was practically pushing her into Byron's arms to dance. The next he was berating her for kissing the boy.

Harris studied her. Another thought seemed to occur to him. His frown suddenly deepened. "Has he declared for you? Is that why you two kissed?"

"What?" she stammered, almost panicking. "Byron and me? It was just a little kiss! A flirtation. Nobody declared anything. No promises were made except that I said I'd see him again."

"Nothing more?" He leaned forward, his hands resting on his desk, his voice full of urgency. "You're certain? I would have some explaining to do to your father if that happened."

"So that's what this was all about." In frustration Alyssa huffed and flapped her arms against her sides. "You're concerned about what to tell my parents? I don't know what Papa told you, but I had the distinct impression that he and Mama would be delighted if, God forbid, something developed between someone like Byron and me."

"Well, I *would not* be delighted," Harris snapped. As the possessiveness of his words echoed in the room, he straightened. He clearly did not like the sound of them. After a long pause, he began to pace in front of the hearth. When he spoke again, his voice was softer. "I forbid you to see Littlefield because, as I said, he is not worthy of you."

Intrigued, she blinked. "And what of Nigel Hawthorne? May I see him?"

"Who?"

"Nigel Hawthorne," she repeated. "I met him at the wedding. He called this morning and asked me to go driving with him next week."

"Hawthorne?" Harris nearly laughed. "Squire Chauncey's son? Nice enough chap, I suppose. But the boy doesn't have a penny to his name. No, you may not see Nigel Hawthorne."

"He may have no fortune, but I *am* quite well provided for," she said, her annoyance and her curiosity growing. "If Papa has not instructed otherwise, there should be no impediment to Nigel and me taking an interest in each other unless," she paused, wondering if she dare utter what had come to her mind. "Unless there is some other reason, such as you being jealous."

"Jealous? Me?" Harris swung around and stared at her, his head down, his gaze intent, and his lips thinned. She wasn't certain whether he was outraged or dumbfounded.

She drew in a quick breath and went on. "Well, jealousy is one explanation for how you are behaving. Of course the other explanation would be some edict from Papa."

There was no mistaking his anger when he spoke. "I received no instructions from your father. I am simply doing my best to protect your reputation and welfare."

She blushed and turned away, ashamed of her petulance and painfully aware that he had neither confirmed nor denied her accusation of jealousy.

"New information has come to light about one of the gentlemen we are discussing and the other simply is not your social equal," he said without looking at her this time. "As you are a guest in my house, I must ask you to comply with my advice regarding these young men."

"Well, then," she began, finally brave enough to glance at him. When he met her gaze she was startled to see a flicker of uncertainty in his eyes, almost as if he thought she might not believe him or he'd not told her everything. "If I am to cancel my appointments with Byron and Nigel," she continued, "I'd best get out of this silk so I can write them."

"Looking down at the rich fabric still draped around her, she reached over her shoulder to begin to unwrap herself.

Harris moved to her side, covering her hand with his. "Let me help you."

She froze. The warmth of his palm covering her fingers flooded through her. She knew she should refuse his help, but she could not.

"Yes," she whispered, turning her back to him as she had when he'd first shown her how to drape the garment.

He slipped an arm around her waist and drew her close against him, pressing her against his groin. This time even through the silk, her skirt, and petticoats, she could feel the solid length of him against her. She released a shaky sigh.

He reached around in front of her with his other hand and tugged on the silk so that it fell away from her breasts. He was so close now, his mouth was against her temple. Her breathing became quick and shallow. He pulled the fabric from between them and held it out in front of her. The pleats remained tucked into her skirt.

She reached to pull them free, but he stayed her hand.

"No, let me," he murmured, his breath hot against her ear. He pulled back the portion of her bodice that overlapped her skirt and began to tug on the pleated silk. "From that first day when you arrived, I wanted to do the best thing for you. I told myself the desire came from my sense of honor and responsibility, but I cannot claim that now. I watched you every day—horseback riding, across the dinner table, and with Meggie when she was here, making a friend of a little girl who wanted to be your enemy, and I knew there was more to my feelings."

All she could do was lean against him in the circle of his arms, allowing his fingers to gently free the silk, pleat by pleat, from her skirt waist. With each pleat freed, he bestowed a kiss on her neck. When he'd reached the seventh one and there were no more, she almost whimpered her disappointment.

He threw the fabric aside. It billowed, then floated to the floor as she made a move to step free of his embrace.

"No, don't go," he said, an appeal. He placed a hand across her middle, fingers spread over her skirt and up beneath her bodice. He held her against him. Even through her stays she could feel the heat of his touch.

"Alyssa, do you see the impossible situation we are in? I'm supposed to protect you, yet I see you every day, I hear your voice, watch you do a thousand little things and I want to touch you, to hold you close—to take complete advantage of your sweet vulnerability."

"What about what I want?" she asked, closing her eyes as she reached upward to slip her hand around his neck to encourage him to bestow more kisses.

He did. At the same time, he began to unbutton her bodice. "Tell me what you want."

"You," she whispered.

Button by button, she watched his fingers work their way up the front of her bodice, mesmerized by their deftness. Kiss by kiss along her neck, he stole her good sense, leaving her weak and helpless, needy and pliant. She stood in his embrace, her bottom against his thighs, willing to watch his hands bring pleasure to her.

As soon as the buttons were unfastened, he covered her breasts, his palms firm against her nipples, his fingers cupping her. Only the silk of her camisole lay between them. She realized how hard and sensitive her breasts had become. Massaging her, he kissed her ear and whispered her name. She closed her eyes, giving herself to the melting sensations his embrace brought, to the liquid heat flowing through her.

He released her, placing his hands on her shoulders and slowly turning her to face him. She gazed up into his face, uncertain of what to do.

"Are you frightened?" he whispered. "Do you want to leave?"

She shook her head emphatically. "I want you to kiss me like you did in the stable."

"I want to do more than kiss you," Harris said, his gaze traveling along her throat and to her breasts covered only by her silk camisole. "Do you understand that?"

"Yes, oh, yes, I do," she whispered, vague images of the men and women in the naughty book playing through her mind. "Touch me," she whispered, eager to know the feel of his hand against her skin again. "Kiss me. Touch me more, and I'll want what you want."

He bent to kiss her—on the lips this time, his hands slipping beneath the fabric of her bodice, slipping it off over her shoulders and along her arms. Then all she knew was that his tongue was tasting her. She wrapped her arms around his neck and tasted him in return, opening wide to him, teasing him with her tongue as he teased her.

He gave a low moan, sat back against the desk, and pulled her between his thighs. They broke apart from the kiss only long enough for her to realize that her bodice was gone and that her skirt and petticoats had slipped down around her ankles. She was pressed between his legs, wearing only her silk camisole, stays, laced-edged drawers, and stockings. Instead of being shocked at her own dishabille, she spread her hands on his hard thighs and gazed up into his face. Still she could not get enough of the heat from his body.

"We're not stopping here, are we?" she asked daringly.

"No, we're not," he said, his hands slipping over her derriere and pressing her against him even more intimately. She knew that the male part of his body was swollen and as eager for her as her body was for him.

He bent to kiss her again, this time his hands moving to the fastenings of her stays. The release of each hook brought her body tingling to life and only made her more eager for the satisfaction of his touch. At last the restrictive garment dropped to the floor. His hands roamed her body freely, stroking through the silk, and molding to her waist, her bottom, along her arms, and up to cup her aching breasts once more.

He teased her nipples with his thumbs. She moaned with pleasure this time.

He pressed his face against her throat and continued the sweet torture. She slipped her arms inside his coat and clung to him, feeling the hard cords of his back beneath her hands.

"I knew you were passionate, my sweet," he whispered, his clever hands working through her silken underclothing, stroking, pressing, rolling her against the pads of his thumbs.

She closed her eyes. She'd never known such sweet powerful sensations—feelings that left her weak and aching with need for him.

His mouth moved to her shoulder and his hands to her waist, seeking the tapes. Suddenly her camisole and her drawers were slipping off of her.

"Over here, my sweet, red-haired Alyssa," he said, gathering her in his arms and leading her toward the sofa.

When she sat down as he urged her to do, he knelt and began to strip off her stockings, his hands as warm and sure as they'd been the night he'd examined her feet for nettles.

"Lie back," he directed gently as he finished with her stockings. He rubbed his hands up and down her calf a few times. Then he stood and stepped back from the sofa, gazing at her, his eyes dark and intent. He began to strip off his coat, waistcoat, and cravat. All the time he was undressing, he studied her. "You are so beautiful, sit back. Let my eyes feast on all of you."

She did as he asked, watching him, understanding at last how mutual a man and woman's desire was, just as the book had pictured it. Regardless of all the things her mother had told her about a wife's duty, when one loved, there was nothing too indelicate to do for her beloved.

As he bared his chest, she drew a sharp breath, eyeing the band of muscles down his torso and the contours of his arms as he shrugged out of his shirt.

When he reached for the buttons of his trousers, she reclined, raising her hands above her head, lifting her breasts and giving him full view of them.

He stepped out of his trousers, clearly prepared to make love—powerful and glorious, narrow hips, strong thighs, shapely calves. And an aroused male member that would have been the envy of every man in the naughty book.

"You are beautiful, too," she said, smiling.

"I'm glad you think so," he said, stepping closer. "Now show me all your loveliness."

She might be a virgin, but she knew exactly what he was asking her to do. His half smile, so approving and loving, gave her the courage and the freedom to open to him, offering herself.

He poised on one knee at the far end of the sofa, his intention blatantly throbbing with desire, his appraisal of her bold. She liked being studied with such ardor gleaming in his eyes. She stirred in an obvious invitation to him.

In a swift move, he snagged a petticoat from the floor and slipped it beneath her.

"I would prefer not to explain stains to the servants," he said, bending over her to kiss the inside of her thigh.

She closed her eyes and savored the warmth of his lips. She wasn't entirely certain what he meant by the remark about the stains, but she trusted him.

Then he was kissing her belly, moving upward with each kiss, his hands skimming over her thighs, his tongue, his breath searing her skin. She closed her eyes, waiting for him to reach her breasts. When he did, liquid fire surged through her. As he teased her with his tongue, the heat spiraled then coalesced in her middle and trickled down into her secret places. Then his fingers found those places, too, and did clever things to her. She sighed, lost in a world of pleasure she'd never imagined existed.

He rose over her, his lips brushing hers, murmuring comforting words. "You are ready, my sweet. So ready. Forgive me for being so greedy," he whispered, his lips against hers, his voice husky with emotion. "I'll be as gentle as I can be."

At first, the pressure of his male member against her was almost pleasurable. She arched her back against him. But then the pressure built, becoming painful. Was this how it was supposed to be? The pressure and pain increased. She tried not to struggle against it. Surely the women in the book hadn't been feeling anything like this. They wouldn't have been smiling if they had.

"Harris?" she murmured, struggling at last.

The next thrust brought a slice of pain and discomfort like she'd never known. A whimper of surprise and hurt escaped her. But he muffled the sound with his mouth and shuddered in her arms. Then he was still.

The song of their passion had died and only the popping and crackling of the fire and the ticking of the mantel clock could be heard in the room.

Harris edged to her side, drawing the length of silk over their nude bodies. He lay still, his eyes closed and his breathing easing back toward normal. She lay stiff and afraid that she'd done something wrong.

"Are you all right?" he asked, his eyes still closed.

"Yes," she said, not really certain that she was. He had that bemused smile on his face like the men and women in the book, but she knew that she wasn't wearing one.

"That was all wrong," he said. "I knew I was being greedy."

She struggled to sit up.

He slipped an arm around her waist. "No, wait. I can do better than that."

"Than what?" she asked, confused and beginning to wonder where all her clothes had gotten to.

"Lie down," he said, his hand pressing her back onto the sofa and throwing a leg across hers.

When she looked into his face again, his eyes were open, and he was still wearing that satisfied smile, but it was focused on her.

"Rest easy," he said. "Lie in my arms just as you were doing before."

She hesitated. The spell was broken, but she didn't know how to tell him that.

"Lie back," he repeated, kissing her ear and beginning to caress her again, his hand skimming over her belly and cupping her breast. He teased her nipple with his thumb. Then he moved down the sofa, his hand trailing a path of tingling heat along her side, until his head was resting on her belly. He slipped one arm beneath her and stroked her thigh; with the other, his fingers began to do oh, such clever things in her secret place.

She fell back against the sofa, raking her fingers through his hair, opening herself again as he urged, fearless and shameless. Let him do what he would as long as it felt as wonderful as this.

The melting heat came again, quick and intense. He made a sound of satisfaction. So she let it come, whatever it was that he was so cunningly drawing out of her. She would give it to him if it pleased him so, and it certainly pleased her into mindless pleasure.

Pleasure broke over her like the crest of a wave. She cried out. A sweet, burning wave, carried her along. Then the heat ebbed, but the sweetness remained, swirling, floating. He was holding her again, his embrace strong. She recalled a light kiss on her lips, then her forehead and the words, "There, my sweet, I told you we could do better."

She slept.

When she awoke, Harris was completely dressed and moving about the room. She lifted her head to take a better look at her lover, to share a smile with him. But he did not see her. Apprehensive, she observed that even his cravat was neatly tied. She pulled the blue silk closer against the chill that had settled over the room and struggled into a sitting position.

The fire was nearly out on the hearth. Icy rain was clicking against the windows. If her stays hadn't been draped over his arm, she would have doubted that their intimacy had ever happened.

But the musky perfume of what she realized was the scent of lovemaking lingered in the air despite the spices in the room. As she glanced at Harris again, he bent down to pick up her camisole and drawers.

She caught his eye as he straightened. The frightening harshness of his expression softened.

"How long did I sleep?" she asked.

"Only a few minutes," he said, handing her undergarments to her. "There is no immediate reason for haste. But you should get dressed."

She accepted the garments, all the time studying his face, wondering what he was thinking.

He reached into his pocket and handed her his handkerchief. "I know this is rather inadequate under the circumstances, but it's the best I can offer for now." Then he turned away.

She stared at the handkerchief, wondering what she was supposed to do with it.

He went to the fire and began putting more coal on it, silent, taking time to stoke the embers carefully, never looking over his shoulder. With a start she understood that he was offering her an opportunity to dress in some privacy.

Hurriedly she began to pull on her camisole and drawers, conscious of a discomfort between her legs that she'd never experienced before, a moistness—from blood and his seed, she realized with wonder. These details were never illustrated in the book nor had her mother mentioned anything beyond wifely submission and duty. Comprehending at last what the handkerchief was for, a hot blush rose in her cheeks. She glanced in Harris's direction, but he remained attentive to the fire. Quickly she tended to herself as best she could and wondered how she'd explain the stains to Jane.

That finished, she began pulling on her clothes, tugging at the stay hooks.

"How are you faring?" He glanced over his shoulder at last. "Do you need help?"

"No," she lied. She could manage on her own; she did it all the time. But in the chill of the room, her fingers were suddenly cold and uncooperative.

Without saying a word, he came to her aid. As he hooked the last hook, he said, "For the record, I'd much rather unhook these things than hook them."

She looked up at him, grateful for his attempt to humor her.

What was he thinking of her now? Did he not feel the same wondrous surge of love and happiness that she did? She tried to smile at him but was unsuccessful.

"Everything is going to be all right, my sweet," he murmured, lifting her chin with his finger so she could see him offer her a smile of encouragement. "Finish dressing, then we'll talk. Your stockings are there on the sofa, and here is your skirt and bodice."

When she finished and was attempting to smooth her hair into place with unsteady hands, he pulled her down on the sofa next to him.

"We must agree on how to deal with what has happened," he began, looking unruffled and self-assured.

She nodded, feeling young and inadequate. She prayed he wouldn't start talking about things as he had after their first kiss.

"I don't think this was a mistake," she hastened to say.

He blinked at her in obvious surprise. Then he took her hands in his and released a slow breath. "Nor do I, Alyssa," he said, gazing into her eyes. "Bad timing, improper behavior, clumsy lovemaking, maybe. But never a mistake. I care very much for you. I have from the first day you arrived and told me of you and your brother and the tableau. Well, there is no rhyme or reason to how I feel. Here you are, a brash American, while I am a staid Brit. And there is such a difference in our ages. Yet, when I saw you with Byron . . . well, one minute I would tell myself it was for the best, and the next I was going mad with the thought of you and him."

Relief flooded through Alyssa. He *cared* about her. He cared about *her*. "And I care for you, too, Harris. And ten years is not so great a difference. I will be twenty in January and you are only thirty."

An indignant frown banished his smile. "I am but twenty-nine."

"Oh." She had given offense. She hurried on. "Well, that's all the better then. There's only nine years between us. Some people think that the perfect difference between husband and wife."

"Let's not move forward too quickly, Alyssa." His frown eased only a bit. "There are many things to settle before we can announce ourselves to the world."

"Of course," she said, feeling light and fortunate to have fallen for such a perfect man. "The Trevells are still in mourning."

"And there are your family's feelings to consider as well," he said. "When the time is right, I want to be able to announce this to your father in the best way possible. He is going to have some questions, as well he should. So there are many reasons why we must keep this afternoon secret. You do understand that, do you not?"

"Not entirely," she said, for the moment caring little about what her mama and papa thought. Harris had just made love to her and vowed that he cared for her. At last she knew how wonderful it was to be loved. Now she understood why her married sisters always looked so smug and complacent. Now she knew that virginity was most certainly overrated. "But the way I feel is so wonderful. How can I hide this?"

He squeezed her hands. "For me, too, believe me." He gazed into her eyes. "Did I tell you I just tasted heaven, and I want more?"

A hot blush stained her cheeks, and she sucked in a breath of pleasure. "I know exactly what you mean," she said, holding his gaze, longing to run out of the room and down the hall shouting his name—and the fact that he loved her.

"But we cannot indulge ourselves in this kind of pleasure again until things are more settled," he said.

"Settled? You mean the suspicion of murder is cleared and the Trevells are out of mourning?"

"Yes, that's what I mean," he said, avoiding her gaze this time. "I hope to talk to some more people. There are things that don't make sense. I need to know the truth."

"So you are investigating," she said, wondering if now was

the time to tell him about her search for the truth on Meggie's behalf. "I can help. I have a list of suspects with notes on motive and where each sat the night of the poisoning. I can ask questions, learn things from people like I did from Lady Cynthia at the wedding."

"No," he said abruptly. "You are not going to help. It's too dangerous. We are dealing with a murderer, Alyssa. If he has murdered even once to gain what he wants, he will have less compunction about murdering again. I want you to leave Penridge." He paused and eyed her. "What did you say you learned at the wedding?"

Twenty

"Oh, no, I am not leaving Penridge," Alyssa said, watching Harris's curiosity grow. She sat back on the sofa, feeling more secure now. "No, not now."

"It is the only safe course, Alyssa," he said, his brow furrowed. "I am thinking of your welfare. But first, tell me what you learned at the wedding that might have a bearing on Alistair's death."

"How interested are you in knowing?" she asked, lifting her chin and regarding him with a challenge. "I am not going to be as easy to pack up and send away as Meggie."

"I should have known." He raised one brow. "You wish to make a deal?"

She shrugged.

He gave a grudging sigh. "I do not like it, not at all, but if you stay, we—us must be kept secret."

"Agreed," she said, not really understanding why secrecy was such a necessity, but willing to consent to most anything to keep him from sending her away.

"Agreed," he repeated with a scowl. "What did you learn?"

"It has to do with Lady Cynthia," she began, secretly relieved by his agreement. "Your cousin Alistair and Lady Cynthia were having an affair just before you returned to Penridge."

"Alistair and . . ." Harris's scowl evaporated and he appeared quite speechless.

"Yes, Lady Cynthia confessed the whole thing to me in the

ladies' cloakroom." When he seemed to have gotten beyond the initial shock, Alyssa went on to tell him what Lady Cynthia had told her at the wedding celebration, including the confession about being discovered by her husband. "In *flagrante delicto,* I believe is the term."

"How do you happen to know that phrase?" Harris shook his head. "Never mind. That must have been a scene. Poor Ralph. Alistair always did have a penchant for another man's woman. Where did all this happen?"

"I don't know," she said. "I was too shocked to ask. But she sounded as though it must have ended about the time you returned from India."

"What else?" he prompted, moving toward her without releasing her gaze. "I suppose you've managed to find out what Byron knows."

"I don't think he knows anything about the affair," she said, relaxing a little, pleased that she could contribute information he did not have. "I don't believe he's capable of murder, even over the threat to his inheritance. He's simply not passionate enough."

"Byron not passionate enough?" Harris repeated with raised eyebrows, the beginnings of a laugh in his tone. He shook his head. "I shall leave that to your womanly estimation."

Alyssa blushed slightly. "I've told you what I know. Now it's your turn."

He regarded her, his lips pursed in consideration.

"It's only fair that you reveal what you know," she said.

"This is not a game, Alyssa." He turned away from her, frowning once more.

"I know it's not," she said, ready to show him how well she understood. "It's a matter of my integrity and your innocence or guilt. It's a matter of knowing that when I told Meggie that her favorite cousin did not murder her father, I was telling the truth."

Slowly, he turned toward her once more. "So Meggie has

heard the rumor," he said, his voice full of disbelief and regret. "I was afraid of that."

Alyssa nodded. "She has. Before she left, she asked me for the truth. She adores you, Harris. The very idea that you might be involved in her father's death horrifies her."

For the first time, Alyssa saw a bleakness in Harris's face that shocked her. He cursed softly, rose, and walked a circle around the sofa before sitting down beside her again. "I was afraid of that. It's part of the reason I sent her away. How did she hear it?"

Alyssa waved the question aside to spare Johnnie. "That's not important. What is important is that I told her the truth."

"You did," he said, taking her hands in his again. "I swear to you that you did."

"I believe you," she said, glad of the reassurance in his grasp. "Now tell me what you learned."

He heaved a resigned sigh and spoke in a tone that said he was replying against his better judgment. "What I've learned is not nearly as interesting as your information. Sir Ralph had filed a lawsuit against Alistair just before my return. Since my cousin's death, however, it has been withdrawn."

"Do you think discovering Alistair and Cynthia together might have prompted the suit?" she asked.

"It looks that way now," he said. "But would a lawsuit satisfy a cuckold husband?"

"Only if it sufficiently hurt the guilty party," Alyssa said.

"Lord, I wish I'd known about Lady Cynthia and Alistair before I started my campaign to settle the differences between him and Sir Ralph." Harris raked his hand through his hair. "I wish I'd known about the lawsuit."

"Harris, you can't let yourself think that knowledge would have made a difference in what happened," she said. "You aren't responsible for a murderer's action."

"But if I'd known, I might have done things differently," he insisted. "I would have asked more questions of Alistair. Pressed Sir Ralph about what he knew. Through all of my negotiations, Sir Ralph never told me he'd taken legal action. Alistair never told me anything about having an affair."

"Maybe because they both knew you would ask questions they didn't want to answer," she said.

"Precisely," he agreed. "But why would Sir Ralph file a lawsuit if he were planning murder?"

"Maybe the idea of murder came up later," she said. "You were there that night at the dinner table. What happened? What was the mood? How could the poison have been given to Alistair?"

"However it was done, I do not believe it was a spur of the moment decision," Harris said. "Too many people were present. And men do not carry poison in their pockets to dispense when the notion strikes. It had to have been carefully planned. Possibly the number of guests was expected to add to the confusion."

"Peter Pendeen was serving that night," she said. "How did he feel about Alistair and the Littlefields?"

"You mean, could someone have bribed him into giving Alistair poison?" he asked and shook his head. "No, Peter's loyalty was unquestionable. He never favored me, but he came here as a boy, years ago, and served the Trevells well. Alistair had given the man his share of dressing-downs, but Peter wouldn't have committed murder over that. The same with Mrs. Brodie. She started here as a scullery maid when she was a girl."

"Then that leaves the people at the table that night as the suspects," she said.

"And the Reverend Whittle," Harris said. "I would wager he had something to do with it. There was no love lost between him and Alistair."

"But what did he gain by Alistair's death?" she asked.

"Power over the miners," Harris said, rubbing his hand over his face. "Despite the difficulties with them, they were loyal to Alistair in their way because Wheal Isabel gave them work just when it looked as if mining was dead in Cornwall. But they hardly feel the same loyalty toward me. I'm like an outsider in their eyes."

"But the reverend was not at the table that night," she said. "If he wasn't there, the only way he could have committed murder would have been to bribe Peter or Mrs. Brodie. Or his brother, Elijah."

"Which is unlikely," he said. "They are all trustworthy. So we are back to where we started."

"Sir Ralph sitting at the foot of the table next to Gwendolyn," she said, silently wondering if he'd thought about Tavi, who was serving behind the screen. "With Lady Cynthia at the head next to Alistair, Lady Penridge at the foot with Sir Ralph, and you, Byron, and the Carburys seated in between, trying to negotiate a peace. Right?"

"The vicar and I were across the table from each other," Harris said. "Nothing seemed unusual about the serving of the food. I asked the vicar later as circumspectly as I could. He saw nothing, either. I want to talk to Reverend Whittle again."

"You mustn't question Reverend Whittle alone," she said, feeling suddenly chilled. "I could go with you."

"No, too dangerous," he said. "I may do the questioning at the mine or somewhere to keep him off balance," he said, squeezing her hand again. "It's a matter of time, Alyssa, I can feel it. We are close to discovering the truth. But until then, no one must know about us. You cannot write of it in a letter to your Aunt Esther or your mother or sisters. Nor Meggie. You cannot tell Jane about us or act in any way to make people think that we are more to one another than guardian and ward. This is very important, Alyssa. Can you do it?"

"I'm not fond of deception," she said, feeling that old weakness to grant him anything he wished creeping over her. "And I'm not very good at it."

"I prefer honesty myself," he said. "But there are good reasons to be cautious for at least a time. We do not want to make the murderer nervous."

"But what could he do?" she said. "Another poisoning would be obvious."

"No, I do not anticipate another poisoning, not with Chef Hugo and Tavi watching over the food," he said, his voice low and grim. "But there are such things as accidents. More than one man has become a widower when his wife seemingly took a fall down the stairs or drowned in her bath."

She frowned; she'd not thought of those dangers.

"I want you to understand that there is risk still," he said, gazing into her eyes. "And it may not take an obvious form."

"So I'm to behave as if you are little more to me than a stodgy guardian," she said lightly. "I'll be safe. The murderer will be lulled into thinking nothing is wrong."

"This is not to be taken lightly, Alyssa," he scolded.

"I do not take it as such," she said, sobering. "You mean too much to me, Harris."

The tenderness that sprang into his eyes touched her heart. She wanted to throw herself into his arms once more.

"And you to me," he said, catching her chin with his thumb. "One last kiss, then, before you go back to your room," he said. "We've been together too long as it is. There might be talk."

He grasped her by the shoulders and took her mouth in a deep, searing kiss that made the melting inside her start all over again. Alyssa wrapped her arms around his waist and deepened the kiss, but he pulled free. "Enough temptation," he said. "Go now. Keep our secret."

She rose, smoothed her skirts. He stood beside her. After another quick embrace, he took her hand and led her to the door. She couldn't resist touching his lips with her finger. "Until later."

"Until later." He kissed her finger and then opened the door.

Alyssa started at the sight of Tavi standing there, enigmatic as ever. He didn't seem in the least surprised to see her. Placing his palms together, he gave his customary bow. Though she couldn't be certain, she prayed he hadn't been standing there long. "Thank you for your advice, my lord," she said. "I shall go write cancellations to Mr. Littlefield and Mr. Hawthorne immediately."

Then she nodded to Tavi and swept down the hall toward the stairs as if she'd concluded a mere social call.

At first, keeping her love for Harris secret had seemed simple, though strange. Her feelings were so wonderful and special, hiding them in her heart where she could savor them almost seemed natural. She was loved. A man knew her in all ways, and he loved her. It was the most wonderful thing in the world. And the knowledge was hers alone. She need not share the miracle with anyone but him. The secret gave her confidence in herself she had not had before. She had nothing to prove to anyone. She had only to be herself and to love him in return.

All she had to do at dinner was smile and nod her head appreciatively as Gwendolyn chattered about the rose she planned to execute in silk embroidery to honor the roses of her garden. Something surpassing all other needlework done in the county, or some such thing, she hinted. It would demand infinite shades of red silk to make the petals come to life, she exclaimed. The same with the green silk.

Alyssa toyed with her food, made a few responsive replies, and glanced at Harris from time to time. How handsome he was, dressed in his dinner coat, his cravat crisp and perfect, his hair combed and in place. A smile touched her lips as she thought of him with his hair fallen across his brow as he covered her on the sofa and loved her.

"It is rather tedious being restricted by mourning from traveling to Launceston to see the silk colors the shops have to offer," Gwendolyn complained. "The catalogs are so inadequate. One can tell nothing of color from their descriptions and illustrations."

"What shop did you wish to visit?" Harris asked, inclining his head toward the widow. He'd hardly glanced in Alyssa's direction during the entire meal. "I shall write to them and have them bring their wares here for you to see."

"Would you, Harris?!" Gwendolyn said, brightening. "That would be so good of you."

"Nothing could be simpler," he said, accepting her gratitude with a smile.

"But perhaps I can help," Alyssa said, inwardly reminding herself that she had no reason to be envious of Harris's attention to the widow. "I'm going with the Carburys to Fowey tomorrow. I can seek samples in the shops there."

"What outing is this?" For the first time during the meal, Harris looked at her, questions in his eyes.

She suppressed a smile of pleasure and gazed at her plate. Though her body was warm and sated from his lovemaking, already she could feel the rising tide of desire again. How many times a day could one feel like doing that?

The difficulty of keeping their relationship a secret was becoming clearer hour by hour, though she wanted to treasure his love and hold it close like a precious thing. Being loved brought such happiness, such discovery of new and wondrous things that she was beginning to realize she would never be able to keep her feelings hidden for long. It was the little things as well as the big that made the secrecy difficult, like wanting to do something special in dressing her hair for dinner, or wanting to wear her best perfume instead of toilet water. She would betray them sooner rather than later. She prayed that truth would be revealed soon.

"Yes, I'd quite forgotten," Gwendolyn said, smiling at Alyssa, her needlework forgotten. "The Carburys sent the invitation round early in the week. I thought Alyssa should go, Harris. It's so dull for her to be confined to the house because we are in mourning. We've discussed this before."

"Yes, of course. I did not know you had made those

arrangements," was all he said, cutting into his salmon. "Will you want the carriage?"

"The vicar is going to drive us," Alyssa said, exchanging a look with him once more. His expression was maddeningly unreadable.

She was glad that she had not told him of her plans, for he would forbid her to carry them out, she was certain. Peter Pendeen, the former butler, may have packed up and left Penridge Hall the day after the death of the late Lord Penridge, but he hadn't gone far. With only a casual question or two of Jane, she'd discovered that he'd gone to Fowey to live with his sister and brother-in-law.

The day Mrs. Carbury and Edith had sent an invitation suggesting a shopping trip to the nearby village, Alyssa had thanked the fates or lady luck or whoever was responsible. She'd been quick to accept and to suggest that they go to Fowey. She had interest in seeing the old church there, as well as the shops, she replied, though she knew nothing of the old church beyond the fact that every village seemed to have one. And it wasn't a complete fib. She did like the old churches—those great caverns of stone that allowed music to soar inside them. And the vicar's wife had agreed to the suggestion.

"So it's settled, then," Alyssa said. "I'll bring back as many red and green silk samples as I can, Gwendolyn."

The widow expressed her delight with the idea. Harris's gaze flickered in Alyssa's direction, but he asked for no explanations, and she gave none. He might have his plans to question Sir Ralph and the Reverend Whittle once more. She had her questions to ask, too.

After dinner, Gwendolyn sank down on a chair by the withdrawing room fire and read aloud another letter from Meggie. The little girl wrote of a new friend named Ellen and a stray cat named Merlin that they had adopted and fed with food sneaked out of the dining hall. Harris stood with his back to the fire, watching as she read the letter. In the firelight, Alyssa sat across the room watching a softness come into his face as he listened to Gwendolyn read Meggie's words.

"She is doing well," Gwendolyn said when she finished. She looked up at Harris and added, her voice full of relief, "Our Meggie is doing well. You made the right choice for her, Harris."

"Yes, so it would seem," he said, smiling fondly at his cousin-in-law. "I'm glad."

The ugly question crept into Alyssa's mind, dark and un-bidden, about the softness in his face—for Meggie or for Gwendolyn? The scene of the three of them—the new lord, the widow, and the orphan—holding each other in the church-yard at Alistair's grave flashed through her mind. The kiss he'd placed on Gwendolyn's head burned into her mind's eye.

Alyssa's heart gave a quick, flutter of uncertainty. She turned away from them, taking a deep breath. Harris and Gwendolyn were family of sorts, she reminded herself once more. His concern for Gwendolyn was only natural and one that he could be open about. Why shouldn't he be? He had ex-plained very logically to her why they must go through this charade, why it was too soon to announce to the world how they felt about each other, but still. . . .

"One day Meggie will look back on the friends she's made and her education and thank us for sending her away," Gwen-dolyn said, dabbing her eyes with her handkerchief. Harris sat down on the chair across from her and took her hands to con-sole her.

The sight was suddenly too much for Alyssa. She jumped to her feet. "I think I should like to study about Fowey before my outing tomorrow. Is there any information about the vil-lage in the library?"

Harris glanced at her, puzzled. "Yes, as a matter of fact, I believe there is. On the south wall, in the lower corner, there is a section of rather recent tour books, I believe. You might find something there."

"Thank you," she said. "Then I believe I'll say good night now and go look."

She found the tour book and went to her room. Jealousy was an ugly emotion, she told herself. She spent the rest of the evening poring over the Fowey entry and refusing to let her mind conjure the image of Harris's handsome, attentive face as he listened to Gwendolyn read Meggie's letter.

She was successful and finally fell into a dreamless sleep.

Twenty-one

St. Fimbarrus' pinnacled tower rose over its two-story porch and soared above Fowey, above the trees, nearly as tall as the hill behind it. Or so it seemed to Alyssa as she tipped her head back to look at the church. According to the tour book, it was a fourteenth-to-fifteenth-century structure, the most recent church on the site since a chapel had first been built there in the seventh century. She was looking at a four-hundred-year-old church sitting where there'd been a place of worship for over eleven hundred years.

"Heavens," she exclaimed softly. She'd been in old buildings before. There were many hundred-year-old buildings in Boston, New York, Salem, and Philadelphia. But the age of this place was counted not in years but in centuries. Her mind struggled to grasp an understanding of that. How many generations had been carried across this ground to be christened at the font or buried in the churchyard where she and Edith now stood? How many couples had crowded into the vestry to make their marks in the record on their wedding day—like she and Harris would do one day at Lanissey?

An odd but welcome sense of peace settled over her. Whatever happened, feast or famine, war or peace, couples would be wed, babies would be christened, elders would be buried and mourned. A church would stand here. The cycle of life would go on and on. Her part in it was a small one, but hers nonetheless. She had promised Meggie to learn the truth, but now she had to learn it for herself, for her future. Harris Trevell was not a murderer. And she would not tolerate the stain of doubt marring her husband-to-be's reputation.

"The pulpit is carved out of wood paneling from a Spanish galleon taken by local pirates in the sixteen hundreds," Edith confided as if the information were the scandal of the week. They were standing in the winter sunlight on the walk leading to the sanctuary door.

"Yes, I read that in the tour book," Alyssa murmured, thinking quickly about how to free herself of Edith's company. She did not believe it wise for anyone near Penridge to know that she had talked with Peter Pendeen, especially after what Harris had said about the danger the murderer still posed.

The strains of organ music reached them. Alyssa decided to go with her instincts.

"Edith, would you mind terribly?" she said, putting on her most apologetic look. "It sounds as if the organist is rehearsing. I'd like to listen for a while. You go on. I'll join you in about an hour at that tea shop your mother said she liked on Fore Street."

"Are you certain, Alyssa?" Edith said, appearing confused. "I can stay with you."

"No need." She patted the girl's arm. "I'll be in a church, listening to music. You can take a little time to go by the bookshop I saw you eyeing."

"Actually, there is a novel I wanted to look for," Edith said. "Well, if you are certain."

"I am." Alyssa nodded. "Go on. I'll see you at the tea shop."

With another word or two, Edith decided it was a good plan and left, seeking out her favorite bookshop.

As soon as the vicar's daughter was out of sight, Alyssa pulled the map she'd traced from the tour book out of her pocket and opened it, searching for Passage Street. That was the street Jane had mentioned as the "direction" of Pendeen's new home.

Fowey, or "Foy," as the Cornish pronounced it, was a maze of steep, cobbled streets hardly wide enough for a horse and cart. Most, except for Fore Street, ended at the water. If she went along the town quay, it shouldn't be hard to find Passage.

It did not take her long to find the house, the only one on the street with red flowers in the window. The woman who came to the door had a kind smile and wispy gray hair escaping from her cap. For a moment, Alyssa was uncertain whether the woman was the maid or the lady of the house. But her manner was such that Alyssa concluded, as she introduced herself, that it must be the latter. She appeared a bit surprised to find an American at her door. But when Alyssa asked to see Peter Pendeen and explained that she brought greetings from Jane at Penridge, the lady invited her in.

"I be Mrs. Bovey," she said, smiling cordially. "Peter's sister. Wait here, Miss Lockhart. My brother is in the garden. He will be pleased to receive greetings from Penridge."

"Thank you, Mrs. Bovey," she said, perching on an ancient fireside settle, scarred from years of use. She'd wondered how she might be received, considering the strained circumstances under which Peter had left the house, but apparently he still bore Penridge and its people no ill will, at least none that his sister knew of. Dropping Jane's name had probably been wise.

She pulled off her gloves and looked about. Though there was no fire on the hearth, the room had a scrubbed-clean warmth about it. It was crowded with plain comforts: the settle, a couple of armchairs, a tea table, and a footstool on a threadbare carpet. No luxuries. A gray cat slumbered in the sunny window behind the lace curtains next to the flowerpot. From the back of the house drifted the aroma of baking bread. Not such a bad place for Pendeen to retreat to.

She heard a door shut at the back and the sound of a man's footsteps coming rapidly through the house. Apprehensive, she rose and faced the door where Mrs. Bovey had disappeared.

A tall, thin, white-haired man with bushy white brows, a white bristle-brush of a mustache, and piercing, dark eyes appeared. He stood in the doorway, appraising her.

"Hello, Mr. Pendeen. I'm Miss Alyssa Lockhart," she began.

"My sister told me," he said, his tone abrupt. "You bear greetings from Jane."

"Yes, she thinks of you often," she stammered. "And when I told her I was coming to Fowey, she asked me to remember her to you."

He nodded. "Jane is a good girl." Still no smile of welcome.

"Yes, I'm fond of her," she said, twisting her gloves. "I'm a houseguest of the Trevells, and she has served me very well. Always cheerful and busy."

At the mention of the Trevells, Pendeen's chin came up and he regarded her with even more suspicion. "What brings you to Penridge? The new lord is still in mourning. They should hardly be entertaining."

Before she could answer, recognition crossed his face. "Yes, I remember now, the Lockharts of Boston. Master Alistair obtained a loan from your family to begin the clay mine business in eighty-one."

She stared at Pendeen, wide-eyed. So that was why the Trevells had been willing to take her as a guest at such an inconvenient time. Her father had loaned Alistair money when it had been unlikely to come from other sources. "Yes, that's my family, the Lockharts of Boston."

"Very generous of them to do that," he said. Somehow, that fact made her an acceptable caller. He smiled at her for the first time, genuine pleasure in his eyes. "Master Alistair was ever so grateful. Please sit, Miss Lockhart."

He gestured to the most comfortable-looking armchair in the room. "How kind of you to take the time to call. Sister, bring us tea. How are Lady Penridge and Miss Margaret?"

"Well, Miss Margaret has been sent to school," Alyssa said, "but she writes that she likes it there."

"Ah, poor little tyke." Pendeen shook his head. "Losing her father like that. It is a sad thing. A sad thing. So, Miss Lockhart, tell me, what brings you to Fowey besides Jane's well-wishes?"

As casually as she could manage, she told Pendeen that she'd come to ask him questions about what had happened at

Penridge. Mrs. Bovey brought in a tea tray bearing fresh bread, butter, and jam; and then she left.

When Alyssa finished, Pendeen's affability had cooled some, but he poured tea and appeared to be willing to talk. "It was a right strange affair, Miss Lockhart, and I'm glad you came to me to ask. You have heard the rumors, no doubt. A murder never declared, a murder of a man who was not an easy man to live with or to serve. No point in listening to rumor, I always say. Go right to the source."

"My thinking exactly, Mr. Pendeen," she said, accepting a cup of tea from him and suspecting that he would expect to learn as much from her as he intended to reveal. "I'm so glad to know that you feel that way." She asked him to tell her about that night.

"It was a foul night, that," he began, his white, bushy brows coming together as he spoke, recalling unhappy times. "After dark, the fog settled in thick—"

"This was in August?" she asked, reluctant to interrupt him, but eager to have all the facts clear in her mind.

"Aye, August—'tis not so strange a thing in Cornwall to see the mist roll in off the sea during any season," he explained. "But the guests had all safely arrived at Penridge and were sitting down at the table."

"The dinner was held at Harris's suggestion?" she prompted.

"His suggestion and the Vicar Carbury's," Pendeen said. "They thought to mend the feud that had grown between Master Alistair and Sir Ralph. It had become so heated that when Sir Ralph saw Master Alistair seated in church on Sunday, he would turn right around and march out again. If Master Alistair were the last to arrive, he would do the same. It was becoming unseemly for the ladies, and you could see how that would trouble the vicar. The two men were making a scene and upsetting his congregation Sunday after Sunday."

"And Harris and the vicar thought they could get those two men to sit down at the dinner table together!" Alyssa knew better than Pendeen how deep the rift was between the two men, but she had not known that they had let it become so public. And Lady Cynthia and Lady Penridge—how embarrassed they must have been by their husbands' behavior. She was beginning to see it all in her mind's eye now—that night around the dinner table. How terrified Lady Cynthia must have been that the truth would come out about her affair with Alistair.

"Master Harris, who was always wanting people to think he was a hero, always trying to make himself look best over Master Alistair," Pendeen said. "I never liked him, even as a boy when he first came to Penridge. Too watchful and quiet by half. But who would have thought it would come to this?"

Alyssa silently noted the old butler's admitted bias against Harris. Arguing with him would not get her the story she wanted to hear. "Go on."

"Well, he and the vicar had gone to each man separately and asked them to sit down to dinner. Each had agreed. At least, that was my understanding. We all expected it to be an awkward occasion, and knew that there might well be a scene. But that did not mean the meal should be served in less than Penridge's best style."

"Of course," Alyssa agreed. "I'm sure you gave every detail of the occasion your closest attention."

"Indeed," Pendeen continued, satisfied she understood how careful he'd been. "Lady Penridge and Mrs. Brodie planned a menu with both men in mind. Shellfish was one of Master Alistair's favorites. Mrs. Brodie fixed the dish for him all the time with no trouble. And Sir Ralph, we were given to understand, fancied lamb and mint sauce. Nobody ever gets sick from that."

"True enough," she said. "What happened after the menu was planned?"

"Well, then there was the wine," Pendeen said. "When I asked Master Alistair about it, he just said for me to select something suitable, but not the best. 'That goatish clout hardly deserves the best from our cellars,' he told me. So I did just that. A good, dry French white for the fish and an Italian red for the lamb. His lordship liked red wine with his lamb.

"Then Lady Penridge and I conferred about the china, silver, crystal, and linen to be used at the table," he said. "In honor of the occasion we chose the green-and-white Wedgwood, and the best sterling and the gold Murano crystal—"

"The stems with the flecks of gold dust in the glass and the gold rims?" she asked, remembering the elegant, if ostentatious, crystal used at Sunday dinner.

"Aye, that sounds like the very ones," Pendeen said. "Master Alistair's favorites. We used the white damask linen. Lady Penridge cut roses for the table. Her roses were at their best then, brilliant deep reds, and petals wide and delicate. It was a wonderful sight, that table. Lady Penridge came down early herself to inspect and approve everything. But she often did that. She likes her tables to look just so. But that night she was especially anxious about everything, as we all were."

"You and Elijah Whittle served that night?"

"Aye, Elijah is experienced in that," Pendeen said, accepting her prompting easily now. "Master Alistair did not approve of women serving at a formal dinner table, so poor Jane and the foreigner, Tavi, helped in the pantry. Jane and Elijah can be trusted not to tamper with the food, but that Tavi . . ."

Pendeen paused to shake his head. "Master Alistair's refusal to allow him to serve offended. Oh, miss, don't allow that bowing and scraping of his to mislead you. There's nothing humble about that foreigner. And with him having a family he wants to bring here from India, and who knows what grudges he holds."

"But I heard that you believed it was someone else who did the poisoning," Alyssa said, trying to steel herself for the part of the story that she knew she would not like.

He paused in his narrative and studied her. "I don't know

where your loyalties lie, Miss Lockhart. You may not like what I have to say."

"My loyalties lie with the truth," she said, concerned that the butler was going to become reticent now. She decided to tell him her own truth. "I promised Miss Margaret to find out who murdered her father. And I intend to do that."

He scrutinized her thoughtfully. "I see. Very brave of you, Miss Lockhart, as a houseguest at Penridge. And a worthy quest. Then I shall do what I can to help. Poor little orphan has a right to know the truth about her kinsman. But I don't think there is any way to make the truth pretty for the child."

"Perhaps not," Alyssa said. "I'll decide what to tell her when the time comes. But I don't intend to lie to her. Please tell me everything that happened that night and in the days up to the late lord's death."

He nodded, leaned back in the armchair, and gazed at the low ceiling above him as he recalled the events of that dreadful night.

"The sweet had been served," Pendeen began. "A trifle. Another of Lord Penridge's favorites and Sir Ralph's, too, we'd been told. Jane's sister works for the Littlefields, did you know?"

"What had it been like during the meal?" Alyssa asked.

"Neither Sir Ralph nor Lord Penridge said much, though they both ate well," Pendeen said. "They are generally known as men of healthy appetites. Master Harris and the vicar encouraged the ladies to talk. And you know those Carbury girls, endless chatter."

"So there was no discussion of the issues at the table?" she asked. "Nothing about the land deal and the mine?"

"No, not in the presence of the ladies," Pendeen said. "I assumed Master Harris would bring it up over cigars and brandy after the ladies withdrew. I was clearing crumbs from the tablecloth, and Lord Penridge stood up and said that he was feeling dizzy. Everyone fell quiet and stared at him. I suppose some were thinking that he just did not want to discuss the issues after all. But when I looked at him, he'd turned quite white and was swaying. It was evident to everyone in the room that he was sick."

"Did he swoon then?"

"No, he did not collapse in the dining room," Pendeen said, "though I think he might have allowed himself to if there hadn't been guests in the room. He was a proud man, and he did not want to be humiliated in front of Sir Ralph."

Alyssa nodded. "Go on."

"The vicar jumped to his feet and excused his family," Pendeen said. "Master Harris went to his cousin immediately. I think he saw that Master Alistair might pass out. Lady Penridge rose from the table, looking confused. Then she saw her guests to the door. I don't think she understood how ill her husband was at that moment. Nor did any of us, really."

"So Master Alistair took sick right at the table," she said. "The poison had to have been in something that he ate there."

"That's what it looked like to me, miss," Pendeen said.

"Dr. Lewellyn was summoned?"

"Yes, as soon as Master Harris and I got Master Alistair to his bed, I sent Elijah for the doctor. He arrived about an hour later, but the vomiting had already started."

"I suppose all the dishes and crystal had been cleared and washed," Alyssa said.

"Jane and Mrs. Brodie saw to that," Pendeen said. "The scrapings were sent down to the home farm for the chickens and pigs like always. No way to test anything for poison, and mixed with other rubbish it wouldn't necessarily hurt the animals. And Dr. Lewellyn announced that it was the shellfish. He'd seen another case in Kerrith just the week before, he said. Master Harris agreed with him. Now, he would, would he not, if he was the murderer?"

"But what evidence do you have to make you think Master Harris is a murderer?" Alyssa asked. "Just because the two men were competitive as boys? Because Master Harris might desire the title?"

"Oh, he wanted more than the title, that one," Pendeen said with a certainty that chilled Alyssa's blood. "He wants much more than that. Why do you think he sent Miss Margaret away?"

"For the little girl's own good," Alyssa said, puzzled. "She was much grieved by the loss of her father."

"Did he tell you that?" Pendeen asked, a light of skepticism in his dark eyes. "You are young. Perhaps you haven't seen it. Perhaps he has seduced you, too. He's a clever one, Master Harris. He wants Master Alistair's offspring out of his way in order to pursue his true desire without distraction. He wants Lady Penridge. She was his betrothed once. Wore his ring on her finger, she did, and he lost her to Alistair. He intends to have her again. Mark my words. No one will stand in his way this time."

Twenty-two

Alyssa stood on the corner at Fore Street amidst the comings and goings of shoppers and delivery boys, taking little notice of them. She stared in the direction of the tea shop where she was to meet the Carburys, but she couldn't make her feet move toward it. She was numb—cold and numb as a block of ice. The cold had crept through her and solidified as she listened to the rest of Pendeen's story. How was she going to go into that shop and sit down with those nice people and act as if nothing in her life had changed?

"Excuse me, miss," a begrimed chimney sweep muttered as he sidled around her on the corner.

She hastily stepped aside to allow him, his black brushes, and sooty toolbox to pass. Seduced or not, life did go on, and she would have to present some kind of appearance to the people she knew—to the Carburys. Hold her head up and act as if Pendeen's story had not ripped her heart out of her being. What else was there to do?

Moving through her emotional fog, she went to the tea shop and seated herself with the Carburys. She even carried on a bit of conversation, fibbing about the fineness of the organ music at St. Fimbarrus. But the numbness persisted, mercifully allowing her to stand apart from herself and go through the motions of being a sane and gracious young lady when she was dying inside. She sipped her tea, tasting none of it, and murmured appropriate phrases as her mind replayed what Peter Pendeen had told her.

"You knew that Master Harris and Lady Penridge had been betrothed, did you not?" Pendeen had said after his remark left her momentarily speechless.

"I understood they'd been sweethearts." She forced a bland expression on her face. There was no way the former butler could know anything about her present relationship with Harris, she reminded herself.

"Not just sweethearts, they were betrothed, ring and all, though the official announcement had not been made," he continued "We called her Miss Gwendolyn when Master Harris first brought her to Penridge Hall."

"Finish telling me what happened after Alistair fell sick and Dr. Lewellyn diagnosed bad shellfish," Alyssa said, brushing aside the shock of the revelation—Harris and Gwendolyn betrothed. "What treatment did he recommend?"

Pendeen tapped his chin with his forefinger. "Broth and coddled eggs, I believe. Mrs. Brodie was packing to leave by then. Jane was in the kitchen doing the cooking, and I personally carried everything up to Master Alistair's room on a tray. Lady Penridge fed him. She was at his side day and night. Devoted until the end. But no food seemed to stay down for him. And the pain! The doctor had left laudanum to dose him with. It helped until the end. Sometimes at night, I can still hear the poor man moaning. Oh, miss, it was an awful way to pass."

Pendeen bowed his head.

Alyssa studied the top of his white head. The scene imagined in her head was a grim one, painful and bleak. It was a difficult tale to listen to, but it was not at an end. She had to know all.

"Jane said that you told them below stairs that you heard Master Alistair accuse his murderer," she said, unable and unwilling to say Harris's name at this point. "Please tell me about that."

"Of course," Pendeen said. "Master Alistair told me from

the beginning, from the night he fell ill, that he did not believe it was the shellfish. He thought the old doctor was daft. He believed he had been poisoned. He said nothing he'd ate ever hurt him like that. The burning, the ache in his throat and in his belly and his bowels. Forgive me, miss, for speaking plain, but if you want the story, these are the facts of it."

"Yes, I understand, go on," Alyssa urged. She'd never been particularly squeamish. Having a brother like Winslow had cured her of that.

"And it was relentless," Pendeen continued. "The pain and the other symptoms. Despite Jane's best broth, the soft eggs, the warm milk. Bad food would have been eliminated, one way or the other, two days later, if you take my meaning. But his lordship just continued to decline."

"I know very little about poison," Alyssa admitted. "But what you describe sounds strange."

"I do not know much about poison either, miss," Pendeen said. "Nor can I tell you how much his lordship knew, but he would ask me, every time I brought up the food tray, who was in the kitchen, and I would tell him, Jane and me. I know that he trusted us. Jane and I had been there a long time and there had been no trouble.

"Then on that last night, and a frightful night it was, too, I tell you. Dark came early because of the heavy clouds. The wind was ahowling round the eaves. Thunder was rumbling across the sky. I went up to his lordship's room to fetch the tray. Earlier, Lady Penridge had nearly swooned from exhaustion. Master Harris had helped her to her room to rest, and he was sitting with Master Alistair. When I was almost at the door, I heard him and Master Harris talking. He had been in and out of his lordship's room all through the illness, hovering over his lordship and Lady Penridge. I had just reached the door and I heard Master Harris say something that I could not make out. He sounded a bit agitated, but he were speaking quiet enough. Then Master

Alistair spoke. I could not hear all that he was saying neither until he began to repeat one word. It was so strange, I could hardly believe I was hearing it. But he was saying, 'Murderer. Murderer. Murderer.' Struck me like a blow in the chest, it did. That's when I knew that Master Harris had killed him."

"And you left then?"

"Oh, no, miss. I burst into that room to be sure that his lordship was all right, I did," Pendeen said with indignation.

"And what did you see?" Alyssa asked, inching forward in her chair.

"His lordship sitting up in his bed and pointing a finger right at Master Harris. 'Murderer. Murderer. Murderer,'" he said, his voice rising in excitement as he pointed his finger at Alyssa to demonstrate. His reenactment was chilling.

"And what was Master Harris doing?"

"Why, he was standing at the foot of the bed, staring at his cousin with this look on his face," Pendeen said, becoming excited as the memories returned.

"What kind of look?"

"A guilty look, miss," Pendeen said. "Like an apple thief caught in the orchard."

"Wait, let's not be too quick with assumptions," she said. This was the part of the story she wanted to explore and discredit, in Peter's eyes, as well as the world's. "What if there was an explanation for Master Alistair using that word? You only overheard part of the conversation. What if he was trying to urge Master Harris to find his murderer?"

"Oh, no, it wasn't nothing like that, miss," Pendeen said, dropping his proper butler's English in his eagerness to refute her explanation. "I know it wasn't anything like that. There'd been clues earlier that Master Harris was up to no good. It was just when I heard Master Alistair accuse him, I knew the truth."

Earlier clues? Alyssa paused, trying to make sense of what he said. "What earlier clues?"

"That's what I was trying to tell you about Master Harris and Lady Penridge," Pendeen said, sitting back in his chair with an I-told-you-so look. "They were sweethearts once, betrothed."

Alyssa twisted her gloves again. "But that was long ago and it didn't last long, did it? Master Alistair and Lad—Miss Gwendolyn took a fancy to each other. Harris was Alistair's witness at the wedding. Jane told me."

"Jane wasn't privy to the family discussions that I was." Pendeen pursed his lips as he set the record straight. "It began with Master Harris and Miss Gwendolyn engaged when they arrived at Penridge with her parents. Mr. Blakethorn was a banker, as I recall. Mrs. Blakethorn had the gleam of ambition in her eye from the start. She did like the look of Penridge. There were several Blakethorn daughters, but they did not accompany their parents. Miss Gwendolyn was the oldest and there was a definite desire on their part to see her well settled."

"Master Harris must have appeared to be a very good match," Alyssa said, envisioning Harris, youthful and handsome in his uniform.

"A mere Army officer a good match?" Pendeen sputtered. "Hardly, when his cousin was heir to a title and also unwed. And I always wondered if Master Harris exaggerated his prospects to impress Miss Gwendolyn. Who knows what tales he might have told. Nothing had been announced about the engagement. All the arrangements and the contracts to be negotiated yet, but her parents had been invited to Penridge for the purpose of making the betrothal official, I'm sure."

"Then she and Master Alistair met," she said, growing more and more uneasy with the prospect of hearing an unpleasant truth.

"I believe Master Alistair was charmed by her at first sight," Pendeen said. "Lady Penridge is a beautiful woman.

What man would not be charmed by her? She is precisely the sort of lady to hold the title. Ten years ago, in the prime of her youth, she was lovely beyond words, especially to two starry-eyed young men."

"She charmed Alistair?"

"Master Harris was proud of her at first, pleased as could be to bring a lovely young woman like that to Penridge on his arm," Pendeen continued. "Nearly strutted like a peacock, as a youth will. But then Master Alistair's eyes lit up at the sight of her. Miss Gwendolyn and Master Alistair took a fancy to each other. That was another matter. The strutting stopped. I believe that's when they really started to hate each other."

"Harris and Alistair, you mean?"

"Master Alistair and Master Harris, indeed," Pendeen said. "Until then, they'd competed for everything. The old lord put them up to it. Have you heard the stories? But winning Miss Gwendolyn's heart, that was no game, no mere contest of wills. It was war, a war Master Alistair won. I was actually afeared it might come to a duel, but nothing like that happened. But one morning the two of them turned up at the breakfast table looking like they had both been in the mill of a lifetime. Cuts and bruises. Master Alistair's right eye was near swollen shut. Said he'd walked into a door, he did. Miss Gwendolyn made a great fuss over him. That afternoon, Master Harris announced he would be requesting assignment to India."

"And perhaps that was the honorable thing to do," Alyssa said.

"I thought so, too, until about two weeks *before* the poisoning," Pendeen said with a wag of his head. "But that day, when I saw Master Harris and Lady Penridge together, I knew Master Harris was up to no good. I held my tongue about it. Master Alistair has been a barnacle to deal with at times, but her ladyship has always been kind to me. I did not want to make trouble for her."

"What did you see?" Alyssa asked, puzzled.

"Master Alistair was away for the day, seeing his banker in Launceston," Pendeen said. "I was up in the grand salon overseeing the maid's dusting. Lady Penridge had always been content to allow me to supervise as housekeeper as well as butler. It was a new girl we had decided to try. I happened to look out the window and saw Master Harris and Lady Penridge together in the rose garden. Alone."

She shrugged. "What of that? Lady Penridge was merely showing Master Harris her beloved roses."

"They were talking, familiar like, their heads together," Pendeen said. "Her hand touching his shoulder, him touching her arm as they walked among the flowers. Finally he said something to her and they walked off toward the garden shed. I went on about my duties. When I glanced toward the garden again, Master Harris was walking along the garden path toward the stable. I did not believe he was going riding because he had not dressed for it. But I thought he might be giving Elijah some instruction or tending to Pendragon himself. He did that sometimes. Old military habit, I suppose."

"Yes, and . . . ?" She realized she'd twisted her gloves into a tangle.

"So I thought, well enough, and went about my business," Pendeen continued. "As I came down the stairs, I found Lady Penridge at the garden door." He paused.

"It was shocking, miss," he said, casting her a sidelong glance. "And I'm not sure that it is fit for a young woman's ears, but you asked—her hair was mussed and her bodice was untidy, and her skirt wrinkled and covered with bits of dried leaves and dirt. Her mouth looked a bit swollen liked she had been well kissed. In short, she looked quite ravished."

That sat Alyssa back in her chair, her heart thumping in denial. "You mean, Master Harris forced—"

"No, I don't think forced or anything like that," Pendeen hurried on, waving his hands in the air. "But I do believe

that Lady Penridge and Master Harris did more than con-
fer about roses in the garden shed that day. And after that.
There were looks exchanged at the table and in the withdrawing room, all when Master Alistair was paying no heed.
If there were more assignations, I do not know. It is not my
business to judge what my betters do, nor my place to chaperone them, but there was opportunity, oh, yes, opportunity."

"You believe that Harris and Gwendolyn plotted Alistair's murder?" Alyssa asked, her words coming out in a
whisper of disbelief.

"No, not Lady Penridge," Pendeen said, aghast at the
thought. "She would never hurt anyone. But the colonel,
yes, I believe he would murder his cousin for the title, but
more importantly, for the woman he always loved. You heed
my words, now that Alistair, Lord Penridge, is gone, and
as soon as a decent period of mourning has been observed,
they will wed. Don't you see? Master Harris never stopped
loving her. Once he knew how to get rid of his cousin with
those things in his medicine chest—have you seen it? Once
he knew that Miss Gwendolyn might still harbor some feeling for him, he did the deed. Careful, well-planned,
thoughtful, and patient. He was always the methodical one
of the two boys. The chess player."

Alyssa sat on the edge of the armchair hardly able to
catch her breath. She'd come here to learn the truth and reveal that the rumor was only misperception—just as Harris
had explained. And so it was. Only *not* the misperception
she had expected. Harris had made it all sound so simple,
as if there were a multitude of others out there who wanted
Alistair dead, but was it really him all along? But she'd seen
him and Gwendolyn exchange looks, touch, murmur to
each other—familiar like people who have been part of the
same family for years. But was there more to it than that?

"Miss Lockhart?" Pendeen reached across the distance between their chairs to touch her arm. "You've gone quite pale.
I hope I haven't frightened you. If you fear for yourself, don't.

As much as I'd like to see justice done on Master Alistair's behalf, I don't believe you are in any danger. Master Harris might poison his cousin for his own benefit, but he would not harm an innocent, unless there was some threat to him personally."

Like discovering he was the murderer, Alyssa could not resist thinking. She attempted to suck in some air, but only succeeded in sipping a shallow breath. She'd told him how she was out to find the truth for Meggie's sake.

"What about Sir Ralph or Reverend Whittle?" she stammered, desperate to discover another possibility. "They had motive to kill the late lord."

"No doubt, Master Harris would be pleased to see the reverend accused," Pendeen said. "That would eliminate a troublemaker for him."

Alyssa nodded, remembering what Harris had said about the reverend. How he wanted him to be guilty.

She looked down at her tea to see that the amber liquid had grown cold and the bread and jam she'd taken one bite from had dried around the edges. She was no longer hungry. When she took her leave of Pendeen, thanking him, and stepped onto the street, she vaguely noted that the cat was gone from the window and the clouds had covered the sun. The day had grown bitterly cold.

Seated in the tea shop with the Carburys, she sipped at the tasteless tea and nibbled at the flavorless sandwiches. Thankfully, Edith, Mrs. Carbury, and the vicar seemed to find nothing amiss about her behavior. They chatted about the goods they'd discovered in the shops. Mrs. Carbury had seen a textiles shop where she thought quality silks might be obtained for Lady Penridge. Alyssa had shared her mission with them and Mrs. Carbury had taken it upon herself to be certain that poor, dear Lady Penridge would have whatever she wanted.

They spent nearly another hour in the textile shop selecting almost a dozen shades of red and green silks for Gwendolyn's needlework roses. Still numb, Alyssa had little interest in the silks as well as little experience with the craft so she deferred to Mrs. Carbury's opinion. The vicar's wife clearly enjoyed making selections with no budgetary restrictions.

Darkness had fallen by the time the Carburys delivered Alyssa at Penridge. She was surprised when Tavi greeted her and informed her that dinner had been held for her. She realized that a cowardly part of her had hoped that Harris and Gwendolyn would have dined already, and she would not have to face them across the table. She wanted to creep up to her room and huddle before the fire for warmth and comfort. What a fool she'd been that day in the study. How could she bear to look into Harris's eyes after what Pendeen had told her about the murder and Gwendolyn?

Packages were set aside while Jane helped her change and tidy her hair. Within a few minutes she stood in the doorway of the dining room, gazing down that long table with the high-back chairs along its sides, her mind placing everyone there as Pendeen had described them. The silver gleaming on white damask, the gold-trimmed Murano glasses adding richness, the green-and-white china giving color, and the blood red of the roses in the center. Had Harris secreted the poison in something on the table that night?

"Alyssa?"

She started at the sound of her name on his lips. She turned to find him standing behind her. He was dressed for dinner, as usual. Warily, she stepped into the dining room, putting several steps between them before she turned to face him again.

He smiled, this man who had been her lover only a day ago. He smiled as if he were truly pleased to see her. "How was your outing with the Carburys?"

"Very nice, thank you," she stammered, her insides aflutter

at the sight of him, as always. Her heart seemed to care little what Pendeen had told her about murder and betrayal. But her head had the good sense to make her back away from him.

"I am glad to hear that," he said, following her into the room. "What did you think of Fowey and St. Fimbarrus?"

"Impressive." She glanced away, unable to meet his gaze, afraid to search his face for fear she might see some hidden truth in his countenance that she had failed to see before—and did not want to see now.

She turned and hurried to her place at the table, wondering if she dared ask him for the truth now. He'd never told her what terms he'd been on with his cousin when he left for India. Dare she ask him if he still loved Gwendolyn? Did she dare ask if he'd seduced her, the skinny redhead, just to keep her from digging into the truth of what happened that night? Would he lie to her?

He certainly would not want to admit what had happened between them in front of Gwendolyn. No wonder he'd sworn her to secrecy, she thought with a pained smile coming to her lips.

Suddenly, Harris was behind her again, pulling out her chair to seat her, something he'd never done for her, only for Gwendolyn.

"What is it, Alyssa?" He leaned toward her ear as she sank into the chair. Husky tenderness filled his voice. "Is something wrong? Did something happen today?"

"I talked to Peter Pendeen," she said, her hands trembling in her lap.

"Pendeen?" He looked shocked and then angry. She knew the frostiness of his disapproval. "I wish you had not done that."

At that moment, Gwendolyn came into the room. He moved away from Alyssa.

"Alyssa, dear, I saw the parcels in the hall." She bubbled with excitement. "I assume your trip was a success. You found some silks for me?"

"Yes, I did," Alyssa said, forcing a polite smile.

Harris crossed to the other side of the table to seat Gwendolyn.

"Then we shall look at them after dinner." Gwendolyn settled into her chair. "A letter arrived from Meggie today. It is one of those horrid things that the teachers assign the students to write, but any word from her is so wonderful, isn't it? Her penmanship is improving, I believe. I will read it to you later."

So the evening passed pleasantly, or so it would seem on the surface. Alyssa ate little at dinner. She saw Harris frown at her plate as it was cleared from the table, but he said nothing.

Her numbness blessedly allowed her to go through the motions of being a pleasant guest while she studied her host and hostess with new eyes. The way Harris turned an attentive ear to Gwendolyn, the way he favored her with the best chair by the fire, and the first glass of sherry after dinner. All these things, these privileges, Gwendolyn was entitled to as the lady of the house.

Before now, Alyssa had dismissed his attentiveness as the thoughtfulness a gentleman would show his kinsman's widow. Yet there was solicitousness about the way he saw to each indulgence that revealed what Alyssa had been blind to before Pendeen had disclosed everything. Harris cared for Gwendolyn. Why had she not seen it before?

Gwendolyn read Meggie's letter aloud, as she had promised. Meggie reported that her school had attended a play and were casting for a production of its own. Alyssa silently prayed that the child would not get caught up in some silly prank like her own tableau escapade that had gotten her expelled. Meggie also reported that she'd done well in her geography class and in deportment.

By then their conversation had moved on to examining the silks that Alyssa had brought from Fowey. Gwendolyn exclaimed with delight at each color, the dark ones and the light ones. Alyssa hardly listened to the words of approval. She

murmured that Mrs. Carbury had given her assistance, but
that did not seem to diminish Gwendolyn's delight. Alyssa
watched the widow finger the silks, sorting them into the
palette she'd planned for her needlework. Harris hovered over
the widow's shoulder, admiring the colors. It was so painful
to watch them; she turned away and gazed into the fire, letting the dancing flames mesmerize her.

"Reverend Whittle called on us today," Harris said, speaking loud enough to wake her from her trance.

When she turned toward him, he was eyeing her intently.

"He asked after you, or so Harris told me," Gwendolyn
said, still sorting her silks. "I refused to receive him, of
course. I simply cannot abide the sight of the man at all."

"Reverend Whittle was here?" Alyssa asked, wondering
why the clergyman would have been asking about her. She
glanced at Harris, remembering that he had wanted to speak
to the reverend again. "Did you invite him?"

"If you are asking, did he have the gall to show his face
here without an invitation?" Harris asked, meeting her gaze
headon. "Yes, indeed he did. I received him on your behalf
and Lady Penridge's."

Alyssa glanced at Gwendolyn to assess her reaction.

She was frowning. "Give the thing to her, Harris."

Harris took a small packet from his inside coat pocket and
brought it to Alyssa where she sat, away from the fire. As he
handed it to her, he said, "The reverend said that this was for
you on behalf of the women of his congregation who appreciated that you and Lady Penridge shared the house stores."

Alyssa stared at him in astonishment.

"He also delivered a similar gift for Lady Penridge." Harris glanced at Gwendolyn.

"It seems Harris is not to receive any credit for the ship-
ments of food now arriving regularly," Gwendolyn said dryly.

"But I certainly didn't do anything," Alyssa said.

"You did more than you know." Harris presented the packet

with a small bow. "I'm glad that the women at least wished to show their gratitude."

She accepted the packet, careful not to touch his hand. In her state of fragile numbness, she could not bear to touch or be touched by him. But their gazes met when she took the package, and she saw the questions in his eyes. He had not believed her when she'd said nothing was wrong, but he would not pursue the matter now.

Hesitantly, she untied the twine and unwrapped the brown paper to find a set of three white linen handkerchiefs edged in handmade bobbin lace. Each was exquisitely embroidered with her initials, "A" and "L", in blue, entwined with daintily worked white alyssum blossoms. The needlework was so painfully beautiful, full of pride and skill and sacrifice, that it brought tears to Alyssa's eyes. She was hardly so sheltered that she did not know where gifts like this came from: A mother or a daughter's treasured best linen swatch saved to be transformed into a special gift and the thread traded and borrowed and the time to do the work, stolen from chores and moments of rest, and the light requiring the burning of precious oil.

"This is much too dear to accept," she murmured, trying to hide her tears.

"The women do fine work when they set their minds to it, do they not?" Gwendolyn said, peering across the room to glimpse the gift.

"It is too dear to refuse, Alyssa," Harris said, still standing over her.

She nodded, understanding perfectly. "Of course—I shall pin one to my lapel and wear it to the miners' cottages the next time the food is delivered to them."

"No, dear, you mustn't," Gwendolyn exclaimed. "Look what happened to me."

"They are good people," Alyssa said, surprised to find that she had no fear of the miners or the women. "Really."

"Do not take the gesture for more than it is, a token of gratitude," Harris said with a tolerant smile.

"I think it is a peace offering," Alyssa said.

"It is both," Harris said, eyeing her uneasily. "The miners and their families are not bad people. They do like you. Nevertheless, do not let their gift deceive you. They can be dangerous when they are unhappy. Send a note to the reverend for him to read at Sunday service and let them be."

"Harris is quite right." Gwendolyn smiled at him. "That is precisely the way to handle it."

"I see the logic in that," Alyssa said, stroking the expert needlework. Then she glanced from Harris to Gwendolyn and back. Still, a note seemed so cold, so distant.

Gwendolyn was regarding her with a polite half-smile. Harris's gaze was sharper, more penetrating, as if he knew she was not convinced.

For a moment she forgot about the handkerchiefs and the note and stared back at them. How innocent they looked. But who were these people, this man and woman? What did they mean to each other, really? What was going on behind the polite façade that she saw? What had she missed? Was Harris Gwendolyn's lover? And she had been blind to the clues. Had they formed an alliance? Before Alistair's death or since? Or was Harris making things happen on his own, for his own benefit, just as the rumors hinted? And Gwendolyn knew nothing?

Alyssa suddenly felt confused, exhausted, and alone. She studied Harris's face closer, longing for answers to her questions.

"I'm glad you see the good sense in writing a note, Alyssa." His eyes, which she knew could be so warm and tender, returned her scrutiny coolly. There were no answers in his countenance. "Write your note tonight or in the morning and Elijah will deliver it tomorrow."

"Yes, of course." She turned from him and forced the mistrustful thoughts from her head. She was tired from the trip to Fowey, she reminded herself. And Pendeen's story had confused her.

Still, a note seemed so inadequate, even condescending. She'd helped Mama and her sisters deliver charity baskets to working people at Christmastime. She understood exactly the work and sacrifice these handkerchiefs had cost the miners' wives. Yet, she knew Harris was probably right, especially in view of the recent unrest.

"I'll write a note," she conceded.

Twenty-three

She fell asleep at her writing desk attempting to compose the note, her head on her arm, the gas hissing in the light fixture above, and the ink drying on the nib of her pen poised over the paper. Her hand relaxed and the pen slipped from her fingers.

Her dream world was a crowded, nonsensical one, filled with images of Harris and Pendeen, Meggie and the reverend, Gwendolyn and Tavi. A medicine chest full of poisons dancing down the dining room table like something out of a child's book of absurdities. Murano glass gleaming and green-and-white Wedgwood spinning like plates on a juggler's stick.

At the head of the table were Harris and Gwendolyn, naked save for the bed sheets wrapped around them, laughing in delight. Laughing at her, the scrawny redhead who believed a man like Harris would love her. Shrill, mocking laughter.

Alyssa awoke with a start. The wind was rattling the windowpanes. The pen clattered from her hand. The arm her head had been resting on was stiff and filled with needles of pain. What nonsense was this? She muttered self-deprecating words to herself as she sat up and rubbed her arm. Pendeen's stories had left her head full of ridiculous suspicions. Dancing medicine chests, indeed.

But the image of Harris and Gwendolyn standing side by side at the head of the table and laughing at her was harder to dismiss. An unpleasant sense of foolishness crept over her. She shivered with the coldness of it.

"Nonsense, nonsense," she muttered in sleepy, singsong fashion. The fire had died on the hearth and the wind had come up. That was all. Without more reflection, without tears, without self-pity, she put out the light and crawled into her bed, praying there would be no more dreams. Her prayers were answered. She fell into a sound, dreamless sleep. Thankfully, no silly fantasies troubled her—nothing about Harris's caresses, his kisses, his intimate touch.

No nightmare about the footsteps that paused for a long time in the dark hallway outside her door, then slowly went away.

In the morning, she awoke knowing precisely what she should do—and this was only the first of several decisions she was going to make. She would deal with each in its time.

First, the note was inadequate. Perhaps it was the way the lady of Penridge manor should handle her "thank you" for the handkerchiefs, but it was not the way Alyssa Marie Lockhart would handle hers. She would offer her thanks in person to the miners' wives and see for herself how they were doing with the food supplies. She had nothing to fear because she was making this visit on her terms, not the Reverend Whittle's.

She dressed carefully in her best dark blue riding habit, requiring Jane's help with the boots. When Jane wasn't looking, she tucked one of the handkerchiefs in a pocket and went down to breakfast as usual. When casually questioned, Tavi told her that his lordship had left already for the morning. He wasn't exactly certain where Lord Penridge had gone. She swallowed a quick bite of toast and tea and left the house. She rode often enough in the morning that no one thought anything was amiss.

As she walked toward the stables, congratulating herself on getting out of the house without having to explain herself, she rounded the garden wall and came face-to-face with Gwendolyn. The widow had wrapped a rich, black cashmere shawl over her elegant mourning gown. Jet earrings hung from her ears, and her golden hair, bound up in a black net, gleamed—even in the dull winter light.

"Good morning, Alyssa," she said, smiling. "It is a rather gray day for a ride, but the air is pleasant enough. Do you have your note for Elijah? I just gave him mine."

Off guard, Alyssa shook her head. She began to stammer some fictional explanation for not having written hers. Of course, after she'd made her call on the miners' wives, she would have to tell Harris the truth. At the moment, she knew that if he knew what she intended to do, in the name of caution he would forbid her to go. However, Gwendolyn saved her from the fib.

"No? No matter, dear," the widow said. "There is no need for haste. Elijah will take it for you later, whenever you like. Do have a nice ride."

Gwendolyn turned away and swept across the gravel toward the house.

Alyssa stared after her for a moment. That had been easier than she expected. The lady didn't seem to suspect anything. With a sigh of relief, she hurried on toward the stables.

Taciturn as ever, Elijah helped her saddle Smuggler. However, he did fuss that Johnnie was not there to ride with her as groom. She dismissed the necessity. She could manage quite well on her own, she told Elijah. Had not he and Johnnie seen that for themselves? She could even mount unaided, she confided in him. It wasn't pretty or ladylike as a leg up from him or Johnnie was, but she could manage. He agreed. She was soon on her way, riding down the avenue of beech trees toward Wheal Isabel and the cluster of cottages where most of the miners lived on Penridge property. Smuggler was in a spirited mood, tossing her head and pulling at the bit to do more than trot.

As soon as Alyssa reached the woods where she knew she was completely out of sight of the house, she halted

Smuggler. Using her teeth, she pulled off her gloves and retrieved the handkerchief. It had not become too wrinkled from its short stay in her pocket. She folded it just so, and using the safety pin, she fastened the linen to the lapel of her riding habit. The blue of the embroidered letters was a perfect match for the blue of her habit. The handkerchief looked quite nice, she thought, craning her neck to admire her lapel just below her chin.

Pleased, she pulled on her gloves and put her heel to Smuggler's side. They were off again, negotiating the woodland bridle path faster than they should. The morning air was crisp and invigorating. She considered throwing her leg over Smuggler's side to ride straddle, but decided it would not make a good appearance before the miners' wives. Still, Smuggler was eager to move and she felt secure in the saddle. It was good to clear her head with a brisk, revitalizing ride.

If she remembered correctly, there was a fallen log across the path farther along the way. She'd put Smuggler to it. Let her take a jump since the old girl was feeling her oats.

"There it is, girl," Alyssa said to the mare, setting the horse toward the higher stump end of the fallen tree. "Let's make this leap a big one," she urged, dropping her weight into her heel for balance and pressing her leg against Smuggler's side to squeeze the horse over.

The mare took the command, ears perking forward, gathering herself, and then reaching for the jump. The moment Smuggler's forefeet left the ground, Alyssa felt the girth give beneath her. There was no time for panic. She grabbed for Smuggler's mane and froze, her knee hooked over the sidesaddle pommel and her heel deep in the stirrup, as it should be. Then she waited for Smuggler's feet to strike earth on the other side.

Smuggler cleared the tree handily. When the mare's forefeet came to ground, Alyssa felt the girth give, and the saddle slid to the side. She pulled back on the reins, attempting to bring the horse to a gentle halt. But the strange feel of the saddle sliding frightened Smuggler. The mare danced off sideways, rolling her eyes and laying back her ears.

Alyssa fought to maintain her balance.

"Easy, girl." Gripping the mane, she attempted to shift her weight and the saddle back into the center of the mare's back. But the action only succeeded in frightening the horse more. The mare's sidestepping turned into a sidelong canter, the saddle slipping farther to the side with each stride. Alyssa knew she either had to jump off or fall beneath the horse's feet.

So when she glimpsed a small clearing ahead, she pushed against Smuggler with as much strength as she could. She had no desire to get kicked in the ribs by one of those shod hooves. Gray sky and bare tree branches whirled above her. She landed with a dull thud on her shoulder in the moss. Her breath whooshed from her. Her head thumped painfully against the ground. A red light flashed before her eyes. Pain washed over her. She was only vaguely aware of the sound of Smuggler's rapid hoofbeats as the mare bolted in headlong panic. The horse was the least of her worries. Smuggler would eventually make her way back to the stable.

Alyssa made no effort to move for several moments. This was hardly her first fall from a horse and most likely not her last. As the initial pain faded and she began to draw steady breaths again, she determined that all her limbs seemed to be uninjured. Little by little she pulled herself up into crawling position. Though she was still shaken and somewhat numbed by the fall, she wasn't in serious pain, not yet anyway.

Satisfied that she was not grievously hurt, she staggered to her feet and looked around. She'd not emerged from the woods near Wheal Isabel yet, and Penridge was some way behind her. She estimated that she was equally distant from the house and the mine.

Should she go on to the miners' cottages and send word back to Penridge that she needed a ride? She looked down at herself. Her skirt was smeared with mud and moss, and she could feel her hat pulling loose, as were tendrils of her hair. She would hardly make a gracious appearance limping into the miners' cottages in this state. There was little choice but to walk home and admit she'd been thrown. It was all rather humiliating. When she reached Penridge, she would take a look at that girth, assuming Smuggler returned home with the saddle. It shouldn't have given way like that.

She reset her hatpin to prevent her hat from falling off. The action of putting her arms above her head made her dizzy and her head ached. When she was finished, she leaned against a tree for a moment until she felt steadier. Then she grabbed the train of her riding habit, threw it over her arm, and set out along the path toward Penridge, ignoring the pain in her right knee.

Smuggler's hoofprints were visible, even in the packed earth of the path. Apparently the mare had headed straight back to the stable. No doubt Elijah would discover the horse, realize what had happened, and send help.

She hobbled along, feeling little aches and pains settling in and her mood souring because she'd been unable to reach the miners' wives. Now she'd have to go back to Penridge and admit to Harris and Gwendolyn what she'd been up to without having the pleasure, at least, of being successful. As her mood darkened, she recognized her little rebellion over the "thank you" note for what it truly was—her anger with Harris—and Gwendolyn. Anger and distrust.

After her interview with Pendeen, she was beginning to wonder if it was possible to learn the truth about Alistair's death. In this house of secrets, would she want to know the truth? Why had Harris been so quick to send Meggie away? And why had he not told her about his past relationship with Gwendolyn?

The pain in her knee was suddenly sharp and she stopped to rest against a tree again until the pain faded. For the first time since the day she'd arrived, she was sorry that she'd come to Penridge Hall. Either Harris was a murderer who had seduced her to win her silence. Or, at the very least, his heart was Gwendolyn's and she was merely an amusement to him.

Regarding the first, she could not bring herself to believe he was a murderer. She simply could not love a murderer. She'd done some foolish things in her young life, but giving her heart to a man who could take a life was not one of them.

Regarding the second, what was she to do if his heart belonged to Gwendolyn? Leave?

She stumbled over a large stone and caught herself against another tree. Leaning against the trunk, she rested for a few minutes to catch her breath, hoping to ease the pain—mostly in her heart.

As she rested against the tree, something on the path ahead caught her eye—her sidesaddle. It had apparently broken loose and dropped to the ground as Smuggler frantically galloped toward home.

Nearly forgetting her aches and pains in her curiosity, Alyssa hobbled toward the saddle. Her knee protested as she knelt, pulling the girth free so she could examine the fastenings. To her surprise, all the buckles were in place, fastened securely just as she'd glimpsed as Elijah tacked up. She turned the saddle over to examine the other side. On the right side, the girth had clearly been cut with a sharp blade, leaving only a few strands connected so that it would pull loose during her ride. *Cut.*

A frision of fear lanced through her. A shallow gasp escaped her as she squeezed the girth in her fists. This was intentional. Someone had intended for her to be thrown. Who?

Beware of making the murderer nervous, Harris had warned her that day she had asked him about the rumor. Could that have been a threat? What was it he had said about danger—and seeming *accidents?*

The thud of rapid hoofbeats reached her. She listened for an instant. Someone was riding down the narrow path pell-mell. Was the rider coming to help or was this the villain coming to see how his plan had fared?

As swiftly as her aching body allowed, she grabbed the saddle, got to her feet, and scrambled for the shelter of the tree where she'd rested earlier.

She peered down the path, but it curved so that she was unable to see the rider until a great black steed burst around the bend. Pendragon.

Despite the fact she'd made some attempt to hide, Harris saw her immediately.

"Alyssa!" Hauling back on the reins, he brought the black to halt, the stallion sitting back on his haunches and his hooves sending divots of earth flying through the air. Harris threw himself from the saddle and ran toward her.

Involuntarily she backed away. Dare she trust him? Maybe her heart believed he wasn't a murderer but the rest of her wasn't at all certain.

Something in her face made him stop before he reached her. He was hatless, his coat was rumpled, and he was breathless from his wild ride. "Dear God! Are you all right?" he asked. "Smuggler came back to the stable—"

"I am quite all right," she said with a calm that surprised her. Could he have cut the girth on her saddle? This man who'd been her lover? Her *secret* lover. Was this the murderer and she'd made him uneasy at last—with her visit to Pendeen?

She studied him, searching for any clue of guilt or innocence in his eyes, in the set of his mouth, in the tilt of his head. She saw only a man who'd ridden at breakneck speed to discover the fate of Smuggler's rider.

"What in the bloody hell happened?" he demanded, taking in the mud on her habit and seemingly puzzled by her wariness.

"I put Smuggler to a jump and the girth gave way," she said, still clutching the saddle.

"When we saw Smuggler gallop in without a saddle, we

feared the worst," he said, a touch of impatience coloring his voice now. "I am glad you are all right, but I wish you had taken Johnnie with you like I asked you to do."

"There wouldn't have been a thing Johnnie could have done even if he'd been with me," she said, her calm giving way to annoyance with his scolding and defiance. "The girth was cut."

"What?" His gaze shifted to the saddle in her arms. "Let me see that."

Before she could say more, he closed the distance between them and seized the sidesaddle. She surrendered it and backed away again.

Holding the girth up to the daylight, Harris examined it closely.

When he saw the condition of it, his perplexed frown turned into cold outrage. He muttered another curse Alyssa didn't quite understand.

"Who would do this?" she asked, studying him closely. She'd come to care so much for him, would her feelings blind her to a lie?

"I do not—" He stopped when his gaze met hers. Astonishment played across his features. "You believe I did this?"

"I don't know what to believe," she said, aware of the anger and pain in her voice. "You seduced me and swore me to secrecy. Then you talked about accidents that aren't truly accidents. Now this."

"I seduced you?" he said, his voice full of surprise and ironic laughter. He reached for her, but she stepped away, separating them by several feet this time. He halted and the frown fell across his features again.

"What did Pendeen tell you?" he demanded, true anger deep and cold in his voice. "He started the rumor that I murdered Alistair, did he not? This is why I did not want you to talk to him."

"He explained things that you have not explained," she said, a part of her longing to hear a logical version from him, but knowing there was none that would make her happy. "Tell me how you wanted to marry Gwendolyn, but Alistair wed her instead, and you went to India. Now Alistair is dead and Gwendolyn looks to you for strength. And Meggie has been conveniently sent away. Why? Explain to me again why you must keep what happened between us a secret."

"Alyssa, I would never hurt you, and—what we have may not be proper—but I am not ashamed of us, if that's what you fear," he said. He dropped the saddle to the ground and reached for her again.

She retreated even farther from him this time. His reassurance had come too late. He'd always been able to read her mind, to know what she needed to hear. She could not allow him to seduce her again even if it was only with words.

He stopped and raked his fingers through his hair. "And I would tell you everything if I thought it would absolve me of murder in your eyes. But it's a long, ugly story about a time in my life that I'm not very proud of. This is not the time or the place."

He glanced around at the wintry woods, obviously uneasy with the fact her retreat had taken them away from the path. "Let's get you back to Penridge and call Dr. Lewellyn," he said with clearly forced calm.

"I don't need a doctor for bumps and bruises," she said, hiding her fear and pain with her fury. "I need the truth. Or I need a train ticket to Southampton."

The words had escaped her without her knowing that she'd made up her mind to leave. But when she heard them, she knew it was what she had to do. She could not go on with things as they were. She did not belong in this gray, rainy moorland country. Whatever dark secrets Harris and Penridge Hall kept—murder, adultery, and lord knew what else—there was no future for her and him together.

His chin came up and he eyed her for a long, silent moment, searching her face for something she knew she did not have to give him.

"Isn't that what you wanted?" she asked to fill the cold silence. "You tried to send me away that day in the study, but I was too stubborn. I thought I could do something to clear your name. I thought I had something to offer. I don't believe that anymore."

"Yes, it is what I wanted." He turned away, staring at the discarded saddle, but she didn't think he truly saw it. Oddly, for a moment there was in his lowered head and the hunch of his shoulders the appearance of defeat. "And I'm glad you've finally seen the wisdom in leaving," he said.

Ignoring the saddle, he walked toward the path where Pendragon stood. "Are you able to ride?" he asked, brusquely, the defeat she thought she'd glimpsed gone.

"Yes, but—"

"I will send Johnnie back for the saddle." He laced his fingers together to give her a leg up. "Let's go, then. There's no time to waste if you are going to catch the train today."

She hesitated.

He frowned and straightened, the lines of his mouth hardening. "I swear to deliver you safely to the house if for no other reason than I have no desire to answer to a rich American relative about what happened to his daughter."

The ride back to the house was long and uncomfortable. She'd thought about refusing it, but after Harris's oath, refusing seemed silly and immature. If he were going to do her in on the bridle path, he'd already had his opportunity. She sat sidesaddle in front of him, his arms around her as he reined Pendragon toward the house. Sitting as erect so as not to make contact with him was nearly impossible because of their proximity and because the soreness from the fall was already making itself known.

Harris seemed unconcerned, his arms brushing against her shoulders from time to time.

"Will your aunt be expecting you?" he asked, his voice practical and his lips dangerously close to her ear.

"I will telegraph her from the train station," Alyssa said, gripping Pendragon's mane to steady her trembling hands and prevent herself from leaning back against him. She wasn't particularly afraid of Harris at the moment, but the consequences of her fall from Smuggler suddenly seemed very real. They made her hands begin to shake. She knew she was lucky to be riding home relatively uninjured.

"Will there be adequate accommodations for you in Southampton?" he asked.

"Aunt Esther and I will manage, thank you," she said.

"I shall see to it that your father is informed that you have returned to Southampton to enjoy the English seaside," he said.

"That would be very kind of you," she said.

They rode around a curve in the path and Penridge Hall came into view, the elegant façade and the fairy gate framed by the gray branches of the woods—stereoscopic picture perfect. Strangely, the sight set her heart aflutter.

Harris halted Pendragon. She was aware of him leaning closer, admiring the house, as she was, the warmth of his cheek near hers.

"I left here once," he began, the sound of his voice making her shiver, "never intending to return. When I returned, I never intended to stay. Now I can't imagine leaving. It is my home and I'm caught in its web of secrets," he said. The sound of longing buried deep in his voice tugged at her heart. "Dare I ask, will you come back to us, sweet Alyssa?" he whispered.

"No, I don't believe so," she said, twisting her fingers deeper into Pendragon's mane to help her resist Harris's powerful attraction. Was she sitting in the arms of a murderer, this man with the ability to say what she needed to hear? How she longed to believe him innocent, but could no longer. How she longed to press her cheek against his and promise that she would return. How she yearned for a future when all would be well, when the shadow of death and deception did not hang over Penridge.

She longed for the impossible, for the storybook ending.

How silly of her. She was an impetuous American who'd foolishly given her body and her heart to a man who'd probably committed murder—who may have even attempted to hurt her—for the love of another. "No, I won't be coming back. I don't belong here."

Twenty-four

"Cut?!" Elijah couldn't have looked more surprised if he'd been told the sun would not rise the next morning. "Who would cut a girth? Oh, Miss Lockhart, I am so sorry. I do not tolerate carelessness in my stable, and I most certainly do not allow tampering with the tack. I cannot imagine who would do this. There has been no one in the stable but Johnnie and me for the past week."

"I want to see the other saddles." Harris nodded toward the tack room, obviously little impressed with the coachman's excuses.

"Right away, my lord," Elijah said, his eyes still wide with surprise and embarrassment. He led the way, throwing open the tack room door and going straight to the other two sidesaddles neatly hung in their proper places. One was Gwendolyn's sidesaddle and another was kept for guests, just like the one Alyssa had used that morning. Upon examination, the girths of both saddles had been cut partially through with a sharp object just as Alyssa's girth had been.

"Our villain was taking no chances," Harris said, holding the cut girths up for Elijah and Alyssa to see. "Whoever the next lady rider was, she would take a nasty fall."

"But why?" Alyssa asked.

"My lord," Elijah began. "Nothing like this has ever happened. I am so ashamed. I will talk with Johnnie straightaway."

"See that you do," Harris said. "Get this tack repaired immediately. And take more heed of what you are doing when you tack up the horses. This should never have happened. Be thankful that Miss Lockhart did not come to any great harm."

"I am grateful for that, my lord," Elijah said. He looked so mortified and humiliated, she took pity on the poor man. He bowed in her direction "Forgive me, miss."

Harris took her hand and mercilessly led her toward the house.

"He didn't do it," Alyssa said, trying to decide if she should free herself from Harris's grasp or not. She limped along as best she could, hardly able to keep up with his long strides on the best of days, and certainly hampered today after the fall.

"But you are willing enough to believe that I did," Harris snapped without looking at her. "But he was careless. It is his job to spot anything amiss with the tack. Purposefully committed or otherwise."

"Then who?" she asked, watching his stony face. "And Gwendolyn is in danger also."

"We are unlikely to find out before you leave," Harris said, marching up the steps to the house. "I will caution Gwendolyn."

Tavi met them at the door, swinging it wide as they started up the steps to the house.

"Ring for Jane," Harris ordered, still leading Alyssa by the hand toward the stairs. "Miss Lockhart is packing to leave on the train today."

Tavi stood with his hand still on the doorknob and the door still open. "But there is no other train today, my lord. I have the schedule here."

Harris stopped and turned to the butler. "Are you certain?"

Tavi took a printed sheet of paper from the drawer of a hall table. "See, here it says the only train left the village at eight o'clock this morning."

Just then, Gwendolyn hurried into the hallway. "What is

it?" she asked, glancing from Tavi to Harris to Alyssa. She frowned at the sight of Alyssa's muddied riding habit. "My dear, what happened?"

"It seems I've been the victim of another prank, Gwendolyn."

"What?" The lady paled. "Are you all right?"

"I will recover," Alyssa said, glancing up to see Harris studying the widow. "But I think a hot bath would do me a lot of good right now."

"Alyssa is leaving us tomorrow, Gwendolyn," Harris announced, still firmly holding her hand in contradiction to his eagerness to see her packed up and on the train.

"Surely not because of this prank?" Gwendolyn asked, her lovely face slack with surprise. "But you have been so brave in the face of all that has happened."

"We have decided it is time," Harris said, his tone short and his expression remote.

Alyssa cast him a cautious look and pulled her hand free of his with as little fuss as she could manage.

"But Byron Littlefield will be so disappointed—" Gwendolyn began, touching Harris's arm.

He covered Gwendolyn's hand with his to interrupt her. "Littlefield will survive."

Alyssa lifted her chin, glad that she was going. She would leave them to their conspiracy. Though her sense of justice was outraged—a murderer was going free—there was nothing more she could do for Meggie now.

"I will write Meggie, of course," Alyssa said, summoning all of her dignity. Suddenly she was eager to be away from the place. From the secrets and the pretensions. The only thing she was sorry to leave behind was Meggie—and her own innocence.

She would plead a headache at dinnertime and ask for a tray in her room. In the morning she would be gone, leaving Penridge and its fairy gate behind her. "Jane, there you are. I should like a bath before we begin to pack. Good day to you all."

She made as graceful an exit as she could with her crooked hat, smudged skirt, and limp.

"But you haven't eaten a thing, miss," Jane said, staring at the supper tray that she'd set before Alyssa an hour earlier.

"I'm just not hungry," Alyssa said with partial honesty. She was sitting at the tea table by the fire where she'd settled when she and Jane finished the packing.

Now that the decision to leave had been made—or made for her—how was she ever going to get through the night torn as she was? Her heart sent up a silent protest against leaving Harris. But her common sense urged her to hurry away from Penridge Hall as fast as she could—urged her to leave before Harris decided that she knew too much and should be silenced.

Jane picked up the tray. "His lordship was asking after you. Concerned he is."

"What did you tell him?" Alyssa asked, fingering the folds of her favorite morning gown.

"That we'd finished the packing and that you were feeling unwell. Wanted to rest. Just like you said to tell him."

"Was he satisfied with that?" she asked.

"He was concerned that you weren't well, and he wanted to send for Dr. Lewellyn, but I explained it was just a few bruises from the fall," Jane said, lingering beside the table. "He seemed satisfied with the explanation, miss. And I can say that those of us below stairs are disappointed, too. It has been a pleasure serving you. Can I get you anything more? Maybe some warm milk to help you sleep?"

"No, but thank you, Jane, for all your help," Alyssa said, smiling weakly, touched by the maid's kind words. "I will miss you, too. I'm quite all right for now."

"I'll be back to stoke the fire later," Jane said, and quietly left the room.

Alyssa returned to staring into the blaze on the hearth, her foolish heart aching. Would she never learn that her impulses were not to be trusted? Harris was *not* her storybook hero. At nearly twenty years of age she should be adult enough to understand and accept that. He was *just* a man, good perhaps in some ways—but flawed and driven by darker motives and desires that she didn't begin to understand.

Was he a murderer? It certainly seemed so. Had he seduced her to gain her allegiance? Probably, but she'd succumbed willingly—she couldn't release herself entirely from that responsibility. She had known what she was doing when she let him make love to her. And, really, she wasn't sorry. Her heart might ache, and she might call herself a dozen different kinds of fool, but she would get over it. Her broken heart would mend eventually, and it might even be stronger for having had such a devastating experience. Maybe she wouldn't be so easily taken in by another man. Certainly she'd know the next time where all those melting, hot feelings Harris aroused in her could lead, and she'd be better prepared not to let them overrule her common sense.

With a sigh, she took up the suspect list she'd begun days ago and stared at it, trying to focus on the words. There was a knock on her door.

"Alyssa, may I come in?" It was Gwendolyn, the last person on earth she wanted to see at the moment.

Alyssa folded up the paper and tucked it behind her in the chair. "Come in."

"My dear," Gwendolyn said when she saw Alyssa in the chair. "We just had to see how you were. If you needed anything."

The sight of Harris standing behind Gwendolyn at the door almost brought Alyssa out of her chair. She'd not expected him to come to her room.

"You do look pale," the lady said, crossing the room to

sit in the other fireside chair. "Sometimes injuries can be worse than we realize. Perhaps we should send for Dr. Lewellyn."

"No, I'm all right, really," Alyssa said, glancing uneasily at Harris and wondering how to look ill enough to have excused herself from dinner, but not so ill as to need a doctor. His expression was one of sober, polite concern. Gwendolyn had talked him into this visit, she was sure. "Dr. Lewellyn will just see my bruises and tell me I need to rest," she added.

"Yes, I suppose so." Gwendolyn was still dressed as she must have been for dinner in black lace, elegant and delicate, like her fine features. Pearls in her earlobes. Her hair swept back from her face. In the firelight her eyes glittered. How pleased Harris must have been to have her to himself at the dinner table, Alyssa thought bitterly.

"I am grateful for your hospitality," Alyssa said, feeling strangely awkward and vulnerable. She glanced anxiously at Harris again, noting that he remained silent. "I hope that everything is resolved for the best," she said.

"Do not trouble yourself over our problems." He moved to the fireside, his hands clasped behind him. Like Gwendolyn, he was dressed for dinner and looked quite handsome, the firelight casting shadows across the aristocratic planes of his face and enhancing the darkness of his hair.

She stifled a sigh to avoid being obvious in her admiration. This was how she wanted to remember him, as lord and master of the house standing by the fire, dressed for dinner, strong—and maybe just a bit dangerous if you stood between him and what he wanted.

"Let us not tire you," Gwendolyn said, rising from her chair. She smiled fondly at Alyssa and took her hand, kissing her cheek so affectionately that Alyssa felt petty and small for suspecting the lady, even for a second, of having even a small part in her husband's death.

"You have a long journey tomorrow, and it starts early. Good night, my dear," Gwendolyn said as she walked to the door. "Of course, I shall be there to see you off."

Harris followed, murmuring good night and hesitating a fraction of a second on the threshold, his hand on the doorknob, his body in the hallway. "Lock your door tonight," he whispered so softly Alyssa almost didn't understand him.

She blinked.

He pointed meaningfully to the key resting in the inside keyhole of the lock. She understood and nodded. Then he was gone.

She was left alone in front of the fire with questions running through her mind—who did Harris fear might threaten her during the night and was that person the same person who'd murdered Alistair? She'd not thought of herself in particular danger until she'd seen the girth, until Harris had frowned over it and insisted she leave, until he'd warned her to lock her door.

With a shiver she realized the night ahead would be a long and sinister one indeed.

Alyssa awoke to the sound of a floorboard creaking in the hallway. She lay still, listening for more sounds, evidence that someone was outside her door. The house was otherwise quiet. The room was inky dark. The fire had gone out earlier, driving her into the warmth of the bed, where she'd finally fallen asleep.

Another sound—like someone twisting the doorknob. Then nothing more. Nevertheless, she bolted up in the bed and listened, holding her breath. She'd locked her door as Harris had told her, so she was safe. Still, who could it be? She heard metal softly slide against metal and lock workings turn and click.

A shiver of fear tingled through her. The intruder had a key.

"Who's there?" she called and frantically reached for the

matches near her bedside lamp. Maybe if the intruder knew she was awake and would identify him, he would go away. "What do you want?" With trembling hands, she struck a match and willed her hand to be steady enough to light the lamp. Thankfully, lamplight flooded the room.

Harris stood in the opened door. "Shh. It's only me," he said, with a warning finger to his lips. Then he turned to take his key from the lock and slipped it into his pocket. Of course, the lord and master of the house would have a key. Why hadn't she thought of that before? Then he closed the door softly and locked it. "Are you all right?"

"Merciful heavens!" Alyssa put her hand to her pounding heart. "What do you want?"

"I'm sorry. I didn't mean to frighten you." He walked to the foot of the bed and put a hand on the bedpost. He was still dressed, but his cravat had been loosened. "I'm not here to seduce you, I promise, but I cannot leave you alone tonight, Alyssa. It is simply too dangerous. After seeing that girth, I have a bad feeling about this. I will just sit here by the fire until morning."

She continued to stare at him, wondering what to do, wondering how much danger she was in.

"To make you feel better," he continued as he reached into his pocket, "I brought you this."

He pulled out a small pearl-handled pistol, a lady's firearm, and laid it in the palm of his hand. "You know how to use a weapon like this, do you not?"

She could feel her eyes growing large at the sight of the gun. She nodded.

"Good," he said, studying her. With a flick of his wrist he threw open the cylinder. "See, it's loaded."

He flipped it closed and he started toward her.

She sucked in a breath and shrank back against the headboard.

He hesitated, holding his hands up in a gesture to indicate he was harmless. "I am going to place the gun here on the table beside you. Use it if you feel the need. If you sense a threat from me or anyone else, use it."

He laid the gun on the table with great care. When he'd done that, he retreated to the fireplace. He reached for the scuttle and began pouring more coal on the embers.

Alyssa eyed the gun with disquiet, her heart thrumming in her chest. "You would give me a gun to use against you?"

"I give you a gun to use against anyone who would do you harm," he said without looking at her as he worked to encourage the fire. "I trust your judgment, Alyssa. You've got a good head on your shoulders."

"Even though I've practically accused you of murder?"

"I know how bad it looks," he said, setting aside the poker and seating himself in the chair by the hearth. "I sent a telegraph ahead to reserve rooms for you at the hotel in Southampton. So if you need accommodations, they are available. I also contacted a bank. There will be funds available if you need them. And Elijah has agreed to travel with you." He turned to her briefly. "You do trust Elijah, don't you? I won't have you traveling alone. I would never have permitted it upon your arrival if I'd known."

She nodded, still clutching the counterpane, completely taken aback by his presence, by the gun, by everything he'd done.

"Do *you* trust Elijah?" she couldn't help but ask.

"Yes, he is not like his brother at all," Harris said, gazing at the fire, his profile toward her.

Alyssa glanced at the gun on the table, suddenly feeling safer, though she wasn't certain she'd have the courage to use the thing against anyone. She sat up straight and tucked the counterpane around her. What else would Harris tell her if she asked? "And what about Captain Dundry? Who is he? Is he trustworthy?"

"Dundry?" Harris repeated with a bit of surprise in his voice, drawing out the syllables as if he was debating what to say. "Captain Dundry is a long-time acquaintance with Bow

Street connections. I hired him to do some investigating for me. A good man. He brought Sir Ralph's lawsuit to light—and Byron's tarnished reputation."

An investigator. That made sense. "Did he learn anything about Zebulon Whittle?" she asked, unable to keep herself from mentally reviewing her list of suspects, though the most probable one was sitting by her fire.

"Nothing particularly useful," he said. "That was a disappointment."

"Yes," she had to agree, unable to resist adding, "It would have been very satisfying to have an investigator discover some foul deed of the reverend's that could be reported to the authorities."

Harris chuckled wryly without looking at her. "Precisely."

She studied him. He certainly didn't look like a murderer or act like one. "Tell me more about Alistair," she said.

He glanced at her. "What do you want to know about my cousin?"

"What was it like for the two of you growing up?" she asked. "Did you play pranks on each other? Did you like each other?"

"No, we didn't play pranks, not in the way you mean it," Harris said. "We did challenge each other. I believe we did like each other after a fashion, more some days than others. But it was never a close relationship. Our temperaments were too different."

"How so?" she asked, though she thought she knew.

"Alistair expected a great deal from others," Harris said, stretching his legs toward the fire that had finally come to life. "And he could be bold, even foolhardy, to prove his point. I remember one summer when we were about fifteen and sixteen we were sailing together when we had a dispute about whether the tide was high enough to tack a certain direction into a cove. I wanted to keep our heading. He wanted to tack. He grabbed the rudder and brought the boat around before I realized that he meant to show me that I was wrong. The boat came about and the reef ripped into the hull. We went down in seconds. Alistair was about as good a swimmer as he was a sailor. The undertow was incredible. I had to drag his sorry soul up onto shore."

As Alyssa listened, she gathered the counterpane around her and crawled to the foot of the bed, closer to the fire, closer to Harris so she could see his face, hear the subtleties in his voice. He could be telling the story just to make himself look good, but she didn't think so. He was talking about the event almost as if it was a fond memory. He even chuckled about Alistair's swimming skills. What murderer chuckled like that?

There were other inconsistencies she knew about Harris. No murderer helped make a pet of a hedgehog for a sad little girl or rode across the wintry moor to get food for miners' families. No murderer worried about a young woman traveling alone. What murderer handed a gun to a possible victim?

She was beginning to think she was not wrong about this man, after all.

"What did your uncle say about the lost boat?" she asked, leaning her shoulder against the bedpost.

"Alistair tried to deny his part, but I think Uncle Seymour suspected," Harris said. "By then I'd become accustomed to my cousin's little frauds, or at least I thought I had."

"Tell me why you sent Meggie away," she said.

Harris turned to scrutinize her over his shoulder. She couldn't be sure what fact he weighed, what truth made him hesitate.

"I did not send Meggie away because I believed she'd put the nettles in your bed," Harris said at last. "Or for whatever nefarious reasons Pendeen might have told you. I did it because when the truth comes out, I thought it best for her not to be here."

"What truth do you fear?" Alyssa leaned toward him. "Be honest with me, Harris. I only want to understand. Is it that you've always loved Gwendolyn?"

Abruptly, he turned in his chair to look at her, his face stark with surprise. "Is that what Pendeen told you?"

"He said he saw you kissing her in the garden before Alistair died," she said. "A lover's kiss. He said that you sent Meggie away so you could carry on your suit of Gwendolyn."

"That's not true," Harris snapped, frowning with indignation. "None of it."

"He said he watched you from the grand salon window," Alyssa said, clutching the bedpost.

"It never happened, Alyssa," Harris vowed, his gaze clear and steady.

"He said that Gwendolyn returned to the house with her hand to her mouth, her bodice rumpled, and her hair mussed," she said, mentally reviewing Pendeen's story. "No, wait. He said that's how she returned to the house after he saw the two of you in the garden. But he clearly thought there'd been a kiss."

"Perhaps that's what Gwendolyn wanted him to think," Harris said with a sigh. He stared into the fire once more.

"Gwendolyn?"

"Tell me about your list of suspects, Alyssa," he said without looking at her. "Now that you trust Elijah, who remains on your list besides me, Sir Ralph, and the Reverend Whittle?"

Alyssa hesitated. There were only two names that she'd purposely not mentioned to him before. "Tavi?"

Harris shook his head. "No, not Tavi. He's completely reliable. He did not like Alistair, but he would not have murdered him. Any others?"

"I thought of Gwendolyn briefly," Alyssa ventured, wary of his reaction, "but . . . "

Harris passed a hand over his face. "Yes, the question is, what if Gwendolyn knew about Alistair's affair?"

Alyssa sucked in a breath of surprise. "But Lady Cynthia said Gwendolyn didn't know. And she certainly has never

given any indication that she knew, has she? But if she did . . .
and she'd said nothing . . . oh, my."

"Precisely," Harris said, continuing to stare into the fire.
"When I returned to Penridge Hall it did not take long to realize that Gwendolyn was unhappy. She was pitiful, starved
for attention. But the past ten years had made me immune to
her appeals. Yet, I felt sorry for her. I made it clear, gently as
I could, that I had returned to see my cousin only. She seemed
to accept that. I decided that Alistair had obviously been ne-
glectful of his wife and needed to mend fences with the
Littlefields."

"So you and the vicar arranged the dinner that night to
bring about a reconciliation between the Trevells and the Littlefields," Alyssa said, drawn into the events of that night
once more. Gathering the counterpane, she climbed off the
bed, tiptoed across the cold floor to the chair opposite Harris's, and tucking her feet beneath her, settled into it. "But
Lady Cynthia, Sir Ralph, Alistair, and maybe Gwendolyn
were sitting at the table wondering if the affair was going to
come to light."

"The vicar and I knew there were bad feelings in the air,"
Harris said, shaking his head. "But neither of us considered
the possibility of an illicit affair or that it would all come to
murder."

"Still, how could it be Gwendolyn?" Alyssa asked, sitting
back in the chair, suddenly chilled to the bone despite her
heavy nightgown and the counterpane wrapped around her.
"She nursed Alistair until the last. Everyone commented on
her devotion."

"She was, indeed, devoted," Harris agreed. "I watched. I
was amazed at her patience and strength. Delicate Gwendolyn. Believe me, nursing Alistair was not a pleasant task
and he made it no better. That night when Alistair swore me
to find his murderer, I thought about her. But I couldn't believe it of her—she was Alistair's wife, for God's sake. I'm
certain he never suspected her. She was the woman he

loved—a woman that I'd loved once. How could she be a murderess?"

"How indeed?" Alyssa said, watching the firelight play across his features, tortured by pain and disbelief. "Yet, it explains everything."

His expression softened. "Alyssa, you will leave tomorrow because it is the only safe thing to do. Then I can go on with whatever I have to do, knowing you are out of danger. But I cannot describe my feelings today when I realized you had lost faith in me."

"Harris." Alyssa groaned with regret. He was right. She'd been quick enough to think the worst of him. She'd listened to Peter Pendeen's story with her head and childishly surrendered to every credible element of it, shutting out every protest of her heart.

"You have been a breath of fresh air in my life," he said with warmth and wonderment in his voice. It made her feel ashamed that she'd given in to her fears. "I'll never forget how you asked me if I knew about the rumor that I'd murdered my cousin and how you waved it aside," Harris continued, smiling. "Do you know how important it has been for me to know a guileless woman? I had come to believe that such a thing did not exist."

She looked down at her hands, uncomfortable with praise she did not deserve. "I want to believe in you, Harris. I have always wanted to."

Slowly he leaned forward in his chair and reached for her hands. She gave them to him.

"Then promise me you will come back to Penridge," he said. "When this is over, and it will come to an end eventually, return to me. Bring your family. Or I'll come to you. Whatever you like. Just promise me that you will see me again."

"Harris?" Alyssa repeated his name because she did not know what to say. Because she knew she'd been wrong to suspect him. Her heart was true. "I promise," she said.

He raised her hands to his lips and kissed her fingers.

"Oh, Harris." She was out of the chair and in his arms in a flash.

He pulled her into his lap, wrapping her in the counterpane and accepting her kisses. She wrapped her arms around his neck and pulled him closer, bestowing a tender kiss that became more passionate as her lips moved over his.

When she released him, they gazed into each other's eyes for a long moment. No words were necessary between them. He swung her up into his arms, counterpane and all, and carried her to the bed.

He fell on her hungrily, his fingers sinking into her hair as he angled her head back and kissed her mouth, her throat, then her mouth again. She responded to the heat of his desire, fighting her way out of the counterpane to arch her body against his. Despite the thickness of her cotton nightgown, she savored the hard, demanding strength of his body pressing her down into the mattress. She wanted to lose herself in their passion.

His kisses became more explicit in what he wanted from her. Parting her lips with his tongue, he blatantly explored her, moving in and out of her mouth, insistent, sleek, and tantalizing. She whimpered.

"I will make it better this time," he said with that huskiness in his voice that fell so wonderfully on her ears. He could make her melt inside with just a few words. He began to unfasten the buttons down the front of her nightgown. Though his hands worked deftly, she grew impatient to have his fingers touch her, and she reached down to help. He brushed her hands away. "No, I am glad you are eager, but this is my privilege," he said.

"Then hurry," she said, grasping his hands and pulling them inside her nightgown to cup her aching breasts. She closed her eyes with relief. His palms were hot. They melted away the heaviness. "That's better," she whispered, her eyes still closed tightly to better enjoy the pleasure his hands brought.

He bent closer, so close his breath tingled on her lips. "There. That's the kind of smile I want to see on your lips."

Briefly his thumbs teased her nipples, then he released her, leaving her bare and open to the cool night air as he returned to unfasten the remaining buttons. She reached for his hands, but he waved them away. "Patience, my sweet."

Then the buttons were free. He pulled her into a sitting position and began to peel the nightgown up and over her head. When she was naked, he laid her back against the pillows, pulling the counterpane back to enjoy the sight of her entire body as once more he cupped her breasts in his hands.

She groaned and reached up to capture his face between her hands. He looked down on her and smiled a devilish smile. "There, now. You are mine to feast on—and to pleasure."

He began to tease her again with his thumbs, making her nipples grow hard. He made small sounds of encouragement and satisfaction. She closed her eyes and arched against the sensations he created in her, praying this would indeed be a long, long night.

He bent over her, slipping an arm beneath her back, lifting her to lave her breasts with his tongue, then finally drawing her into his hot mouth and sucking. When his lips closed over her, he brought the most incredible awareness spreading through her body that she'd ever known. But it was not complete.

He lifted his head and glared at her, his eyes filled with a mixture of bewilderment and anger all at once. "I can hardly bear the thought of you leaving, sweet Alyssa. I know it is the right thing. But I cannot get enough of you."

"It won't be for long," she said, taking one of his hands and guiding it down to her secret place where she knew she was moist and needy. Where she knew her heat would seduce him.

His fingers found her and began their cunning strokes.

"Harris," she responded, helpless to do anything else.

He groaned again, his surrender, and he captured her mouth. When she fumbled for his trouser buttons, he pushed her hands away and undid them himself. He rolled off the bed without his gaze leaving her. With hasty but efficient motions he shrugged out of his coat and shirt, flinging them across the room, and shed his trousers.

She rose up on one elbow to catch sight of his male member, proud and obvious in its eagerness to perform.

"Do you like what you see, my sweet?" he asked, looking arrogant and amused as he put one knee on the bed and loomed over her.

"Yes, but I have so much to learn," she said, vaguely recalling images she'd seen in the book in his study, things that seemed much more feasible and pleasurable now than they had before he'd introduced her to the delights of a man's physical attentions.

"I'll teach you," he said, lying down beside her and throwing a long thigh over her hips, pressing himself intimately against her. He bent to kiss her lips, then her neck. "But we'll take our time."

Then he began working his way downward, planting kisses on her breasts, down her middle between her ribs, nipping at her soft, pale skin with his teeth. Then his tongue flicked over her navel. Her reaction was thrilling and involuntary. Raising her knees, her thighs parted. He pressed his fingers into her supple flesh and found her center. She threaded her fingers through his thick hair. Mindless as she was, and drowning in ecstasy, Alyssa realized that Harris wanted her in the most intimate of ways. When his kiss came, his lips, his tongue against her, the knowledge was not a shock, but an unbearable thrill. She pulled on his hair.

Suddenly he was bending over her face.

"Are you on the edge, my sweet?" he asked hoarsely.

The edge was the only possible description of how she felt, poised on the verge of a drop, waiting for the great lightness of the fall. "Yes, the edge," she murmured, gripping his shoulders as if to pull back from a life-threatening plunge.

"Then, let go," he said against her ear. "Let me take you over the edge this time. Together this time."

Gently he parted her knees with his and thrust into her, shuddering as he sank deep, stretching her, the cords of his back hard and tight, his breath short and shallow. Alyssa arched up to meet him and each thrust that followed. Again and again. Their bodies meshing perfectly each time. The completeness of him filling her was perfect, yet frustrating. Her need for him grew. Soon her breathing matched his. When the fall came, she clung to him. He pressed his face against her cheek, and they soared together. Sweet brightness. Shimmering air.

Harris murmured her name.

Sparks tingled from her fingertips to her toes. Then she was falling gently, like a leaf, back and forth. Rocking like a baby.

She was cradled in his arms. He smiled down at her, brushing his thumb across her lips.

"I love you," he whispered.

"Me, too," were the only words she had the energy to say. Closing her eyes, she drifted off to sleep, certain that her life was complete at last. She loved Harris. And he loved her.

She awoke later, when the fire had died, and she realized that Harris was lying next to her awake. Smiling to herself, she snuggled closer to him. She felt him kiss the top of her head. She'd almost drifted off again when she realized what must be on his mind still.

"Gwendolyn?"

"What?" he asked.

"You're thinking about Gwendolyn," she said, sighing heavily. "I remember now meeting her yesterday morning as she returned from the stable."

"Yes, she must have cut her own girth to divert suspicion from herself," Harris said.

"What are you going to do?" she asked, laying her head on his chest and listening to the strong, steady beat of his heart. "If she is Alistair's murderer, you can't go to the sheriff with what you know. There's no proof. And what about Meggie?"

"I've been thinking about that," he said. "I may offer Gwendolyn a choice: the sheriff or a settlement to go live in Brussels or Paris."

"And Meggie?"

"Meggie will stay at Penridge," Harris said. "I can arrange it legally. The less the child knows, the better. For the moment, the important thing is to get you safely away from here."

He turned to her, cupping his hand around her neck and kissing her, sweetly. She stroked his body, and they made love again, slow and tender.

Twenty-five

They made love again before dawn, a gentle, incredibly sweet mating without the urgency of the first, yet just as satisfying. When Alyssa awoke to Jane's knock at her door, Harris and his clothes were gone. Disappointment dampened the glow that lingered inside her.

Harris had left her early to be discreet, of course, she told herself. In the gray light of dawn she leaped from the bed to snatch up her nightgown and pull it on over her nakedness. How awkward it would have been if the maid had walked in on them in each other's arms. "Come in, Jane."

Jane bustled into the room with hot wash water. She set it down and busied herself with lighting the lamp and then stoking the fire in the grate. "His lordship is in a great rush. He is already after Elijah about hitching up the horses and the carriage. He says you are leaving in an hour. He is eager to be off, with no chance for you to miss the train. We best get you dressed and downstairs for your breakfast."

Jane went into the dressing room, where Alyssa's traveling clothes had been hung out the night before.

Eager for her to be off? Alyssa stood in the middle of the floor, sleep-muddled and, after their declarations of love, too astonished by the thought of leaving to move. How could he still plan to send her away? Surely last night had changed everything.

Jane came back into the room carrying Alyssa's gray gabardine suit over her arm. "Wot's this, miss?" she said, staring at a piece of paper that was lying on the floor near the door. Neither of them had noticed it before the lamp was lit. The maid crossed the room and picked it up. The plain stationery was folded and they could both see Alyssa's name scrawled across it. "Why, it appears to be a note for you. Here."

Alyssa took it and went to stand by the lamp to read. It was written in a scrawl much like Harris's.

> *Meet me at the dower house in a half hour. We have much to say to each other yet. Burn this note before you leave.*
>
> > *H*

She read it through one more time before she glanced around at Jane, who was seemingly busy with the fire again. Well, it was too late if Harris wanted her to burn the note so Jane didn't know it had been received, Alyssa thought, folding the paper and tucking it under the foot of the lamp. She thought about taking the pearl-handled gun with her to return it to him, but decided to put it in the bedside table drawer and return it later.

Woodside, the dower house, seemed like an odd place to meet. It stood empty and secluded in the woods a quarter of an hour's walk from Penridge. Why did they need to be as circumspect as that? Why not meet in his study?

But he was right; they did have more to say to each other, especially if he still thought he was going to send her away. Now that she knew he felt about her as deeply as she felt about him, she would stay at his side until he was proven innocent. How could he even question that?

Wide-awake and determined now, Alyssa turned to the maid. "I must be on my way quickly, Jane. Help me dress."

A light burned warmly in the dower house window as she approached along the path from Penridge. She stopped at the edge of the woods, studying the place. Since the morning of her first visit, she'd only glimpsed Woodside cottage from a distance when she was out riding, a quaint fairy-tale cottage tucked into the forest. On this frosty morning with the grass and trees covered in white crystals, white smoke curled up from the main chimney. The light in the window and the comforting scent of a wood fire added an inviting touch to the cottage that she'd only seen deserted before.

Pendragon was nowhere to be seen, but then Harris had probably walked just as she had. Again she wondered why he'd chosen this place to meet, unless he felt it offered them more privacy than his study. Privacy for lovemaking? Her body warmed at the thought, though the cold morning had chilled her. Heated memories of the previous night's activities coursed through her. Harris's hands and lips against her skin. His body filling hers. Though there was little cottage furniture left after Gwendolyn's removal of her favorite pieces, it might be just the perfect lovers' tryst. All they needed was a mattress.

At Woodside, there would be little chance of Jane or Tavi interrupting them. Smiling in anticipation, she started toward the cottage again, reconsidering her hasty judgment about it as a meeting place.

When she entered the garden, mournful and fuzzy with frost, she noticed for the first time that the cottage door was standing open and the reflection of orange firelight danced on it.

"Harris?" she called as she walked up the flagstone path and through the doorway. The heat in the room struck as soon as she set foot on the threshold. It felt more like an oven's blast than the warmth of a cozy room. At the moment it felt good. "I'm glad you built a fire," she called, "because it is quite chilly out here and I didn't wear my jacket."

No one answered, and in the play of the firelight, she thought the keeping room was empty except for the old wooden fireside settle with a homespun throw draped across its back.

Alyssa stepped farther into the room. "Harris?"

"Harris is not here, my dear," Gwendolyn said from behind her.

She whirled around to face Lady Penridge as she'd never seen her. Not the sad beauty, but a creature with narrow and cold eyes, her lips pursed in irritation, her features smooth and oh, so hard. She held a shotgun with familiarity, the twin barrels gleaming in the orange light and twin hammers cocked.

An icy chill pooled in Alyssa's belly.

"Gwendolyn? I—" Her mind raced to make sense of what she saw and what she knew. The pieces did not fit. "What's the shotgun for?"

"You will see soon enough, dear." Gwendolyn's dulcet tones contradicted the evil in her face. She swung the gun barrel toward the fireplace. "Go stand over there. I was beginning to think you would disappoint me, Alyssa. That you would never come. But I should have known that anything signed with Harris's name would bring you, sooner or later. You lack subtlety, my dear."

"So I've been told," Alyssa said, surprised to find that this time the criticism had no power to hurt her. She moved toward the fireplace as Gwendolyn instructed and gathered her wits. *"You* sent that note? Why?"

"Because, as I wrote, we have things to discuss, you and I," Gwendolyn said, the firelight glinting demon-like in her eyes. "But we must wait a bit. Not everyone is here."

"Harris?" Alyssa asked. It had always been plain enough that Gwendolyn coveted Harris. What woman wouldn't? But surely not enough to murder for him. "Are we waiting for Harris?"

"No—you are so simple," Gwendolyn said, her mouth relaxing into a malevolent smile. "You only see the obvious. All will unfold shortly."

The fire roared in the great old fieldstone hearth, its heat burning into Alyssa's side. Flames licked up and out of the hearth, blackening the stones and singeing the wooden mantel mounted above it.

"We are waiting for another lover of yours," Gwendolyn said.

Mystified, Alyssa glanced around the room for a clue to what was going on, for an escape route or a diversion.

"Do you not know who I mean?" Gwendolyn laughed, low and vicious. "Byron, of course, my dear. Do you have so many lovers you cannot remember them? But Byron was your lover last week, was he not?"

Alyssa had no idea what to say.

"Then last night . . ." Gwendolyn eyed her with a sidelong glare. "Last night Harris slept with you."

Alyssa remained silent.

"Have you nothing to say for yourself?" Gwendolyn baited, holding the shotgun in the crook of her arm and stroking the barrel. "When you came to Penridge, I actually welcomed your visit. It was a relief in the tedium of mourning and a distraction for the gossipmongers. Of course, I could see that Harris found you attractive. And you clearly had a *tendre* for him. He was better at hiding it than you. It didn't bother me at first. You were pretty, but you were also young and quite lacking in the necessary sophistication to hold a man. Yet, a woman cannot expect a virile man to let a pretty girl go unnoticed. Untouched, yes, but not unnoticed. And Harris is only a man. Soon I began to hope that you would leave Penridge and that he would forget his infatuation with you. I did not mind Meggie's little pranks at all. But I quite underestimated you. It seems you seduced Harris with your novel red hair and your tomboy ways after all."

"And *you* want Harris for yourself," Alyssa said, understanding at last that which should have been so obvious before.

"No, you are wrong." Gwendolyn stared at Alyssa in astonishment. "Harris wants *me*. You saw how he came to my rescue the day the miners held me prisoner in their church. You saw it. He held me in his arms. He would have come to me that night, too, if I had wanted him to. Wake up to the truth about the man you slept with last night. The rumors are all true. He murdered Alistair *for me*. To have *me*."

Alyssa said nothing.

"I see he told you something last night," Gwendolyn said. "Did he swear his undying love? Men do that, you know, to get a woman into bed. They will tell her anything. Alistair certainly lied to me. And lord knows what lies he told that poor, frumpy Cynthia."

"So you knew about the affair," Alyssa said.

"About Cynthia and Alistair?" Gwendolyn said with disdain. "Yes, and I see you knew, too. Did she tell you? Cynthia is such a weak thing. She takes great pleasure in her guilt. So she must confess. But no matter. When Harris came back from India, he saw what a poor excuse of a husband his cousin had become. Coldhearted. Tyrannical. A penny-pincher. An adulterer. An indifferent father to Meggie." Gwendolyn paused to shrug. "So it was necessary to do away with Alistair."

"How?" Alyssa asked. "That night at the dinner, Harris was trying to mend the feud between Sir Ralph and Alistair."

"Such a clever ruse." Gwendolyn smiled slyly. "The white arsenic powder I sprinkled into Alistair's gold Murano goblet went quite unnoticed that night. Then a few more doses proved necessary while Alistair was recovering from his food poisoning."

"You continued to poison him while he was recovering?" Alyssa said, wide-eyed and stunned.

"One dose was not going to be sufficient," Gwendolyn said. "Alistair never suspected nor has anyone else."

A shiver of revulsion coursed through Alyssa. And poor Meggie—her heart ached for the little girl. Meggie's mother had committed the ultimate betrayal—she'd helped make her child an orphan.

"Now that Alistair is dead, we must observe the proper mourning period to avoid too many questions," Gwendolyn continued. "I am so thankful black flatters my coloring. We are fortunate that poor cuckolded Sir Ralph is not going to make trouble. He's content with Alistair's end. Then there will be mourning for you, of course. A minor complication. You are a very distant relative. By the time the year is up for Alistair, we will have satisfied any mourning obligations to you."

"Mourning?" Alyssa repeated, barely comprehending. Death? Hers? "How are you going to explain to my parents?"

"It has all worked out rather nicely," Gwendolyn said, "with Harris forbidding you to see Byron. I heard the poor boy was terribly disappointed when you wrote him that you would not see him again. Frightfully disappointed. How pleased he must have been to receive a note from you this morning asking to see him at Woodside."

"With instructions to burn the note?" Alyssa asked, thinking of the piece of paper she'd left tucked under the lamp foot.

"Of course, dear." Gwendolyn smiled icily again.

"But you can't expect anyone to believe that Byron and I—" Alyssa began. Her hands had become cold and stiff despite the heat in the room. Her heart pounded erratically. She understood at last. Gwendolyn intended to kill her and Byron and make the deaths look self-inflicted. "There was never anything between us of that magnitude. Never."

"Of course there was," Gwendolyn said, her smooth skin covered with a sheen of perspiration. It made her look even more evil. "Everyone saw you dancing at Lucy's wedding. Nearly everyone below stairs saw the two of you kiss on the steps of Penridge the day you went riding. You know, that kiss grows more wanton with each telling of the story. And it will soon be common knowledge that you two have been secretly trysting here at the dower house for weeks. Byron has a rather checkered reputation. It is why he was sent down from university."

"So you have it all worked out," Alyssa said, frantically reviewing all the things that had happened in the past few weeks, wondering what she had missed, what she had not understood. "And Reverend Whittle. What does he have to do with this?"

"Whittle?" Gwendolyn blinked at her and then laughed. "The reverend has ambitions beyond his means and a dreadful *tendre* for me, poor man. But he has served his purpose. He wanted to weaken Harris's influence with the miners. I wanted to be rescued. I knew if Harris faced the crisis of losing me, he would realize how important I am to him. The near-riot worked out rather nicely, did it not, even with your interference?"

Then Alyssa understood. "It was you the reverend expected to find in the Trevell carriage."

"What?"

"The day I arrived at Penridge, the reverend waylaid the carriage," Alyssa said, remembering the clergyman's warning about murder and secrets. The pieces of the puzzle had all been there in front of her. "He told me he'd expected to find someone else riding inside, not me."

"Perhaps," Gwendolyn admitted with a pleased smile. Her chin came up and victory gleamed in her eyes. "Zebulon likes to catch me alone when he can. And you realize, of course, that I cut the girth on your saddle and the others. To make myself look endangered as well. And I would have been content to see you scamper away from Penridge, afraid for your life. But I should have known from your reaction to the nettles in your bed, a mere fall from a horse would hardly frighten you off."

"And the nettles in my bed? You were responsible for them?"

"I was, though poor Meggie took the blame." Gwendolyn paused, narrowing her eyes again as a new thought came to her. She lowered her head and glared at Alyssa. "Last night, Harris could not stay away from you," she hissed. "I will not have you come between us!"

Alyssa remained quiet, silently fighting back the panic. If Gwendolyn was not mad, she was at the very least obsessed—with Harris.

"I could not poison you," Gwendolyn said. "That would raise too many questions after Alistair's death. And that Tavi is always watching the food. So I decided on fire. When they find Byron's and your charred bodies here in the ashes, everyone will know that you were enjoying one last lovers' assignation! Either the fire got away from you or you decided never to be parted."

"I should have realized," Alyssa said, glancing at the flames. Yellow-red tongues flicked up and out of the hearth like an enraged monster smacking its lips over the prospect of a meal.

"I've always hated this cottage." Gwendolyn glanced around at the four walls. "This is where they came, you know. *Alistair and Cynthia.* They met here in a room upstairs, Alistair huffing and puffing. Cynthia yowling like a cat in season. I heard them, listened to their animal noises.

"Then, after Alistair died, Harris actually talked of me moving in here—a meager cottage. Imagine the mistress of Penridge shuttled off to the dower house! I belong at Penridge, do you not agree? Your visit saved me from that move, at least. Our American kinswoman could not stay at Penridge without a lady in residence. But now your visit is over and this place will serve a good purpose. I needn't worry about anyone relegating me to a dower cottage.

"Where *is* Littlefield? I expected him to come running to your invitation. He is nearly as besotted with you as you are with Harris."

"I believe this is rather early in the day for Byron," Alyssa said, glad of his tardiness and praying that Harris would realize that something was terribly wrong. That he would find the note. "Perhaps we should go back to the house and have a talk with Harris."

"About what?" Anger flashed across Gwendolyn's face. "Our plans are laid and you have no part of them."

"What plans?" Harris asked from the open doorway, a hand on either side of the doorframe. He was dressed for riding. His face was stony, his body rigid.

Alyssa started at the sight of him, relieved and apprehensive.

Astonishingly, Gwendolyn's face brightened at the sight of him, but the aim of her gun toward Alyssa's heart never wavered. "Harris, darling, I was not expecting you."

He glared at the widow. "What's going on, Alyssa?"

"Darling, Alyssa knows about us," Gwendolyn said before Alyssa could answer.

"Of course she does," Harris said, releasing the doorframe and stepping into the keeping room. "I told her last night. My lord, it is hot in here! Why the fire? And is that gun necessary?"

"Naturally, darling," Gwendolyn said. "Alyssa knows about our plot to murder your cousin, Alistair."

"Our plot?" He glanced at Alyssa, his gaze resting on her only briefly.

"Well, yes, so it was mine," Gwendolyn said. "But I knew you would understand it. And most effective it was, too, do you not think?"

"Gwendolyn, give me the gun," Harris said, stepping into the room and reaching out for the weapon. The widow immediately backed away, staying just beyond his reach. Her aim remained on Alyssa.

"Do not be coy, darling." Gwendolyn's eyes glittered with hysteria. "Do not play the hero for her. We are very close to having everything, you and I. We will be Lord and Lady Penridge and Meggie will have you as her true father at last."

True father? Alyssa glanced at Harris. "What is she saying, Harris?"

He ignored her, his gaze fixed firmly on Gwendolyn.

"You and I need to talk, Gwendolyn." Slowly he held out his hand to Alyssa and beckoned her toward him while his gaze remained intent on the widow.

"Let Alyssa go," he said, his voice quiet.

Alyssa stared at him for an instant, uncertain what to do. Then, with her heart pounding loud enough for all to hear, she started toward him. At the same time he took a few steps toward her, moving into Gwendolyn's aim.

"What are you doing, Harris?" the widow demanded, her aim momentarily swinging toward the man she claimed to love. "Stop that. Leave her alone."

The gun blast flashed in the room.

Pellets whistled by Alyssa's ear, teasing tendrils of her hair. Deafened, she closed her eyes. Clutching her hands into fists, she stood her ground, afraid to look anywhere, at anything. The stinging scent of ignited gunpowder nauseated her. Her knees threatened to give way, but she managed to remain on her feet. If she was hurt, she could not feel it. If Harris was hit, she could not bear to know it.

Twenty-six

"Alyssa?" Harris's voice reached her over the roar in her ears.

She opened her eyes and turned to see him standing closer to her this time, his calm not quite so firmly in place.

"Darling, do not let this infatuation get the best of you," Gwendolyn began, as if she hadn't just fired a shotgun at her lover. Her aim was on Harris this time. "Do not make me shoot you over a light skirt. I have it thoroughly planned. How to get rid of her and go on. When it is over, we will be together and no one will be the wiser. The way it was meant to be."

"Gwendolyn, if you think that's what I want, you are mad," he said, real anger in his voice now. "Give me the gun."

A furrow formed between Gwendolyn's elegant brows and her voice grated. "What do you mean? You wanted to be together well enough when Alistair proposed marriage to me. You were crushed when I accepted. You and Alistair fought. Remember?"

"That was a decade ago, Gwendolyn," Harris said, stepping toward her again and in front of Alyssa. "I was nineteen years old and the fool of fools."

"Do not move," she ordered, backing away and waving the gun once more. She had one shot left. "Indeed, you were a fool, *over me*. Fool enough to sleep with me when I was a bride. Now, are you going to be a dupe over her?"

Alyssa's head had cleared. A diversion was needed. If the woman's frenzy grew worse, she would shoot Harris. Alyssa touched Harris's arm to warn him, then stepped out from behind his body and moved toward the window and the door.

"Stop!" Gwendolyn swung the gun in her direction.

Harris was on Gwendolyn in an instant. He attempted to knock the gun barrel wide with his left arm and grabbed for her right hand. He was too late. The second barrel went off. The blast shattered the window and the burning lamp.

Lamp oil sprayed in all directions—walls and floor. In the heat of the room, flames sprang up instantly.

Heedless of the fire, Harris and Gwendolyn fell to the floor in a tangle of limbs, grappling for control of the gun. Alyssa scurried around them and reached for the throw on the old fireside settle. Frantically, she swung the woolen blanket at the flames. She'd smothered small fires before. But this time no sooner had she beaten out the orange tongues than others appeared. It was like fighting a blistering creature that scaled the draperies and slithered across the old wood. Hot and hungry, devouring all. Like a scorned woman's fury.

She glanced toward Harris and Gwendolyn, glimpsing the widow's contorted face and Harris's countenance harsh with determination. At last he wrestled the weapon from her and leaped up. Gwendolyn screeched in anger. She glared up at him, her fair hair straggling loose, her eyes glittering with rage.

"You bastard!" she shouted, crawling to her feet and leaping at him.

"Get out, Alyssa," Harris shouted, holding Gwendolyn by the wrist as she tried to claw his face. "The fire is out of control. Go."

She looked to see the flames lick upward again, reaching for her skirt. She staggered backward, but the fire followed, caught on the gabardine. With a small cry, she dropped the throw. A mistake. Instinctively, she beat at the flames with her hands. But the unrelenting conflagration stretched upward.

She searched the floor for the throw again, but the heat was searing through to her petticoats.

Harris shoved Gwendolyn away and was across the room in an instant. He grabbed the throw, dropped to his knees, and wrapped it around Alyssa's skirt. Smoke billowed into her face. She clutched at his shoulders to keep from falling.

"Leave her, you dunce," Gwendolyn cried. She came at them across the room, wielding the shotgun by the barrel. "This is how she is meant to die."

Harris leaped to his feet and pulled Alyssa aside. When the gun butt swooshed through the air, it caught his body instead of hers. She heard the air rush out of him. He staggered, but regained his balance. He released her and went after Gwendolyn again.

"Get out," he shouted, as he wrestled with the widow, their forms barely visible amid the smoke and flames.

This time Alyssa did what she was told. There was nothing she could do to help him. She was choking and nearly blinded by the smoke. Remaining only endangered herself and him. Without looking back, she clutched the throw against her skirt and hobbled toward the door. She fell once, tripped by her ragged skirt. But she climbed to her feet again and stumbled on, grabbing the doorframe to steady herself.

Suddenly he was there, lifting her up in his arms, and carrying her out the door. She clung to him, grateful to know he was escaping, too.

Blessed fresh air struck her in the face, cool and clean. She sucked it in, and then coughed. He hurried down the path and out the garden gate, coughing and choking as he went, bearing her weight as if it was nothing. He did not stop until he reached a tree. He lay her down on the ground and grabbed at the throw.

"Is it out?" he demanded, kneeling beside her and tugging at her skirt and petticoat to find any flames. His face was smudged with soot and his hair had fallen over his brow. "How badly are you burned?"

"Singed only, I think," she said, peering down at her charred gown and scorched knickers. The fire had penetrated only the first three layers of clothing.

"Thank God," he breathed, examining the fabric to be certain the fire was dead. "Thank God." He pulled her into his arms and pressed his lips against her hair.

Alyssa wrapped her arms around him, equally grateful.

Abruptly, he released her and got to his feet. "I've got to go back for Gwendolyn. She panicked and went farther into the cottage."

"No!" she cried, catching at his coat in fear. He was safe with her, and she did not want him to risk his life again. She scrambled to her feet. "Not without help."

"There's no time for that," he said, starting back toward the cottage.

Alyssa followed him as far as the gate, where he paused. The heat of the flames seared her cheeks. The entire cottage was engulfed now. Orange tongues licked out of the ground-floor windows. Glass shattered and smoke poured from the upstairs windows. Beyond the open door was a wall of fire like a portal to hell.

"Harris, you can't go in there. It's impossible. If she couldn't get out on her own, you won't survive, either."

"Give me the throw," he ordered.

Reluctant to obey, she gave it to him.

"I have to do this. Stay here," he said, throwing the small, heavy woolen blanket over his head. He started up the path toward the door. She stayed as he ordered, knowing there was little she could do to help, knowing there was no stopping him. He had to do this—not for Gwendolyn, but for Meggie.

Over the roar of the fire, she heard the ancient cottage timbers groan, the sound like a low scream. Anguished, deep, bone-chilling, yet sharp and painful. The place might start to collapse at any minute.

A movement caught her eye and she turned to see Byron Littlefield gallop up on horseback. From the direction of Penridge, Tavi and Elijah Whittle appeared, running along the path.

"Alyssa, what's Penridge doing, for God's sake?" Byron demanded, his gaze following Harris toward the cottage.

"Lady Penridge is in there," she said, relieved to see help arrive. "Can you help him?"

"Help him?" Byron shouted as he swung down from his horse. "Are you mad?"

Tavi rushed past her and Elijah followed. They had no qualms about following Harris into hell. Finally, not to be outdone, Byron went, too.

Just as they reached the front steps, another screeching groan issued from the cottage. Part of the slate roof sagged, and then collapsed into the gable over the entrance. Like an avalanche, slates slid downward on the men.

Alyssa cried a useless warning. She knew they couldn't hear her over the noise. Tavi grabbed the back of Harris's coat and pulled him back just as the slates were about to crush him.

Another loud groan and the main roof beam sank into the blaze with a roar. Angry flames shot upward, victorious, released from the confines of the cottage. Smoke and embers spiraled into a gray sky that shimmered with heat. Alyssa prayed that Gwendolyn had met her end quickly. The dower house and whatever, whoever, was left in it, was lost. The fire burned on, but its wrath was spent.

Still the heat drove Alyssa back to the tree where Harris had first taken her. The men retreated there to watch with her.

Harris turned away from the fire long enough to issue orders. "Go get your uncle and bring him here," he said to Byron. Without question, the young man mounted his horse and galloped away.

"Tavi, summon the fire department to be certain that this doesn't spread," he said. "I don't think it will, but let's not chance it."

"Yes, sir." Tavi headed down the path toward the house.

Then, staring helplessly at the fire, Harris pulled Alyssa close. "I couldn't do it. I couldn't get in there to help her."

"'Twas impossible, my lord," Elijah said, his gaze still fixed on the burning cottage. "Nobody could go in there. If Lady Penridge was in there, she were probably gone already anyway. Weren't nothing you could do."

"That's true, Harris," Alyssa said, touching his arm. "You know it."

He pulled her closer, and they watched the fire until the officials came. Elijah returned to the house and brought them blankets to wrap themselves in and camp stools to sit on. Alyssa made no effort to leave Harris's side.

"We must talk before Sir Ralph arrives," he said in a low voice as they waited. "There will be difficult questions to answer."

She nodded.

"I believe in honesty," he began. "Most of the time. But in this case—it is not even about the family reputation."

"It's about Meggie," she said for him.

"Precisely. She loved her mother. She's too young to understand all that has happened."

"I agree," Alyssa said. "What purpose would it serve for the world to know that Gwendolyn killed her adulterous husband?"

"Gwendolyn came out here to select some additional pieces of furniture to take back to Penridge," Harris said. "She apparently knocked over the lamp and the fire got away from her before help came."

"The note to Byron?" Alyssa prompted. "She told me she wrote a note to him and signed it with my name asking him to meet me at the cottage. That's why he was here."

"Explain that you sent it to ask him to meet you to say good-bye," Harris said. "Is that believable?"

"I'll do my best," Alyssa said. She threw her arms around him again. "I'm so glad you found the note."

"Tucked under the foot of the lamp," he said. "I was damned glad you had the good sense not to burn it."

"Me, too," she said, leaning her head against his shoulder. "How much of what she told me did you hear?"

"Enough to know that we were right last night," he said.

Then, summoning her courage, she asked the question that troubled her most. "And Meggie? Is it true? Are you her father?"

"It is possible," Harris said, passing a hand over his face. She could hear the apprehension in his voice. "I told you that was a time in my life I'm not very proud of."

"Why didn't you tell me last night?" she asked.

"I couldn't be certain, Alyssa," Harris said. "I couldn't take the chance that you would be mortified by the fact and I would lose you again."

"Harris, I'm sorry I doubted you once," she said, touching his face with the back of her hand. "I love you. I trust you. Trust me."

"When I brought Gwendolyn to Penridge, we were engaged," Harris said. "The final contracts had to be drawn up and the announcement made. But then Gwendolyn and her mother realized that Alistair was eligible and the heir. It was so painfully apparent I could hardly believe it. Oh, Alistair was only too glad to play his part in the sorry affair. Stealing away a beautiful banker's daughter pleased him to no end. Within a week, Gwendolyn returned my ring and latched onto my cousin. I was disgusted with her and with myself.

"Then it happened just before I left for Calcutta. She appealed to me. It was only days after she had married Alistair. Said she was sorry about marrying him, and in a weak moment—still angry and vengeful, envious—well, I'm not even certain that Gwendolyn knew for sure whether Meggie was my child or Alistair's. I do not know whether she ever told Alistair. He said nothing to me and surely he would have if he had any idea that we . . . in any case, she hinted to me over the years at the possibility.

"As time passed and I built a career and a life in India, I began to see her for what she was. Ambitious. Greedy. Shallow. I was skeptical of her claim. Was it just another calculating way to hold influence over me as she once had?

"When I returned to Penridge, it was not for her. I did not return for the estate or title. I'd lost interest in vengeance years ago. Life is too short for such things. My plan was to settle in London and get the import business under way. I wanted to come to terms with Alistair, if I could. If he would. I swear that to you on my soul, Alyssa."

She gazed into his eyes and knew he meant everything he said. "I believe you."

"But when I came to Penridge and I saw Meggie," he continued, a soft smile coming to his lips, "I was smitten. She was adorable. To my horror, Alistair had become a tyrant like his father, and Gwendolyn was as calculating as ever and pitiable. But there was Meggie, sweetness and innocence. I began to think maybe I could organize the business from Exeter so I could be close by. She was my niece, at the very least. I had a right to take an interest in her life. To be perfectly honest, I thought she deserved better than my cousin Alistair and Gwendolyn."

"So you stayed?" Alyssa said. "And in staying, you gave Gwendolyn hope of having the man she truly wanted."

"She admitted poisoning Alistair?" he asked.

"Sprinkled the arsenic in the Murano goblet before the meal when she inspected the table," Alyssa said.

"Elegant. Simple. Just like Gwendolyn," Harris said. "She liked to put on the last touches herself."

"No one would have noticed that night," Alyssa said. "She examined the place settings. Rearranged a glass, Alistair's, slipped a little poison into it. Later, the wine is poured, and he drinks it with his meal."

"That must be what happened," Harris agreed with a nod.

"Before he died, Alistair was convinced that Sir Ralph had done it somehow. Alistair was calling Sir Ralph *murderer* when Pendeen stopped at the door."

"She also told me that she and the reverend were co-conspirators," Alyssa said. "She told me that he and she planned her kidnapping."

Harris stared at her. "Gwendolyn and Whittle?"

"Remember the day I arrived?" Alyssa continued. "Reverend Whittle stopped the carriage. He was expecting to find Gwendolyn. They were already planning their little food riot to make you look bad to the miners and so you could rescue Gwendolyn."

"So that's what the reverend intended," Harris said. "But a rescue? What did Gwendolyn get out of it?"

"Your sympathy and attention," Alyssa said. "They were using each other, each for their own motives."

"Neither one of them counted on you," Harris said, kissing her temple.

"Or the miners responding to your quick action on their behalf," Alyssa said.

"Here comes our magistrate," Harris said, rising to greet the man.

Sir Ralph arrived, pale and frowning, with his cravat askew. A subdued Byron trailed him. Sir Ralph asked Harris a few questions. He told the story they had agreed upon. Alyssa agreed with it and explained her note to Byron. The man made a few notes in a notebook. Satisfied there was no more information that he needed, Sir Ralph told them they could go.

"I will stay until the undertaker has arrived and the body is found," he said, and turned to join the firemen who'd arrived to contain the fire.

Harris and Alyssa began to walk through the woods toward Penridge, their arms around each other. Tavi followed at a distance with the blankets and camp stools.

"When I realized that Gwendolyn had tricked you into

going to the dower cottage," he said. "I berated myself for not sending you away from Penridge Hall sooner. I should have seen what she was up to."

"She was very clever, Harris. Very clever. She knew how to hide her feelings. She knew how to use people to get what she wanted. She even used her own daughter."

Harris nodded sadly. "I should have been more discerning."

Alyssa's heart went out to this man with singed hair and burned hands who had carried so many dark secrets for his family and Meggie's sake.

When they reached the edge of the woods where they could see Penridge, they continued across the lawn, walking slowly.

"Go on to the house, Tavi," Harris said over his shoulder.

"Yes, my lord, I will see that food and clothing is ready for you," the butler said, silently slipping away.

Harris stopped within sight of the house and the gatehouse and pulled her into a tight embrace. "I am so glad to be alive with you in my arms. I do not give a bloody damn about what is proper or improper—ward or guardian—at the moment, and I intend to have a lot less respect for propriety in the future."

"Propriety is definitely overrated," Alyssa said, smiling up into the handsomest smudged face that she knew.

"Good," he said. "Then you will consider marrying me?"

"Considered," she said, her heart racing with happiness. "And accepted."

He paused, studying her face.

"Was that too impulsive?" she asked, frowning, afraid her youthful enthusiasm had offended once more. She hoped she'd outgrown that. "I've known since the food riot that I loved you, and that I wanted to spend my life with you. Some decisions are made in your heart."

He put a hand over her heart. "I love your heart, Alyssa,

and your impulsiveness. Keep as much of it as you like," he said, bending down to kiss her. It was a sweet, loving kiss, his firm lips urgently moving over hers. She returned the sweetness and the eagerness. It was a heady kiss, even with the scent of smoke clinging to both of them.

"Tomorrow, is that too soon?" he asked, the moment he released her mouth. "Sir Ralph and the vicar will frown and bluster about the timing, but they will help us get the special licenses. We'll marry in the morning and telegraph your parents afterwards."

"Perfect," she said, breathless from his kiss and with the excitement. He loved her. He loved her. But she would not dance across the lawn like an impetuous girl. "We'll sign the ancient Lanissey Church registry together, just like Lucy and her groom did, our names side by side for all to see through the ages."

"I will gladly sign," he said with a broad grin. "We'll start a new life together and leave the past and its secrets behind in the dark where it belongs."

He kissed her again, more passionately this time. Neither of them cared who was watching.

Epilogue

"There he is," Alyssa cried softly, peering over the rose-bush. The May moon was nearly full and bright enough to make keeping lookout in the garden easy. That was why Harris had suggested they initiate their plan on this particular night. She pointed to where a small, spiny creature scurried across the gravel from one shadow to the next. "See him, girls? He is waddling down the path over there. He can smell the food."

"You should know," Harris whispered, slipping a hand over her rounded belly. "You are our expert on waddling."

"I see him." Then Meggie whispered to her school friend from her rosebush hiding place. "See him, Ellen? There."

"Shush," Alyssa scolded her husband, afraid the girls might hear him. "You sound like my brother, Winslow."

"Oh, that's an insult," he said, mock pain in his voice. "But I adore your waddle, my sweet. Do you really think you can lure that fuzz-peg back?"

"Maybe," Alyssa said. "It's worth a try, for Meggie's sake. And she's the one who brought it up."

Everything was in place. Tavi was in his rooms with his wife and little girl, who had recently arrived from India. So Elijah had helped the girls set out the pan of bread and milk and a clay pot with straw and a couple of spools.

"That is not King Arthur," Meggie said finally, certainty in her voice.

"How can you tell him from any other hedgehog?" Ellen

asked. She was a tiny little thing with dark hair and eyes and an engaging manner who Meggie had befriended. Alyssa liked the girl. Like Meggie, Ellen had lost her father during the past year. So when Meggie returned home, Alyssa had invited Ellen to join them. Her mother had agreed. Ellen had become a well-liked and frequent visitor at Penridge, almost a member of the family.

"It is easy to tell them apart," Meggie explained to Ellen. "King Arthur has a white stripe down his right side. That one has a white spot near the left ear."

"So it seems we have a different hedgehog in our garden," Harris suggested to the girls across the way. He was sitting on a stool behind Alyssa. "Maybe King Arthur found greener pastures," he added.

"I guess that would be all right," Meggie said, sounding doubtful.

"We will keep watching," Harris said, pulling Alyssa closer, a thing he did often.

He'd taken up his role as father figure easily and with pleasure, Alyssa thought as she shifted uncomfortably on her stool. And he'd continued to try to solve the problems at the mine. Blessedly, Reverend Whittle had suddenly packed up and gone off to preach to the Welsh miners.

But Harris had also insisted on redecorating the house right away. Alyssa agreed, changing the fashionable reds and greens to lighter blues, creams, and gold. Gwendolyn and Alistair were cleared away, symbolically at least. Then Harris turned to getting the import business truly under way.

But that never kept him from devoting time to the girls, seeing to the proper mounts and saddles for them, asking them for their opinion, and instructing them on the finer points of pony selection and horsemanship. He was also instructing them in chess and once, on a rainy day, she'd caught him, the proper Lord Penridge, playing a rowdy game of hide-and-seek with them in the grand salon. And why not? They didn't use the room for much else. Though he promised her that would change after their baby was born, when mourning for Meggie's parents was over and the new year was ahead of them. Her parents had already invited themselves for an extended stay when the baby arrived.

She shifted on the stool again. At six months she was growing large enough that finding a comfortable position, sitting or lying down, was becoming a challenge.

"Are you all right?" Harris asked over her shoulder, bussing her neck. He was a fine husband, too—and lover. She could not imagine ever being satisfied with a separate bed from her husband. There was too much delight to be found in each other's arms at night. And he'd taken the news of her condition well. When she'd told him, he'd given her a staid smile, told her how pleased he was, and then he'd commenced to strut and swagger in an aloof British way, as if he were the only Englishman who'd ever helped conceive a child.

She still wasn't certain whether that had happened their first time together or later when they'd declared their love, but she preferred to think it had been the latter.

"It is late, my sweet," Harris continued, nibbling her ear. "Why don't you go into the house and get ready for bed? I will stay here in the garden with the girls until we sight the old fuzz-peg."

"No, I want to find him, too," Alyssa said, afraid to admit to herself or Harris that she feared that Gwendolyn might have done harm to the poor thing. The woman had poisoned her husband—why would she spare an annoying hedgehog? Elijah had told her that Lady Penridge had released the creature into the garden, but upon questioning, he'd admitted that he hadn't actually witnessed the event. He had only seen her carrying the cage near the pond behind the stable.

In a strange way, Gwendolyn continued to haunt them. There were moments when someone addressed Alyssa as Lady Penridge and she caught herself glancing around for Gwendolyn. And the dreams. She still had them, nightmares about standing in a searing-hot room facing the cleverest, evilest woman she'd ever known—and she feared that she would lose this time. That the witch would win, would drag them all into a fiery hell. Her husband and baby.

That's when Harris would awaken her and kiss away the dark imagining. "She is gone, my sweet. She will never use any of us again unless we allow her to," he would whisper and she would know he was right.

The night of Meggie's mother's funeral, Alyssa and Harris had told the child the "truth." It was one of the most difficult things she'd ever had to do. But they laid out the facts. That Harris had *not* murdered her father. Alistair had died of food poisoning just as the magistrate and Dr. Lewellyn had declared. And they told her that her mother had died because of an awful accident.

Meggie had accepted it dry-eyed. Her tears were gone by then, shed brokenheartedly at the church service and at the burial. When she heard all they had to say about her parents, she'd asked where she was going to live then. They told her they would like to have her at Penridge. From that day on, she'd been a contented, sweet-natured child.

"Look, there is something else moving," Ellen whispered, pointing into the darkness and pulling Alyssa from her reveries.

"That is too small to be King Arthur," Meggie said with expert authority. Alyssa heard the disappointment in her voice.

"And there goes another one," Ellen continued, pointing frantically at another little shadow that scurried along the garden path. "Maybe they are babies."

The pair of creatures stopped at the pan of bread and milk and ate briefly, then went on.

"So we have a mother with her babies in our garden," Alyssa said, trying to make the best of it. "Elijah will be pleased."

"Wait," Harris said. "Look farther up the path. There. Do you see it, Meggie?"

"Yes, there is something else, a hare maybe—no, it is a hedgehog," Meggie said, excitement returning to her tone. "Wait. Here it comes."

They all fell silent. In the expectant stillness they could hear four little feet running across the gravel. Its side was in the shadow so that they could not tell much about the fuzz-peg's coloring, but he was larger than the previous three. He kept coming toward them, his nose twitching in the air, sniffing out the food he seemed to know was there.

Finally, he reached the pan and began to eat noisily, slurping and sucking at the bread and milk with just as much racket as King Arthur had ever made.

Meggie moved silently around to get a better look at him.

Alyssa held her breath and prayed the little girl wouldn't be too disappointed.

Meggie made a muffled sound. Then she clamped her hand over her mouth and froze.

The animal heard her and stopped eating. It glanced around warily. Satisfied with the silence, it returned to its meal.

Meggie turned to them. "It's him," she whispered, her eyes gleaming with joy in the moonlight. "It's King Arthur. I can see the white stripe down his side. He's come back to us."

"Let me see," Ellen said. The girls crept closer to spy on the hedgehog.

Unexpected tears began to roll down Alyssa's cheeks, and she bit her lip to stifle a sudden sob.

"What is it?" Harris asked, suddenly on his knees at her side. "Is something wrong?"

Alyssa shook her head. She wasn't sure she could explain. Maybe it had something to do with her impending motherhood. "She didn't kill him, Harris. She didn't kill Meggie's pet. I'm so happy she didn't kill him."

Harris frowned at her. "I believe you are overtired."

"Don't you see?" Alyssa said, waving her hands uselessly in the air, still at a loss to express her feelings. "Gwendolyn used us all, but she loved Meggie, enough to let King Arthur live. Whatever else we think of her, we must remember that. Even if she orphaned Meggie, in her own way, she loved her daughter. If she hadn't, she would have done away with what she considered a nuisance."

"Alyssa," Meggie called, delight and laughter in her voice. "The babies are over here. They have stripes, too. Almost like King Arthur's. He has a family. Just like us."

"That's wonderful," Alyssa called back, smiling through her tears, which she hoped the children did not see.

"I see what you mean," Harris said, holding her hand, stroking it. "And when the time comes for us to tell Meggie the truth about Gwendolyn, we can tell her truthfully that whatever demons possessed her mother, she did love her daughter."

"Yes," Alyssa said, thankful that that revelation lay years away. She stroked Harris's hand in return and gazed into his face. "Until then, we will love and take care of each other, giving and taking, laughing and crying, through trials and joys, caring and being cared for, accepting what we must— even the hedgehog—because we love each other."

"Yes, we do." Harris chuckled and kissed her. "Now and forever."

ABOUT THE AUTHOR

When not at home in the Flint Hills of Kansas with her family, acclaimed novelist Linda Madl loves to travel. Among her destinations have been the wild moors and shores of Cornwall, the setting of *Silk and Secrets*. As author of many historical romances, she loves to hear from her readers. You may contact her c/o Zebra Books with a self-addressed stamped envelope or at her Web site: www.lindamadl.com.